Praise for Elin Hilderbrand's

The Island

"Wildly successful.... As escapist beach reads go, Hilderbrand's latest is consistently smarter and more compelling than it needs to be. This tale of a middle-aged divorcée's monthlong sojourn on tiny, rustic Tuckernuck Island with her art-world sister and two troubled daughters zips along with the kind of well-limned romantic drama that keeps poolside readers out of the water for hours." —Leah Greenblatt, *Entertainment Weekly*

"It's not just Hilderbrand's covers that say 'perfect beach book.'... She has the romantic drama down as well.... Her juicy ninth novel sets newly divorced Birdie Cousins, her daughters, Chess and Tate, and her widowed sister, India, on an island that just happens to be home to hot handyman Barrett Lee." —*People*

"A steamy maelstrom of broken hearts, divorce, secrets, and lots of romance."

—CK Wolfson, *Martha's Vineyard Times*

"This never-neverland portrait of the rich and randy will please those looking for a satisfying beach read."

—*Publishers Weekly*

"*The Island* is a summer treat.... An appealing story.... Hilderbrand's books are perfect beach reads. She captures the daily rhythm and the magic of island life, providing an escape from the daily grind. *The Island* goes down as easily as a cold glass of white wine on a hot summer day. The characters are believable and likable, and their relationships with each other ring true with frequent tension and flat-out fights between the sisters. Predictably, but satisfyingly, these squabbles and dramas resolve themselves as the women rediscover how to trust each other with their greatest fears and secrets."

—Catherine Mallette, *Houston Chronicle*

"Chess's sister, mother, and aunt take her to the family's ancestral home on Tuckernuck Island for a month in the summer. Their time together promises love, both lost and found, secrets, and intrigue."

—*Idaho Statesman*

"For those looking for a slower-paced novel to savor, this latest by Hilderbrand will fit the bill.... It's an island vacation with a difference—good summer reading."

—*Library Journal*

"*The Island* is an enjoyable story, with humor, drama, and interesting characters."

—Sue Bond, *Courier Mail* (Australia)

"Queen of the summer novel.... Hilderbrand's portrait of the upper-crust Tate clan through the years is so deliciously addictive that it will be the 'it' beach book of the summer."

—*Kirkus Reviews* (starred review)

"Fast-moving, often eye-popping, and sometimes salacious. Hilderbrand's stories revolve around loving and losing...and loving again, and how four women in the Tate family figure out how to make life's miseries fly in formation.... The author does an admirable job depicting the upper-crust characters. The island is a character unto itself.... If you want one last beach book to toss into your sandy tote, this could be it."

—Mims Cushing, *Florida Times-Union*

The Island

BY ELIN HILDERBRAND

The Beach Club

Nantucket Nights

Summer People

The Blue Bistro

The Love Season

Barefoot

A Summer Affair

The Castaways

The Island

Silver Girl

Summerland

Beautiful Day

The Matchmaker

Winter Street

The Rumor

Winter Stroll

Here's to Us

Winter Storms

The Identicals

Winter Solstice

The Perfect Couple

Winter in Paradise

Summer of '69

What Happens in Paradise

28 Summers

Troubles in Paradise

Golden Girl

The Island

A Novel

Elin Hilderbrand

LITTLE, BROWN AND COMPANY

NEW YORK BOSTON LONDON

The characters and events in this book are fictitious. Any similarity to real persons, living or dead, is coincidental and not intended by the author.

Little, Brown and Company
Hachette Book Group
1290 Avenue of the Americas, New York, NY 10104
littlebrown.com

Little, Brown and Company is a division of Hachette Book Group, Inc. The Little, Brown and Company name and logo are trademarks of Hachette Book Group, Inc.

The publisher is not responsible for websites (or their content) that are not owned by the publisher.

Printed in the United States of America

Originally published in hardcover by Little, Brown and Company, July 2010
First Little, Brown and Company mass market edition, May 2012
Updated premium mass market edition, April 2022

10 9 8 7 6 5 4 3 2 1

To my mother, Sally Hilderbrand,
who gave me my roots and my wings

The Island

THE TATE HOUSE

It had sat abandoned for thirteen years. This had happened without warning.

It was a summer house, a cottage, though it had been built well, with high-quality lumber and square-headed steel nails. This was back in 1935, during the Depression. The carpenters had been eager for work; they were careful when aligning the shingles, they sanded, swept, then sanded again with high-grit paper. The banister was as smooth as a satin dress. The carpenters—brought in from Fall River—stood at the upstairs windows and whistled at the views: one bedroom looked out over the mighty ocean, and one bedroom looked out over the bucolic pastures and wide ponds of this, Tuckernuck Island.

The house was occupied only in July and sometimes August. In the other months, there was a caretaker—poking his head in, checking that the windows were tight, removing the small brown carcasses from the mousetraps.

The house had been witness to a wide range of behavior from the members of the family that owned it. They ate and they slept like everyone else; they drank and they danced to music picked up off the shortwave radio. They made love and they fought (yes, the Tates were screamers, one and all; it must have been genetic). They got pregnant and they gave birth; there were children in the house, crying and laughing, drawing on the plaster with crayons, chipping a shingle with a well-hit croquet ball, extinguishing a sneaked cigarette on the railing of the deck.

The house had never caught fire, thank God.

And then, for thirteen years, nobody came. But that wasn't entirely true. There were field mice and an army of daddy longlegs. There were three bats that flew in through the open attic window, which the family had forgotten to close when they left and which the caretaker had overlooked. The window faced southwest so it deflected the worst of the wind and the rain; it served as an aperture that allowed the house to breathe.

A quartet of mischievous kids broke in through the weak door on the screened-in porch, and for a moment, the house felt optimistic. Humans! Youngsters! But these were trespassers. Though not, thankfully, vandals. They hunted around—finding no food except one can of pork and beans and a cylindrical carton of Quaker oats, rife with weevils (which frightened the girl holding the carton so badly that she dropped it and the oats scattered across the linoleum floor). The kids prodded one another to venture upstairs. Around the island, word was the house was haunted.

Nobody here but me, the house would have said if the house could talk. *Well, me and the bats. And the mice. And the spiders!*

In one of the bedrooms, the kids found a foot-high sculpture of a man, made from driftwood and shells and beach glass. The man had seaweed hair.

Cool! one of the kids, a boy with red hair and freckles, said. *I'm taking this!*

That's stealing, the girl who had dropped the oatmeal said.

The boy set the sculpture down. *It's stupid anyway. Let's get out of here.*

The others agreed. They left, finding nothing more of interest. The toilet didn't even have water in it.

Again, silence. Emptiness.

Until one day the caretaker used his old key and the front door swung open, groaning on its hinges. It wasn't the caretaker, but the caretaker's son, grown up now. He inhaled—the house knew it couldn't smell terribly good—and patted the door frame with affection.

"They're coming back," he said. "They're coming back."

BIRDIE

Plans for the vacation changed, and then changed again.

Back in March, when arrangements for Chess's wedding were falling into place as neatly as bricks in a garden path, an idea came to Birdie: a week for just the two of them in the house on Tuckernuck Island. As recently as three years earlier, such an idea would have been unthinkable; ever since Chess was a little girl, she and Birdie had clashed. They didn't "get along." (Which meant that Chess didn't get along with Birdie, right? Birdie had tried everything in her power to gain her daughter's good graces, and yet she was perpetually held in contempt. She said the wrong thing, she did the wrong thing.) But lately, things between mother and daughter had improved—enough for Birdie to suggest a week of bonding in the family cottage before Chess embarked on the rest of her life with Michael Morgan.

Birdie had phoned Chess at work to see if the idea would fly.

"I have to call you back," Chess said in the tight voice that meant Birdie should have waited and called Chess at home. Chess was the food editor of *Glamorous Home* magazine. She was the youngest editor on the magazine's staff; she was the youngest editor working for the Diamond Publishing Group, and she worked extra hard to prove herself. Chess's job was one Birdie secretly coveted, being an enthusiastic and accomplished at-home gourmet cook. She was so, so proud of Chess, and envious of her, too.

"Okay, honey!" Birdie said. "But just put this in your stew pot: you and me in the house on Tuckernuck the week of Fourth of July."

"You and me?" Chess said. "And who else?"

"Just us," Birdie said.

"The whole week?" Chess said.

"Can you?" Birdie asked. Chess's job had seasonal flexibility. The summer was slow; the holidays were insanity. "Would you?"

"Let me think about it," Chess said, and she hung up.

Birdie paced her house, agitated and tense. She felt like she had in 1972 when she was waiting to find out if she'd gotten a bid from Alpha Phi. Would Chess consider this trip? If Chess said no, Birdie decided, she wouldn't take it personally. Chess was busy, and a week was a long time. Would Birdie have wanted to spend a week alone with her own mother? Probably not. Birdie picked up her cup of tea, but it had gone cold. She put it in the microwave to reheat and sat down at her computer, which she kept in the kitchen, where she could get the news and recipes. She checked her e-mail. Her younger daughter, Tate, was a computer wizard and sent Birdie at least one e-mail each day, though it was sometimes a forwarded joke, or a chain letter, which Birdie deleted without reading. Today, her in-box was empty. Birdie chastised herself. Chess would never want to spend a week with her alone. She shouldn't have asked.

But then, just as she was about to sink into the self-doubt that plagued nearly every interaction with Chess (why was her relationship with her elder daughter so fraught? What had Birdie done wrong?), the phone rang. Birdie snapped it up. It was Chess.

"July first through seventh?" Chess said. "You and me?"

"You'll do it?" Birdie said.

"Absolutely," Chess said. "It sounds great. Thanks, Bird!"

Birdie sighed—relief, happiness, elation! A week on Tuckernuck *did* sound great. One of the benefits of being divorced now, after three decades of being married, was that Birdie could do whatever she damn well pleased. The house on Tuckernuck had been in the Tate family for seventy-five years—*her* family, not Grant's family. Whereas Birdie had grown up with memories of simple, carefree summer days on Tuckernuck, Grant had not. He had pretended to like Tuckernuck for the two summers of their courtship, but once they were married and had children, he revealed his disdain. He loathed the place—the house was too primitive, the generator unreliable. He wasn't a pioneer; he didn't want to work a pump by hand for water that was then heated over a fire for his bath. He didn't like mice or mosquitoes or bats hanging from the rafters. He didn't like to be without a television or a phone. He was lawyer to half of Wall Street. How could Birdie reasonably expect him to live without a phone?

Grant had suffered through two weeks a summer in the house on Tuckernuck until Tate was a senior in high school, and then he put his foot down: no more.

Birdie hadn't been to Tuckernuck in thirteen years. It was time she returned.

And so, in addition to planning Chess's wedding to Michael Morgan, Birdie also planned a week's vacation on Tuckernuck. She called their caretaker, Chuck Lee. As she dialed the number—long forgotten and yet familiar—she found herself singing with nerves. Chuck's wife, Eleanor, answered the phone. Birdie had never laid eyes on Eleanor, much less had a conversation with her, though Birdie was aware of Eleanor's existence and she was sure that Eleanor was aware of hers. Birdie decided not to identify herself to Eleanor now; it would be easier that way.

She said, "I'm looking for Chuck Lee, please. Is he available?"

"Not at the moment," Eleanor said. "May I take a message?"

"I have a caretaking question," Birdie said.

"Chuck doesn't do caretaking anymore," Eleanor said. The woman had a pleasant enough demeanor, Birdie thought. In Birdie's younger imagination, Eleanor had weighed four hundred pounds and had skin the texture of a squid and a faint mustache.

"Oh," Birdie said. She wondered if Chuck and Eleanor's phone had caller ID, but decided not. Chuck was a man firmly embedded in 1974 and always had been.

"My son Barrett has taken over the business," Eleanor said. "Would you like his number?"

After Birdie hung up, she had to sit down and take a moment. How mercilessly the years flew by! Birdie had known Barrett Lee all his life. She remembered him at five years old, a towhead in an orange life preserver sitting beside his father on the Boston Whaler that picked up Birdie and Grant and the kids from Madaket Harbor on Nantucket and delivered them to the slice of beach, as white and soft as breadcrumbs, that fronted their property on the tiny neighboring island of Tuckernuck. Was Barrett Lee old enough to take over a business? In age, he had fallen somewhere between Chess and Tate, who were thirty-two and thirty respectively, making Barrett thirty-one or so. And Chuck had retired like a normal sixty-five-year-old man, whereas Grant still rode the train into the city every morning and, for all Birdie knew, still took clients to Gallagher's for martinis and sirloins after work.

Birdie called Barrett Lee's cell phone, and sure enough, a man answered.

"Barrett?" Birdie said. "This is Birdie Cousins calling. I own the Tate house on Tuckernuck?"

"Hey, Mrs. Cousins," Barrett Lee said casually, as though they had spoken only the week before. "How's it going?"

Birdie tried to remember the last time she had seen Barrett Lee. She had a vague memory of him as a teenager. He had been quite handsome, like his father. He played football for the Nantucket Whalers; he had broad shoulders and that white-blond hair. He had come out on his father's boat alone early one morning to take one of the girls fishing. And then another time he had taken one of the girls on a picnic lunch. For the life of her, Birdie couldn't remember if he had taken Chess or Tate.

How's it going? How was she supposed to answer that? *Grant and I divorced two years ago. He lives in a "loft" apartment in Norwalk and dates women he calls "cougars," while I bounce off the walls of the family homestead in New Canaan, six thousand square feet filled with rugs and antiques and framed photographs documenting a life now gone. I cook an elaborate meal on Monday and eat it all week long. I still belong to the garden club. I go to a book group once a month and frequently I'm the only one who's read the selection; the rest of the women are just there for the wine and the gossip. Chess and Tate are grown up, with lives of their own. I wish I had a job. I spend more time than I should feeling angry at Grant for never encouraging me to work outside the home. Because now, here I am, fifty-seven years old, divorced, becoming the kind of woman who inflicts herself on her children.*

"It goes well," Birdie said. "I'm sure hearing from me is something of a shock."

"A shock," Barrett confirmed.

"How is your father?" Birdie asked. "He's retired?"

"Retired," Barrett said. "He had a stroke just before Thanksgiving. He's fine, but it slowed him way down."

"I'm sorry to hear that," Birdie said. This also gave her pause. Chuck Lee had had a stroke? Chuck Lee with his military buzz cut, and the cigarette clenched in the corner of his mouth, and his biceps bulging as he pulled the ropes of the anchor off the ocean floor? He was slow moving now? Birdie imagined a land turtle, bald and lumbering, then quickly erased it from her mind. "Listen, Chess and I are going to spend the week of the Fourth of July in the house. Can you get it ready?"

"Well," Barrett said.

"Well, what?"

"It's going to need work," Barrett said. "I stopped by there back in September and the place is falling down on itself. It needs to be reshingled and it probably needs a new roof. You'll need a new generator. And the stairs down to the beach have rotted. Now, I didn't go inside, but..."

"Can you take care of it?" Birdie asked. "I want it to be usable. Can you buy a good generator and fix the rest of the house up? I'll send a check tomorrow. Five thousand? Ten thousand?" In the divorce, Birdie had gotten the house and a generous monthly stipend. Grant had also promised that if she had larger expenses, he would cover them, as long as he deemed them "reasonable." Grant hated the Tuckernuck house; Birdie had no idea if he would deem the cost of fixing it up reasonable or not. She smelled a possible battleground, but she couldn't let the Tuckernuck house fall to pieces after seventy-five years, could she?

"Ten thousand to start," Barrett said. "I'm sorry to tell you that..."

"No, don't be sorry. It's not your fault..."

"But if you want the house back to where it was..."

"We have no choice!" Birdie said. "It was my grandmother's house."

"You'd like it ready by July first?"

"July first," Birdie said. "It's just going to be Chess and me for one last hurrah. She's getting married in September."

"Married?" Barrett said. He paused, and Birdie realized that it must have been Chess that he'd taken on the picnic.

"On September twenty-fifth," Birdie said proudly.

"Wow," Barrett said.

By the middle of April, tax time, every last detail of Chess's wedding to Michael Morgan had been tended to—including the dress for the flower girl, the catering menu, and the selection of hymns at the church. Birdie called Chess at work much more frequently to get her opinion and her approval. Most of the time what Chess said was, "Yes, Birdie, fine. Whatever you think." Birdie had been both surprised and flattered when Chess had asked her for help with the wedding. She had essentially dropped the thing in Birdie's lap, saying matter-of-factly, "You have exquisite taste." Birdie happened to believe this was true; her good taste was a fact, like her green eyes or her attached earlobes. But to have Chess's confidence was gratifying.

Three hundred people would be invited to the wedding; the service would be held at Trinity Episcopal, with Benjamin Denton, the pastor of Chess's youth, presiding. The ceremony would be followed by a tented reception in Birdie's backyard. The landscapers had started working the previous September. The pièce de résistance, in Birdie's opinion, was a floating island that would be placed in Birdie's pond, where the couple would take their first dance.

Grant had called only once to complain about cost, and that was in regard to the twenty thousand dollars for the engineering and manufacturing of the floating island. Birdie had patiently explained the concept to him over the phone, but he either didn't get it or didn't like it.

"Are we or are we not paying for a regular dance floor?"

"We are," Birdie said. "This is a special thing, for the first dances. Chess dancing with Michael, Chess dancing with you, you dancing with me."

"Me dancing with you?"

Birdie cleared her throat. "Emily Post says that if neither of the divorced spouses is remarried, then...yes, Grant, you're going to have to dance with me. Sorry about that."

"Twenty thousand dollars is a lot of money, Bird."

It took a phone call from Chess to convince him. God only knows what she said, but Grant wrote the check.

At the end of April, Birdie went on her first date since the divorce. The date had been set up by Birdie's sister, India, who was a curator at the Pennsylvania Academy of Fine Arts in Center City, Philadelphia. India had been married to the sculptor Bill Bishop and had raised three sons while Bill traveled the globe, gaining notoriety. In 1995, Bill shot himself in the head in a hotel in Bangkok, and the suicide had devastated India. For a while there, Birdie had feared India wouldn't recover. She would end up as a bag lady in Rittenhouse Square, or as a recluse, keeping cats and polishing Bill's portrait in its frame. But India had somehow risen from the ashes, putting her master's degree in art history to use and becoming a curator. Unlike Birdie, India was cutting edge and chic. She wore Catherine Malandrino dresses, four-inch heels, and Bill Bishop's reading glasses on a chain around her neck. India dated all kinds of men—older men, younger men, married men—and the man she set Birdie up with was one of her castoffs. He was too old. How old was too old? Sixty-five, which was Grant's age.

His name was Hank Dunlap. Hank was the retired headmaster of an elite private school in Manhattan. His wife, Caroline, was independently wealthy. The wife sat on the board of trustees at the Guggenheim Museum; India had met Hank and Caroline at a Guggenheim benefit years earlier.

"What happened to Caroline?" Birdie asked. "Did they get divorced? Did she die?"

"Neither," India said. "She has Alzheimer's. She's in a facility upstate."

"So the wife is still *alive,* they're still *married,* and you dated him? And now you want *me* to date him?"

"Get over yourself, Bird," India said. "His wife is in another world and won't be coming back. He wants companionship. He is exactly your type."

"He is?" Birdie said. What *was* her "type"? Someone like Grant? Grant was the devil's attorney. He was all about single-malt whiskey and expensive cars with leather interiors. He was not the kindly headmaster type, content with a salary in the low six figures. "Does he golf?"

"No."

"Ah, then he is my type." Birdie swore she would never again be romantically involved with a golfer.

"He's cute," India said, like they were talking about some sixteen-year-old. "You'll like him."

Surprise! Birdie liked him. She had decided to forgo all of the "I can't believe I'm dating again at my age" worry-wart nonsense and just be a realist. She *was* dating again at her age, but instead of fretting, she got showered and dressed and made up as she would have if she and Grant were going to the theater or to the country club with the Campbells. She wore a simple wrap dress and heels and some good jewelry, including her diamond engagement ring (it had been her grandmother's and would someday go to one of *her* grandchildren). Birdie sat on her garden bench in the mild spring evening with a glass of Sancerre and Mozart playing on the outdoor speakers as she waited for old Hank to show up.

Her heartbeat seemed regular.

She heard a car in the driveway and proceeded inside, where she rinsed her wineglass, checked her lipstick in the mirror, and fetched her spring coat. With a deep breath, she opened the door. And there stood old Hank, holding a bouquet of fragrant purple hyacinths. He had salt-and-pepper hair and wore rimless glasses. He was, as India had promised, cute. Very cute. When he saw Birdie, he smiled widely. He grinned. He was darling.

"You're even prettier than your sister!" he said.

Birdie swooned. "God," she said. "I love you already."

And they laughed.

The evening had gone from good to better. Hank Dunlap was smart and informed, funny and engaging. He picked a new restaurant on a trendy street in South Norwalk, among the art galleries and upscale boutiques. This faux SoHo (they called it SoNo) was where Grant now lived. Birdie wondered if he hung out on this trendy street (she had a hard time imagining it); she wondered if she would see him, or if he would see *her* out on a date with cute, erudite Hank. It was warm enough to sit outside, and Birdie jumped at the chance.

The food at the new restaurant was extraordinary. Birdie loved good food and good wine, and as it turned out, so did Hank. They tasted each other's meals and decided to share a dessert. Birdie didn't think, *I can't believe I'm dating again at my age.* What she thought was that she was having fun, this was easy; it was easier, perhaps, to have dinner with this man she barely knew than it had ever been to have dinner with Grant. (Beyond his penchant for aged beef, Grant didn't care what he ate. He ate only to stay alive.) In the last few years of their marriage, Birdie and Grant had barely spoken to each other when they went to dinner. Or rather, Birdie had chirped away about the things that interested her, and Grant had nodded distractedly as he watched the Yankees game over her shoulder or checked his BlackBerry for stock reports. As Birdie ate with Hank, she marveled at how nice it was to spend time with someone who not only interested her but found her interesting. Who not only talked but listened.

Birdie said, "I would run away and marry you tonight, but I understand you're already married."

Hank nodded and smiled sadly. "My wife, Caroline, is in a facility in Brewster. She doesn't recognize me or the kids anymore."

"I'm sorry," Birdie said.

"We had a good life together," Hank said. "I'm sorry it's going to end for her away from home, but I couldn't take care of her by myself. She's better off where she is.

I go to see her Thursday afternoons and every Sunday. I bring her chocolate-covered caramels, and every week she thanks me like I'm a kind stranger, which I guess, to her, I am. But she loves them."

Birdie felt tears rise. The waiter delivered their dessert—a passion fruit and coconut cream parfait. Hank dug in; Birdie dabbed at her eyes. Her marriage had ended badly, though not as badly as some, and Hank's marriage was also ending badly, though not as badly as some. His wife no longer recognized him, but he brought her chocolate-covered caramels. This was the kindest gesture Birdie could imagine. Had Grant ever done anything that kind for her? She couldn't think of a thing.

Hank kissed Birdie good night at her front door, and that was the best part of the evening. The kiss was soft and deep, and something long forgotten stirred inside Birdie. Desire. She and Grant had had sex right up to the bitter end with the help of a pill—but desire for her husband's body had evaporated by the time Tate went to grammar school.

"I'll call you tomorrow at noon," Hank said.

Birdie nodded. She was speechless. She stumbled inside and wandered around her kitchen, looking at it with new eyes. What would Hank think of this kitchen? She was a big believer in small details: always fresh fruit, always fresh flowers, always fresh-brewed coffee, real cream, fresh-squeezed juice, the morning newspaper delivered to the doorstep, classical music. Always wine of a good vintage. Would Hank appreciate these things the way Birdie did?

She made herself a cup of tea and arranged the hyacinths he'd brought in one of her cut-glass vases. She was floating. The perfect life, she decided, would be a life filled with first dates like this one. Each day would contain electric promise, a spark, a connection, and desire.

God, desire. She had forgotten all about it.

She undressed and climbed into bed with her steaming mug of tea. She picked up the novel her book club was reading, then set it down. She was levitating like a magician's assistant. She closed her eyes.

The phone rang in the middle of the night. Three twenty, the clock said. Birdie sat straight up in bed. Her bedside light was still on. The tea was cold on the nightstand. The phone? Who called at such an hour? Then Birdie remembered her date and she filled with warm, syrupy joy. It might be India calling to find out how the date had gone. India kept ridiculous hours. Ever since Bill died, she had suffered from mind-blowing insomnia; she occasionally went seventy-two hours without sleeping.

Or the call was from Hank, who had, perhaps, not been able to sleep.

Birdie grabbed the phone.

A woman, crying. Birdie knew immediately that it was Chess; a mother always knew the sound of her child crying, even when her child was thirty-two years old. Birdie intuited the rest of it right away, without having to hear one lurid word. It crushed her, but she knew.

"It's over, Birdie."

"Over?" Birdie said.

"Over."

Birdie drew the covers up to her chin. This was one of her defining moments as a mother and she was determined to shine.

"Tell me what happened," she said.

Michael Morgan was six foot six, clean cut, and handsome. He had sandy hair, green eyes, and a smile that made others smile. He had played lacrosse at Princeton, where he had graduated summa cum laude with a degree in sociology; he was a whiz at crossword puzzles and loved black-and-white movies, which endeared him to people of Birdie's generation. Instead of taking a job at J.P. Morgan, where his father was managing partner, or going to Madison Avenue, where his mother oversaw the advertising accounts for every smash hit on Broadway, Michael had taken out a staggering business loan and bought a failing head-hunting company. In five years, he had turned a profit; he had placed 25 percent of the graduating class of Columbia Business School.

Chess had met Michael Morgan at a rock club downtown; Birdie couldn't remember the name of the place. Chess had been at the bar with a girlfriend, and Michael had been there to see his brother, Nick, who was the lead singer in a band called Diplomatic Immunity. This was how young people met each other; Birdie understood that. But unlike the other young men that Chess met socially, she and Michael Morgan got serious right away.

The beginning of Chess's relationship with Michael Morgan coincided with the end of Birdie and Grant's marriage. When Birdie and Grant met Michael Morgan for the first time, they were, technically, separated. (Grant was staying in a room at the Hyatt in Stamford. This was before he rented and then purchased the loft in South Norwalk.) Chess knew her parents were separated, but Chess wanted Birdie and Grant to meet Michael *together* as a *unit*. Birdie balked at this. It would be awkward; it would be what amounted to a date with Grant, whom she had so recently and unequivocally asked to leave her life. But Chess insisted. She believed that her parents could be civil and congenial to each other for one night on her behalf. Grant was open to the idea; he made a reservation for four at La Grenouille, their former favorite restaurant. Grant and Birdie drove to the city together;

it wouldn't make sense not to. Grant smelled the same; he was wearing his khaki suit and one of the Paul Stuart shirts that Birdie had bought for him, and the pink tie with the frogs that he always wore when they went to La Grenouille. Birdie remembered having the reassuring yet sinking feeling that nothing had changed. The maître d' at La Grenouille, Donovan, greeted them as a married couple—he had no idea they'd split—and showed them to the table they preferred. On the way to the restaurant from the parking garage, Birdie had filled Grant in on Michael Morgan. He and Chess had been dating for three weeks.

"Three weeks?" Grant said. "He got an audience after only three weeks?"

"This is it, I think," Birdie said.

"It?" Grant said.

"Just be nice," Birdie said. "Make him comfortable."

Chess had looked beautiful in a flowery lavender dress, and Michael Morgan was stunning in a charcoal suit and a lavender-hued Hermès tie. (They had color-coordinated their outfits! This struck Birdie as cute at first; then she worried that they were secretly living together.) Chess and Michael Morgan looked like they had just stepped off the pages of *Town and Country*. They looked like they were already married.

Michael Morgan greeted Grant with a strong handshake; he kissed Birdie's cheek. He gave them both that brilliant smile that made them smile. (That square jaw, those perfect teeth, the light in his eye—he was magnetic!) Birdie had gone into that dinner feeling very jaundiced about romance and relationships, but even she had been won over by Michael Morgan, and by Michael and Chess together. Michael had beautiful table manners, he stood when Chess rose to use the ladies' room and when she returned, he told Grant and Birdie about his business and plans for future growth in a way that was both impressive and pleasingly self-effacing. He appreciated the wine, he drank scotch with Grant after dessert, he thanked both Grant and Birdie profusely for the meal, he praised them for bringing up a beautiful, smart, accomplished daughter like Chess. What was not to like?

So what Birdie heard over the phone surprised her. Chess had broken the engagement. Chess had been out to dinner at Aureole with her friend Rhonda; from there, she and Rhonda had gone to the Spotted Pig for cocktails, and then on to a nightclub. Chess had left the nightclub without telling Rhonda. She had walked sixty-seven blocks uptown to her apartment (Birdie shuddered at the danger of it) and had called San Francisco, where Michael was with candidates interviewing for the head of a prestigious tech company. She had called off the wedding. Michael was flying home in the morning, she said, but it wouldn't do any good. The relationship was over. She would not be getting married.

"Now wait a minute," Birdie said. "What happened?"

"Nothing *happened,*" Chess said. "I just don't want to marry Michael."

"But why *not?*" Birdie said. She wasn't naive. Had Chess taken any mind-altering drugs while she was at the club? Was she still feeling their effects now?

"I don't have a good reason," Chess said. She started to cry again. "I just don't want to."

"You don't want to?"

"That's right," Chess said. "I don't want to."

"You're not in love with him?" Birdie said.

"No," Chess said. "I'm not."

What could Birdie say?

"I understand."

"You do?"

"I support whatever decision you make. I love you. If you don't want to marry Michael Morgan, we will undo all the wedding plans."

Chess exhaled. She hiccuped. She whispered, "God, Birdie, thank you. *Thank* you."

"Okay. Okay, now," Birdie said.

"Will you tell Dad?" Chess asked.

"Me?" Birdie said.

"Please?" The tears threatened. "I just can't do it. I am not strong enough."

What Chess meant was that she didn't want to do it. Who in their right mind would want to call Grant Cousins, whose job it was to intimidate everyone from the at-home investor to the SEC, and tell him that he may have wasted $150,000 on things like hand-engraved invitations and a floating island in his ex-wife's backyard pond? Birdie was aware that her greatest flaw as a mother was not holding the children fully accountable for their actions. She had never made them do the dirty work. When Tate, at age six, stole crayons from the five-and-dime, Birdie hadn't marched her back to the store to confess to Mr. Spitko, the owner, as she should have. She had let it slide with a lecture and had then put five dollars in an envelope, which she slid under the door of the five-and-dime after hours.

"I think you should call your father and explain your decision in your own words," Birdie said. "I won't be able to do it justice."

"Please?"

Birdie sighed. The hour weighed upon her, as did the reality of No Wedding—all that work for naught!—as did the prospect of speaking to Grant about this catastrophic turn of events. But she mustn't think of it as a catastrophe. She would think of it as Chess saving herself from a lifetime of unhappiness. A catastrophic event would have been Chess getting married, bearing three children, and then realizing that any one of a hundred other options would have been better than marrying Michael Morgan. You only got one life, and Chess was going to treat hers with thoughtful care.

Birdie was exhausted.

"Let's talk in the morning, and then talk again after you speak to Michael in person. Then we'll worry about your father. This thing might reverse itself."

"No, Birdie, it won't."

"Okay, but—"

"Birdie," Chess said. "Trust me."

Chess was steadfast in her decision. Michael came home from California exhausted and frantic, willing to do absolutely anything to get Chess to change her mind, but Chess shut him down. She would not marry him in September. She would not marry him at all. Michael Morgan, former King of the World, former Golden Boy, former All-Ivy athlete, and one of *Inc.* magazine's Young Entrepreneurs of the Year, was reduced to gravy.

Michael called Birdie early the following evening. It was Sunday, cocktail hour, and Hank Dunlap was in Birdie's living room with a glass of wine, eating her savory *palmiers,* listening to Ella Fitzgerald on the stereo. Birdie had invited him over for a springtime supper of roast chicken and asparagus, despite the fact that her world was tumbling down around her. Or not her world, exactly, but the world of people she loved.

When Hank had called Saturday at noon, what Birdie said was, "I find myself in the middle of a startling family crisis."

And Hank said, "Would you prefer company or space?"

The wonderful thing about dating again at her age

was that she was dealing with a partner who was emotionally mature. She could choose either company or space, and Hank would understand. She decided she wanted company. She barely knew Hank Dunlap, but she sensed he would give her a sound perspective. He had been a school headmaster. He had dealt with students, teachers, parents, money, emotions, logistics, and, most likely, dozens of thwarted love affairs. He might be able to help, and if not, he could just sit there and Birdie would feel better for looking upon him.

He had arrived at her door with a bottle of Sancerre, her favorite wine, and she had poured two glasses immediately, pulled the *palmiers* from the oven, and told Hank the story. *My daughter Chess called in the middle of the night with the news that she'd broken her engagement. She gave no reason. She simply isn't in love with him.*

Hank nodded thoughtfully. Birdie had begun to feel slightly embarrassed on Chess's behalf. Why on earth had she agreed to marry Michael Morgan in the first place if she wasn't in love with him? Michael had proposed to Chess onstage at a rock concert, which had seemed rash to Birdie, bordering on unseemly, but Chess and Michael had met at a rock concert and he was after some meaningful symmetry. He had thought it through; he had asked Grant for Chess's hand the week before. Chess hadn't seemed bothered by the public nature of the proposal, or had seemed bothered only slightly. What she'd said was, *How could I say no?* But she said this lightly, and what Birdie thought she meant was, *Why would I want to say no?* Michael and Chess were made for each other.

Hank interrupted Birdie's thoughts by putting his hands on her waist and pulling her to him. She felt a light-headed rush. She set her wineglass down. Hank kissed her. Instantly, she was aflame.

He stopped and said, "I feel like the guy who is only thinking about sex when we're supposed to be studying."

"Sex?" Birdie said. "Studying?"

Hank took off his glasses and started kissing her again.

And then the phone rang. Initially, Birdie ignored it. *Nothing* was going to tear her away from... but then she realized she had to answer. She pulled back. Hank nodded and put his glasses back on.

"Hello?" she said.

"Mrs. Cousins? It's Michael Morgan."

She had told him at least half a dozen times to call her Birdie and he had never complied—his Ivy League sense of decorum stopped him—though now she was glad.

"Oh, Michael," she said, and Hank repaired to the living room sofa with his wine and the tray of *palmiers*.

Michael's voice was shaky, then stronger, then shaky again, with high-pitched, boyish breaks. What did he do wrong? What could he do to change Chess's mind? It seemed Chess had failed to come up with a convincing argument. She didn't want to marry him but she didn't have a reason. He wasn't buying it.

"It doesn't make any *sense,*" Michael said. "At eight o'clock, everything was fine. She called me on her way to Aureole. She told me she loved me." He paused, allowing Birdie to express her sympathy with a clucking noise. "Then at ten o'clock her time, I got another text saying she was leaving the restaurant and going out to a bar."

Birdie said, "I see."

"Four hours later, she had taken off her ring." His voice grew stronger, angrier. "Mrs. Cousins, I want to know what happened at that club."

"Oh, goodness," Birdie said. "I don't know what happened."

"She didn't tell you?"

"She didn't say a word about the club. Other than that

she left without telling the other girl. She walked all the way back to Sixty-third Street in the middle of the night by herself."

"Are you sure she was by herself?" Michael said.

"That's what she told me," Birdie said. "Why? Do you think there's someone else?"

"Why else would she break the engagement?" Michael said. "There is no other reason, is there?"

Is there? He was asking Birdie for her opinion. She was torn between wanting to comfort Michael and wanting to fairly represent Chess's point of view. She was, she realized, being plopped right in the middle of this.

She said, "I can't speak for Chess, Michael. She told me she doesn't want to get married. Her feelings have changed. You proposed in a very public way." This came off as an admonition, and it was: if Michael Morgan had proposed privately, Chess might have answered differently. "Maybe Chess felt like she had to say yes when what she meant was that she wanted to think about it."

"I proposed six months ago," Michael said. "She's had time to think about it."

"She's had time to think about it," Birdie said. "And I know this comes as cold comfort, but having her realize now is much better than having her realize in ten years when you have four kids and a mortgage. This is a perspective that comes with age, and you're going to have to take my word for it."

Michael said, "I can't give up hope. I love her, Mrs. Cousins. I am madly in love with your daughter, and I just can't turn it off like a faucet. My heart..." Here, he started to sob, and Birdie cringed. The boy was used to getting whatever he wanted, but he couldn't have Chess. He didn't know it, but this kind of earthshaking disappointment would be good for him. "My heart is in a thousand pieces."

"You need to talk some more with Chess," Birdie said.

"I was just with her for four hours."

"A little later, maybe. Once she's had time to reflect."

"I have to go back to San Francisco," he said. "I left two candidates for a seven-figure job sitting at the Marriott."

"Go back to San Francisco," Birdie said. "Talk to Chess when you get home."

"If she doesn't change her mind, I don't know what the hell I'm gonna do," he said.

"You'll survive," Birdie said, looking at Hank on the sofa, wiping crumbs from his lips with a cocktail napkin. "We all do."

In the week that followed, there were all sorts of other conversations, conversations upon conversations. Birdie had never had so many conversations. One of the most difficult, predictably, was Birdie's conversation with Grant, which she chose to undertake at nine o'clock at night when he would be at home in his "loft" rather than at the office.

She said, "Grant, I'm calling to tell you that Chess has broken the engagement. The wedding is off."

"Off?" he said.

"Off."

Silence. Birdie had wondered how Grant would meet the news. It was telling that after thirty years of marriage, she had no idea. She figured his main concern would be for Chess's welfare, and once he realized the murder had come at Chess's own hand, he would be worried about his money. Birdie waited for his questions, but none came.

"Grant?"

"Yes?"

"What do you think?"

"What am I supposed to think? You want to tell me what the hell happened?"

Of course, she should have guessed that he would not react at all until Birdie told him how he was supposed to feel. She had always done his emotional work for him.

"Chess wanted out. She's not in love with him."

"Not in love with him?"

"That's the gist of it." It was no longer Birdie's job to shield Grant from the unpleasant realities about his children. Birdie had to deal with it, and now so did he. "She's not in love. She doesn't want to spend the rest of her life with him."

"I don't get it," Grant said.

Of course he didn't get it. This was why Chess had wanted Birdie to call; Birdie was supposed to make him understand. Grant was eight years her senior; he had been thirty-one to her twenty-three when they got married. Grant had just made partner at the firm; he was expected to marry, start procreating, move to the suburbs, join a country club. He had come after Birdie like a bull charging; he had tracked her like a hit man. *I want you, you, you.* There had been dinners and musicals and weekends skiing in the Poconos, where they kept separate rooms for the sake of appearances. Birdie had an entry-level job at Christie's, where she showed a proclivity for carpets. She idolized the head of fine carpets, a man named Fergus Reynolds, who was always dashing off to Marrakech or Jordan. He spoke fluent French, Spanish, and Arabic and wore silk scarves in the style of Amelia Earhart. Birdie wanted to be a female incarnation of Fergus. She wanted to smoke clove cigarettes and appraise estates on the French Riviera. But instead, she succumbed to Grant. Within a year of marrying, she had quit her job; within two years, she was pregnant with Chess. The ways in which Grant Cousins had curtailed her potential were too numerous to name.

And then, once they were married and the girls had been born and the household established, Grant vanished. He was still present physically—sitting at the head of the dinner table with his tumbler of scotch and his benevolent, slightly baffled smile—but his mind was elsewhere. He lived in a state of constant distraction. The office, the cases, the clients, the billable hours, his handicap, the Yankees game, the Giants game. Birdie had grown to feel that anything and everything was more important to Grant than she and the girls were. He was kind to them, and generous, but they could never quite capture his full attention.

"I don't know how else to say it," Birdie said. "She's not going to marry him. And rather than beating her up, we should be praising her for calling it off before it was too late. If she'd gone ahead and married him, she'd regret it."

"The way you regret marrying me?" Grant said.

Birdie inhaled. Honestly!

"I do not regret it," Birdie said.

"Sure you do."

"I do not regret raising our children. And for many years, I didn't regret marrying you."

"You regretted being hemmed in to a certain life," Grant said. "You wished your life had contained more than PTA open houses and garden club. I do listen when you talk, Bird."

Infuriating. He was playacting now, trying to fudge the exam when he hadn't read the book. "Well, this will come as a surprise to you, I'm sure, but I'm not exactly dead yet. In fact, I'm dating someone."

"Congratulations," Grant said.

He was so patronizing. Birdie chastised herself for telling him. Her love life was none of his business, and no reaction—not even one of jealousy, which would have been disingenuous—would have satisfied her. Dating Hank was a source of private delight; to make it public would poison it.

"So anyway," Birdie said, "there are the matters of the wedding arrangements. I assume you'd like me to try to get your deposits back?"

"Yes, please," Grant said.

"All I can do is try," Birdie said. She had half a mind to simply let Grant's cash sink to the bottom of the ocean, but his money was her money, and wasting it was foolish. "And Grant?"

"Yes?"

"Call your daughter, please."

"And say what?"

"What do you think?" Birdie said. "Tell her you love her."

In the days and weeks that followed, Birdie had a hard time reaching Chess. When she called Chess at work, she was stonewalled by Chess's assistant, Erica, who claimed that Chess was no longer accepting personal calls at work.

"But she's there, right?" Birdie said. "She's alive?"

"Affirmative," Erica said.

When Birdie tried Chess's cell phone, she was inevitably shuttled to voice mail, where her messages stacked up like newspapers in the driveway of someone who had moved away.

"Call me," Birdie said. "I'm worried."

Birdie sought refuge in conversations with her daughter Tate. Birdie didn't love Tate any more than she loved Chess, but Tate was easier.

"Have you talked to your sister?" Birdie asked.

"A couple of times," Tate said. "Mostly I just leave messages."

"Oh, good," Birdie said. "I thought I was alone in that."

"You know I'd never leave you alone, Mama," Tate said.

Tate—Elizabeth Tate Cousins—was, at the age of thirty, a computer genius who was flown in by the biggest companies in America to fix glitches in their systems. She had such specialized knowledge and expertise that she was able to call her own shots: She wore jeans to even the swankiest workplaces, she worked with her iPod blaring Bruce Springsteen at top decibel, she ate lunches of tuna fish sandwiches and creamy tomato-basil soup from Panera and, in cities where there was no Panera, from Cosi. She demanded an astronomical fee.

"Where are you today?" Birdie asked. Technically, Tate lived in Charlotte, North Carolina, a place that Birdie didn't understand. It was a "new" city, known as a banking capital. Charlotte was the first place Tate had worked on assignment, and she had spontaneously plunked down money on a condo in a complex that had a beautiful swimming pool and a state-of-the-art fitness center.

Why Charlotte? Birdie had asked.

And Tate said, *Because it was there.*

There had been a period of time in junior high school when Tate had dressed like a boy. She had worn jeans and a boy's white undershirt and a red bandanna wrapped around her wrist or her ankle; she had cut her hair very short, spiking it some days and slicking it back on others. She even sounded like a teenage boy; she was constantly making flip remarks. She had been caught engraving the lyrics to "Darlington County" into a desk at school, and when asked why, she had shrugged and said, *Because it was there.* Birdie had wanted Tate to see a therapist, but the guidance counselors at school assured Birdie that Tate was experiencing a phase and it would pass. It had passed, but the teenage boy lived on in Tate. She was still fanatical about Bruce Springsteen, and about computers, and about NFL football. She had bought her first piece of real estate in a city where she knew no one "because it was there."

"I'm in Seattle," Tate said.

"Microsoft has computer problems?" Birdie said.

"I'm at a conference," Tate said.

"What did Chess tell you?" Birdie said.

"The same things she told you, I'm sure," Tate said. "She changed her mind. She doesn't want to marry Michael." Tate paused. "And she said you were completely cool about it. Not a freakazoid at all."

Birdie fought a sense of disquiet. She didn't love the idea of Chess and Tate discussing her, though of course Birdie and her sister, India, had parsed and deconstructed their own mother from the time they were conversant, at ages three and five.

"Did she say if anything had happened?" Birdie said.

"Happened?"

"Did anything precipitate her decision? Or it all just came out of thin air?"

"Out of thin air, I guess," Tate said.

"Okay," Birdie said. "Because Michael thinks there's something else going on. Something Chess might not be willing to tell him. Or her mother. Like maybe she's met someone else?"

"She didn't mention anyone else," Tate said. "But we're talking about Chess. I'm sure she has men hounding her day and night. I'm sure she has men following her home from the subway like stray dogs, trying to sniff up her skirt."

Birdie sighed. "Really, Tate, must you be crude?"

"I must," Tate said. She paused. "So...what about Tuckernuck?"

"Oh," Birdie said. She had forgotten about Tuckernuck. "What about it?"

"Chess said that you two are going, and I want to come, too," Tate said. "I want to stay two weeks like we used to. Can we? Chess said she would."

Birdie was caught off-guard. Amazing, at the age of fifty-seven, that she could still feel so many surprising emotions at once. Both girls on Tuckernuck for two weeks? It was an embarrassment of riches; it was a lavish gift, one Birdie never would have dared wish for. And yet the motivating factor behind this trip had been for Birdie and Chess to spend quality time alone together. Now that Chess wasn't marrying Michael Morgan, Birdie supposed the need for one-on-one time with her daughter was less pressing. And the trip to Tuckernuck would be more fun with Tate along. Birdie decided to let herself be happy. She would have both of her girls on Tuckernuck for two whole weeks!

"Can you swing it?" Birdie said. "What about work?"

"I am my own boss," Tate said. "Two weeks is nothing. I could take the whole month off if I wanted to."

"You're sure you want to come?" Birdie knew that both her girls loved Tuckernuck as much as she did. But they were adults now, with responsibilities. There was no Internet on Tuckernuck, no TV, and very poor cell phone reception.

"God, yes!" Tate said. "Of course I want to come. The house is still a total dump, right? I think about it all the time. The cobwebs? The bats? The stars at night, bonfires on the beach. And the Scout? I love that vehicle."

"I spoke to Barrett Lee," Birdie said. "Do you remember Chuck's son, Barrett? He's taken over the caretaking business."

"Do I *remember* Barrett Lee? Yes, I remember him.

He was the object of my private fantasies until Clooney and Pitt did *Ocean's Eleven*."

Birdie said, "Was it you, then, who went on a date with him? The lunch date, in the boat?"

"No, he took *me* fishing. He took *Chess* on the picnic. Good old Mary Francesca scored a date with my fantasy man, then proceeded to drink a six-pack of beer, get seasick, and upchuck her ham sandwich off the stern."

"Really?" Birdie said. She knew there had been a date, but she'd had no clue what transpired.

"Classic Chess, right? The woman gets whatever she wants and then ruins it. That's her modus operandi, present situation included."

"Well, Barrett is fixing up the house. He's reshingling it and repairing the roof. Buying a new generator. Refinishing the floors in the attic, and painting all the trim, I guess. I'll buy new linens and towels. Perhaps a few pots and pans so we don't get Alzheimer's from the corroded aluminum..."

"Don't bring too much," Tate said. "The whole point—"

"I know the point," Birdie said. "I invented the point." This wasn't exactly true; her grandparents had invented the point and her parents had refined it. The point was to live simply. "So we'll go, then, the three of us, for two weeks?"

"I can't wait," Tate said.

Thus followed a second conversation with Barrett Lee.

"Chess and I will be coming for two weeks instead of one," Birdie said. "And my other daughter, Tate, will be joining us."

"Swell," Barrett said. "It'll be nice to see everybody again."

Birdie said, "The reason for the switch is that Chess's engagement was canceled. The wedding is off."

"Ouch," Barrett said.

"It was Chess's doing," Birdie said. "She wasn't ready."

"She's still really young," he said. Then he cleared his throat. "And Mrs. Cousins? I sent you a bill. It's for twenty-four thousand dollars."

"You got the check I sent you? For ten?" The ten thousand had come out of Birdie's personal savings account. She had not wanted to ask Grant for the money until she knew what the total would be.

"Yes, ma'am, thank you. This bill is for twenty-four beyond that. The house needed a lot of work, the generator alone was eight grand, and I hate to say this, but I think it's going to be ten to twelve grand more, at least."

Birdie calculated. Fifty thousand dollars fixing up the Tuckernuck house. Birdie tried not to panic. Tuckernuck was her ancestral summer home; it had been left to her by her parents and someday would go to her children. But Grant, most certainly, would never set foot on Tuckernuck again. So why would he shell out fifty grand for upkeep and improvements? Would the kids' interest be enough for him? Birdie would have to grovel for it. It wasn't fair: Thirty years Birdie had supported Grant, and hence, the divorce lawyer reminded her, she was entitled to half of what Grant had earned during that period. Grant had earned millions. Fifty thousand dollars was negligible. It was a sneeze.

Furthermore, in the past two weeks, Birdie had recouped 75 percent of Grant's deposits from the wedding. She had pleaded and begged, negotiated—and, in one instance, cried—on behalf of Grant's money. She would remind him of this.

"Fine, Barrett, no problem," Birdie said. "The house needs a roof, it needs walls, it needs electricity. Thank you for all your hard work."

"My pleasure," Barrett said. "And hey, I'm sorry about Chess's wedding falling through."

"It's for the best," Birdie said, for what felt like the thousandth time.

The last conversation, one Birdie was dreading and had practically talked herself into believing was unnecessary, was with Evelyn Morgan, Michael's mother. Birdie had never met Evelyn Morgan, half of the aggressively branded couple Cy and Evelyn Morgan, but Birdie knew through Chess that Evelyn was a hurricane. She was not only the managing partner of a behemoth Madison Avenue advertising agency, but she was also on the board of directors at Bergen Hospice, an elder at the Presbyterian church, and president of the Fairhills Country Club. She was a tireless power walker and she read six newspapers a day. She had two sons—Michael and his younger brother, Nick—and a daughter, Dora. Evelyn Morgan was perpetually moving at amphetamine-rocket speed—wheeling, dealing, exercising, overseeing, singing, and dancing.

Birdie had sensed this from Evelyn's manic and overdetailed e-mails regarding the rehearsal dinner, which was to have been held at Zo, the hottest new restaurant in the Flatiron District. It was to be caipirinhas and Brazilian tapas for all out-of-town guests; Evelyn had hired a samba band with a transsexual lead singer. *We could have had the dinner at our country club,* Evelyn wrote. *But really, how dull—sauced tenderloin, martinis, sprinklers dousing the eighth green in the sunset. Certainly the kids would rather be in the city!*

All plans in the city were now off; the rehearsal dinner had been thrown in the recycling bin along with everything else. Chess and Evelyn had gotten along famously; they were better friends, Birdie had to admit, than Chess and Birdie were. They met for lunch on the seventh floor of Bergdorf's, they walked in Central Park after work, they cruised art galleries downtown in search of paintings for the apartment that Chess and Michael would inhabit after the wedding. But Chess hadn't spoken to Evelyn in person about the breakup. Calling Evelyn Morgan was one more thing that Chess should have done but refused to do. And so, it fell to Birdie.

Birdie wasn't sure how she envisioned the one and only phone call between her and the woman who would not become Chess's mother-in-law; she thought maybe she and Evelyn would commiserate a little, express regrets that they would not be grandmothering the same future children. But what niggled at Birdie was the thought that she might be expected to apologize to Evelyn. Her daughter had hurt Evelyn's son. How was this call any different from the call Birdie had had to make to Helen Avery when Tate pushed Gwennie Avery from the top of the slide and Gwennie Avery broke her arm?

Birdie tackled the call at the civilized hour of ten o'clock on Saturday morning. Birdie had a hair appointment at eleven, followed by a manicure, a pedicure, and a massage. She had a date with Hank at six that evening. Her day would be so, so pleasant once she got this phone call over with.

She dialed the number at the kitchen counter and then stared into her fruit bowl at the pineapple, the lemons, the Granny Smith apples.

Evelyn picked up on the first ring. "I was wondering if you'd have the guts to call," she said.

"Hello?" Birdie said.

"I've been wondering if you, Birdie Cousins, mother of Mary Francesca Cousins, would have the guts to call me, Evelyn Morgan, mother of the heartbroken, yet admittedly overprotected, Michael Kevin Morgan."

Was the woman drunk? Her voice was loud and theatrical, as though she were speaking not only to Birdie but to an audience of people that Birdie couldn't see.

"I have the guts," Birdie confirmed. "I'm calling."

"You are a better woman than I," Evelyn sang out. "In a similar position, I would have found a way to talk myself out of calling."

Birdie sighed. "I'm sorry, Evelyn."

"You have no reason to be sorry," Evelyn said. "*You* did nothing wrong."

"Chess is sorry, too," Birdie said.

"If she's really sorry, she would call me herself and tell me so," Evelyn said. "I've left the girl God knows how many messages. I even called her at work, and they told me she's no longer accepting personal calls."

"If it makes you feel any better, she won't take my calls either," Birdie said.

"I just don't get it," Evelyn said. "This came out of *nowhere.* I was there when Michael proposed. You've never *seen* a girl so happy. And that's why I'd like to talk to her. I'd like to find out what happened."

"I don't think anything *happened,*" Birdie said. "She just changed her mind."

There was a pause on Evelyn's end, and Birdie wondered if her last comment had been too glib: Chess broke Michael's heart because she changed her mind? Was Chess that flighty? That insensitive?

When Evelyn spoke again, her voice took on a normal timbre. "Chess feels how she feels, there is no right or wrong. We can't make her marry him. She has to want it. I applaud her for being brave enough to speak up."

"You do?"

"I do," Evelyn said.

"How is Michael?"

"He's devastated. He's not eating, not taking care

of himself. He works all the time because when he's working, he doesn't have time to think, and as I'm sure you know, it's thinking that hurts. He does have a trip planned. He's going rock climbing with his brother in Moab over Memorial Day."

"That'll be good for him."

"He'll survive," Evelyn said. "But he's lost something. All of the Morgans have. Chess is a wonderful girl. I love her like my own. We're the ones missing out."

"You're sweet to say so," Birdie said. She was shocked to find that she *liked* Evelyn Morgan. Birdie might have enjoyed a life tethered to this other woman, as they lived their lives on either side of the reflecting pond that was New York City.

"It was good of you to call," Evelyn said. "Thank you."

"You're welcome," Birdie said. She didn't want the conversation to end. She might never speak to this woman again. "I just thought—"

"You thought correctly," Evelyn said. "And please encourage Chess to call me when she's ready. I'd like to talk to her."

"I will," Birdie said. "Good-bye."

On the twentieth of May, which happened to be Birdie and Grant's ex-anniversary, Chess called to say she had quit her job at *Glamorous Home.* From the background noise of traffic and sirens, Birdie could tell Chess was calling from the street. Birdie was dumbfounded.

"So you *quit* quit?" Birdie said. "You walked out?"

"I walked out," Chess said. "We just put the July issue to bed and I thought, *That's that.*"

Birdie wondered what was going on here. Was the fact that her elder daughter had marched out on two major commitments in a row—seemingly without planning or forethought—a sign of encroaching mental illness?

"I can't believe it," Birdie said. "You've been there so long."

"Eight years," Chess said.

She had been at the magazine for eight years; she had been named food editor a month shy of her thirtieth birthday. Birdie had been so proud. Her daughter was a prodigy; she was the Yo-Yo Ma of food magazines. One day she would be the magazine's creative director or editor in chief. But now a sideways move might not even be possible. If Birdie understood her, she had walked out without giving two weeks' notice.

A prevalent worry of Birdie's since the children were small was that her kids would suffer from their privilege rather than benefit from it. This worry surfaced now: Breaking her engagement and then quitting her job? What did Chess plan to do for money? Ask her father? (Internally, Birdie cringed. This was, of course, what *she* did when she needed money.)

Birdie longed to call Hank to ask his opinion. She had continued to see Hank every weekend, and often he spent the night. He was the warmest, kindest, most evolved man Birdie had ever met. He not only brought Birdie flowers but spent two hours on his knees in her garden helping her weed. He took her to see *Jersey Boys* and then they drank champagne and shared french fries from a paper cone at Bar Americain. Hank serenaded her all the way home, and then he carried her upstairs to bed like a bride. Another weekend they had wandered around Greenwich Village and he had encouraged Birdie to enter clothing boutiques meant for women twenty years younger and try on clothes. It had been something of an erotic fashion show, with Hank occasionally peeking at her over the top of the dressing room door. Birdie didn't want to weigh down her relationship with Hank with her concerns about Chess. She didn't want him to think Chess was a complete mess. Chess was her marquis, gold-standard daughter. She would leave her job at *Glamorous Home* only after securing a more fabulous job at *Bon Appétit* or *Food and Wine.* But she had called from the street. *Was* she a complete mess?

"What are you going to do?" Birdie asked Chess now. "Do you have anything lined up?"

"No," Chess said. Her voice was so indifferent that Birdie wondered if this was really her daughter. Maybe this was some kind of prank? "I'm thinking of traveling."

"Traveling?" Birdie said. "What does that mean?"

"I'm thinking about India," Chess said. "Or maybe Nepal."

"India?" Birdie said. She was trying not to become hysterical. "*Nepal?*"

"Listen, Bird, can we talk about all this when I get home?"

"Home?" Birdie said.

"I've sublet my apartment for the summer. I'm coming home to you next weekend."

"Next weekend" was Memorial Day, and Birdie had plans to go to the North Fork of Long Island with Hank. Reluctantly, she canceled. She said to Hank, "Chess has quit her job and sublet her apartment, and she's coming home. And I should be there for her. I'm her mother."

Hank said, "Do you want to talk about it?"

Birdie thought for a second. Hank had handled Chess's broken engagement artfully, convincing Birdie that if Chess was no longer in love with Michael, then breaking the engagement was the only decent and humane thing to do. He might be able to make sense of these new developments. But Birdie held back. "No," she said. "I don't think so."

"You're sure?"

"I'm sure."

"Okay, well then, we'll go to the North Fork another weekend. I promise. Now go take care of your little girl."

Birdie changed the sheets in Chess's room and put roses in a vase by her bed. She made Tuscan lemon chicken, Chess's favorite dinner, for Friday night. Birdie had half a mind to plan a barbecue for Sunday afternoon, inviting some of Chess's high school friends, but thought better of it. And how wise! Chess, when she arrived, looked, not like a beautiful thirty-two-year-old newly liberated from fiancé and high-powered job, but wan and puffy eyed and painfully thin. Her long blond hair was greasy and tangled; her shoulders were hunched. She wore a ratty T-shirt featuring the logo of the band Diplomatic Immunity, and a pair of surplus army shorts. She hadn't bothered with makeup or jewelry; the holes in her pierced ears were red and swollen. She looked like a homeless person.

Drugs, Birdie thought. *Or a cult. India? Nepal?*

Chess pulled her cell phone out of her incongruously elegant Coach purse and dropped it into Birdie's kitchen trash. "I am done with phone calls," she said. "I am done with e-mails and done with texting. I don't want to talk to Michael or to anyone else about Michael. I don't want to talk to anyone from work about why I left or where I'm going. I am all done talking. Okay?" She looked to Birdie as if for permission, and her eyes filled with tears. "I'm just really confused, Bird. The way this has all played out... the things that have happened... honestly? I'm done with other people. I want to be a hermit and live in a cave."

"What's wrong?" Birdie asked. "What 'things' have happened?"

"Are you not listening?" Chess said. "I don't want to talk about it."

Birdie, not knowing what else to do, poured Chess a glass of Sancerre and led her to the picnic table, which was set for two overlooking the garden. (Would it make Chess uncomfortable to gaze at the acreage where her wedding reception was to have taken place? Probably, but what could Birdie do? It was her backyard.) She plied Chess with Tuscan lemon chicken and a gratin of potatoes and fennel, and haricots verts sautéed with garlic, and rolls and butter. And a wedge of rhubarb pie for dessert. Under Birdie's hawklike gaze, Chess ate four bites of chicken, one green bean, a bite of roll, and two bites of pie. She didn't want to talk, and Birdie—despite four or five really important topics hovering over the table like hummingbirds—wouldn't make her.

After dinner, Birdie rescued Chess's phone from the trash can. She checked the display—fourteen new messages. Birdie was tempted to see who the messages were from. What kind of "things" had happened? Birdie supposed her curiosity was natural, but she was determined to shine as a mother, which meant respecting Chess's privacy. She wiped the phone off and set it on the counter next to the house phone.

Upstairs, she drew her daughter a lavender-scented bath in the claw-foot tub and turned up Pachelbel's Canon. She laid a fresh white eyelet nightgown on Chess's bed. She set a copy of her reading group's latest selection on the night table.

Before retiring to her own room that night, Birdie peeked in on Chess, after knocking lightly and waiting to be invited in. She was happy to find Chess tucked between the crisp linens, reading. The light was soft; the roses by the bed were fragrant.

Chess looked up. "Thanks for everything, Birdie."

Birdie nodded. It was what she did, it was who she was: a mother. Chess was home. She was safe.

Which was a good thing, because three days hence, on Monday, Memorial Day, the call came saying that Michael Morgan was dead.

He fell a hundred feet while rock climbing in Moab. He broke his neck and died instantly.

This was crisis. *This* was hysteria. Upon hearing the news—from Michael's brother over the phone—Chess screamed like she was being stabbed. Birdie rushed into Chess's bedroom, where Chess was sitting on the floor in her wet bikini. (Chess and Birdie had spent the majority of the weekend at the country club pool, picking at club sandwiches and hiding from acquaintances behind copies of *Vogue.*) Birdie said, "Chess, what is it?" And Chess put the phone down and looked at Birdie and said, "He's dead, Mommy! He's dead!"

For one stricken second, Birdie thought she was talking about Grant. She thought, *Grant is dead,* and felt a vertigo that nearly pulled her to the floor as well. The children had lost their father; she was all they had left, and she had to be strong. But how could she be strong when Grant was dead? Birdie wasn't quite sure what led her to understand that it was Michael Morgan who had died and not Grant. It was something Chess said over the phone to Nick, or perhaps the fact that it was Nick on the phone clued Birdie in. Birdie got the story straight: Michael and Nick had been rock climbing in Moab. Everything had been fine; the rock climbing had been going well. They had good weather, perfect conditions. On Monday morning, Michael had arisen at dawn and gone for a climb by himself in Labyrinth Canyon. He had not been harnessed properly; he had lost his footing and fallen. A park ranger found him.

The funeral would be Friday at the Presbyterian church in Bergen County.

Birdie didn't know what to do. She called Hank, but he was on his way to Brewster with his children to see Caroline at the facility and couldn't be interrupted. She called Grant and was shuttled to his voice mail, which meant he was golfing. (Of course: Grant golfed every Memorial Day.) Birdie called their family physician, Burt Cantor, at home. Burt, too, was golfing, but his wife, Adrienne, was a nurse practitioner and she called in a prescription for Ativan to the pharmacy. Chess was screaming deep into her pillow, she was wheezing and hiccuping, and Birdie sat on the bed next to her, put a hand on her back, and felt as useless as she ever had in her life. She thought: if Chess was this upset now, how upset would she have been if Michael Morgan were still her intended? Or maybe this was worse somehow; Birdie didn't know.

Tears flooded Birdie's own eyes as she thought of Evelyn Morgan. What kind of hell must she be experiencing right now? To lose a child. To lose her big, handsome, smart, talented, charming, athletic firstborn—who would only have been a little boy in Evelyn's mind. Birdie rubbed Chess's back and smoothed her pretty hair, which was stiff with chlorine from the pool. It was the world's greatest privilege to be a mother. But God knows, it was a punishment as well.

Birdie said, "Adrienne Cantor called in a sedative. I'm going to run to Fenwick's and get it."

Chess raised her head. Her face was melting. She was trying to speak, but the words were gibberish. Birdie shushed her and handed her a tissue. Chess blew out a faceful of snot and said, "This is *my* fault."

"No, Chess, it isn't." She reached for Chess and rocked her. "Honey, it isn't. He fell. It was an accident."

"But there are things you don't know."

"We can talk about it if you want to. We can look at

it sixteen different ways, and in none of those ways will this be your fault."

Chess buried her head under the pillow. She was moaning.

"Okay," Birdie said, and she stood up. Was it safe to leave her? She needed a pill, that was for sure. "I'll be right back."

Birdie was trembling as she got into her car. It was a spectacular late afternoon, as green and golden as a day could be. Birdie smelled charcoal. Her neighbors were having the first cookout of the year. Birdie had been thinking of grilling hamburgers herself just an hour before, when she and Chess pulled into the driveway. It wasn't fair how things happened without warning. Someone fell, a neck snapped, a phone call came, and your whole reality was changed forever. Birdie backed out into the street, incredulous.

Going to the pharmacy to get sedatives reminded her of something. *It's my fault.* The beautiful day mocking what was happening inside the house. It reminded Birdie of... what? And then it came to her: it reminded her of India.

The next day, Tuesday, Birdie phoned India at her office at the Pennsylvania Academy of Fine Arts. India's assistant seemed to want to screen the call; she claimed India was down in the vault until Birdie said, "This is her sister and it's urgent." Then the assistant, magically, put her right through.

Birdie said, "India, it's me."

India said, "What's wrong?"

And so Birdie explained it frankly, the way she could only explain something to her sister: the broken engagement, Chess quitting her job, Michael Morgan dead.

"Dead?" India said, as though maybe Birdie had gotten this detail wrong.

"Dead."

"How old?"

"Thirty-two." They both paused for a moment, and Birdie imagined herself at age thirty-two: married to Grant, the mother of Chess, age seven, and Tate, age five. Still so, so young. Then Birdie said, "I have a proposition."

"Oh, God," India said.

Birdie said, "I'm taking the girls to Tuckernuck. It was going to be for two weeks, but now I want to stay the whole month of July. Chess is going to need time... away, really *away* away...and I thought...well, you've dealt with things like this before. You can help Chess in ways that I can't. I want you to come with us."

"To Tuckernuck?" India said. "For the month of July?"

"It's crazy," Birdie said. "I know you have work. But I had to at least ask you."

"You don't know how lucky you are," India said. "Because it just so happens I *need* to get away. Don't get me wrong—I was thinking Capri or the Canary Islands. I was not thinking dowdy old Tuckernuck. I was thinking cold limoncello, not a month of cold showers."

"Please?" Birdie said. "Would you come?"

"Are you sure you want me? Are you sure I'm not going to be infringing on your time with your girls?"

"I don't want you," Birdie said. "I need you. And they're your girls, too, you know that."

India sniffed. Birdie could picture her polishing the lenses of her late husband's reading glasses the way she did when she was at a loss for words. "Who are we kidding?" India said. "It's me who's lucky."

* * *

Later, Birdie cracked open the door to Chess's bedroom. Chess was asleep, snoring like the old man who bumped his head. Birdie heard bells. She hunted around the room and found Chess's cell phone in the trash. Birdie checked the display: Nick Morgan calling. Gently, Birdie set the phone down and waited until the ringing ceased. (She had a vision of India and Bill's driveway once the news broke that Bill had killed himself. There had been so many cars: lawyers, reporters, art dealers, all of them on the phone. India had looked out the picture window and screamed. *What could they be saying? Make them stop, Bird! Make them stop!*)

Thirty days on dowdy old Tuckernuck, Birdie thought. It would do them all some good.

CHESS

Before she left for Tuckernuck, she cut off all her hair.

And when she said all her hair, she meant *all her hair:* twenty-six inches of honey blond was wound around the stylist's forearms like a skein of yarn. Chess had made him shave her scalp, and the last bits of downy fluff floated to the polished floor like out-of-season snowflakes.

She was at an expensive salon in Nolita where anything went and nobody asked questions. She had felt compelled to tell the stylist she was donating to Locks of Love. She paid at the receptionist's desk; the girl handed her the credit card receipt and smiled as though nothing were wrong. Chess's skull felt as thin and exposed as a helium balloon. She'd brought along a blue crocheted cap, which she put on, not out of vanity, but because she didn't want anyone to pity her. She didn't deserve anyone's pity.

Her mother had looked upon her in fright, or revulsion, or sadness—Chess couldn't identify her own emotions, much less anyone else's. Shaving her head had been—what? Some kind of statement? An alternative to slitting her wrists? A denunciation of her beauty? A shedding of her identity? A tantrum? As a child, Chess had once cut her own hair out of anger, using a pair of blunt-nosed scissors. The bangs had been hacked down to a mere quarter inch at her part. Her mother had reacted with openmouthed shock then, too, but Chess had only been five years old.

"Your hair," Birdie said.

"I cut it," Chess said flatly. "I shaved it all off. I gave it away."

Birdie nodded. She reached out and touched the crocheted cap.

Now, Chess, along with her mother, her sister, and her aunt India, was in her mother's Mercedes, cruising north on I-95 toward Cape Cod, toward Nantucket, toward Tuckernuck Island, where they would live in rustic simplicity for a month. Neither Tate nor Aunt India had said one word to Chess about her shaved head, which meant that Birdie had intercepted them and given them fair warning. What had Birdie said?

She's worse off than we imagined.

Chess touched her head under the cap, a new, irresistible habit. Her scalp was rough and bumpy; it itched. Her head felt so light she had to check that it was still there, attached to her neck. She supposed she had wanted to *do* something, something big, something drastic, something to express a small fraction of her pain. She might have set herself on fire in front of the Flatiron Building, or dangled by both hands from the top deck of the George Washington Bridge, but she had settled for visiting the Nolita salon, which was, Chess understood, a cowardly option. Her hair, after all, would grow back.

For the past twenty-eight days, Chess had seen a therapist named Robin. Robin told Chess that she should put "all that had happened" in a silk-lined drawer and revisit it when it was less painful. In the meantime, Robin said, Chess should try to think about other things: what she would have for lunch, the color of the sky.

Robin was a psychiatrist, a real doctor of the mind with a degree from Johns Hopkins. Chess's father had insisted on the very best, and for Grant Cousins, the very best translated to the most expensive. And yet, for $350 an hour, Robin (she wanted Chess to call her Robin and not Dr. Burns) talked about silk-lined drawers, a mental exercise that was beyond Chess. Telling her not to think about "all that had happened" was the equivalent of telling her to spend all day standing on her hands, when the most she could manage was three or four seconds.

They should turn the car around now. Chess couldn't handle this trip. She was "depressed." The label had been slapped across her forehead; it had been whispered between her mother and sister and aunt. (And with the trip to the salon, "depressed" had taken a step closer to "crazy," even though everyone in the car was taking great pains to make all this seem normal.) Chess was taking an antidepressant, which, Robin promised, would make her feel like her old self.

Chess knew the pills wouldn't work. Antidepressants couldn't turn back the clock; antidepressants couldn't change her circumstances. And this drug wasn't particularly effective at quelling the voices in Chess's head, soothing her panic, easing her guilt, or filling her emptiness. She had thought that "depression" would be like sitting in a rocking chair and not being able to make it move. She had thought it would descend over her like a fog, turning things fuzzy, coloring them gray. But depression was active, it paced back and forth wringing its hands. She couldn't stop thinking; she couldn't find her way free from apprehension. Everywhere she turned, it was there, the situation, all that had happened. Chess felt like she was swimming through an endless jungle of seaweed. She felt like her pockets were filling with rocks: she was growing heavier and heavier, she was sinking into the ground. Robin had once asked her if she harbored any suicidal thoughts. Yes was the answer, of course; all Chess wanted was to escape her present circumstances. But Chess didn't have the energy to commit suicide. She was doomed to sit, mute and useless.

In her rare moments of clarity, she realized that her situation wasn't original. She had been an English major at Colchester. Her situation was Shakespearean; it was, in fact, *Hamlet*. She had fallen in love with her fiancé's brother—madly, unreasonably, insanely in love with Nick Morgan.

Acknowledging this love had been like throwing a grenade—killing Michael, leaving Chess emotionally amputated. If surgeons sliced her open, they would find a time bomb where her heart used to be.

Put that in your silk-lined drawer and revisit it when it is less painful.

How had this happened to her? She, Mary Francesca Cousins, had lived easily in the world. She'd belonged; she'd succeeded.

From the time Chess was young, she had been marked as a shining star. She was pretty and she smiled, she was graceful and she twirled and curtsied. Her ballet teacher placed her up front, in the center. She had the best posture, the most compelling presence. She excelled at school, she outscored all the boys, hers was always the first hand in the air; teachers who taught two and three grades above hers knew her name. She was well liked, a queen bee; she was a kind and benevolent leader. She edited the yearbook, she was on the pep squad, she was president of the student council. She played tennis, the country club variety, social rather than competitive, and she played golf with her father. She was a good swimmer, a great skier. She had been accepted at Brown but went to Colchester because it was cuter. She was the social secretary of her sorority; she wrote for the college newspaper for the first two years, then became the editor. She aced all her classes and graduated Phi Beta Kappa, despite the fact that she could be found on any given Saturday night drinking keg beer and dancing on the bar at the SigEp house.

After college, Chess moved to New York City. She got a job in the advertising department at *Glamorous Home;* then she was promoted to editorial, where they could make better use of her talents. She indulged her lifelong love of cooking by attending the French Culinary Institute on the weekends and learning the proper way to dice an onion and how to measure in metric. She discovered Zabar's and Fairway and the greenmarket in Union Square. She threw dinner parties in her apartment, inviting people she barely knew and making difficult dishes that impressed them. She went to work early and stayed late. She smiled at everyone, she knew all her doormen by name, she joined the Episcopal church on East Seventy-first Street and worked in the soup kitchen. She got promoted again. She was, at age twenty-nine, the youngest editor in the Diamond Publishing Group. Chess's life had been silk ribbon unspooling exactly the way it was supposed to—and then it was as if she'd looked down and the ribbon was a rat's nest, tangled and knotted. And so Chess threw the ribbon—spool and all—away.

Chess's therapist suggested that she keep a journal. She needed an outlet for her feelings while she was away. Chess bought a regular spiral-bound notebook at Duane Reade, seventy pages, with a pink cardboard cover—the kind of thing she had written her chemistry labs in during high school. She could write about "all that had happened," Robin said, but she didn't have to. She could write about the scenery on Tuckernuck; she could write about the sound of the birds, the shape of the clouds.

Silk-lined drawer, the shape of the clouds. Robin Burns was a *medical* doctor? A diploma from Hopkins hung on her wall, but Chess was skeptical. Chess wasn't sure she would be able to write at all. It was a yoga position she couldn't achieve.

Try, Robin and her medical degree said. *You'll be surprised.*

Okay, fine. There, in the car, Chess pulled the notebook out of her bag. She found a pen. The effort of this was enough to leave her short of breath. To express a thought or feeling in writing...she couldn't do it. She couldn't swim out of the seaweed. It was thick, bright green, and twisted like crepe paper, strangling her, binding her wrists and ankles. She was a prisoner. Michael. Nick. One dead, the other gone. Her fault. She couldn't write about it.

She glanced at her sister. For the first ten years of their lives, they had been constant companions; for the second ten years, they had not. In that seminal decade—say, when Chess was ten to twenty, Tate eight to eighteen—they did the best they could to disentangle the burrs of their identities. This was easier for Chess because she was older and more at home in the wide world. Chess was smart and popular and accomplished, and so the predictable way for Tate to distinguish herself was to underachieve and hang out with complete losers. Tate was good at math and a genius on the computer; at the age of fourteen, she acquired a bordering-on-freakish taste for the music of Bruce Springsteen. While Chess was participating in Junior Miss and spearheading the senior class trip to Paris, Tate was hanging out in the computer lab, wearing ripped jeans, communing with the school's population of nerds and geeks, all of them boys, all suffering from poor eyesight, acne, and cowlicks.

To look at Tate now, you would never guess the severe degree of her loserdom. Now, she was thin and toned, she had great hair—blond and thick, cut well—and she had a career that knew no limits. She was single and hadn't had a boyfriend that Chess could remember since her senior year of high school. Did Tate care about this? Was Tate lonely? Chess had never asked; since they had grown up and moved out of their parents' house, they talked only when circumstances required it—about their mother's birthday present, holiday plans, and, more recently, their parents' divorce. Tate had been leveled by their parents' divorce. She just didn't get it: They had made it so far, thirty years, they had made it through the years when the kids were small and Grant was building his practice. Now they were rich and the kids were out of the house. Why did they have to split? There had been some tough conversations, with Tate crying and Chess comforting, and these conversations had knit the two girls together closely enough so that when Michael Morgan proposed, Chess asked Tate to be her maid of honor.

Tate said, "I'll do it as long as you promise never to get divorced."

"I promise," Chess had said.

"Okay, then," Tate said.

Since "all that had happened," Tate had been unstinting with her support and love, despite the fact that Chess hadn't told her anything. Tate wasn't known for her emotional depth. If Chess told her about the seaweed jungle or the stones in her pockets, Tate wouldn't get it. Chess was going to have to come up with a reasonable explanation about her hair. A friend with cancer. Temporary insanity.

Chess's heart slammed in her chest. *This* was depression: the constant urge to escape herself. To say, *I'm done here,* and step out of her life. Outside the car window, the landscape—endless trees punctuated by obnoxious rest stops (McDonald's, Nathan's, Starbucks)—streamed by. Robin had promised that getting away would feel good, but Chess experienced a sick panic rising in her throat like vomit.

"Bird?" Chess said. Her voice was barely a whisper, but Birdie was so attuned to any sound or movement from Chess that she immediately turned down the radio and said, "Yes, darling?"

Chess meant to ask Birdie to slow down; they were driving like they were on the lam. But Chess couldn't form the sentence; she couldn't find the tone that would do the trick. If Chess asked Birdie to slow down, Birdie would stop the car altogether. She would pull over to the shoulder to make sure Chess was okay. Did she need air, or ice water? She would offer Chess India's seat up front.

Chess said, "Nothing. Never mind."

Birdie eyed her in the rearview mirror, her voice already an octave higher with concern. "Are you sure, darling?"

Chess nodded. *Your mother is very worried about you,* Robin had said. Worried, yes; Birdie was treating Chess like she had a terminal disease. But things between Chess and her mother had always been unbalanced. How to explain? When Chess graduated from college, her mother handed her a thick binder, painstakingly prepared, replete with all of Chess's accomplishments. The binder contained every single report card from twelve years of school, the program from every dance recital and every awards ceremony; it contained the short story she'd published in the high school literary magazine, her valedictory speech, her first byline in the college newspaper. It contained letters of recommendation from her high school teachers and her letters of acceptance from Brown, Colchester, Hamilton, and Connecticut College. Her mother had *saved* all this stuff? She had included snapshots of Chess throughout: in her sleek black dress before prom, on the diving board at the country club pool, as a toddler in a diaper, holding a dripping Popsicle. Chess paged through the binder, amazed and embarrassed. Her mother had believed that her life was worth careful documentation, whereas Chess hadn't given her mother's life a single thought. Her mother, Chess realized, had never *interested* her.

Chess had started calling her mother "Birdie" at the age of twelve, which was the age Chess felt like her mother's equal—and neither her mother nor her father had commented. Birdie might have thought Chess would grow bored with it, or that it meant she and Chess were becoming friends, when in fact it was Chess asserting her adolescent power. Now, she continued the practice out of habit.

Things between Chess and Birdie changed with the divorce. Chess gained a new admiration for her mother: Birdie had thrown Grant Cousins out. At the age of fifty-five, she had changed her life. She had said no to unhappiness; she had opened herself up for other possibilities. Chess had encouraged her mother to get a job, and her mother seemed receptive to the idea, if understandably hesitant.

What would I do? Who would hire me at my age? If I go to work, who will take care of you?

Chess had said, *Birdie, I'm a grown woman. I can take care of myself.*

And yet now that Chess had run her life through the meat grinder, she was a full-time job for her mother.

Could Chess tell her mother about "all that had happened"? Could she tell her mother she had fallen in love with Nick Morgan? If she told her mother this, her mother would love her anyway. After all, Birdie was her *mother.* But Birdie would be mortified, and the vision that Birdie held of Chess—the glowing, golden girl celebrated in that binder—would be tarnished.

Put that in the silk-lined drawer and revisit it when it is less painful.

The person that Chess felt the closest to now was her aunt India. India had been to hell and back on her own express train. Chess remembered the October morning when India had called to say Uncle Bill killed himself. It had been Chess's senior year, the weekend of the homecoming dance. Birdie had received the call at four in the morning; she had climbed into the family minivan in her nightgown. She was going to drive all the way to Pennsylvania even though the sun was not yet up. It was Tate, at age fifteen, who had run out to the driveway with an overnight bag haphazardly stuffed with their mother's clothes. Chess had wanted their mother to wait until the following day, Sunday, because of the homecoming dance. Chess was a senior and both her parents were expected to be at the dance to present her when her name was announced. If her mother wasn't there, it would look weird.

Chess implored her mother to stay. She remembered the stricken look on Birdie's face through the open car window in the breaking dawn. Her mother had said, "I am going because India is my *sister. There is no one else.*"

It was only later that Chess understood what it meant for Uncle Bill to commit suicide and leave behind a wife and three sons and a hulking artistic legacy. And it was only now that Chess realized what it must have felt like for her aunt. Yet look at India: She was laughing at something Birdie was saying. She could laugh! She was a whole person. She had been as badly broken then as Chess was now, or worse, and yet you couldn't even see the cracks.

Chess slid her notebook and pen back into her bag, and the vision came to her unbidden: Michael, slipping, letting go, falling. *Falling! Letting go!* His arms flailing, his eyes popping. *Wait! Wait!* He was dead at the age of thirty-two. Death sometimes made sense—when a person was old, when a person had been sick for a very long time. Michael dead—his new business dissolved, his careful plans rendered meaningless. *This did not make sense!*

Chess thought of Nick with a spray of cards in his hand, his eyelids hooded, his fingers worrying his chips. When she pictured him, he was always gambling. Why? Chess needed air. She could hear the tinny sound of Bruce Springsteen playing on Tate's iPod. She couldn't do this! She couldn't pretend she was okay. She needed her mother to pull over. She would get out of the car and walk all the way back to Nick. But Nick wouldn't have her. Put that in the silk-lined drawer.

She breathed in through her nose and out through her mouth. This was the breathing pregnant women used for pain management. She rested her head against the window, where it vibrated with the tires speeding over the highway.

A chicken salad sandwich, she thought. *Blue,* she thought.

TATE

Tate had never been in love before, and this, she felt, was for the best. What did love get you? Misery. Exhibit A in the seat beside her was her sister: Mary Francesca Cousins. Chess fell in love, Chess fell out of love, and then—wham! Instead of her being able to pick herself up, dust herself off, and move on, her jilted boyfriend *died.* When Tate had heard Chess was getting married, Tate had felt sorry for her (and sorry for herself for having to wear a four-hundred-dollar Nicole Miller bridesmaid dress in ruched bronze satin). When Chess had announced that she had thrown Michael Morgan off her back like she was a feisty bronco in a rodeo, Tate had felt a sense of kinship. Maybe she and her sister were related after all and, much to their mother's dismay, would, by choice, spend the rest of their lives as single women. When Michael Morgan died, in an accident that Chess believed to be her fault even though she was twenty-two hundred miles away, Tate thought, *Oh, shit.* Drama followed Chess around like a smell. Some people, Tate had learned, were like that, and it was for people like her to sit and watch the show.

Tate was going to Tuckernuck out of love and concern for her sister. Because look at Chess now: she had shaved her head down to the scalp like an NBA star or a white supremacist. Birdie had been stricken by this. She had called Grant, who told her to call Chess's therapist, and Robin had told Birdie not to overreact. Shaving her head was just Chess's way of letting the world know she was hurting. Chess had always been vain about her hair, for good reason (long, thick, naturally wavy, the color of spun gold), and so to shave herself bald, she must have been in some exquisite pain indeed. And yet, Tate thought, it was damage she did to herself. It wasn't as though she had cancer and had lost her hair to chemo. This was an ungenerous thought, and since Tate was here out of love and concern for her sister, she tucked that one away.

Tate had her own agenda for Tuckernuck, and that agenda was to run the circumference of the island each morning, swim across North Pond and back, do 150 sit-ups a day while hanging by her knees from the branch of the only tree on their windswept property. She was going to lie in the sun, do Sudoku puzzles, drink wine, and let her mother feed her. Just like Chess, Tate wanted to escape the world. On Tuckernuck there would be no screens, no keyboards, no interfacing with anyone's god-damned crashed system, no hackers, no viruses, no hardware, no software, no incompatibility. No checking her iPhone for e-mails or texts, no checking the weather, no checking the stock market, no playing beer pong, no streaming E Street Radio. Good-bye to all that.

Tate was a level 4++ computer programmer, she was a wizard, she could fix absolutely anything short of a martian blowing your system away with his beta gun or a system overtaken by saltwater (it had happened once, at a five-star hotel in Cabo). But what Tate Cousins really did for a living was travel. She was constantly en route to Toledo, Detroit, Cleveland, San Antonio, Peoria,

Bellingham, Cheyenne, Savannah, Decatur, Chattanooga, Las Vegas. Her life was one long concourse; it was an endless string of Au Bon Pain and Hudson News. It was barf bags and foil packs of square pretzels and in-flight magazines. Shoes on, shoes off. Any liquids or gels? There was a stocky, red-haired TSA employee in Fort Lauderdale who remembered Tate and called her "Rosalita" because that was the song she had been listening to on her iPod when she first came through his security line. Tate had 1.6 million frequent-flier miles; she had enough bonus package points to buy either a time-share in Destin or a Range Rover. She was sometimes struck by images of Home: a house somewhere in the suburbs, Mom, Dad, kids, dog—all out on the front lawn, washing the car or throwing the Frisbee. It occurred to Tate that this was what she was supposed to want: a home, an end point. She was not supposed to be constantly in transit. She was supposed to stop somewhere and feel a sense of belonging.

The noteworthy thing about today, July 1, was that there was an end point. There was a home. Tate's mother, Birdie (which was short for Elizabeth, which was also Tate's given name), delivered them safely to Hyannis and nestled her Mercedes into long-term parking. The four of them then hopped the short flight to Nantucket. They took a taxi from the airport to Madaket Harbor. Once they were in Madaket, Tate's heart started to settle, like a dog on its canvas Orvis bed, like a baby in its quilted Moses basket. She had crisscrossed the United States of America dozens of times with little expectation or fanfare, but the mere sight of Madaket Harbor, sparkling blue and green in the July sun, smelling salty and swampy, and presenting itself *exactly* as she remembered it when she was last here at seventeen years old, was turning Tate to jelly.

Home!

And there, whistling, waving his bronzed arm in an arc, cutting a frothy swath through the placid water of the harbor, was her prince on a white horse—it was Barrett Lee on a thirty-three-foot Boston Whaler Outrage with dual 250s off the back. In gold letters across the back of the boat, it said, *Girlfriend, NANTUCKET, MASS.*

"Barrett Lee," Chess said. Her voice sounded surprised, as if he'd appeared out of the recesses of her deepest memory. Tate, meanwhile, had thought about nothing but Barrett Lee since her mother had first mentioned his name.

She wondered if Barrett Lee was married. She had searched for him on Facebook and come up empty handed. She had googled him but had been unable to find evidence of her Barrett Lee amid the 714 other Barrett Lees who had left footprints in cyberspace. She searched the online archives of the *Inquirer and Mirror,* the Nantucket weekly newspaper, and discovered—aha!—that Barrett Lee had been in the Thursday night dart league in 2006 and 2007.

Tate wondered if she would still have feelings for Barrett Lee, and if she did, would these be new feelings, or old, resurrected feelings? She wasn't the same person she'd been thirteen years ago, and he wouldn't be either. So did resurrected old feelings even count, if she didn't know him anymore?

This was all pretty deep thinking for Tate. She preferred to work in tangibles, and what was tangible was this: Barrett Lee was more attractive than ever. The kind of attractive that made Tate feel like her heart was being pulled out through her nose. Was that tangible enough for you?

"I got his girlfriend right here," Tate said. Chess may have been heartbroken, medicated, and shorn, but there was no way she was getting Barrett Lee. Tate planted her feet, removed the earbuds of her iPod, and waved back.

Barrett Lee was the person from Tate's past who evoked the deepest and most poignant longing. In Tate's memory, she had loved him since he was six and she was five. At six, Barrett had been what her parents called a towhead; his hair was white, like an old person's. Tate's most intense memories centered on the summer she was seventeen, the last summer she'd been to Tuckernuck with her family. It was for Tate, as it no doubt was for many other seventeen-year-olds, the seminal summer of her life. She had been headed into her senior year of high school. Barrett Lee, she remembered, had just graduated, and although Plymouth State had expressed interest in him as a wide receiver, he wasn't going to college. Tate found this very exotic. Chess had just finished her freshman year at Colchester in Vermont, which epitomized the New England collegiate experience that absolutely everyone in Tate's New Canaan high school was seeking: the scholarly brick buildings with white pillars, the green quadrangle, the flaming orange maple trees, the cable-knit sweaters, the ponytails, the keg parties, the a cappella singing groups strolling among the tailgaters as Colchester took on rival Bowdoin in football. Instead of going to college, Barrett Lee was going to work for his father; he was going to learn to build houses and then take care of them once they were built. He was going to tile bathrooms, plumb dishwashers, wire stove burners. He was going to build bookshelves and window seats. He was going to make money, buy his own boat, fish for striped bass, ride his Jeep to Coatue on the weekends, go to the Chicken Box, drink beer, see bands, pick up girls. He was going to live life. God, Tate could remember clear as day how much better that had sounded than going to college, sharing a dorm room, sponging off her parents.

She had spent that whole summer watching Barrett Lee. He was the one who brought the family their groceries, their firewood, their newspapers and paperback books. He picked up their bags of trash, which he took to the dump, and their laundry, which he took to Holdgate's and returned in neat white boxes like treats from the bakery. On very good days, he did repairs around the house, usually without wearing a shirt. Tate couldn't get enough of him—the deep tan of his back, the impossible sun-bleached lightness of his hair. He was gorgeous, and that would have been enough for Tate; she was, after all, only seventeen. But he was nice, too. He smiled and laughed with all of the members of the Cousins family—even Tate's grouchy father, who in that final summer demanded a *Wall Street Journal* by 10 A.M. each day, crisp, so that Barrett took to bringing it in a Wonder bread bag. Barrett Lee made their vacation on Tuckernuck pleasant; he made it possible. Everyone remarked on it.

It had been Aunt India who said that having two teenage daughters lying on the beach in bikinis helped to keep Barrett Lee on-task. Tate's heart trilled at the insinuation, but in the back of her mind, fear and jealousy festered. If Barrett Lee was interested in one of the Cousins girls, it would be Chess—and really, could Tate blame him? Chess had the long, wavy, honey blond hair, she had magnificent breasts, she had college-level expertise about how to smile and chat guys up, how to flirt, how to exude the confidence that came with acing her art history survey course and mastering the beer bong. She was reading thick books that summer—Tolstoy, DeLillo, Evelyn Waugh—that gave her an aura of intelligence and inapproachability, which Barrett Lee was attracted to. Tate, on the other hand, was stick thin and flat chested. She bounced a tennis ball incessantly on an old wooden racquet she'd found in the attic; she listened to her *Born to Run* tape on her Walkman until the Walkman ran out of batteries and Bruce warbled like a ninety-year-old man after ten shots of whiskey. Whenever they needed something from the store on Nantucket, they were to write it, in Sharpie, on "the list," which was most often kept on a panel of brown grocery bag. But Tate's grouchy father refused to pay for the sixteen-pack of AA batteries to power Tate's Walkman until she had finished her summer reading, *Their Eyes Were Watching God,* which Tate found impossibly tedious. Tate didn't do her reading, and Barrett didn't bring the fresh batteries that would have so improved her summer.

Tate had been a tomboy and a late bloomer. One night after dinner, she overheard Aunt India ask Birdie if she thought Tate might be a lesbian. Birdie said, "Oh, heavens, India, she's just a child!" Tate had filled with embarrassment, shame, and rage. In high school, she had once been called a dyke, but that was by an extremely ignorant girl who didn't understand Tate's devotion to the Boss or to the Macs in the computer lab. To have Aunt India, a woman of the world, suspect her to be a lesbian was confusing on another level. Tate lay in bed in the dark house—and darkness on Tuckernuck was far darker than in other places—listening to the rustle of what she knew to be bat wings (Chess slept with a blanket pulled over her head even though Tate had explained that bats echolocate and therefore would never accidentally brush her face or hair), thinking of how ironic it was that Aunt India would question her sexual orientation when she was suffering from the worst crush of her life. She came to the conclusion, too, that whatever it was that made Aunt India think that she, Tate, was a lesbian, was exactly the same thing that was keeping Barrett from looking at her the way he looked at Chess.

Predictably, that summer, things came to a head. One day, Barrett was invited to stay for lunch, an hour involving the whole family eating char-grilled burgers around the picnic table on the bluff that overlooked the beach, during which Tate's father interrogated Barrett about his aspirations and plans for the future. The answers formed the sum of what Tate knew about Barrett Lee. During the lunch, Barrett looked at Chess fourteen times. Tate counted, and it was like fourteen nails in the coffin of her hopes for love.

She had spent her entire life losing out to Chess, but she couldn't stand the thought of losing out to Chess with Barrett, and so she employed the only tactic that had ever been successful for Tate with a boy: she showed an interest in what he was interested in. This had worked organically for Tate at school—she liked Lara Cross, she liked Bruce Springsteen, and so did certain boys. These boys paid her attention; they thought she was "cool," unlike the rest of the female high school population, who only cared about makeup and Christian Slater.

What did Barrett like? He liked fishing. Toward the end of that fateful lunch, Tate had proclaimed several times, too loudly to be ignored, her burning desire to go fishing. She was *dying* to go fishing. She would do *anything* to go fishing. If only she knew someone who could take her . . . fishing.

Her father said, "We get the hint, honey. Barrett, would you be willing to take my daughter fishing?"

Barrett smiled uncomfortably. He flicked his eyes at Chess. "Uh, both of you, or . . ."

"God, no," Chess said. "I think fishing is just one more form of animal cruelty."

Tate rolled her eyes. This sounded suspiciously like

one of the radical positions Chess had picked up, like a flu bug, at the Colchester Student Union. "You *eat* fish," Tate pointed out. "Is that cruel?"

Chess glared at her. "I don't *want* to go fishing," she said.

"Well, I do," Tate said. She grinned at Barrett, not caring how transparent she was. "So you'll take me?"

"Yeah, I guess," he said. "Or my father could..."

Tate's father said, "I'm sure Chuck is too busy to take Tate fishing. If you agree to do it, Barrett, I'll be happy to pay you."

Tate was mortified.

Barrett said, "Okay, yeah, sounds good. So... we'll have to go pretty early. I'll pick you up at seven, okay?"

She was nothing more to him than an hourly wage, but what could she do now?

"Okay," she said.

That night, Tate didn't sleep. She closed her eyes and imagined Barrett's arms encircling her as he showed her how to cast. She imagined kissing him, touching his bare chest, warmed by the sun. She sighed and relaxed in the fact that she was most definitely attracted to the opposite sex.

She was up at dawn, dressed in a bikini, a pair of jean shorts, and a skimpy T-shirt that she had stolen from Chess's drawer. Chess was sound asleep and wouldn't notice until Tate got back, at which point it would be too late—the magic of the T-shirt would have worked. If Chess wanted to bitch about Tate borrowing her T-shirt without asking, she could go right ahead. Tate would be anesthetized by the power of Barrett's love.

At quarter to seven, Tate carried a waterproof bag containing a sweatshirt, three peanut butter and honey sandwiches, two bananas, and a thermos of cocoa down to the beach to wait. The bikini and Chess's skimpy T-shirt didn't offer much in the way of warmth, and Tate waited on the misty shore with her arms crossed over her chest, her nipples as hard and cold as the pebbles under her feet. When she heard the motor of Barrett's boat, she tried to appear sexy and enticing, even though her teeth were chattering and her lips, she was sure, were blue.

Tate's heart was hammering in her chest as she waded out to the boat; she was convulsing with the chill.

Barrett offered her a hand up. They were, for one sweet second, holding hands! He said, "I packed a picnic lunch, some beers and stuff, for after fishing."

It was, Tate saw now, a testament to her low self-esteem that she never once considered that the picnic had been meant for Barrett and *her*.

"And you're going to..."

Barrett nodded. "Ask your sister if she'll go with me. What do you think she'll say?"

Tate pressed her lips together to keep from screaming. "She'll say yes."

"You think?"

"I know," Tate said. Although Tate and Chess had not spoken about how insanely attractive Barrett Lee was, they were sisters, and therefore the whole novel of how Tate loved Barrett Lee and how Barrett Lee loved Chess and how this would eventually be revealed to Tate's horror and Chess's embarrassed delight was understood but left unspoken.

"Great," he said.

The fishing was ridiculously successful. Barrett caught three bluefish and one striped bass, and Tate caught two bluefish and two striped bass, one of which was a whopping forty-two inches long. Tate's dream of having Barrett wrap his arms around her as he showed her how to cast didn't materialize because Tate's first cast on her own whizzed out thirty yards.

"You're a natural!" Barrett said. "You look like you've been casting all your life."

Barrett was in good spirits—not because he was fishing with Tate, but because he was being paid (handsomely: Tate's father was very generous) to do what he loved. And they were slaying them out there. "This is the best fishing I've seen in years," Barrett said, though he was only eighteen, so how many years could he have been talking about? And he was happy, Tate knew, thinking about his imminent lunch date with the beautiful and standoffish Chess. When Tate caught her final fish, the monster striper, and Barrett measured it at forty-two inches, he gave a low, impressed, almost sexy whistle.

"That's a keeper," he said. "But I'm afraid seeing it will upset your sister." He threw the fish overboard.

When Barrett and Tate pulled back into the cove, Chess was lying on the beach in her bikini, reading. She looked up as Barrett beckoned to her. "Come on!" he said. "Your turn for a ride!" Tate's only hope was that Chess would turn Barrett down, but no sooner had Tate disembarked than Chess was up on her feet. She and Tate passed each other in the shin-deep water without a single word—not even an admonition about the pilfered T-shirt—and then, just like that, they had switched places. Chess was on Barrett's boat and Tate was on the shore.

The difference was, their father hadn't paid Barrett to take Chess anywhere.

Tate trudged up the stairs. She decided she would hang herself by the nonlesbian neck from the branch of the only tree on their Tuckernuck property.

* * *

Instead, Tate stole one of her father's cold Michelobs and two batteries from the transistor radio that her father kept around with hopes of catching part of a Yankees–Red Sox game (fruitless), and she spent the afternoon in the attic drinking, burping, crying, and softly singing "Thunder Road" to the bats sleeping in the rafters. This was predictable. What was not predictable was that Chess was more nervous about a date with Barrett Lee than Tate would have guessed. Chess drank an entire six-pack in two hours. Just as Barrett was making his move—placing his hand on Chess's bare waist and keeping it there—the swell and bump of the ocean got to Chess, as did the suspicion that the mayonnaise on the ham sandwich out of the picnic basket had gone bad, and she puked off the back of the boat.

She later detailed her disgrace to Tate. "It was so gross," she said. "The beer came out in one long stream, like a power washer. And then there were the chunks of the sandwich and the potato salad floating in the water, and Barrett made a comment about how my puke would draw the fish, and I barfed again."

They were lying in bed and Tate was glad for the darker-than-dark because she didn't want Chess to see her gleeful expression. Chess puking and Barrett's subsequent rebuff thrilled her. Chess said that Barrett had offered her a wintergreen Life Saver but hadn't touched her again, he hadn't kissed her, and he hadn't mentioned another date. This was the best outcome Tate could have hoped for. She was evil, she knew. She had no chance with Barrett Lee, but at least Chess had no chance either.

Barrett was an adult now. His hair was golden brown rather than the platinum of his youth; he had a day of stubbly growth on his face. He wore a visor with his sunglasses resting on the bill, and a blue T-shirt trumpeting a shark-fishing tournament. Tate checked his hand: no ring.

Birdie was the first one down onto the boat. Barrett reached out to shake her hand. "Hey, Mrs. Cousins, good to see you."

"Give me a hug," Birdie said. "I've known you since you were a baby."

Barrett laughed and kissed Birdie on the side of the mouth.

India said, "Ooohh, give me one of those. I've known you just as long, and I smoked a cigarette with your father when I was only fourteen!"

Birdie swatted her sister. "That's a horrible thing to say, India!"

"Is it?" India said. "Well, it's true."

Barrett laughed. He hugged and kissed India.

Then it was Tate's turn. She was nervous. Hug? Kiss? Shake hands? She said, "Hey, I'm Tate."

He said, "Like I could ever forget you. I haven't seen a forty-two-inch striper since that day we went fishing together."

"Really?" she said. He took her hand and helped her down into the boat and she thought, *Oh, what the hell,* and said, "Well, it's good to see you." She stepped in closer and kissed him somewhere between the side of the mouth and his cheek, no-man's-land for a kiss, which was awkward. She chastised herself. *Idiot!* Already, she was pushy. He probably remembered that about her.

Tate moved to the back of the boat, where there was a horseshoe of white cushions. There were white cushions encircling the bow as well, and two captain's chairs at the controls. One for Barrett, Tate supposed, and one for girlfriend. Tate watched as Barrett took notice of Chess's blue crocheted cap covering what was clearly a bald egg.

He touched Chess's shoulder and said, "I'm sorry to hear about your troubles."

"Thanks," Chess said. She looked for a second like she might cry, and Tate could see Barrett teeter with worry.

Tate said, "Chess, come sit by me! This is going to be so great!"

Chess sat next to Tate, and Tate reached for her hand. Chess was hurting, and for a second Tate wondered if Chess should be given the first shot at Barrett Lee. But no, Tate decided. What Chess needed was a *break* from men. For her to dive headlong into another relationship would be the worst thing.

Barrett loaded their luggage onto the boat, and Tate watched the muscles in his forearms straining. She looked at his fine legs, the frayed hem of his khaki shorts, the sliver of oxford blue boxer peeking out from below the hem of one leg. He was too perfectly himself, the boy-now-man of Tate's dreams. He was *here,* she could reach out and touch him.

Barrett took the wheel and eased the boat away from the dock. Tate inhaled the diesel fumes, which, mixed with the sun and the swampy harbor water, gave her a heady feeling of well-being. Barrett puttered out of the harbor—Tate didn't take her eyes from his strong shoulders—and then he let the engines loose.

Tate squeezed her sister's hand. They flew across the open water toward Tuckernuck Island. Tate leaned her head back so her face got direct sun. The boat hit waves, and a fine spray of saltwater came over the side. Tate loved summer in New England. It was so different from summer in Charlotte, where everyone moved from one air-conditioned venue to the next, where "swimming" meant laps in a heated, chlorinated pool.

Tate decided she was never going to spend another summer day working. Next year, she would take off not only all of July but all of August as well. She would live in the Tuckernuck house. God, she wanted to ask Barrett to anchor the boat right here so she could strip off her clothes and dive in. She wanted Barrett Lee to see her swimming naked like a native creature—a seal, a Tuckernuck mermaid. Okay, she was happy, she was high. Would it be inappropriate of her to shout? They were here! Barrett cut the motor by half. Their crescent of perfect, pale beach was in front of them. Their house waited on the bluff.

Tuckernuck Island was a stone held in the ocean's palm. The name meant "loaf of bread," and it did look a little like a loaf of bread—it was vaguely oval—though Tate had always thought it looked like a fried egg. The coastline was amorphous, shifting over the years, depending on storms, she supposed, and global warming. The island was only nine hundred acres, all of them privately owned by the residents; there were two large ponds—one in the northwest called North Pond, and one in the northeast called East Pond. Tuckernuck had thirty-two homes, as well as a firehouse, which held a fire truck with a 250-gallon tank. There was no electricity on Tuckernuck other than that provided by generators, and no running water other than from wells powered by generators. The Tate house sat on the somewhat flattened eastern shore, facing Eel Point on Nantucket. Just south of them was the spit of sand called Whale Shoal. The next closest house was a quarter mile to the southwest.

The drill for disembarking hadn't gotten any easier or more glamorous. Barrett anchored the boat and then hopped into the knee-deep water to help them down. Poor Birdie! She was okay; she was only fifty-seven, still small and spry and, as her name implied, birdlike. She removed her white tennis shoes, hopped down into the water, and waded to shore. Aunt India was wearing a gauzy skirt with an asymmetrical hemline, which probably cost six thousand dollars; it made disembarking gracefully a challenge. She ended up sort of falling into Barrett's arms like a new bride, and what could Tate do but admit she felt jealous?

There was a new set of stairs from the beach to the bluff. The staircase, always treacherous and rickety, was now sturdy, built from bright yellow pressure-treated lumber.

"Wow!" Birdie said. "Look, girls!"

They ascended to the bluff. There was the lone tree with its gnarled branches, the very same tree Tate had meant to hang herself from. Nice to know they had both survived. In the yard, the old picnic table was centered in an oval of dirt, and from the oval was a white shell path that led to the front door of the house. The house had been reshingled and it smelled like resin. The door was the same weather-beaten blue, and next to the door hung the driftwood sign that Birdie and Aunt India had made when they were girls. Using thumb-size slipper shells, they had formed the word *TATE*. The sign was the closest thing the house had to an antique; it was taken down when they left for the summer, stored in a kitchen drawer, and brought out again to harbinger their arrival. *TATE*.

On the far side of the house, where the white shells widened to form a driveway, sat their jalopy, a 1969 International Harvester Scout with a white vinyl roof and a stick shift that was longer than Tate's arm. The Scout had, once upon a time, been fire-engine red, but it had faded to a grayish pink. Tate looked upon the Scout as a long-neglected pet, a trusty though beat-up veteran of

Tate family summers on Tuckernuck Island. The Scout had been brought to Tuckernuck on a car barge by Tate's grandfather in 1971; Tate and Chess and all three of the Bishop boys had learned to drive in that car at the age of twelve. Tate remembered her own initiation, with her father in the passenger seat coaching her about the gear-shift and the clutch. Despite its appearance, shifting the Scout was like cutting through butter, which was good because the Tuckernuck "roads" were challenging; they were dirt, gravel, or grass, potholed and ridged, a bitch to navigate. Tate had always had an affinity with machines; she had learned to drive with incredible ease and had savored every second of freedom behind the wheel. Freedom! At thirteen and fourteen, she had taken the Scout out by herself, she had explored every inch of Tuckernuck's roads, she had given her mother a heart attack, staying out until after dark when the Scout had only one working headlight.

Tate ran her hand over the hood. Did it still run? She believed it would, like a magic car—Herbie the Love Bug, or Chitty Chitty Bang Bang. It would run for her.

Birdie had discreetly mentioned that the girls' father had agreed to put "some money" into the house for necessary improvements as prescribed by Barrett Lee, and Tate had feared this meant the house would be different—shiny, new, unrecognizable. But the house looked the same. Tate was the first one inside; it *smelled* the same—like mildew and mothballs and pine sap and ocean air. She walked right into the galley kitchen—long and narrow, with a working sink and a gas camp stove and a half-size fridge lining one wall, and a Formica counter over the cabinets on the other side, with three feet of pale linoleum separating them. The "dining room table," which sat three, four in a pinch, and therefore was never used except when it rained, was pushed up against the outside kitchen wall. Beyond the "dining room table" was the "living room," which featured a braided rug, a sofa and two chairs upholstered in an abrasive bottle-green fabric meant to survive a nuclear holocaust, and a "coffee table" fashioned from a slab of glass over a lobster trap. The "coffee table" was another house antique; it had been made by Birdie and India's grandfather, Arthur Tate.

Birdie and India both sighed when they saw the table, and Tate sighed, too. Chess didn't sigh. Chess, Tate realized, wasn't in the house. She was outside, sitting at the picnic table with her head in her hands.

Tate pushed open the screen door. "Hey," she said to Chess. "We're sharing the attic, right?"

Chess nodded morosely. Well, okay, it wasn't great, sharing a room with your sister for a month, but wasn't there a certain slumber-party appeal for all of them in this venture? Wasn't part of the idea that they would all have constant sisterly-motherly-auntish comfort? They would never be alone, and because they were all related, there was no need for Tate to shower, clip her toenails, worry about deodorant. Tate could fart or burp or pick her teeth with abandon. The others would love her anyway.

There wasn't much of an option in the way of bedrooms. On the second floor of the house, there were two bedrooms—the Cousins bedroom and the Bishop bedroom. The Cousins bedroom was slightly bigger; it was "the master," though incongruously it had two twin beds. This was where Tate's parents had always slept. (Had they ever had sex in those narrow, spinsterish beds? They must have, though Tate didn't want to imagine it.) The Bishop bedroom had a queen bed with a squishy mattress that was low to the ground. This was where Aunt India and Uncle Bill had slept when Uncle

Bill was alive. Tate peeked inside on her way up to the third floor. She was delighted to see Roger, the name given to the quixotic sculpture of a man that Uncle Bill had fashioned out of driftwood, shells, seaweed, and beach glass. Roger was recognizable as a Bishop sculpture, though far smaller than Uncle Bill's other works (which were made of copper and glass and which populated nearly every major metropolitan area in the first and second worlds). Roger could have been sold to a museum for tens of thousands of dollars, and that was what was remarkable about having him just sitting on the dresser in the long-abandoned family summer home.

Tate heard footsteps and turned to see Barrett coming up the steps with the bags.

"Third floor?" he said.

"You guessed it," Tate said. "Kids sleep in the attic." She reached for her bag.

"Allow me," he said.

"You've done so much already," Tate said. "The place looks amazing."

"I hope you weren't expecting Jacuzzi tubs and granite countertops," he said. "I think maybe your mother was..."

"No, she wasn't," Tate said.

"It cost a fortune just to get the place back to zero," Barrett said. He took the narrow stairway to the attic, and Tate followed him. The attic was, as ever, hot and gloomy, ventilated by one small window, too high up to provide any breeze. The attic slept six: there were two double beds and a set of bunks. The idea was that all five cousins (Cousins cousins and Bishop cousins) could sleep here at once if need be, though the three Bishop boys—Billy, Teddy, and Ethan—had preferred to sleep downstairs on the screened-in porch. Easier to sneak beer from the icebox and piss in the yard, Tate supposed. The screened-in porch was awful in rain, so the attic beds had gotten used in inclement weather. Tate noticed a large cardboard box from Pottery Barn at the foot of the bunks. She peeked inside and found brand-new summer linens in bright sherbet hues.

"What's this?" Tate said. The sheets and blankets of the Tuckernuck house were supposed to be threadbare and as full of holes as Charlie Brown's Halloween costume—that was part of the charm. "Does UPS deliver here?"

"They deliver to me. I brought them over last week. Your mother ordered them. She wants you to be comfortable, she said."

"I don't need six hundred thread count to be comfortable," Tate said. She sat on the double bed that had traditionally been hers, the one farther from the door (Chess had a bladder the size of a golf ball, and she needed to be closer to the door, too, to escape from the bats).

"The other sheets *were* really bad," Barrett was saying. "I used them as drop cloths when I painted downstairs."

Tate took a deep lungful of the stuffy attic air. "So how *are* you, Barrett Lee?" she said. She had her own business, two hundred thousand dollars in the bank, a condo, a plasma TV, sixteen pairs of True Religion jeans, and a million frequent-flier miles. She was going to be direct with Barrett Lee.

He laughed, as though she were telling a joke. "Ha!" His blue eyes settled on her for one uncertain second, and she thought—ecstatically!—that he was going to say something she could muse over later. Perhaps tell her how great she looked. He took off his sunglasses, ran a hand through his sandy hair, replaced his sunglasses on top of his head.

He said, "I better get the rest of the stuff." And he disappeared down the stairs.

Tate wondered if she should be offended. Barrett Lee was no more interested in her now than he had been at eighteen. *Yet!* Tate told herself. After all, this was only the first hour of the first day. There was plenty of time.

INDIA

She had made a terrible mistake in coming.

And goddamn it, it wasn't *like* her to have lapses in reason. She was the only person whose judgment she trusted. She, India Bishop, made decisions based on the one thing that had never failed her: her common sense. She didn't compromise her standards; she didn't get "talked into" things. So what was she *doing* here?

India was the widow of one of America's premier sculptors and the mother of three handsome and successful sons. At one time, her wife- and motherhood had been her entire identity. But then Bill shot himself in the head (fifteen years ago now) and the boys grew up, graduated from college, embarked on careers. Billy was married and expecting his own child, a boy, to be named after his father (of course), at the end of the summer. The boys needed India less and less often, and that was as it should be. India had been free to reinvent herself. She had become the most revered woman on the arts scene in the city of Philadelphia. She was a curator at the Pennsylvania Academy of Fine Arts—which was not only a museum but a university—and she consulted for the Philadelphia Museum of Art and the Barnes Foundation. There were those people (small-minded, emotionally one-dimensional people) who believed India had acquired her position and accolades solely because she was Bill Bishop's widow. And while it was true that Bill's far-reaching fame had allowed India to know all the right people, and while it was true that everyone in the City of Brotherly Love and its bucolic suburbs felt sympathy for India after Bill's suicide, these two things did not a brilliant curator make. India held a master's degree in art history from the University of Pennsylvania. She had traveled the world with Bill—to Peru and South Africa, Bombay, Zanzibar, Morocco, Copenhagen, Rome, Paris, Dublin, Stockholm, Shanghai—and in each place, she was exposed to art in its many forms. Plus, India was smart—in an IQ way and in a practical way and in a social way. She dressed well, she said the right things to the right people, she drank white Burgundies and listened to Mahler. She used the money from Bill's estate—and there was a fuckload of it—to surround herself with exquisite things (a low-slung Mercedes convertible, Jonathan Adler lamps, a slender Patek Philippe, first editions of *Madame Bovary* and *Anna Karenina,* season tickets to the Pennsylvania Ballet and the Philadelphia Orchestra). Success had not been given to her out of pity. She had earned it.

But enough tooting her own horn. Today, she should be scolded! Today, she had messed up. She had agreed to spend a month on Tuckernuck, an island the size of Central Park. It was as remote as one of Jupiter's moons, and she would be here for thirty &%$# days! (India loved to swear, a bad habit learned from Bill that she had not shed, although she knew Birdie abhorred it.) Under the best circumstances, when Bill's psyche had been healthy and the boys were good ages for this kind of outward-bound adventure, they had stayed on Tuckernuck for two weeks. When India had come the two summers following Bill's death, she hadn't been able to last more than five days.

So what was she *doing* here?

India had fielded Birdie's phone call at a weak moment. India had, only hours before, discovered that the most promising young artist at PAFA, Tallulah Simpson, had withdrawn from the four-year certificate program and absconded with her considerable talent to Parsons in New York. Tallulah Simpson, who was known throughout PAFA as "Lula," was a protégé of India's, and not only a protégé but a friend, and not only a friend but an intimate friend. And yes, it did get more complicated than that, and yes, something had transpired between Lula and India that had, most likely, instigated Lula's defection to PAFA's biggest rival. If Lula made what had happened public, it would become a scandal. The news of Lula's withdrawal came as a shock to India—a literal, hair-raising, body-buzzing, 150-volt *shock*—but she hadn't let on that this was the case. When India's secretary, Ainslie, delivered the news, gently, along with India's usual latte, India didn't flinch, or she flinched only a little. (She couldn't be taken by surprise ever again, she believed, after receiving the news that her husband had put a bullet in his brain.) India had to pretend that she had seen this coming. She had to be nonchalant and dismissive, when inside she was hurt and frightened, and filled with regret.

PAFA was on fire: Lula's departure was all anyone wanted to talk about. India had quietly closed her office door and smoked ten cigarettes while she tried to figure out what to do. Should she contact Lula? Meet her for a drink at El Vez—or somewhere in New York? Should she go to Virgil Seversen, the director of the academy, and explain what had happened? Should she go over Virgil's head, to her ultimate boss, Spencer Frost, president of the board of directors? India's actions had been beyond reproach. She had, even in the most intense moments with Lula, followed her doctrine of impeccable behavior. But Lula was young (twenty-six), she was fiery, she was an artist, and she had fallen madly in love with India. Who knew how she would present things?

The hallowed halls and galleries of PAFA, which for the years since Bill's death had served as India's inspiration and her refuge, was now a field of land mines. Was Virgil Seversen looking at her oddly? Did Ainslie suspect? Had Lula posted gossip on Facebook? Foremost on India's mind when she fielded Birdie's phone call was how to escape the awkwardness of her present situation, and there was Birdie with the answer: Tuckernuck. India couldn't hope to get much farther away than Tuckernuck. Birdie had been convincing: Chess needed her. And so, India agreed. A tragically dead ex-fiancé fell exactly within India's sphere of emotional expertise; she *could* help. She had more than enough vacation time stored up; summers at PAFA were slow. India would connect with people she loved but didn't see often. Her sister. Her sister's daughters.

Her intentions had been good, and they had made sense at the time, but the reality was, India couldn't stay here. She had never loved Tuckernuck the way Birdie did—and that was why her parents had left the house to Birdie and given India the equivalent in cash. India was too urban for Tuckernuck. She needed action. She needed cappuccino.

They sat around the picnic table writing up a grocery list for Barrett Lee. Barrett Lee was as ruggedly handsome as his father had been at that age. India looked between Chess and Tate; one of them would snag him. Which one?

"Bread," Birdie said. "Milk. Special K. Sugar. Blueberries, American cheese, saltines." She was dictating for Tate, who was writing everything down.

"American cheese?" India said. "Saltines? Let's think like grown women here. When the kids were small, we bought American cheese and saltines, but now we can get camembert and a baguette. And a stick of good Italian salami. That, and some nice, ripe apricots and a pint of raspberries and half a dozen green figs."

Birdie looked at India. India thought, *Five days from now is Wednesday. Can I make it to Wednesday?* She had not had a cigarette since leaving Philadelphia, and her body was craving nicotine at red-alert levels. She had a carton of Benson and Hedges upstairs in her suitcase. As soon as possible, she would sneak one.

"You're right," Birdie said. "We can eat figs and cheese if we want to. And we should get some wine."

"God, yes," India said.

"Chess?" Birdie said. "Is there anything *you* want?"

Chess shrugged. India recognized the slump to her shoulders, the far-off expression. Here they were, wrapped up in the Camp Fire girl task of making a list of provisions, and Chess couldn't have cared less. India knew all too well how Chess felt. India hadn't shaved her head after Bill died, but she had done other self-destructive things: She had subsisted on Diet Coke and toast for months, until she fainted behind the wheel of her car (thankfully, she was in her driveway). She had refused to return the lawyer's calls until her bank account was overdrawn and a check for Ethan's high school football uniform bounced. She and Chess would have a long, frank talk before India escaped this barren hell, and India would tell her... what? *You will survive. This will pass, like absolutely everything else.*

But right now, all India wanted was a smoke. She was a bad girl.

"Bluefish pâté," Birdie said. "A bag of those Tuscan rosemary crackers. Lobster salad, butter lettuce, corn on the cob, aluminum foil."

India removed her reading glasses. They had been Bill's and were, without exception, her most valued personal possession. She regarded their Brad Pitt boy Friday. "Barrett," she said, "are you married?"

Birdie stopped her litany. Tate's cheeks flared an attractive pink.

"Um, no. Not anymore."

"Divorced?" India said.

"No," Barrett said. "See…uh, it's tough. My wife, Stephanie? She died. She had Lou Gehrig's disease?" The way he said it made it sound like a question. India nodded, and thought, *Ooooh, Lou Gehrig's disease. The worst way to go.* "She died two years ago. A little more than two years."

Everyone at the table was silent. India felt like an ass for asking. This was further proof that she didn't belong here. She never put her foot in her mouth; she never made other people uncomfortable. Now, she wanted to hide under the table. Here she had just crowned herself Queen of the Widows, with a deep emotional reservoir for those who had lost a loved one, and she had managed to fry Barrett like a bug under a magnifying glass.

"I'm very sorry to hear that," she said. "Do you have children?"

"Two boys, five and three."

"Names?"

"Cameron and Tucker. Tucker after Tuckernuck."

"Wonderful," India said. "I have a particular fondness for little boys! You'll bring them sometime? So we can meet them?"

"Maybe," he said. "They're with my mom during the day and Stephanie's parents in Chatham every other weekend." He was quiet for a second, looking off at the water. "Yeah, I'll bring them over sometime."

There was silence then; it was either respectful or awkward, India couldn't quite tell. The girls were no help. Chess was picking at a knothole in the picnic table, and Tate stared at Barrett the only way one could stare at him—with sympathy and wonder.

"Are we done with the list, Birdie?" India said. "There's so much stuff here, Barrett's boat is going to sink."

"No worries," Barrett said. "Finish the list. I'll have everything back here later this afternoon."

India let out a breath. Having Barrett Lee around would make things bearable. He would be their romantic hero this summer the way Chuck Lee had been her and Birdie's romantic hero in the late sixties. Chuck Lee had been India's initiation to a certain kind of man; he had a crew cut and a tattoo and a thick New England accent. India had desired him before she even knew what desire was. Now here was his son: handsome and helpful and tragically widowed. Barrett Lee and his surprising revelation energized her.

As he walked toward the bluff, India let out a sharp wolf whistle. The others sucked in their breath, scandalized.

"India," Birdie scolded. "Really!"

Barrett turned around and waved.

"He better get used to it," India said.

CHESS

Day one.

Here is my confession.

I met Michael and Nick on the same night, the first Friday in October, less than two years ago. I had just put the Thanksgiving issue to bed—a very big deal in the world of food magazines—and I was out to celebrate with my best friend from the city, Rhonda, who was a perpetual student and lived on the floor below mine in an apartment that was subsidized by her influential father. I invited Rhonda up to my apartment for martinis. We played Death Cab for Cutie, we drank, we put on makeup and fixed our hair and checked our outfits. It was finally autumn weather after a hot and breezeless summer. We were ready to go.

We went to the Bowery Ballroom to see a band called Diplomatic Immunity. There was a line around the block, but Rhonda's father was a hotshot at the United Nations, a recipient of some kind of diplomatic immunity himself. He knew someone everywhere in the city, it seemed, including at the Ballroom, and we strolled right in. Plus, Rhonda was gorgeous. She had been naturally gorgeous, and then she got her boobs done, after which we could cut any velvet rope in Manhattan and beyond.

Michael was standing at the bar. He was six foot six, impossible to miss, a head taller than everyone else. He was handsome in the way that I liked—clean cut, smart, bright eyed—and I smiled at him.

He said, "You look happy to be here."

I said, "God, yes, I am. I am so happy!"

His face lit up. Happy begat happy. "Let me buy you a drink, happy girl."

"Okay," I said. It had taken five seconds, and I was his.

The band had yet to begin, so we talked. He told me Princeton, Upper East Side (renting), started his own business (head hunting, not as violent as it sounded, he promised). He said Bergen County, New Jersey, parents still married, one brother, one sister. He said jogging in the park, food and wine, New York Times *crossword puzzle, poker on Wednesdays.*

I told him Colchester, food editor at Glamorous Home, *West Sixty-third Street (renting). I said New Canaan, Connecticut, parents just announced they were splitting after thirty years, one sister. I said jogging in the park, food and wine, reading, shopping, skiing, and the beach.*

He said R.E.M., Coldplay. He said Mr. Smith Goes to Washington, GoodFellas. *He said Hemingway, Ethan Canin, Philip Roth.*

I said Death Cab for Cutie, Natalie Merchant, Coldplay. I said The English Patient, Ghost, American Beauty. *I said Toni Morrison, Jane Smiley, Susan Minot.*

He said, "Are we a match?"

I said, "You're a man, I'm a woman. If you'd said your favorite movie was Ghost, *I would have walked away."*

He said, "You have beautiful hair."

I said, "Thank you." This was a compliment I was used to.

When I introduced Michael to Rhonda a few minutes later, he stuck out his hand and said, "I'm Chess's boyfriend, Michael Morgan."

I swatted him. I said, "He is not my boyfriend."

Michael said, "I'm her fiancé."

The band started playing. I had heard that they were good, and they were good. Michael led Rhonda and me through the mayhem to the front row. That was when I got my first look at Nick. What to say? My heart melted away. He was beautiful in a brooding, rock-star way. He had light brown hair that fell into his eyes, which were blue. His nose was a little crooked, as if it had been broken. He was wearing a Death Cab for Cutie T-shirt. He was tall, though not as tall as Michael, but he was leaner and more fit. His voice was a mystery, it was textured and rich, husky at some moments and clear as a choirboy's at others. At the time, I didn't know he was Michael's brother. I only knew he was the lead singer of the band, and he seemed focused on me. There was eye contact and I drank it in like cold water. He was singing a song that I thought must be called "Okay, Baby, Okay," because those were the most oft-repeated lyrics, and when he sung those words, he looked at me. He sung them to me. *Michael shouted above the noise of the crowd, "I think he likes you." It was quite a position to be in: I had just met an amazing man custom made for my bright side, and I was face-to-face with a rock star who was sexier and more intriguing, a soul mate for my dark side.*

Michael, to his credit, didn't try to touch me while the band was playing. He was into the music; he knew every word to every song.

I said, "Are you a fan, then?"

He grinned. "You could say that."

At the break, Michael said, "Let's go backstage."

"Backstage?" I said.

He said, "Nick, the lead singer, is my brother."

"Your brother?" I said. His brother? It was either good news or it was bad news, I couldn't tell which. If the lead singer had been anyone else, he would have disappeared from my life and the next time I saw him would have been on VH1. As it was, I was going to meet him.

Michael led Rhonda and me backstage. The band was sitting on the grotty greenroom sofas drinking bottled water and toweling themselves off. Michael shook hands with the other band members—Austin, Keenan, Dylan, we were all cursorily introduced—and then he hugged it out with Nick. Nick seemed much more interested in Rhonda and me.

"Which is yours?" he asked Michael.

"Chess is mine," he said. "We're getting married."

Nick looked at me. I would never forget the way that look penetrated. *And he said, "Bastard."*

Rhonda, never a shrinking violet, said, "But I'm free."

Chess considered suicide on Tuckernuck: She could weight the pockets of her grandfather's yellow rain slicker with rocks and walk out into the ocean. She could plug the tailpipe of the Scout with her Diplomatic Immunity T-shirt and start the ignition. There was a box of rat poison in the bottom of the utility closet. She could slit her wrists with the rusty corkscrew in the kitchen drawer; if she didn't bleed to death, she would give herself tetanus. She was able to joke about it; that much was good. She was choosing to stay alive; that much was good. Each day, that was something accomplished.

She had five pages of her confession penned in the notebook. She tucked the notebook between her mattress and box spring, away from prying eyes.

Tate was happy. Upon their arrival, she had put on her bikini and run down to the beach. Now she was sitting on her unmade bed, dripping wet, poring through the musty book of flora and fauna she'd found on the shelf of the living room. Chess eyed the box of cheerful new linens her mother had purchased, and then she squinted into the rafters to look for the bats that had populated the nightmares of her childhood. She didn't see any bats, but she knew they were there. Or they would come.

Tate said, "I just love it here. And I love it that we're here together. This is home for me. This is more my home than my condo in Charlotte. Or even the house in New Canaan."

The attic was cavernous, dusty, sour smelling, and hot. Chess unzipped her suitcase, which was the size of a coffin. Michael had not, thankfully, been buried in a coffin. He had been cremated and his ashes were placed in an expensive-looking mahogany box with brass fittings. At the funeral, his parents had jointly carried this box down the aisle of the church while everyone stood. Chess had been numb; before the service, she had taken three Ativan. It was the only way. Evelyn Morgan had invited Chess to sit with the Morgan family. This had taken Chess by surprise. In her drug-muddled state, she couldn't figure out Evelyn's motive. Did Evelyn feel sorry for Chess? Did she want to put on appearances by having Chess among the rest of the family, as though the breakup had never happened? Did Evelyn want to be seen as the bigger person? Was she the bigger person? Did Evelyn think that having Chess sit up front with the family was what Michael would have wanted? Had Nick lobbied on her behalf? Chess didn't know, but she couldn't bring herself to accept the offer. She sat on the opposite side of the church with her mother and father flanking her like the Secret Service. She was hoping for anonymity, but the people who attended the funeral were many of the same people who would have been attending the wedding. That was the first bad thing; people she didn't know pointed at her and whispered, and Chess turned around, thinking there was someone important or noteworthy behind her, but it was her they were noticing. The ex-fiancée. The second bad thing was the eulogies. The preacher started off. He spoke about what a full life Michael had lived for someone who was so young.

"He had loved," the preacher said. "And he had lost love."

Chess felt her heart go up in flames, like a ball of gasoline-soaked trash. Her father coughed into his hand.

And then it was Nick's turn. Chess found it difficult to look at Nick at all, though she could feel his eyes on her. Nick recounted the happiest moments of his late brother's life: beating Englewood High School in the lacrosse championships junior year, buying his own business, and proposing to Chess at the Knitting Factory in front of a mob of strangers.

Nick had cleared his throat and addressed her directly. "He wanted the whole world to know how much he loved you, Chess."

She met Nick's gaze for one atrocious second, feeling confused and betrayed. Had Nick really just *said* that? Birdie reached for Chess's hand, and the program for the service that had been resting on Chess's lap fell to the floor. Her father coughed again. Chess bent down to retrieve the program; blood pounded in her ears. She wanted to run from the church, to weave through the old tombstones of the graveyard until she could find a place to hide.

Nick.

She had remained seated, thanks to the effects of the sedatives and out of a sense of decorum. She didn't want to embarrass her parents. But when the final hymn played, she beat a hasty retreat out the side door of the church, leaving her parents to make her excuses. She waited for them in the backseat of her father's Jaguar, whimpering like a child. They submitted when she said she couldn't possibly attend the reception at the country club, and then, on the way back to Connecticut, her father asked her if she wanted to stop for ice cream. Ice cream? Chess was stunned. Did he think her problems could be fixed with *ice cream?* But it was early June, the day was hot, and ice cream, she thought, would taste good. So they stopped at a Dairy Queen and sat at a picnic table in the shade. Chess and her two divorced parents in their funeral blacks ate soft-serve cones dipped in chocolate. They didn't speak—what could they possibly say to one another?—but Chess was grateful for their company. She didn't know how to feel about anything else, but she knew she loved her parents, and they, of course, loved her.

Chess pulled back the flap of her suitcase to reveal her entire summer wardrobe, neatly folded.

Tate said, "Jesus, you brought a lot of stuff."

Chess said, "Fuck you."

Tate looked at her wrist, where she wore a chunky

black plastic running watch with so many knobs and dials she could probably use it to land the space shuttle. "That didn't take long."

"Sorry," Chess said.

"You don't sound sorry. You sound angry."

"Angry, yes," Chess said. "My anger is general and not specific to you."

"But you're taking it out on me because you can," Tate said. "Because I'm the one in the room with you. Because I'm your sister and I love you unconditionally and you can say whatever you want to me and I will accept it and forgive you." Tate stood up and peeled off her wet bathing suit top. "That's fine. That's what I'm here for. To be a place where you vent your general anger." Tate shucked off her bikini bottoms. How long since they had been naked in front of each other? Tate's body was sleek and muscular. She reminded Chess of a gazelle or an impala. All that contained energy and power. "I'm here for you. If you want to fight, we can fight. If you want to talk about it, we can talk about it. But you cannot alienate me. I love you with hair and without hair. You are my—"

"Only sister," Chess said.

Tate put on shorts and a T-shirt. "I'm going for a walk," she said. "Would you like to come?"

"No," Chess said.

She left, and Chess was glad. Along with anger, she was hosting a hundred other emotions like unwanted party guests—among them sadness, despair, self-pity, guilt, and jealousy. The jealousy had arrived at the moment it became clear that Tate was happy. Tate had every reason to be happy. Tate ran her own extremely successful business; she was, in all ways, her own boss. And she was beautiful now. But Tate's happiness came from somewhere else; it came from the elusive place that happiness comes from. She could afford to be kind because she wasn't the one who was hurting.

Chess had never once, in her thirty-two years, been jealous of Tate. It had always been the other way around; that was the direction the river flowed. Chess did everything first; she did everything better. She was pretty and smart and accomplished in a way that caused Tate to give up without even trying. Chess was engaged to be married while Tate had yet to date anyone more than three times since graduating from college. Chess was the bride, Tate the bridesmaid.

The neatly packed suitcase mocked her. Chess shoved the suitcase across the dusty wooden floor to the ancient dresser that had traditionally been hers. Inside, the shelf paper was dried out and curling at the edges; there were mouse droppings that made Chess sigh. This, however, was life in the Tuckernuck house. Everything was just as she remembered it from thirteen years earlier, just as it had been for decades before that. Tate had called the Tuckernuck house "home," and Chess knew what Tate meant. Every inch of the place was familiar and sturdy and unchanged. Chess knew exactly where she was. Why, then, did she feel so lost?

BIRDIE

When Barrett arrived back with the eight bags of groceries, he caught Birdie fiddling with her cell phone at the dining room table. She was so surprised when she saw him that she gasped and then clutched the phone to her chest. If she had been fast enough, she would have slipped it into her bra.

"Whoa, sorry," he said. "Didn't mean to startle you."

She didn't even try to collect herself. She was frazzled, it was hot, they had risen at six that morning, and Birdie had done all the driving. It was nearly five o'clock now and she was beat.

"Is there wine in one of those bags?" she asked.

"The wine is still on the boat," Barrett said. "I'll go get it now."

"Would you?" Birdie said.

"For you, madame, anything." Barrett smiled at her and she felt herself flush, more out of shame than anything else. Barrett Lee had been back and forth between Nantucket and Tuckernuck dozens of times this week on their behalf, and then Birdie discovered that the poor boy had lost his wife and had two small children at home to raise on his own, and yet he managed to be charming and upbeat. Birdie needed to pull herself together.

When Barrett left to get the wine, Birdie found his check. The repairs to the house had cost $58,600. Birdie had donned her linen suit and driven to the city to Grant's office to present him with the bills. Since Michael Morgan's death, Grant had called the house every day—to talk to Chess, to check in with Birdie about Chess. He had gone with Chess and Birdie to the funeral, and he had paid an exorbitant hourly fee for Chess to see a psychiatrist each day. Dr. Burns thought Tuckernuck was a good idea, and hence the repairs to the house were validated. If Chess needed Tuckernuck, then Tuckernuck would have to be fixed up. Right? Birdie wasn't sure Grant would see it that way; she was confronting him in person to plead her case.

Grant's office was painted oxblood red. Birdie had picked the color herself nearly two decades earlier when Grant became managing partner. She had picked out all of the appointments in his office; it was amazing, two years after their divorce, how nothing had changed. There were still the photographs of her and the children, and there were still the golf landscapes—Pebble Beach, Pinehurst, Amen Corner at Augusta.

Birdie handed Grant the bills. She felt like a sixteen-year-old. "I'm sorry it was so expensive," she said.

Grant looked over the bills, then tossed them in his in-box, which meant he would pay them. "Don't you get it by now, Bird?" he said. "It's just money."

Birdie placed the check before her on the dining room table. Barrett appeared with the wine; the bottles clinked against one another. Birdie fetched a corkscrew and two glasses.

"You'll join me?" Birdie said.

"I'll let you enjoy your family," Barrett said.

"Please?" Birdie said. "Everyone else has scattered."

Barrett paused. His eyes swept over her and perhaps took in the check on the table.

"Okay," he said. "I'll sit for a minute."

"Good," Birdie said.

"Let me," Barrett said, and he took the wine and corkscrew from her. He opened the bottle like a professional. "I waited tables at the Boarding House for a few summers there. Got pretty good at this."

"I see," Birdie said.

He poured two glasses of the Sancerre. "This isn't as cold as you'd like it, probably. And you know the fridge isn't exactly a Sub-Zero. I'll bring ice tomorrow in a good cooler. And I'll bring gas for the Scout. It still runs. I started her up last week."

"Amazing," Birdie said. "You know, I got the Scout stuck out on Bigelow Point when I was pregnant with Tate. Chess was just a baby. She was crying while Grant tried to dig the tires out with a plastic bucket and the tide was coming in. I thought we were going to sink the car for sure, but Grant dug and pushed and we must have had a little help from above, because we got it out of there. I remember that like it was yesterday."

Barrett smiled. Was she boring him?

"Here's a check for the house," she said. "And we agreed on seven hundred and fifty dollars a week for you while we're here, plus expenses, plus gas for your boat. I know it isn't cheap."

"That's more than fair," Barrett said.

"And you'll come every morning and every afternoon?"

"I will," Barrett said.

"It'll be all the usual stuff," Birdie said. "Groceries, newspaper, gas, ice, trash, firewood, laundry back and forth to Holdgate's, plunge the backed-up toilet..."

"Remember not to flush toilet paper or anything else," Barrett said. "Put up a sign if you have to."

"The outdoor shower works?" Birdie asked.

"It's a spritzer, cold water only," he said.

Birdie smiled. "That used to drive Grant nuts."

"Part of the Tuckernuck charm," Barrett said.

"And..." She paused long enough to get his attention, but once she had his attention, she felt bashful. "Oh, I don't know how to say this..."

"What is it?" he said.

"Well, I don't want your time here to be all work," she said. "You're not our servant, after all. I want you to relax, have a glass of wine, bring your boys over if you can. I know Tate and Chess would love to...spend some time with you. Especially Chess. I told you she was getting married and I told you her wedding was called off, but what I didn't tell you was that over Memorial Day weekend, her fiancé, or ex-fiancé I guess he was by then, died in a horrible accident."

"No," Barrett said. "You didn't tell me that."

"He was rock climbing in Moab," Birdie said. "He fell and broke his neck."

"Oh, man," Barrett said.

"He was a good boy," Birdie said. "And Chess feels guilty because she didn't treat him very nicely at the end." She clamped her mouth shut. Two sips of wine had gone straight to her head.

Barrett nodded.

"Chess is depressed, she needs help, and I'm not sure what to do. You noticed she's shaved her head?"

"I noticed."

"I'm worried sick about her," Birdie said. "Earlier, when you said you lost your wife..."

Here, Barrett looked at the table.

"It occurred to me that you and Chess had something in common. Sort of. And maybe talking with you would help her."

Barrett sipped his wine, then set the glass down and twirled the stem. "I'm not really into the whole support-group thing."

"I wasn't thinking of anything so structured..."

"I'm into survival," Barrett said. "I have two little boys to think about. They require a lot of me. I don't have time to sit around commiserating with other people who've lost significant others..."

"I understand that," Birdie said.

"Maybe you do," Barrett said. "But probably you don't."

Birdie looked at him. "Oh, God, you're right. I probably don't. I just thought maybe the two of you could hang out."

"Hang out?"

"Maybe you could take her out on your boat."

Barrett stared at Birdie over his wineglass.

"Didn't you take her out when you were teenagers?"

"I took her to Whale Shoal for a picnic," Barrett said. "I had quite a crush on her back then."

Birdie tried not to appear anxious. She tried not to think of Chess as she had seen her twenty minutes ago—alone in the dim attic room, staring into space, looking as forlorn as Sylvia Plath or some other tortured soul. She had taken her cap off, and her bald head was exposed. Birdie had to avert her eyes. Without her hair, Chess looked sick, she looked alien. She looked like a full-grown baby. Birdie needed someone to help her. She tried not to appear like she was paying Barrett Lee $750 a week to be her daughter's male escort, though nothing would make Birdie happier than to see a friendship spark between Chess and Barrett Lee. He could help restore her confidence, make her laugh. If Grant knew she was thinking this, he would reprimand her. *What in God's name are you thinking, Bird? Stay out of it!*

Birdie pushed the check across the table. "It would be nice if you hung out," she said. "We all like you."

"Well, I like you, too," Barrett said. He nodded at Birdie's cell phone, which was on the table. Birdie had forgotten about it. "There's no hope for that here."

"Oh, I know," Birdie said quickly. She picked up her phone and studied it. "Really? No hope?"

"Actually," Barrett said, "there is one place on the island that gets reception."

"There is?" Birdie said. "Where's that?"

"If you're good, I'll tell you." Barrett stood up, pocketed the check, and said, "Thanks for the wine, Mrs. Cousins. I'll see you tomorrow."

"Oh," Birdie said. "God. I hate to be pushy..." She did hate to be pushy, but she was desperate in a way she couldn't explain or defend. He turned to her with a wary look in his eye; he probably thought she was going to bring up Chess again. "Can you tell me where the place is that I can get reception? Please?"

Barrett chuckled. "Someone you want to call?"

Birdie didn't know how to answer. On her last night with Hank, he had taken her to Lespinasse for dinner, and then they had gone to the top floor of Beekman Tower and drunk champagne and danced. Hank had gotten them a room at the Sherry-Netherland for the night and they had made love on the exquisite sheets. The window at the foot of their bed overlooked Fifth Avenue. Hank had roses sent up in the morning on the breakfast tray, along with champagne and melon and strawberries. They asked for a late checkout so they could enjoy the champagne and each other and then go back to sleep for a while. Birdie had worried that the whole thing was costing a fortune, and Hank said, "It very well may be, but we are alive and in love and I would happily go bankrupt romancing you, Birdie Cousins." Birdie almost wished they had spent their last night at a bingo hall or a pizza joint, because then perhaps her heart wouldn't ache this way. Just thinking about the pink roses in the sweet little vase on the tray made her want to cry.

"Yes," Birdie said to Barrett.

Barrett said, "Bigelow Point. Probably right where you got stuck in the Scout, at the very end. Reception clear as a bell. But don't tell anyone. The last thing anyone on this island wants is to see the four of you ladies standing on that beach using your cell phones."

Birdie said, "Of course not. Thank you, Barrett, for everything. I mean it."

"No problem," Barrett said.

She was sad to see him go, but grateful that he'd told her where to use her phone, grateful that he had admitted to having had a crush on Chess years ago, grateful that he hadn't flat-out refused to spend time with Chess. That was all she was asking as a concerned mother; she couldn't make them confide in each other. If Barrett thought she was a nut, he was right: she was. She was tired and addled from travel, she had yet to get her bearings, and she was worried about her daughter. She wondered how it was that she could feel more alone here when she was living with three other people than she did when she was at home in New Canaan by herself.

She missed Hank in a way she hadn't thought possible at her age.

Thank God there were eight bags of groceries to unpack. Thank God there was dinner to make. Birdie stood up and got to work.

The Tuckernuck house had been built seventy-five years earlier by Birdie and India's paternal grandparents, Arthur and Emilie Tate. Arthur Tate was trained as an orthopedist, and he had written a seminal medical text used by bonesetters across the country. He held an endowed chair at Harvard Medical School, and he and Emilie lived in a glorious brownstone on Charles Street. They took their summers on Nantucket. They owned a yellow clapboard house on Gay Street; the front porch was hung with fuchsias and ferns. Emilie's half sister, Deidre, from her father's second marriage, had wed a wealthy Parisian businessman, and they, too, spent summers on Nantucket, in a house on the side of Orange Street that overlooked the sparkling harbor.

Emilie hated Deidre. This was family legend, but Birdie's father had saved Emilie's diaries, so Birdie could see for herself: *abhor, detest, nouveau riche, unmannered, inconsiderate, French, Franco, froggy, faux, faux, foe!* The half sisters saw each other only on Nantucket, and even that wasn't often because Gay Street society and Orange

Street society didn't commingle. Arthur was a sailor. He and Emilie were members of the Nantucket Yacht Club, where they ate their dinners out, attended dances, sailed, and played tennis. Problems between Emilie and Deidre arose only at the onset of the Great Depression. No one had any money, the country was sinking, the currency devalued. Somehow, Deidre's French husband, Hubert, was able to procure a membership to the Nantucket Yacht Club with money, rather than with connections as had been the custom—or at least this was Emilie's suspicion. And so, in the summer of 1934, when Arthur and Emilie arrived on Nantucket, they found Deidre and Hubert sitting at the next table at dinner and playing doubles on the neighboring tennis court. Emilie found her mortal enemy *in her club!* At the end of the summer, a scene ensued between the two sisters on the parquet dance floor during the Commodore's Ball. The orchestra had stopped playing. Emilie insulted Deidre. Deidre raised her hand to Emilie. Both women left the club in tears.

The next summer, the summer of 1935, Arthur and Emilie sold the house on Gay Street and bought a parcel of beachfront land on Tuckernuck for $105. They built the house, grandiose for its time. In her diary, Emilie noted that they wanted *something simpler. A simple life.* Town life on Nantucket had become fraught with social obligations. *It has become not so different from life in Boston,* Emilie wrote. *We seek a quieter place, a more remote escape.*

Tuckernuck.

But the truth was, Emilie had come to Tuckernuck to escape her sister.

Birdie reminded India of this story as they lingered outside their respective bedrooms with only their flashlights to see by. Birdie was flat-out exhausted, but India seemed to be looking for something to do at nine o'clock at night. She knew there were no clubs on Tuckernuck, right? No bars, no restaurants, no whorehouses. There was only peace and quiet, and the weight of their family history. They had come here as girls, their father before them, their grandparents before him.

"Emilie built this house to get away from her sister," Birdie said. "But now the house is bringing sisters together. You and me. And Chess and Tate."

India snorted. "Are you always such a Pollyanna, Bird?"

Birdie didn't take the bait. She would not squabble with India on this, their first night. "You know I am," she said. She smiled sweetly. "Good night."

TATE

She woke up in the morning and thought, in a panic, *Only twenty-nine days left!*

Chess was cleaving to her back like a bug. Tate was both irritated and touched. Last night, after a quiet, nearly somber dinner (*What's with everyone?* Tate had wondered. Even Birdie had seemed subdued and distracted), she and Chess had come upstairs with a flashlight and put the prettiest sheets on their beds. Tate had planned on initiating a long, meaningful conversation with her sister—that, after all, was the main mission here—but Chess made it clear she didn't want to talk.

Tate had said, "You won't get better if you don't let it out. It's like not cleaning a sore. It will fester. You know that, right?"

Chess tucked a pillow under her chin and slipped it into the case. No response.

Tate had thought three words: *Okay, fine, whatever.* She hadn't felt Chess climb into bed with her last night, but she wasn't surprised that she had. Chess was afraid of the dark; all their lives, she had crawled into bed with Tate.

Tate slid out of bed without waking Chess. It was hard for Chess to fall asleep and hard for her to wake up. But not Tate. Tate was a morning person. She put on her jogging bra (gingerly, because she had gotten too much sun at the beach the day before), her shorts, and her running shoes and went down to the second floor to use the bathroom.

The Tuckernuck house had only one bathroom, squeezed in between the two bedrooms. It had been installed when Tate was a child, and everyone marveled at the flush toilet. (Before, there had been an outhouse.) The sink and tub ran only cold water. If you wanted a hot bath, you had to heat the water over the gas stove in the kitchen and carry it upstairs. Water from the bathroom sink had a brownish tinge and tasted like rust. (*Perfectly safe to drink!* Birdie always assured them.) Tate was the only one who didn't mind the water. She was a traditionalist; the water in the Tuckernuck house had always been dingy and metallic, and if she had come this year and found that the tap yielded clear, tasteless water at remarkable pressure, she would have been disappointed.

She brushed her teeth and did a quick scan of all the products crowding the back of the toilet (the only level surface in the bathroom). There were young women's products—Noxzema, Coppertone—and older women's products (Tate tried not to examine these too closely). She noticed a new sign hanging on the wall opposite the toilet. In her mother's handwriting, it said: *Do not flush paper or anything else (please!).*

Birdie's bedroom door was open, the curtains were tied back, and the twin beds were made so tightly that Tate couldn't tell which one her mother had slept in. The sun was bright. (In the attic, you couldn't even tell the sun had risen.) A breeze came through the window. Birdie's room had a zillion-dollar view over the bluff and the ocean. It was such a clear day, Tate could almost make out the figures of the early morning fishermen on the shores of Nantucket.

Down in the kitchen, Birdie had made coffee in a French press. When Tate's parents had divorced and Birdie first made noise about wanting to get a job, Tate had entertained the idea of hiring Birdie to live with her and be her . . . mother. Because that was what she needed, a mother. Someone to make her coffee in the morning (Tate spent a small fortune at Starbucks), someone to do her laundry, someone to cook for her, someone to call her and check in when she was spending the night in a hotel.

"Come live with me and be my mom," Tate had said. Birdie had laughed, though Tate could tell she was considering it.

Tate poured herself a cup of coffee.

"Cream?" Birdie said.

Tate hugged her mother and lifted her off the floor. The woman weighed nothing. Birdie gurgled out a laugh or a cry, and Tate set her down.

"I love it here," Tate said.

Birdie cracked two eggs into the ancient blue ceramic bowl that she always made pancakes in here on Tuckernuck.

"Blueberry pancakes?" Birdie said.

"When I get back," Tate said. "I'm going running."

"Be careful," Birdie said.

Tate took her coffee out to the picnic table to stretch. There was nothing to fear while running on Tuckernuck, but Tate liked hearing her mother say, *Be careful.*

It would be nice to hear when she was in New York City, say, heading out to Central Park at five in the morning. Or when she was in Denver, where she nearly fainted from the altitude. Or Detroit, where she ran in the wrong direction and very quickly ended up in a sketchy part of town. Or San Diego, where she encountered a gang of drunken sailors wearing navy blue uniforms with white trim like nursery school children; they looked like they would have eaten her if they could have caught her.

Be careful!

She raced down the new stairs to the beach. She was ready to go! She took off.

The circumference of the island was five miles; it took Tate an hour to run it. It had been harder than she thought. It was rocky in some places, and it was swampy around North Pond, where she sank to the tops of her ankle socks. But for the most part, the run was magnificent and exhilarating. She saw two seals in the water off the western coast; she saw oystercatchers and piping plovers and flocks of terns. She saw two seagulls as big as terriers fighting over the remains of a beached bluefish. She wondered if the seagulls were sisters. One seagull would tug at the fish carcass while the other one squawked at her—her beak opening and closing, making a nearly human and definitely female protest. Then the other bird would peck at the fish and the first bird would yap like Edith Bunker. Back and forth they went, taking turns at eating, taking turns at complaining.

Just like that, Tate remembered something about the night before. She remembered Chess climbing into bed, throwing her arm over Tate, and asking, "Have you ever been in love?"

Tate had opened her eyes. It was very, very dark and she was confused. Then it came to her: Tuckernuck attic, Chess. Tate hadn't responded to the question, but Chess must have sensed the answer was no. Or maybe Chess believed the answer was yes; after all, what did Chess know about the details of Tate's life? Tate could be in love with the CEO of Kansas City Tool and Die, whom she had done hundreds of hours of work for this year; she could have been in love with the concierge at the Hard Rock Hotel and Casino, which was where she liked to stay when she was in Vegas. Tate came in contact with dozens of men daily; she took, on average, six flights a week. She could have fallen in love with the married father of four girls who sat next to her in first class on her way from Phoenix to Milwaukee, or the cute United Airlines pilot with the cleft chin.

But the answer was no, Tate had never been in love. She had never even been close. She had had a boyfriend in high school named Lincoln Brown. Lincoln Brown was the only black student in Tate's graduating class. He was handsome, he was the cleanup batter for the baseball team, he was, like Tate, a computer whiz. Tate had loved Linc, yes, she had, but it was a brotherly love, it was a protective love, it was a proud love. (She was proud that Linc was black and she was white, she was proud that her parents didn't care either way, she was proud to call a person who was so utterly fabulous her boyfriend.) She lost her virginity to Lincoln Brown and liked it. But she was not in love with Lincoln Brown. He was not her heart's one desire.

There had been other guys in college—Tate's taste ran to nerdy computer geeks and funny, outspoken fraternity guys—but these guys were for sex and goofing around only. She had not fallen in love with any of them.

She hadn't fallen in love as an adult. Sometimes a man at Company X would hit on Tate as she was trying to work, and she would look up from the screen at so-and-so's bland pudding face, his Van Heusen shirt and Charter Club tie and pleated-front pants, and she would think, *Are you kidding me? I'm trying to fix your system here.*

No, she had never been in love. But last night she had been too tired to say so. Plus, with Chess in her current condition, Tate feared it would sound like she was bragging.

At the end of her run, Tate raced up the beach stairs, pumping her arms like Rocky, expecting to find her mother and her sister sitting at the picnic table ready to indulge her in some applause—but the house was quiet. Tate, breathless, entered the kitchen. Her mother was juicing a crate of oranges by hand. Tate was so thirsty that she drank straight from the pitcher. Gross, she knew, and uncouth. If her aunt or Chess had been around, she would have exercised restraint, but being with her mother was like being with herself. Birdie didn't scold and she didn't sigh.

She said, "Isn't it good?"

Tate needed a mother to squeeze her orange juice fresh each morning.

"Water?" Tate said.

Birdie pulled a bottle of water from the dinky fridge. "It's been in there overnight and it's still not cold," she said. "Sorry. Barrett is bringing ice in a cooler today."

Tate inhaled the water. She burped enthusiastically. The pancake batter was foaming in the blue ceramic bowl. "Everyone else asleep?"

"Asleep."

Tate nodded as an unspoken understanding passed between her and her mother. It was nearly nine o'clock! How could anyone still be sleeping? Life was far superior when you enjoyed the top of the day.

She said, "I'm going outside to do my sit-ups."

Birdie smiled. "Be careful."

Tate hung by the knees from the longest, sturdiest branch of their one tree. She had visualized herself doing this back when she was in her air-conditioned state-of-the-art fitness center in Charlotte, but she'd really had no idea if the branch she was thinking of was going to be strong enough or high enough off the ground to make sit-ups feasible. She was delighted to find the branch was ideal. She pulled herself up once, up twice. Her abs were screaming in protest after five ups, and the juice and water churned in her stomach. After ten ups, the backs of her knees were sore from the abrading bark. She couldn't do 150 sit-ups. She could maybe, with fortitude, do 25. But at 25, it was easier. She did 30, 32.

Then she heard a voice say, "Wow."

She dropped back down to hang by her knees. Even upside-down, he was beautiful. Damn it. Her thighs were weak; her heart was encroaching on her throat. She grabbed the branch with both hands, inverted into a skin-the-cat, and hit the ground with a thud.

"Morning," she said.

"I'm impressed," Barrett said. He was staring at her in a way that made her sizzle. She worked out in a fitness center where the walls were made of mirrors; she knew how she looked. Sweaty, red faced, lank haired, bug eyed. And she smelled worse than that. But Barrett's expression was bright and interested, she thought. She had him captive.

But quick, what to do with him?

"I ran around the island," she said. Okay, that was bad. That sounded like bragging.

"The whole thing?" he said. "Really?"

She was out of breath. It was hard to sound adorable

and fetching when she was panting like a Saint Bernard. "What you got there?" she asked. Though she knew it was a cooler filled with ice.

He said, "A cooler filled with ice."

She said, "Can I lie down in it?"

He laughed and said, "You'd better not. It's for your mother's wine."

They were both laughing. Barrett was wearing a darker pair of khaki shorts with blue gingham boxers peeking out from the bottom, and he wore a red T-shirt with a logo for Cisco beer. He wore a visor and flip-flops; his sunglasses hung around his neck by a blue foam strap. Every detail of Barrett Lee was endlessly fascinating. And now Tate knew that his wife had died. Tate found this romantic in some inexplicable way. And he had two little boys. He was a father. Was there anything sexier? When he turned toward the house, Tate stared at him. She had twenty-nine days left. Would she kiss him? Would she sleep with him? It seemed impossible, but what if the answer were yes?

What if the answer were yes?

"Good morning." At that very second, Chess stepped out of the house wearing a white eyelet nightie and the blue crocheted cap. Barrett's color heightened, and when he spoke, his voice was husky.

"Hey, Chess. How goes it?"

Chess was holding two plates of blueberry pancakes.

"One of these is for you," she said.

"For me?" Barrett said.

"Birdie insists," Chess said.

"Okay," Barrett said. "Let me set this down."

Tate watched in horror as Barrett hurriedly placed the cooler in the shade of the house and settled at the picnic table with Chess. What was Birdie thinking? Birdie was supposed to be on *Tate's* team, the early riser team. But she had made pancakes for Barrett and *Chess?* This was wrong. This was, day one, off on the wrong foot. Chess had taken a seat at the far end of the picnic table from Barrett and on the opposite side. If it were Tate, she would have sat right next to him; she would have fed him his pancakes. Barrett asked Chess what she did for a living.

Chess said, "Well, I *was* the food editor at *Glamorous Home,* but I quit."

"Did you do any writing?" Barrett asked. "I remember back when you were at Colchester, you said you wanted to write."

He remembered that from thirteen years ago? Tate tried not to panic. Barrett Lee was the person from Tate's past who evoked the deepest and most poignant longing—but what if that person, for Barrett, was Chess? What if even as Barrett got married and had children, he had been thinking of Chess, wondering about her, pining for her? What if, in the nights after his wife passed away and he was left a lonely widower, he had thought of Mary Francesca Cousins, the Tuckernuck two-week-a-summer girl with the beautiful body and the grouchy father and the big, thick novels? What if when Birdie called him up in the spring to say, *Fix up the house, Chess and I are coming,* his heart had leaped with anticipation, just the way Tate's heart had leaped when Birdie said the name "Barrett Lee"? What if Barrett Lee's feelings mirrored Tate's own except that they were for the wrong sister?

She watched them eat. She didn't know what to do. She smelled smoke and looked up and saw India framed in the upstairs window like a picture on an Advent calendar. She was holding a cigarette. It was a momentarily distracting thought: India still smoked. (Tate remembered India and Uncle Bill smoking when she and Chess were children. They smoked in an elegant way; it went with the fact that they vacationed in Majorca and went to parties in SoHo lofts and knew famous people like Roy Lichtenstein and Liza Minnelli.) But now India was smoking inside the Tuckernuck house, which was a pile of tinder and which would absorb the smell of her cigarettes and hold on to it for the next seventy-five years. Birdie was going to have an aneurysm. Tate nearly shouted this up to India, but India wouldn't give a shit.

Tate was also quieted by the way India was looking down on the three of them, by the way she seemed to see *exactly* what was happening. She was connecting the dots to make . . . a love triangle.

Tate was angry now. She announced, in a loud voice, that she was going to shower.

Chess and Barrett both looked up at her. She smiled. She said, "Chess, would you be a doll and get me one of those yummy new towels that Birdie bought?"

Chess said, "Okay, in a minute."

Tate said, "Please? I'm a dirt sandwich. I need to hop in *right now.*" She strode over to the outdoor shower and enclosed herself inside. The outdoor shower had the same picket walls with eighth-inch gaps between each board, and a slatted "floor," which was a pallet set in the grass. The showerhead and knobs were frosted with mineral deposits. Tate turned on the water, and out came a fine spray of cold.

"Whoo-hoooo!" she screamed. "It's freezing!"

Barrett said, "Ah, the joys of Tuckernuck living."

Tate could see him pivot on the bench of the picnic table, looking her way now. Imagining her nude and wet? Could he see the shape of her through the gaps in the wood? Had she done it? Had she trumped Chess?

Chess reappeared and flipped one of the fluffy new polka-dot towels over the side of the shower. "There."

"Thanks, lovey!" Tate said. "How about shampoo? Or a sliver of Irish Spring? There's nothing in here."

"Forget it," Chess said. "Birdie might be your slave, but I'm not." She picked up her plate and headed for the kitchen.

"You barely touched your food," Barrett said.

"I need soap!" Tate cried out, but no one was listening.

Chess said, "I don't have much of an appetite these days."

Barrett said, "Yeah, I know what that's like."

Chess nodded once, curtly, then disappeared into the house. Barrett looked after her. He opened his mouth to speak, then closed it again. He worked on his plate of pancakes. He had forgotten about Tate in the shower.

Tate leaned her head back and let the water flow over her face. Barrett was a lost cause. But Tate loved him. She couldn't make herself stop.

She emerged from the shower wrapped in the towel, her hair wet and sleek. At that second, Chess emerged from the house with a bar of soap.

"Here you go," she said.

"I'm done," Tate said. She sat down at the picnic table next to Barrett.

"Aren't you going to put clothes on?" Chess asked.

"Aren't you?" Tate asked.

They glared at each other.

Barrett stood up with his syrup-smeared plate. "Those were good pancakes," he said. "Do either of you ladies need anything from the big island?"

Tate smelled smoke again. She looked up. Aunt India waved.

INDIA

Bill was everywhere on this island. She heard his voice, smelled the smoke from his cigarettes and the lime from his gin and tonic. She saw him from behind on the beach—his hair dark as it used to be before it thinned and grayed, his back and arms strong enough to carry one or another of the boys piggyback. She could even picture his bathing suit—fluorescent orange trunks. Those trunks had been loud. *Jesus, Bill, turn down your bathing suit! I can't hear myself think!*

He had been happy here, on Tuckernuck, for the two weeks that they stayed each summer. He, unlike Grant, had loved being unplugged. No dealers calling, no deadlines looming, no pressure to be a great artist. Here, he was a father. He built the bonfires, he whittled the marshmallow sticks, he told the ghost stories (always with ridiculous, goofy endings so the kids wouldn't go to bed scared). He organized footraces and gin rummy tournaments and nature walks. He gave driving lessons in the Scout. He collected shells and driftwood and beach glass and made things from them (because he couldn't *stop* being an artist). He had made the sculpture they called "Roger" for India the day after a terrible fight. The fight had emerged from India's happiness rather than from her unhappiness. This was right when Bill's sickness began to present itself in a way that she could no longer ignore. On Tuckernuck, Bill was relaxed and unfettered. He was able to laugh and to be her lover. They made love on the squishy mattress (filled with jelly, they used to joke), they made love out of doors—on the beach, in the Scout, at the end of the dirt road, and once, recklessly, in the old schoolhouse. *Why couldn't Bill be like this at home?* India had asked. She was crying. She was so happy here, right now, like this! And at home, in their real life, things were miserable.

At home, in their real life, Bill would work in fits and bursts. He went for days without sleeping and eating. He stayed out back in his studio, and India would bring him cigarettes and bottles of Bombay Sapphire, which he drank straight over ice. He had hired a fabricator out in Santa Fe to construct his larger pieces; the pain with the larger pieces was the sketch—first the overall effect, and then the excruciating detail—and the measurements had to be exact. Bill was a perfectionist—all great artists, all great people were—but perfection could only be judged in his eyes. Something that looked gorgeous to India would look not quite right to Bill. He would swear at the top of his lungs, throw things and break things; even from his closed-up studio a hundred yards away, the boys would hear him. India tried to intervene, but he wouldn't allow it. He was his own slave driver.

That was Manic Bill, a real monster, someone to be feared and avoided like a hurricane. Please use all evacuation routes.

Manic Bill was always shadowed by Depressive Bill, who was even more unwelcome. Depressive Bill was sad and pathetic. He didn't work, couldn't work, couldn't take a phone call or eat a sandwich or get an erection or, many times, rise from bed except, thankfully, to go to the bathroom. The very first depressive episode came at a convergence of events in 1985: The *New Orleans Times-Picayune* published a scathing review of a sculpture of Bill's that had recently been installed in City Park. The paper called it "hideous and inorganic" and lambasted the city council for spending two hundred thousand dollars of the taxpayers' money on "a grotesque misstep by an otherwise laudable artist." Although the review was bad, it had been published in New Orleans, so no one

Bill and India knew personally would see it, but then the *Philadelphia Inquirer* got hold of the review and ran a feature piece about what happened when great artists put out "bad product," and named Bill and the New Orleans piece specifically. At the same time, Bill contracted bronchitis, which turned into pneumonia. He was bedridden for days, then weeks. He was dirty and bearded. India took to sleeping in the guest room. She was a decent nursemaid, she thought. She brought him homemade Italian wedding soup and focaccia from his favorite deli on South Street, she made sticky date pudding from his British mother's recipe. She brought him his antibiotics every four hours and kept his water glass fresh and filled with ice. She borrowed books from the library and read them at his bedside. He got better physically; the fluid cleared from his lungs. But he didn't get better mentally. He stayed in bed. He missed the kids' soccer games; he missed a benefit at MoMA where he was being honored. One night, India heard a noise coming from their bedroom, and when she opened the door, she found Bill sobbing. She sat on the side of the bed and smoothed his hair and contemplated leaving him.

Then, his favorite hockey player, Pelle Lindbergh, was killed in a car crash, and somehow this provided the impetus Bill needed to get out of bed. He wasn't saddened by Lindbergh's death; he was angry. *Goddamned waste of talent.* He was back in the studio, returning phone calls, sketching a new commission for a private garden in Princeton, New Jersey.

Between Manic Bill and Depressive Bill there was a normal man, on an even keel. It was Bill Bishop of 346 Anthony Wayne Way, owner of fourteen acres and a stone farmhouse and barn-cum-studio, husband of India Tate Bishop, father of Billy, Teddy, and Ethan.

Bill and India lived in the suburbs, and their boys

attended Malvern Prep and played sports. Bill and India attended functions and parties, they went to movies and restaurants, they celebrated holidays. They took their trash to the dump and raked leaves and mowed the lawn. It was all well and good that Bill was a "famous artist," but they had a life to live and it required sanity.

In those days, India had depended on Tuckernuck to clear Bill's mind. Bill was good on Tuckernuck. He was strong; he was sane. Back then, when the final day arrived, India had never wanted to leave.

India lay back on the mattress—filled with jelly, Jell-O, toothpaste, lemon curd, caviar, something impossibly squishy—and studied Roger. They called him Roger, but really the little man with the driftwood torso and the blue beach-glass eyes and seaweed dreadlocks was Bill when he was happy.

God, she missed him.

She had made up her mind to leave Tuckernuck on Wednesday. First of all, she was smoking. Smoking helped calm her nerves, it kept her hands occupied, it allowed her to think—but when Birdie found out India was smoking, she would kick India out of the house. Just as the headmistress at Miss Porter's School had kicked India out for smoking when she was fourteen. (India then went to Pomfret, where smoking was tolerated, and then to college at Bennington, where smoking was mandatory.)

There was a knock at the door. India panicked. She sat up in bed and tried to wave the smoke out the open window—but it was pointless. Anyone who entered would know she was smoking. She was fifty-five years old; she had to be accountable for her actions. But Birdie was such a Goody Two-shoes. This had always been the case. She hadn't married a tempestuous, mentally ill sculptor, she had never snorted cocaine at two in the morning at an underground club, she had never romantically kissed another woman. Birdie made pancakes and squeezed the juice from oranges; she went to church. She was the reincarnation of their mother.

"Come in!" India said, praying for one of the girls.

The door opened. It was Birdie.

"You're smoking?" Birdie said.

India inhaled defiantly and nodded.

Birdie sat on the corner of the gelatinous mattress. "Can I have one?"

"One what?"

"A cigarette."

India smiled. She couldn't help herself. This was *funny*. Birdie might have been joking, but the woman couldn't pull off sarcasm or irony; her voice was full of its usual earnest. Little Birdie, Mother Bird, wasn't going to send India home for smoking. She was going to join her in the filthy vice.

India didn't remark. She didn't want to scare Birdie away. She plucked a cigarette from her pack and handed it to Birdie. Birdie placed it between her lips, and India lit it with her gorgeous jeweled Versace lighter. Birdie inhaled. India watched, fascinated. Birdie had the smooth mannerisms of a practiced smoker. India realized then how little she knew about Birdie's adult life. Birdie and Grant hadn't smoked at home; of this, India was certain. Grant had puffed his cigars on the golf course and with brandy at the steak house, but when did Birdie find occasion to smoke? At the country club dances, perhaps, in the ladies' room when the women were all fixing their hair and thinking about sleeping with one another's husbands? Or maybe the smoking was new since the divorce. Maybe it was a sign of further rebellion. Because although Birdie was a Goody Two-shoes like their mother, she had done that which would have been unthinkable to their mother: Birdie had left her husband. It amazed India now how little she knew about Birdie's divorce.

There had been one phone call to India's office at PAFA. India knew something was up; Birdie didn't call unless someone had died or was sick.

"What's going on?" India had said.

Birdie said, "I'm divorcing Grant." Her voice was bloodless, matter-of-fact.

"You are?" India said.

"I am," Birdie said. "It's time." Like she was talking about putting the dog to sleep.

"Did you catch him cheating?"

"No," Birdie said. "I don't think women interest him. And that includes me."

"Is he gay?" India asked. This couldn't be true—not Grant!—but she lived in the art world, where she had seen the most unlikely people come out of the closet.

"God, no," Birdie said. "But he has his golf, the Yankees, the stock market, work, his car, his scotch. I'm sick of it."

"I don't blame you," India said. "You have my full support."

"Oh, I know I do," Birdie said. "I just wanted to tell you first. You're the first person to know other than the kids."

"Oh," India had said. "Well . . . thanks."

That had been the extent of their conversation on the topic, though now India wished she had asked more questions. What had the deciding factor been? Had something happened, had they fought, did Grant check his BlackBerry one too many times, did he fail to look up from the *Wall Street Journal* when she called his name, had he not thanked her for his eggs (over easy, perfectly salted and peppered)? Or had something shifted in Birdie's own mind? Had she read a book, seen a movie? Had one of her New Canaan friends asked for a divorce? Had Birdie fallen in love?

India hadn't asked then, but she could ask now. Now they were alone, face-to-face, with a string of empty hours ahead of them. They were smoking together.

"What was it?" India said. "That made you leave Grant?"

"Oh, God...," Birdie said.

"No, I mean the one thing. The moment."

"The moment?"

"The moment when you knew. When you were spurred to action." India was high from the nicotine and from this unusual closeness with her sister. "Because you know Bill and I had our problems, big problems, huge fucking problems. How many times did I contemplate throwing him out? Leaving him on the subway in Stockholm? Serving him with papers on the squash court? And yet, I couldn't. I never had the guts. I didn't want to turn our world upside down. I didn't want to disrupt the status quo." India exhaled. "And then, of course, he did it for me."

Birdie nodded thoughtfully, and India felt ashamed. Here, she'd asked Birdie a question and then she'd talked about herself. She was a selfish bitch and always had been, and that, ultimately, was why Bill had shot himself.

Birdie said, "Well..."

India leaned forward. She wanted to know.

"It was a couple of things in succession. First, there was the trip we took to Charlotte to visit Tate. She had just moved to the city on her own, and I wanted to see how she was faring. We arrived on Friday night and left on Sunday, but it killed Grant, you know, because it was what he liked to call 'forced family fun.' He had to interact with us; he had to be present. So Friday night was fine—Tate drove us around the city a little, we saw the stadium lit up at night, that kind of thing. Saturday we met Tate at the park where she liked to run, and then we went to lunch and did a little shopping. I wanted to buy Tate some new clothes, pretty clothes...get her out of her jeans. The whole afternoon, Grant was like a huge, reluctant Saint Bernard that I was yanking on a leash. Then, that night at dinner—we were at a steak house—Grant got up from the table and I thought he'd gone to the men's room, but he never returned. So Tate and I finished up, I paid the bill, and we went to find him. He was in the bar, of course, where there was a television. He was talking to a complete stranger about the Giants' chance the next day against the Panthers."

"That sounds like Grant," India said.

"It *was* Grant, *is* Grant. But it hurt. He loved us, but he didn't like us."

"You know that's not true..."

"He liked us but he didn't want to be with us," Birdie said. "So that was the precursor to 'the moment.' 'The moment' came a few weeks later."

"What happened?" India asked.

"It was a beautiful autumn Sunday. Grant had golfed all day Saturday, and our agreement was, only one day of the weekend could be devoted to golf. So on Sunday, he was mine, right?"

"Right," India said.

"So we woke up and we...made love."

"How was that?" India asked.

"Oh, it was *fine,*" Birdie said. Here, Birdie blew a stream of smoke out the window. It was weird watching her smoke. It was like watching President Obama smoke. Or the pope smoke. "But it wasn't like I was hearing 'Unchained Melody' play in my head. I'd been married to the man thirty years. I was hoping for some other kind of connection, something deeper. I wanted to *do* things with Grant. I wanted to be his friend."

"Gotcha," India said.

"He wouldn't go to church with me because he said he didn't *feel* like it... the only thing he worships, as you and I know, is money. Okay, fine, to each his own, but then I asked if he would go to brunch with me after church. I was talking about a nice brunch at the Silvermine Tavern, with mimosas and Bloody Marys. Since when has Grant ever turned down alcohol? But he said no, he didn't want to eat a big brunch and he didn't want to drink because he had plans to go jogging with Joe Price at two o'clock. And that was it. The moment."

"It was?" India said.

"Grant had never jogged in his life. But on that Sunday, he was going jogging with Joe Price. Because he would accept any offer to avoid spending time with me."

India exhaled and picked a fleck of tobacco from her tongue. What could she say? Birdie was probably right. Grant was a guy's guy. He excelled at the manly. He wrote the handbook.

"I didn't want to do it. I spent a lot of time thinking about the Campbells and the Olivers and the Martinellis and the Alquins and all our other friends who had weathered the first storm of divorce that came through when we were all in our late thirties. We were the survivors, we thought. We had skirted stepchildren and alimony payments. We were proud of that; I was proud of that. I was proud to still be married. But the only thing I was holding on to, I realized, was my own misery. So before he could even tie up his running shoes, I asked Grant to move out. And he said, 'Are you sure, Bird?' As nice as can be, but in a way that let me know the marriage wasn't something he valued enough to fight for. And I said, 'I'm sure.' And he was gone—not that night, but a couple of nights later."

"Did it feel weird?" India asked. "Watching him move his stuff out?"

Birdie tapped ash into the clamshell that India was using as an ashtray. "What was weird was that he had so little to take. What was there? His suits, his toothbrush, his bathrobe and slippers. His humidor. His tennis racquets and his two sets of golf clubs. A few pictures of the kids, but these I suggested. He took the flat-screen TV and his really good scotch from the liquor cabinet. He made only one trip and all of it fit into the Jaguar. And that was it."

"That was it," India said. God, Bill had had so much stuff. His studio was filled with sketchbooks, clay, rolls of copper wire, copper sheeting, canvases, paints, color palettes stolen from the hardware store, and half-finished studies for sculptures. He had hundreds of CDs—from Mozart to the Beatles to the Cure. He loved music; he always wanted to know what the boys were listening to. He had the things he bought in other countries—a Tibetan prayer shawl, a flute from India, masks and blowguns and kris knives, a tea set from China. He had other artists' sculptures and other artists' paintings. He had his own set of chef's knives and his special Indian spices ordered from Harrods. He had a library filled with books. Thousands and thousands of books. If India had asked Bill to leave, it would have taken him months to gather his shit. As it was, after he died, India kept it all. This was her attorney's suggestion. *Do not throw away anything that personally belonged to Bill Bishop.* Someday, down the road, they could talk about donations. Or about a foundation. Or about turning the house into a museum.

"A regular person would have walked through the house and not noticed anything missing," Birdie said. "And that spoke volumes. Grant had never been vested in our home life. His life was elsewhere—at the office, on the golf course. He was more at home at Gallagher's than he was at our house. So when he left, what I felt was regret that I hadn't asked him to leave earlier."

"Really?" India said.

"Really," Birdie said. She stubbed out her cigarette, then reached for another, and India scrambled to light it for her. "I wasted my life with him."

"You didn't waste your life," India said. "You have two beautiful children."

"And what else?"

"A lovely home."

"Don't you think I expected more from myself than that?" Birdie asked. "We were educated. I went to Wellesley, for God's sake. I expected great things from myself."

"You did great things."

"I won the women's member-guest in 1990," Birdie said. "A golf tournament. Golf, which I despise, which I took up solely to spend time with Grant, who didn't like to play with me anyway, because I wasn't good enough. I won that tournament just to spite him. I started a book group, the first of its kind in Fairfield County, because I wanted to read really good contemporary literature and talk about it, and what happened? It devolved into being just like everybody else's book group—drinking Kendall-Jackson chardonnay and reading *The Secret Life of Bees*."

"You raised the girls," India said.

"The girls are the girls," Birdie said. "I'm not going to take credit for the girls."

India said, "You're a wonderful person, Birdie. You're being too hard on yourself."

Birdie said, "I look at Chess and I feel *so jealous.*"

"Jealous of Chess?" India said. "The girl is miserable."

"Miserable now," Birdie said. "But happier in the long run. She stood up for herself. She stood up for her *life.* What if I had done that? What if I had fended off Grant Cousins and all his money and focused on myself? I could have been an expert in fine carpets."

India lit herself another cigarette. "That's right, you always liked carpets."

"The language in carpets is fascinating," Birdie said. "I used to know a little about it. Now—well, it's like trigonometry. I've forgotten it all."

"You're a wonderful gardener," India said.

"See? I could have been a landscape architect. I could have made a fortune in New Canaan alone. I could own my own business. I could be a landscaping *mogul.*"

"You're talking like you're all washed up," India said. "You can still do it."

Birdie stood up from the bed and looked out the window. India's window looked northwest, toward North Pond and Muskeget. "I want to go home," she said.

"You *do?*" India said.

"Yes," Birdie said.

When Birdie first walked into the room, India had been wondering how to tell her that she would be leaving on Wednesday. But over the course of the conversation, she realized she was enjoying herself, and she was connecting with her sister, which was far superior to dealing with the potential bullshit transpiring in the cauldron that was Center City, Philadelphia, in July. (Independence Mall on July Fourth, mobbed with tourists from Kansas and Bulgaria: India shuddered.) And now, just as India had pretty much decided to stay put, Birdie announced that *she* wanted to leave?

"Give yourself a chance to settle in," India said. "Please?"

Birdie exhaled smoke, said nothing. Her eyes were far away.

CHESS

Day two.

That night, I left the Bowery Ballroom with Michael, and Rhonda left with Nick. My heart was sliced and diced like an onion, or maybe not that neatly. I liked Michael, I did. On paper, he was perfect for me. He was what I thought I'd always been looking for: an Ivy League scholar-athlete with plans to conquer the world. He would, someday, be rich and successful; he would pass on his excellent genes to our children. He was earnest and kind. But I desired *Nick; I knew that the first night. Nick was chocolate and cigarettes and whiskey and danger, everything I should stay away from. I asked Michael about him in the taxi to my apartment. He had always been in trouble, Michael said. His life lacked a clear direction. He had barely graduated from high school, and then it took him seven years to get through Penn State. He played the guitar in bars in State College; he recorded an album with a band, then the band broke up. He currently lived in a studio on 121st Street. The apartment was paid for by their parents, but Nick didn't have any money for furniture, or the cable bill, or food. He spent whatever he made on new guitars, on recording space, on expensive equipment for rock climbing, which was his second obsession after music. But the new band, Diplomatic Immunity, was good, it was great. Nick had to hold steady and not blow it. He drank a lot and he was temperamental. Michael worried about him.*

I nodded. "Mmmmm," I said. Nick, as expected, was not the brother I should be after.

But I wanted him.

I was distraught that Nick had left the bar with Rhonda. Rhonda was irresistible and I couldn't stand the thought of Nick and Rhonda, together, a floor below me. But as it was, Rhonda reported that Nick had been a gentleman. He delivered her to the lobby of the building but wouldn't escort her up. ("Which sucked!" Rhonda said. "What better way to end the evening than with some really hot rock-star sex?") He kissed Rhonda at the elevator bank, then left without asking for her number.

"I think he was kind of into you," Rhonda said. "He asked me a lot of questions about you."

"Me?" I said.

I started seeing Michael. I liked Michael. We had fun together. We jogged together after work, then went out for Vietnamese food. I cooked for him in my apartment. He was a good eater, he appreciated the ingredients and the technique, he helped me in the kitchen. We liked the same movies; we started reading the same books and talking about them. He was romantic—he sent me flowers, he took me to Café des Artistes, he made coffee and brought me a cup in bed. He was a good lover, considerate, earnest, eager to please. Too eager? I thought about Nick in bed more times than I cared to admit. I wanted to smolder. There was no smoldering with Michael. With Michael, sex was clean and athletic.

Michael met my parents and it was a tremendous success. My father loved him. My father would not have loved Nick.

I met Michael's parents. This happened in their house in New Jersey, and Nick was there. He was in jeans and a paint-splattered T-shirt; to earn some money, he was painting the upstairs bedrooms of his parents' house. This was the first time I had seen Nick since that night at the club, but Michael had a Diplomatic Immunity poster framed and mounted on his kitchen wall, so Nick stared at me and I stared at Nick as I made Michael dinner and as I ate my eggs in the morning.

I said to Nick, "It's nice to see you again."

He said, "It's nice to see you.*" Again, the penetrating stare. He wanted me, I was sure of it, but then not sure at all. I felt lucky to be liked by Michael. I wasn't vain or confident enough to believe that I could be attractive to Nick, too.*

That dinner was tense, and it had nothing to do with Cy and Evelyn. Cy and Evelyn were easy, they were delightful, they liked me, I could tell, and I liked them. I answered all their questions correctly; I got a gold star. Nick stared at me. I would look at him and his eyes would hold me like I was in his arms.

The tension was present between Michael and Nick. They sniped at each other all through dinner. Nick called Michael a corporate ass kisser and Michael called Nick a ne'er-do-well nitwit sponge. Cy and Evelyn didn't seem to notice, or maybe they did notice and were just used to it. As Evelyn was clearing the plates, she let it slip that the reason Nick's nose was crooked was that Michael had punched him in the face, back when they were in high school.

I gasped. "Why?" I said.

Michael and Nick didn't answer. They were glowering at each other.

Evelyn answered from the kitchen, "They were fighting over some girl."

Before dessert, I excused myself to go to the bathroom and I wandered down the long hallway looking at pictures of Michael and Nick and Dora as children. I loved the eighties hair and clothes, Michael in his lacrosse uniform, Nick in his corduroy suit, his nose straight and perfect. I found the powder room. It was elegant and refined, much like the powder room in Birdie's house. There was a bowl of soap meant to look like river rocks.

When I opened the powder room door, Nick was standing there. I was startled. He kissed me. His lips were warm, salty, tangy. Then he pulled away. He said, "You taste just like I dreamed you would." And he disappeared into some nether part of the house. He didn't reappear for the chocolate mousse. I didn't see him again that night.

Chess threw the notebook across the attic. It skidded under the dresser, disturbing who knew how many spiders. The confession was hurting, not helping. Robin was a quack.

A few seconds later, Chess lifted herself out of bed to retrieve the notebook and put it back between the mattress and box spring. She didn't want Tate to find it.

Robin and her medical degree had told Chess that the most important thing to do upon her arrival on Tuckernuck was to establish a routine. The routine should not be complicated or stressful. This made Chess laugh. Nothing on Tuckernuck was complicated or stressful; it was simple and boring.

Still, she tried. Chess woke up between nine and ten in the morning, at which point Tate had already been awake for three hours, run around the island and done six hundred sit-ups hanging by her knees from the tree branch, taken a shower, eaten a robust breakfast prepared by their mother, changed into her bikini, put on lotion, and made her way to the beach. Tate urged Chess to join her.

"I'll be down in a little while," Chess said. She brushed

her teeth and oozed down the stairs like a slug, still in her nightgown. Sleeping in didn't make a person feel good; it made a person feel slovenly. Birdie always lingered in the kitchen long after everyone else had finished breakfast so that she could make Chess's breakfast fresh and it would be hot. And what did Chess do by way of thanks? She picked at her food and let some drop to the ground on purpose, where the ants would get it. After not eating breakfast, Chess returned to the sweltering attic, where she wrote her confession in the notebook.

She then put on her bathing suit, trying to ignore the fact that her body was changing in the most unfair way. She was skeletal in the rib cage, and her breasts were shrinking. The skin at the sides of her breasts, which used to be taut, was slack; she could pull at it. And yet, Chess's ass didn't fit in her bikini bottom properly; she had to pull at it to keep the suit secure. The Tuckernuck house had no full-length mirror—in fact, the house had no mirrors at all except for the badly tarnished mirror above the bathroom sink—which was a good thing because Chess was, for the first time in her life, ugly. Her hair was gone. Each morning, she woke up thinking she had long, silken hair, the envy of every woman she had ever met, only to discover that her head was as scruffy as a vacant lot. Her scalp itched. This led to further thoughts: It didn't matter if she was ugly. She loved only one man and that was Nick, and Nick was gone. And Michael was dead. Dead? No. But yes. She hated thinking. She needed to stanch her mental bleeding.

Her routine included rising late, picking at breakfast, writing down the pain, and indulging in some negative self-image.

To the beach, Chess wore her ill-fitting bikini, her stretched-out Diplomatic Immunity T-shirt, her army-surplus shorts, and her blue crocheted cap. She carried a towel, a book, and a bottle of water. She had decided she would read only the classics while on Tuckernuck, and so the two books she had brought were *War and Peace* and *Vanity Fair.* She had thought that because the books were set in olden times, the characters would have quaint, outdated problems. She started with *War and Peace.* She slogged through the war scenes, and she identified way too closely with the affairs of the heart suffered by Natasha. Reading *War and Peace* was alternately dull and painful. She should have brought something light and funny, but Chess didn't like light and funny books; she liked deep and meaningful books, which, now, her psyche couldn't handle.

As it turned out, this hardly mattered because after five or possibly ten minutes of reading, Tate interrupted her. "Jesus, Chess, all you do is read." And Chess put her book down because Tate needed lotion rubbed into her back or Tate wanted to swim or Tate wanted to throw the Frisbee or Tate wanted to take a walk to see if she could identify any of the shorebirds from the book she was "reading," which was the same flora and fauna guide she'd picked off the shelf the minute they arrived at the house. Being at the beach with Tate was like being at the beach with a five-year-old boy. She couldn't sit still, she couldn't be quiet. She wanted conversation, movement, activity. Chess was grateful when Birdie and India made their way down the steps with their upright chairs, carrying a small cooler with lunch, and a thermos of iced tea. Birdie and India wore one-piece suits and they both looked better than Chess looked in her bikini. Birdie and India now smoked like flappers, a discovery that had initially shocked Chess, then comforted her, because it was a self-destructive behavior that she had not indulged in (yet). Between cigarettes and smearing chunks of baguette with camembert, Birdie and India took turns entertaining Tate. They walked with her, they swam with her, and Aunt India even played Frisbee with her, throwing and catching quite adeptly with one hand while holding a cigarette in the other. This allowed Chess to stand at the water's edge and throw rocks in the water, a symbolic exercise meant to lighten her load. *Get rid of the heavy stuff,* Robin had told her. At first, Chess assigned the rocks names: *grief, guilt, eulogy, harness.* And then she would throw the rock as far as she could. The act of throwing was therapeutic in and of itself; three dozen rocks left her exhausted. Aunt India started referring to this as Chess's "shot-put practice," but Chess was pretty sure India understood. Afterward, Chess would fall asleep in the sun.

Routine included five or ten minutes of tortured reading of classics, reluctant beach activity forced upon her by sister suffering from ADD, picking at prosciutto and butter sandwich wrapped in wax paper, "shot-put practice," and nap.

They left the beach at three thirty, at which point they all took "showers." Chess couldn't abide the freezing cold water, and the soap didn't adequately lather in it anyway, so all she got was a cursory rinse. Thankfully, she didn't have to worry about her hair. After showering, Tate convinced Chess to take a "nature walk," which ended up being a three-mile tramp across Tuckernuck on the dirt-and-gravel road. It was hot, there were mosquitoes and horseflies, and if she took one step off the path into the brush, she was standing in poison ivy, to which she was grossly allergic. Why did Tate insist on this hike when she had already run five miles that morning? There was no nature to be seen other than seagulls, which were as prevalent as rats in the Bastille sewer, and red-tailed hawks, one of which dive-bombed into the scrub a few yards in front of them and came up with a wriggling field mouse. Tate found this display thrilling, whereas Chess found it sad and disturbing. They walked past all the houses they recalled from childhood, including the "scary house," which had been owned, in their grandparents' day and maybe before, by Adeliza Coffin. Adeliza, the girls had been told, used to stand in front of her house with a shotgun, to scare off interlopers. She and her husband, Albert, were buried right there in the front yard; their gravestones jutted crookedly out of the ground like buckteeth. Out of habit, Tate and Chess hurried past the scary house with just a quick glance.

For the most part, the citizens of Tuckernuck were hearty, salty, happy-looking people, whose families had all owned their houses for two hundred years and who were all somehow distantly related.

"Life is good!" a gentleman wearing a tattered fishing hat called out to them.

And Tate, the ambassador, eagerly called back, "Life is good!"

"Life is good" was the accepted Tuckernuck greeting. It was a password. By calling out, "Life is good!" Tate was announcing that they belonged there, despite their thirteen-year absence.

The best part of Chess's day was arriving home from the nature walk feeling sweaty and spent and sitting down at the picnic table with Birdie and Aunt India for a glass of wine. It was, officially, happy hour, Chess's favorite time of day. This had always been the case, but it was especially true now. What did this say about her? Tate preferred the morning, as did their mother, when the day was new and filled with possibility. Chess, however, liked it when the day was done, morning and afternoon survived, and as her reward, she could sit down and have a glass of wine—which, because she'd eaten next to nothing, went straight to her head. Birdie set out dishes of Marcona almonds and smoked bluefish pâté with rosemary crackers, and although Chess had not had an appetite all day, she ate these snacks. This "happy hour" was only compromised when Barrett Lee joined them.

Barrett Lee made Chess uncomfortable, and not only because he was a member of the male species and as such was someone she should stay away from. She was uneasy around him because of their past, which included one ill-fated date here on Tuckernuck and one even more ill-fated road trip that Barrett Lee had taken the following autumn. Chess had treated him as badly as she had treated anyone in her life, Michael Morgan included. And even though Barrett had been nothing but friendly and kind since she arrived, she suspected it was an act. She had hurt him, and men didn't forget things like that. Or maybe they did. Maybe Barrett had forgiven her; his life had certainly held bigger challenges than rejection by a recalcitrant college girl.

Chess had been surprised to hear that Barrett had lost his wife. In everyone else's eyes, this made Barrett Lee a hero and a saint. Birdie and India treated him with kid gloves. And Tate, well, Tate wore her heart on her sleeve; it was easy to see how Tate felt. Chess wasn't sure that losing someone you loved made you a hero or a saint. It turned you into a figure of pity; rising above the pity was what made you admirable. Barrett had risen above the pity. He had kids; he had to get on with it.

Chess had always known that Barrett was a worthy person. She knew his compass pointed true north; she knew he was made of finer stuff than she was. And that, perhaps, was what made Chess uncomfortable in Barrett's presence.

Barrett only stayed for one beer. Tate and Birdie and India leaned toward him and asked the appropriate questions to keep Barrett talking. As six o'clock approached, the sun achieved a mellow slant and Barrett said, "Well, I should shove off. I have little mouths to feed."

He left, hauling two bags of trash and their laundry and the list for the next day, and the others watched him go. Aunt India, as part of her own routine, gave a wolf whistle, which made Tate swear under her breath and Birdie shake her head with a delighted smile. "Honestly, India."

And India said, "He'd better get used to it."

As happy hour waned, Birdie started on dinner. If Birdie had said it once, she'd said it a hundred times: "Chess is the real cook in the family. Are you sure you don't want to cook, Chess?" Chess declined. Cooking, just like everything else, had lost its allure. She remembered the hours of planning and preparation she used to put into dinner parties—she had made her own pasta from scratch, her own sauces, her own bread. For herself and Michael on a weeknight, she'd whipped up chicken piccata, a Thai *laksa,* an elaborate Indian curry with eight garnishes. Why had she gone to all that trouble? She couldn't imagine.

Birdie was a good cook, and the meals were simple. She grilled steaks or chicken or fish, she boiled corn on the camp stove, she prepared a lettuce salad or cucumbers marinated in tarragon vinegar, and she served the rolls that Barrett brought from the bakery each morning. India usually pitched in to help, and sometimes Tate, too, while Chess sat and drank her wine.

I am a parasite, she thought. But she didn't lift a finger.

Between dinner and dessert, Tate and Chess got into the Scout and drove out to North Pond to watch the sun set. They took their plastic cups filled with more wine—really, by this time, Chess was too drunk to drive and Tate probably, too. But that was the beauty of Tuckernuck:

there was no one else on the road. They only had to watch out for deer. The car radio picked up an alternative station out of Brown University, so they were able to listen to music. The sunset itself was an otherworldly event. In New York the sun came up and went down, and between all the people and the cabs and the Korean delis and the stock market, no one seemed to notice. Which was too bad. Of course, it was far superior to watch the sun sink into the ocean than it was to watch it set over Fort Lee, New Jersey. It gave Chess peace, perhaps her only real peace of the day, once the sun was gone, extinguished like a candle. She had survived another day.

When they got back to the house, Birdie served them blueberry pie, which Barrett had bought at Bartlett Farm, topped with whipped cream from a can. After dessert, they all retreated to the screened-in porch, which allowed them to feel like they were outside, while at the same time keeping them safe from bugs. There was a card table on the porch, and some new wicker furniture with comfy cushions that Birdie had purchased—the old wicker furniture had disintegrated and the old cushions had been as inviting as stale slices of bread. Tate wanted to play gin rummy, but Chess couldn't focus. (She closed her eyes and saw Nick bathed in the green light of the poker table, cards fanned in his hand.) Birdie was working on a needlepoint Christmas stocking for India's soon-to-be grandson, William Burroughs Bishop III, who would be called Tripp. India indulged Tate in rummy for half an hour, and then she took what she called "me-myself time," which she spent smoking one last cigarette and reading in her bedroom. Chess tried to read on the porch, though it was difficult to concentrate with Tate swearing over the lie of the cards (after India retired, she played solitaire). Chess would not go up to the attic without Tate because she was afraid of the bats. Chess hadn't seen any bats yet and Birdie had made a point of mentioning that Barrett had somehow gotten rid of the bats in the attic. But Chess was afraid nonetheless.

She and Tate went upstairs together, they brushed their teeth and peed in front of each other, saving the poor toilet a flush, and then they each climbed into bed. Chess had a flashlight, and a LightWedge for reading, but once she was in bed, she lay there, feeling the dark. Twice that day, Tate had tried to initiate conversations with Chess about "all that had happened" with Michael Morgan, but Chess wouldn't speak on the topic. *I don't want to talk about it.* Now, under the blanket of complete darkness, Chess thought she might be able to share at least part of the story; she could start at the beginning, like she had in her journal, and see how far she got. As Chess arranged the thoughts and words in her mind, Tate, who had had a full and exhausting day, fell fast asleep.

Chess lay awake, thinking that this darkness, the absolute black, was what Michael was experiencing now. Michael had been warm and whole, he had been able to cradle a lacrosse ball and jog around the Reservoir, he could look you in the eye and shake your hand—but now he was dead and gone. There was no greater inequality than that between the living and the dead. It took Chess's breath away, thinking about it. It terrified her more than the proximity of any bat could, until she could stand it no longer and she climbed into bed with Tate. It was the most basic comfort: her sister's body, warm and breathing, keeping her safe.

On the third day, Chess was too miserable to write. She threw the notebook across the room.

The fourth day was the Fourth of July. The routine

remained the same except Birdie put blueberries *and* strawberries in the pancakes and she wore a silk scarf printed with American flags around her neck, despite the fact that such a scarf was too fancy for Tuckernuck. Tate and India teased her about being a holiday junkie. Birdie wore the flag-printed scarf with the same enthusiasm that she wore her embroidered Christmas sweaters. Chess didn't weigh in one way or the other.

There was a distraction during the ho-hum-reading-and-needlepoint-and-solitaire hour on the screened-in porch, and that was fireworks. On Nantucket, the town shot fireworks off the north shore and they were visible from the east coast of Tuckernuck: big, bright pyrotechnic posies, overlapping and unfolding. Chess heard the crackle. She wasn't a huge fan of fireworks, but they seemed beautiful and important because she was alive and she could see them and Michael was dead and he couldn't. His body was cold ash in a mahogany box.

Barrett didn't come because of the holiday. Tate was in a pissy mood. She said it was because she was getting her period. She sang "Independence Day" by Bruce Springsteen at lunch, but she was painfully off-key.

BIRDIE

She had her role: she was the mother. She was the girls' mother, of course, which was both gratifying and frustrating (gratifying in regard to Tate, who appreciated every little thing Birdie did for her, and frustrating in regard to Chess, who didn't notice anything Birdie did because she was so miserable). She was also India's mother. She made India's breakfast, she did India's breakfast dishes, she washed India's cotton Hanro underwear and hung it on the clothesline, she made the sandwiches that India liked, mirroring the ones served in the gourmet cafeteria at PAFA (goat cheese with red pepper, prosciutto with herb butter), she cut the corn off the cob for India, as she used to those summers when the kids had braces, because something was the matter with India's bridgework. She did all the thankless tasks around the house—wiping the counters, brushing crumbs from the sofa cushions, trimming the wicks of the citronella candles, cleaning the toilet, and wiping toothpaste sludge from the sink. She kept the list for Barrett and made sure they had enough of everything. Really, there was nothing worse than running out of something on Tuckernuck—because, unlike on the mainland, one couldn't just run to Cumberland Farms or Target to get more. In past summers, there had been days when Nantucket was fogged in and the planes didn't fly and Grant hadn't been able to get his *Wall Street Journal*—that was bad. They ran out of calamine lotion but only discovered it when Tate got stung by a wasp. They had run out of butter for the corn on the cob; they had run out of bread and English muffins and had to eat peanut butter straight from the jar. The Scout had run out of gas half a mile from the house when India and Bill were using it for one of their midnight sex jaunts. They ran out of toilet paper and had to use pages of the *Wall Street Journal.* They ran out of Kleenex and had to blow their noses on rags torn from old sheets. These were minor inconveniences and they had all turned into good stories, but it was Birdie's responsibility as mother to make sure they had enough of everything at all times.

Birdie didn't resent her role as mother, even when she was mothering her own sister. (Although this did occasionally give her pause. India was a mother, too, right?

She had raised three boys and in less than two months would become a *grandmother,* and yet her maternal instincts were nonexistent. Perhaps she lost them when she went back to work in the fabulous Philadelphia art world, or when Bill died and she had enough money to hire people to do everything for her.) Birdie would say, however, that she was tired of being a mother, just as she had tired, three years earlier, of being a wife. Birdie wanted to be a person, the way India was a person. India was important, she had a career. Birdie didn't have a career, but she could still be a person, right? She was trying. She had recently (four days earlier) taken up smoking, a fact that she was sure shocked and appalled her daughters (though neither of them had mentioned it) because they hadn't known Birdie when Birdie was a smoker. Birdie had started smoking at the age of sixteen for one reason only: Chuck Lee smoked. Chuck Lee, who had been twenty-four to Birdie's sixteen, smoked Newports aggressively and without thought. Birdie remembered being rendered speechless when she saw Chuck Lee flick a butt into the clear water that surrounded Tuckernuck, the water he was the guardian of. But instead of being disenchanted with Chuck for polluting a pristine ecological system, Birdie assumed that Chuck Lee was the captain of Tuckernuck's waters and that therefore he was allowed to do as he wished upon them. Still, on more than one occasion, she had leaned over the side of the boat and plucked a soggy, bloated butt out of the water and stuffed it into the pocket of her shorts. Chuck caught her at this once and shook his head.

There was one occasion the summer Birdie was sixteen and India fourteen when Chuck Lee had delivered them to the island of Nantucket without their parents. Birdie and India had some school friends who had invited them over to Nantucket for croquet and lunch, and it was Chuck's job to ferry the girls back and forth. Birdie had been far more excited about the time alone with Chuck in the boat than she was about either croquet or seeing her friends, and she knew India was, too. No sooner had the white crescent of their beach vanished than Chuck offered them each a cigarette. The gesture had been nothing but gallant back then; these days, it might have landed him in jail.

"Either of you smoke?" He held out the crumpled pack of Newports.

India accepted first, while Birdie stared on, as gape-mouthed as a bluefish. Chuck invited India back behind the windscreen so he could light her up with a match. India inhaled dramatically, then blew a stream of smoke out of the side of her mouth like a fifty-year-old truck stop waitress. Birdie realized in that instant: India had smoked before. Probably behind the public middle school with her miscreant friends. It was a good thing their parents were sending her to Miss Porter's, Birdie thought. They didn't allow so much as bad grammar at Miss Porter's.

Chuck then looked to Birdie. He offered the crumpled pack. Birdie had never smoked in her life; she was afraid of choking or coughing or otherwise demonstrating her naïveté. But she couldn't let herself be outdone by India, who was still weeks shy of her fourteenth birthday. Birdie accepted a cigarette and imitated India as best she could, though the cigarette felt foreign in her hand. Chuck might as well have handed her a baton and told her to conduct the orchestra. She inhaled shallowly; she blew smoke right into Chuck's face.

Chuck indicated that the girls should take their cigarettes and sit up on the bow. They did. India said, "You have to *inhale.*"

"Shut up," Birdie said. She sucked deeply on the cigarette,

then sputtered out a terrific cough. India giggled. Birdie wanted to throw her overboard. She glanced back at Chuck. His eyes were over the girls' heads, on the intricacies of Madaket Harbor. He didn't notice Birdie breathing fire. She inhaled again. It was better.

Birdie had smoked the following six summers (only when Chuck offered her a Newport, out of view of her parents), and then she smoked more seriously the year she worked at Christie's. Then she met Grant. Grant despised cigarettes; his father had smoked two packs a day and died, gruesomely, of emphysema. So Birdie gave up smoking for Grant, and in quitting she had probably saved her own life. However, in retrospect, it felt like one more thing Birdie had had to cede to Grant, along with her career and her individual wants and desires. She had liked smoking and she was glad to be back at it, everyone else be damned.

The other thing that Birdie did to assert her personhood was against the Tuckernuck rules: she used her cell phone. If she was feeling energetic, she walked to Bigelow Point, though one day, after too much wine the night before, she drove the Scout. As Barrett had promised, if she took off her flip-flops and walked all the way out to where the water lapped at her ankles, she could get a signal. She could dial a number and the phone would ring and Hank would answer, and when Birdie spoke, he could hear her.

It was astonishing to Birdie from the moment she pulled onto I-95 at Exit 15 how much she missed Hank. Her missing him was like a sickness. Her heart ached; it was difficult to focus. India would be talking about a certain artist or about an Italian film she'd seen, and Birdie would be looking into India's eyes, nodding, but not hearing a word. She could think only of Hank. Hank on his knees in her garden, throwing dirt-clumped weeds in the bucket, Hank asleep in the hotel bed. (Unlike Grant, who snored, Hank slept silently. When Birdie watched him, she was filled with the desire to touch him, kiss him, wake him up!) He was everything she wanted in a man. Birdie had been guilty of thinking, as they lay in bed after making love, that she wished she'd married Hank when she was young instead of Grant. This felt true but probably wasn't. Would she have been happy with a young Hank, who started out as a history teacher at the Fleming-Casper School before becoming headmaster? Would she have risen to the responsibilities of being the headmaster's wife—having to at once represent the elitist values of "the school" while at the same time kowtowing to the parents? Caroline, Hank's wife, had done this brilliantly, but she had the advantage of personal wealth and of sitting on two other boards during her adult life (the Guggenheim and the New-York Historical Society), so that Caroline's involvement at the Fleming-Casper School was, to her, just one more philanthropic duty. Birdie and Hank would have been an altogether different couple. They would have been forced to live someplace like Stuyvesant Town, in a rent-controlled apartment, or in Hoboken, or on Long Island. Their children would have gone to Fleming-Casper on scholarship rather than paying full tuition as Hank and Caroline's children had. Birdie and Hank's union, while potentially lovely, would have been hobbled by economics. They might have gotten divorced; Birdie might have been dreadfully unhappy.

But now Hank was retired and very comfortable. His children would inherit Caroline's money, but he would keep the house in Silvermine and the four-bedroom prewar apartment on East Eighty-second Street. He was at a place in his life where he knew what made him happy:

food and wine, literature, painting, film, travel, the politics of President Obama, music, gardening. These were the exact things that made Birdie happy. And he was so cute, with his hair and his glasses and his smile. He chewed a certain kind of fruit gum that she liked. He was a wonderful lover. They were not in their thirties or even their forties anymore, but that didn't matter because they had chemistry.

She had been dating Hank only three months, but it was fair to say she was in love. When he pulled into her driveway on the final day, she saw the tears gathering in the corners of his eyes and she nearly canceled her trip. She couldn't leave him! She couldn't walk away from the roses, the romance, the companionship. Here, on Tuckernuck, the days she spent with Hank seemed cruelly distant. The night at the Sherry-Netherland felt fictional, like something she'd read in one of her book club selections. She missed him. It was killing her.

Birdie's phone calls to Hank were not altogether satisfactory. She had placed the first call on the Fourth of July. Hank had picked up the phone and said, quizzically, "Hello?"

Birdie had said, "Hank?"

Hank had said, "Birdie?"

Birdie said, "Yes! It's me! I'm calling from Tuckernuck!"

Hank said, "How? Why?" She had explained to him that she would be incommunicado for thirty days. Not only was it against family rules to use a cell phone (Grant had broken this rule liberally; he spoke to the office four and five times in a day and would have done so using a ham radio), but it was nearly impossible to get reception.

She said, "There is one funny little place where I can get reception. You can hear me, right?"

"I can hear you fine," Hank said. "But I thought it was against the rules."

"Oh, it is," Birdie said. "I had to sneak away." This was true: she had waited until Chess fell asleep on the beach and Tate and India wandered off in search of oyster-catchers, and then she'd slipped up the stairs to the bluff. Back at the house, she'd left a note on the table that said, *Went for a walk.* Which wasn't a lie. Still, Birdie had felt a twinge of guilt and attendant panic that something would happen while she was gone. A rogue wave would come in and sweep Chess away.

"Well," Hank said, "I don't know what to say. I'm speechless." He sounded uncomfortable, or perhaps he was just taken by surprise. Or perhaps he was embarrassed that she had broken the sacred family rules on his account. Or perhaps he was disappointed in her.

"I just wanted to wish you a happy Fourth of July," she said. "And tell you that I miss you." She tried to emphasize the words "miss you" because that was why she was calling. It had nothing to do with the Fourth of July; she had only called on the Fourth because she couldn't make it another day without hearing his voice.

"That's very sweet," Hank said. He didn't say, *I miss you, too.* Why did he not say it?

"Where are you?" Birdie asked. "What are you doing?"

"I'm at a picnic at the Ellises' house," he said. "I was getting my ass handed to me in horseshoes, but you saved me from that."

The Ellises had been friends of Hank and Caroline's for decades. There were other couples Hank had mentioned—the Cavanaughs and the Vauls and the Markarians—whom Birdie couldn't meet because they would not approve of Hank dating while Caroline was still alive. He hadn't seen much of these friends since he and Birdie had started dating, but he was at the Ellises' now and this stung for some reason.

"Well, I don't want to keep you from your game," she

said, though she had walked two miles in the heat of the day to do exactly that.

"Okay," Hank said. "I hope you're having fun..."

Birdie said, "Oh, I am..." If waiting on everyone hand and foot could be considered fun, if watching your daughter's depression up close and not knowing what to do about it could be considered fun, if cold showers and a twin bed and lukewarm milk were fun, then yes, it was fun.

"Well, it's good to hear your voice," he said.

This, she sensed, was as loving and tender as he was going to be. He was probably standing only a few yards away from his old friends. "Yours, too," she said.

"Take care," he said, as if she were an acquaintance from childhood he had bumped into at the airport.

"Okay," Birdie said, heartbroken. "Bye-bye."

"Bye."

Birdie hung up. She was staring across the water on a magnificent stretch of beach on an island that she had called home all her life. There was nothing before her but more water, calm and blue, a few seagulls, half a dozen distant boats, and the shoreline of Muskeget. She was devastated. Was this too strong a word? She didn't think so. What about dancing to Bobby Darin, Hank's arms strong and possessive around her back, his face nuzzled into the side of her neck? Had he forgotten? Birdie's insides were disintegrating. She doubted she would be able to make the walk back to the house.

Hank!

He didn't love her, and he didn't miss her. He sounded fine without her. He was at a picnic at the Ellises' house, playing horseshoes, laughing, drinking a beer or a glass of wine, socializing with the friends he'd neglected since he'd met Birdie. He wasn't talking to these friends about

Birdie because they didn't know she existed; they only knew Caroline existed.

Birdie headed back, and with each step she grew angrier at herself. She had told Hank she wouldn't call, couldn't call, and what had she done? She had thought of nothing since leaving New Canaan except how to call. It had been a mistake to call; it had been weakness. She looked at her cell phone. She wanted to call back right that second and ask him, *Do you miss me? Do you love me?* But no, she wouldn't do it. She wouldn't call him again.

But calling Hank turned out to be like scratching a mosquito bite. She knew she shouldn't, but she did. And scratching felt so good at first. Then, not so good. But it always led to more scratching.

She had to call in the middle of the day; it was the only time she could sneak off. And in the middle of the day, Hank was busy. On the fifth, he was swimming laps at the pool. Birdie left a message, then called back twice more, and when she finally reached him he was in the hardware store and seemed preoccupied with locating the garden hoses. On the sixth, he was in the car with his son and daughter-in-law on his way to Brewster to see Caroline. He couldn't talk freely; he barely said anything at all. Was this the same man who said he would gladly go bankrupt romancing her?

"I miss you so much," Birdie said.

"I hope you're having fun," Hank said. "You'll be back before you know it."

"Do you miss me?" Birdie said.

"You bet," Hank said. "Bye-bye."

On that day, the sixth, after Birdie had been rejected a third time (though feeling rejected was silly, she knew.

Hank wasn't rejecting her. She was just calling at a time of day that was inconvenient for him to talk), she hung up the phone and stared at the ocean. The water was flat, the day brutally hot. There were flies on Bigelow Point and they swarmed Birdie's face. No sooner would she swat them away than they would land again on the bridge of her nose or the sensitive skin above her lip. She remembered the old joke. *How do you know Tuckernuck is so great? Fifty thousand black flies can't be wrong.*

On a whim, she called Grant.

She called his cell phone, even though she knew he would be at his office, but he answered on the second ring.

"Hello?"

"Grant?"

"Bird?" he said. "Everything okay?" His voice was concerned and kind, and Birdie felt tears rise. She had the bizarre sense that Grant was her father. He would protect her, he would put to rest all the crazy doubts that her conversations with Hank were causing.

She said, "Everything's fine, everything's great."

"You're on Tuckernuck?"

"Yes!" she said. "Can you believe the reception I'm getting? Barrett Lee told me the trick. You have to stand at the tip of Bigelow Point and it's clear as a bell."

"Wish I'd known that years ago," Grant said.

"I know," Birdie said. She pictured Grant on his cell phone, back in the day. He called from the edge of the bluff, and he would just have gotten his secretary on the phone when he would lose the line. He would have to call back ten or twenty times to get through one conversation. "You remember Bigelow Point, right? I'm standing in the spot where we got the Scout stuck. Remember? When Chess was a baby?"

"Oh, God, yes," Grant said, chuckling. "And I was

pushing and the tide kept coming in, burying the back tires with wet sand. I thought that car was a goner."

"Me, too," Birdie said. She could picture what she'd been wearing—a daisy-print caftan over her white maternity bathing suit. She sat behind the wheel of the Scout with a howling Chess on her lap and she steered while Grant pushed. It was amazing to think that they were those very same people.

Grant cleared his throat. "How are the daughters?"

"Tate is fine, takes each day by the horns. Chess worries me. I'm not sure what to do for her."

Grant said, "You don't have to do anything, Bird. Just being there is enough."

Birdie thought, *You have no idea what you're talking about.* But she hadn't called to be uncharitable. She said, "And India's hanging in there better than I expected. She said she hasn't gone a week without a cosmopolitan or take-out Indian food in fifteen years, but she's doing fine. We're both sitting for hours in the sun, just waiting for the cancer to come get us."

Grant laughed. "I wish I was there."

"Oh, heavens," Birdie said. "You do not. You hate it here."

"I don't hate it there."

"You do so. You never once enjoyed yourself."

"That's not true, Bird. That sounds like more of your revisionist history. Plus, back then, when we were going every summer, I was distracted with work. Now, it would be a different story. I'd be out surf casting at first light. I'd be gossiping with you and India on the beach."

He was full of nonsense, but Birdie didn't want to argue. She said, "What's going on there?"

"Here?" Grant said. "It's been only me here this week and a few ambitious associates. Everyone else is off on vacation. On the Fourth, I was here alone."

"You worked on the Fourth?" Birdie said.

Grant coughed dryly as he had for the past thirty years whenever he was uncomfortable. "I had some things to finish up."

He had nowhere else to go. Birdie felt a wave of empathy. She thought of Grant putting on a suit and tie and driving in to work on the nation's birthday. She thought of him sitting behind his desk while the rest of the firm's offices remained quiet and dark; everyone else was at picnics or barbecues, at the country club or the beach.

"Why on earth didn't you play golf?" Birdie asked.

"I was going to, but my foursome fell apart. It's hard to find people with as much free time as I have. The other guys have families to see and lawns to mow."

Birdie nearly asked Grant if he was lonely, but she refrained. Clearly the answer was yes. Birdie felt sorry for him, then battled this feeling. She had spent thirty years feeling lonely. She had spent countless Fourths of July at the country club pool with the kids while Grant golfed or spent three hours on a conference call with Japan. Still, she could understand being lonely. Would she have called him if she weren't lonely herself?

She said, "Would you like to come up here, Grant? Spend a few days? It would be easy. If you get yourself to Nantucket, Barrett will bring you over."

"I thought it was women only. I thought that was the point."

"The daughters would love to see you."

Grant was silent, and Birdie panicked. What if he said yes? What if Birdie had just ruined the trip by inviting her ex-husband along? She wasn't at all sure the girls would appreciate his presence, and India would most certainly protest. And where would Grant sleep? In the other twin bed in Birdie's room? Good Lord. It was unthinkable.

Grant said, "Thanks for asking, Bird, but I'm going to let you gals do what you went there to do. Bang your drums and chant and share your secrets by moonlight. You don't need me around."

"Okay," Birdie said. She was relieved!

"It was good talking to you, Bird."

"You, too," Birdie said.

"No, I mean really good," Grant said. "You made my day."

"I'm glad," Birdie said. She filled with warmth. These were the words she wanted to hear. Hank hadn't been able to say them, but Grant had. Life was endlessly perplexing. "We'll talk soon," she said, and she hung up. The water was halfway up her shins. She was okay to walk home now, and when she got to the house, she would make herself a Perrier with ice and lime. It wouldn't be great, but it would be okay.

TATE

Prayer worked. Sometimes, when Tate was trying to fix a really bad problem in someone's system, she closed her eyes and said a prayer. And more times than a rational person might imagine, the God that lived inside the computer responded. The screen would clear or jump to life, and she took over from there.

And so, she thought, why not call on the God that lived on Tuckernuck to help her with Barrett Lee? She said a little prayer every day and hoped for the best. *Pick me, pick me, pick me, PICK ME!*

She was trying to become Barrett's friend. This was difficult because her mother and Aunt India were always around, so there wasn't a good opportunity for a one-on-one chat.

The only time of day when Tate and Barrett got a few minutes alone was in the morning. Barrett normally arrived while Tate was doing her sit-ups in the tree, and the sight of her hanging from her knees was clearly too much to resist because he always stopped to tease her. He took to calling her Monkey Girl, not a flattering moniker by any means, but she would take what she could get. One day, she challenged him to try it. *No, really, I'm serious. I bet you can't do one!* And Barrett, handsome goddamned devil, set his visor and his sunglasses on the picnic table, pulled himself up into the tree, and hung by his knees. His shirt fell, revealing a perfect abdomen. He did ten sit-ups with his hands behind his head, then he flipped down and said, *Not bad, but I prefer the gym.*

Yeah, well, I prefer the gym, too, Tate said, *but look where I am.*

I'll give you one thing, Barrett said. *You're resourceful.*

That was right, she was resourceful! The following morning, she left fifteen minutes later than usual for her run. And sure enough—she was finishing just as Barrett's boat was puttering into their cove. Tate had her hands on her hips and she was panting. She chugged from the bottle of water she left on the beach stairs; then she stretched her hamstrings on the steps. Barrett anchored the boat. Tate sat on the bottom step, waiting for him. Her face was hot and red, she smelled like moldy cheese, but this was it—her chance!

He jumped off the side of the boat, then lifted out a bag of groceries and a ten-pound bag of ice. Tate waved to him; he smiled.

He said, "Good morning, Monkey Girl. Did you sleep in?"

She said, "I decided to run around the island twice."

His eyes widened. "You are *kidding* me."

She said, "I *am* kidding you."

He got closer. She made no move to get up. He... looked like he was going to head past her up the stairs, but then he turned and sat on the step next to her. Tate didn't know where to look, so she stared at her running watch. Eight fourteen, it said. The hour and the minute of her first real conversation with Barrett Lee. Tate fidgeted with the buttons of the watch; the face turned a ghostly blue. It was a man's running watch and truly hideous, though Tate remembered ogling it at the sporting goods store in Charlotte—all the things it could do! Now, she wished she'd bought something more attractive, more ladylike. Sitting next to Barrett, she was self-conscious beyond belief.

She said, "So how goes it on this fine day, Barrett Lee?"

He said, "Oh, you know."

"No, I don't know," Tate said. "What is your life like over there? What do you do? Aside from getting my mother her beach-plum jam, I mean."

"Well, last night I went fishing with my old man," Barrett said.

"How is Chuck?" Tate said. "I can remember him from when I was a little girl. I thought he owned this island. I thought he was its president."

"Chuck Lee, president of Tuckernuck. He'll get a kick out of that."

"He's okay? Birdie said he had a stroke."

"He had a mild stroke. His left arm is affected and his speech is slow, but he gets around a little bit still—one outing a day, the post office or his Rotary lunch. He can't golf anymore, and taking him fishing is tricky, but I do it. He loves being out on the water. I cast the line and he holds it, and if he gets a bite, I reel it in, and he snaps the line."

Barrett was a saint, Tate thought. But to say so might embarrass him. "So did you catch anything?"

"Three stripers, one keeper."

"Are you going to eat it?"

"Tonight, maybe," Barrett said. "Course, my night went downhill from there. I have one client who is very needy. Her husband is in Manhattan all week, so she's in the house alone. She heard a noise that she thought was an intruder, so the police came, and they heard the noise, but it turned out to be her pipes knocking. So she called me."

"Are you a plumber?" Tate asked.

"I'm a little of everything," Barrett said. "I fixed it."

"What a pain, though, to have your night ruined."

"Yeah," Barrett said. "This particular woman has a problem with boundaries." He was sitting next to Tate; their arms were practically touching. Tate had dozens of questions. *What do you do aside from working and fishing? Do you ever get to do fun stuff? Do you ever get to go on dates?* As Tate was debating which question to ask, Barrett said, "So what's the deal with Chess?"

It was like the sting of the cold shower. It was her seventeenth summer all over again.

"The deal?" Tate said.

"Yeah. Your mom told me the fiancé or the ex-fiancé died. And she's destroyed. Is that why she shaved her head?"

"That would be the logical conclusion," Tate said. "Although who knows?"

"It's none of my business," Barrett said. "But God, she used to be so pretty. Her hair...and she used to be so together. Mature, you know, and cool."

"I'd love to fill you in," Tate said, "but she hasn't even told me how she's feeling. Not really. So if you want further details, you'll have to ask Chess yourself."

Barrett said, "Okay, fair enough." He stood up, then turned back. "I just get the feeling she doesn't like me very much."

"She doesn't like anyone very much these days," Tate said.

Barrett looked skeptical.

"Honestly. That's the best I can do," Tate said. "She's in a bad place right now. And that's why we're all here."

Tate did her sit-ups from the tree branch in a haze of sickly green jealousy. When Birdie asked if Tate was all right, she said, "Uh-huh," and stormed for the shower. The cold water felt good, but it didn't cool her down. Birdie had made a skillet of scrambled eggs with cheddar and a plate of crispy bacon, Tate's favorite breakfast, and yet Tate breezed by her darling mother and the beautiful breakfast. She squeezed past India on the stairs when the customary thing to do was to wait at the bottom for the person coming down to descend. The staircase was narrow and could only handle single file. Tate didn't say good morning to her aunt. When India got to the bottom of the stairs, Tate heard her say to Birdie, "Is she all right?"

Tate stopped in the bathroom for deodorant and lotion. And there, out the bathroom window, she saw Chess and Barrett leaning against the front of the Scout. They were facing the water, not looking at each other. There was no reason for them to be out by the Scout except that the Scout was on the far side of the house, out of view and earshot of anyone in the kitchen or eating at the picnic table. Tate knew she shouldn't, but she spied mercilessly. The bathroom window was open and she could hear their voices, but she couldn't quite make out what they were saying.

Then Barrett turned to face Chess and he said, "You're sure?"

She said something back, but the words were lost to the wind and the ocean. Barrett walked away.

He'd asked her out.

Tate scowled at herself in the dingy mirror. It wasn't fair. Chess had won *again,* and the thing that pissed Tate off and demoralized her at the same time was that Chess wasn't trying. She looked like Telly Savalas, she was *bald,* for God's sake, and yet Barrett was still attracted to her. Meanwhile, Tate was athletic and smiling and happy and a gung ho positive life force. Tate weighed 111 pounds, she was tan, and she had straight white teeth. Tate was gainfully employed in the world economy's leading industry. This summer, Tate was the better choice. Could he not see that?

Is she all right?

Yes, Aunt India, I'm fine, Tate thought as she stepped into her bikini. *Except for where my sister is concerned.*

When she descended to the kitchen with her backpack (containing lotion, her iPod—which she had not listened to since she'd arrived—two towels, and the Tuckernuck house copy of John Irving's *Cider House Rules,* which Tate had read already but would happily read again because she knew she liked it), Birdie, Aunt India, and Chess were all sitting around the "dining room table," ostensibly reading the newspaper. But Tate could tell they were waiting for her. She decided to pounce on them before they could pounce on her.

"Nobody needs the Scout, right?" she said. "I'm going to take it to North Pond and hang out there today."

"I'll go with you," India said. "I haven't gone anywhere yet, my bones are so lazy."

"I'd like to go alone," Tate said. They all stared at her. "I need some me-myself time."

Birdie said, "Tate, is something the matter?"

She didn't like being put on the spot like this. "Can I plead the Fifth on that?"

Birdie said, "By all means. Let's all plead the Fifth on everything while we're here and have a very quiet and unproductive month. And then when we get back to the mainland, we'll be seething with all the things we've kept inside." Tate was taken aback. She looked at Chess, who had her forehead in her hands.

Tate said, "It's not a big deal, Mom. Would you mind packing me a picnic?"

Chess made a kind of snorting noise, perhaps indicating that she found the request for a picnic audacious, because their mother was neither Tate's personal chef nor her slave. (They were sisters; Tate could read her mind to the word.) But Tate didn't take the bait.

Birdie said, "I will, if you'll apologize to your aunt about being rude on the stairs."

Tate looked at India. "I'm sorry," she said.

India waved a hand. "Accepted."

When Birdie stood up, Tate sat down in her chair, and Birdie brought her a plate of eggs and the brittle bacon and a glass of fresh-squeezed juice and a buttery English muffin, and then she clattered around in the kitchen making a picnic for Tate. Chess rested her face on the table, and India read the paper and smoked a cigarette. Tate was getting used to the smell.

She said, "I hope you're not offended that I want to go alone?"

India said, "Heavens, no. I can go tomorrow, or the next day, or the next day. Or the day after that."

Birdie said, "Are you absolutely certain that you want to go to North Pond?"

"Yep," Tate said.

"Because the undertow is bad there," Birdie said.

"It's a pond, Mom," Tate said.

Chess said nothing, but Tate didn't care.

Barrett had asked Chess on a date, but Tate wouldn't think about it.

The Scout was a magic vehicle; it could deliver her to a different frame of mind. Tate drove the dirt roads very slowly, because she enjoyed the ride and because someone from the homeowners' association would complain about any vehicle topping eight miles per hour. Tate parked out at North Pond and then hiked to the end of Bigelow Point. The sand was golden and granular, and even on the ocean side, the water was clear to the bottom and as warm as bathwater. Tate spread out her towel and put in her earbuds. She listened to "Tenth Avenue Freeze-Out," "For You," "Viva Las Vegas," "Atlantic City," "Pink Cadillac," and "The Promised Land." There wasn't another soul for miles. It was liberating, being so alone. Tate went for a swim on the ocean side; she swam a couple of hundred yards, then a couple of hundred yards farther. She was a quarter mile out; she could see the entire west coast of the island. The water was calm and Tate was tempted to go even farther. But there were sharks out here. Well, there was an occasional shark, one sighted every forty years or so. As Tate treaded water, her legs felt tingly and vulnerable. She was angry, yes, and she was jealous. She loved Barrett, but Barrett loved Chess. Still, Tate didn't want to get eaten by a shark. She loved life too much. She loved Bruce Springsteen and her mother's cooking. She loved running on the beach and driving the Scout. She loved sleeping in the hot attic and she loved her sister. Yes, she did; it was undeniable. The bitch crawled into bed with her every night, and every morning Tate woke up happy to find her there.

She swam back to shore.

She read the first few pages of *Cider House Rules,* but

then she tired of it. She had never been a great reader; she had never been able to concentrate and think about what the words meant and what subtext might be lurking between the lines. Reading, for Tate, was too much work. Chess thought this was a flaw in her personality. But Tate hadn't had any of the good high school English teachers, and Chess had had them all. Chess read all the time. She owned thousands of books—her "library," she called it—she read the fiction in the *New Yorker* and the *Atlantic Monthly.* She had poems taped to her bathroom mirror in her apartment in New York. She was that kind of person, but Tate wasn't. Tate liked computers, she liked flashing screens, information made clear and interesting with pictures. Click on this link and the screen changed, click on that link and you were somewhere completely new. The Internet was alive, it was an animal that Tate had trained, it was a planet where she had learned the terrain. The world was at her fingertips. Who needed books?

She used *Cider House Rules* as a pillow.

But she wasn't tired, and lying in the sun gave her too much time to think. She didn't want to think.

Barrett had asked Chess out on a date. It looked like Chess had said no. But she hadn't said no out of loyalty to her sister. She'd said no because she didn't feel like going out with Barrett and having fun. Fun was beyond her.

Tate pulled out the picnic Birdie had packed her: a mozzarella and tomato sandwich with pesto that had grown warm and melty in the sun, a bag of potato chips, a plum, a Tupperware of raspberries and blueberries, a bottle of lemonade, a brownie. Tate thought about how much she loved her mother and how perfect it would be if Birdie agreed to come live with her. Even for just a month or two in the winter. Charlotte never got really cold, not like the Northeast. It rarely snowed. Tate's condo complex kept the outdoor pool heated; her mother could swim laps in January. But Tate was never home; she was always on the road. Her mother would grow bored in Charlotte; she would have no friends and little to do. Tate's apartment didn't have a garden. It barely had furniture; Tate owned a fifty-two-inch flat-screen TV and a queen-size futon that sat on the floor in front of the TV. Tate couldn't imagine Birdie spending one night in the condo in Charlotte in its current condition. Birdie and Grant had come to Charlotte once, a couple of years earlier, when Tate first moved there. Tate's parents had stayed in a Marriott and the three of them had eaten dinner at a steak house whose name Tate couldn't remember. Tate's connection to Charlotte was tenuous. Maybe she should move someplace else. Las Vegas appealed—all those flashing lights.

Tate needed to get a life.

She needed a boyfriend.

Barrett!

She didn't want to think about it.

After lunch she swam in the pond, ignoring common wisdom to wait an hour for her food to digest. She was floating on her back when she saw something move in her peripheral vision. She stood up—the water was chest deep—and squinted. It was another person trekking out to Bigelow Point. Tate recognized the blue terry-cloth cover-up and the floppy white hat that had belonged to her grandfather.

It was Birdie!

Tate waved. She was relieved. She had wanted company, though she was too proud to admit it to herself. Spending all day at the beach alone was beyond her. Her mother realized this and had come to the rescue. She was such a good mother.

Birdie didn't wave back. Her face held an expression that Tate couldn't place, though one thing was for sure: she didn't look happy. She picked her way out onto the slender sandbar that jutted into the water.

Tate called out, "Mom! I'm over here!" Surely her mother had seen her? She didn't look over. "Mom!" Tate squinted. That *was* her mother, right? It was her mother's blue cover-up and her grandfather's floppy white hat, which he used to wear when he took Tate and Chess crabbing in the flat-bottomed rowboat.

It was her mother. And now Tate noticed that she was on the phone. That couldn't be right. But yes, Birdie was on the phone. She was talking to someone. She was gesturing. The phone call was brief. Two minutes, maybe less. She folded up her phone and slipped it into the pocket of her cover-up.

Tate waited. Her mother gazed out at the ocean for a moment, then took a heaving breath and walked toward the pond. Tate swam to shore.

Birdie approached without a word or a smile. What was wrong? When she was close enough to speak to, Tate found she didn't know what to say. And rather than say something stupid, she was quiet. She waited.

Together they walked to Tate's towel and sat down. Birdie said, "I'm sorry. I know you wanted to be alone today."

"Actually," Tate said, "I was dying for company."

"I was just on the phone with Hank," Birdie said.

"Who's Hank?" Tate asked.

"He's a man I'm dating," Birdie said.

"Really?" Tate said. She felt a sharp, clean slice through her gut. She had held out hope that since neither of her parents were seeing other people, they might someday reunite. She knew it was juvenile, wanting them back together, but that was how she felt.

"Really," Birdie said.

"Why have I never heard of him?" Tate said.

"He hasn't been around very long," Birdie said. "I met him at the end of April. I met him at the same time that your sister broke her engagement. So there have been a lot of distractions. And I'm not sure how serious it is."

"Are you in love?" Tate said, praying the answer was no.

"I'm in love," Birdie said. "At least, that's what I'm calling it in my head. He is not in love with me, however. I thought he was, he said he was, but our conversations since we've been here tell me otherwise. He sounds positively uninterested."

Uninterested, Tate thought. Like Barrett.

"Hank is married," Birdie said.

"Mother!" Tate said. She tried to sound shocked, though she wasn't at all. She knew how the world worked; she knew that betrayals were as common as anthills.

"His wife has Alzheimer's," Birdie said. "She's in a facility. She'll stay in the facility until she dies."

"Oh," Tate said.

"So here's the thing I don't understand, still, at my age," Birdie said. "In the two years between the time your father and I split and the time I met Hank, I was fine. I was reasonably happy, I had hobbies and interests—my gardening, my reading, the house, you kids, my friends. Then I met Hank. And he likes to do things—go out for dinner, go to the theater, spend the night in nice hotels, go dancing. God, it was intoxicating to have someone to *do* things with. You have no idea. I'd always been alone, throughout my marriage, alone, alone. The problem is that my happiness, now, depends on Hank." Birdie clenched her fists. "It's not fair that someone should be able to affect me this way! But I don't want to go back to how things were before I met him. I was lonely. Then, with Hank, I was not lonely. And now, without Hank, I'm even lonelier than I was before."

Tate watched her mother. She wasn't happy to hear about Hank, but she understood. She felt the same way. She had been in love with Barrett Lee either since she was seventeen or for the past six days—but either way, it wasn't fair.

"I don't understand why he won't talk to me," Birdie said. "I don't understand why he's pulling away. Just now I called and he was with his three-year-old granddaughter at the farm at Stew Leonard's. I want him to tell me that he misses me and he loves me, and all he wants to tell me is that it's ninety-two degrees in Connecticut and the cow's name is Calliope."

"You got him at a bad time," Tate said.

"It's been a bad time every time I've called."

"Have you called him every day?"

"Every day since the Fourth."

Tate had noticed that Birdie wandered off around this time each day, but she figured her mother was on some typical Birdie mission: picking wildflowers for the dinner table, or hunting down chives for the salad.

Tate said, "If it makes you feel any better, I'm in love with Barrett Lee."

Birdie gasped. "You *are?*"

"Oh, come on, Mom," Tate said. "Tell me it's not obvious. I've loved him forever. I've loved him since I was a child."

"You have?" Birdie said. "I always thought it was Chess who was interested in Barrett."

"Of course you did," Tate said. "Chess always gets to play the romantic lead. Why is that?"

"Oh, Tate—"

"No, I'm curious. Why is she always the one who gets to fall in love and have relationships, and never me?"

"It will be you, soon enough," Birdie said.

"I'm thirty years old," Tate said. "How much longer do I have to wait?"

"I didn't know you were in love with Barrett Lee," Birdie said. "I'm sorry. It helps to know now. I've been trying to throw him and Chess together."

"Can you stop?" Tate said. "Please?"

"It's not working anyway," Birdie said.

"He asked me about Chess this morning, and then he asked her out—I saw them talking by the Scout—but I think she said no. Did she mention it?"

"Not a word," Birdie said. "You'll be glad if she said no?"

"It doesn't change the fact that he wanted to ask her."

"Love is perfectly awful," Birdie said. "I'd forgotten how awful it was. I don't remember feeling like this with your father. Grant and I found each other, and we knew. There wasn't any game playing. We joined forces and we moved through life—he worked, we bought the house, I had you and Chess. Then I lost those two pregnancies right in a row, which was upsetting, but I recovered. Your father was free to worry about making money and playing golf and I could worry about returning the library books on time and getting you girls to dance class. I never remember feeling this addled. Loving your father was frustrating, but it wasn't painful."

"Until the end?" Tate said.

"It wasn't even painful at the end," Birdie said. "I just ran out of rope. I didn't want to stay with your dad anymore. I wasn't getting anything out of the marriage."

Tate nodded. This felt like a conversation she should have had with her mother two years ago, but it had never happened. Tate hadn't wanted to know what went wrong; she just wanted them to fix it.

"Grant was my big relationship. He was the co-president of the corporation of our life. But what I realized when I met Hank"—here, Birdie rested her chin on her tented knees—"was that there might be a chance to have another kind of relationship. A dessert, if you will. Hank already has his family, and I have mine; Hank is finished with his career. We both have money. All that remains is possibility: ten, twenty, thirty years to enjoy life with someone. I never got to enjoy life with your father because we were so damn busy. Hank likes all the same things that I like—he cooks, he gardens, he enjoys the same music and the same wine. And that is what makes my love for him so terrible. I don't want to gallivant about with just anyone. It has to be Hank. Before I came here, we were inseparable. I cried when we parted, and he cried, too. But now... I'm losing him." When she looked at Tate, her eyes were watery. "Oh, honey. I feel like a girl."

"That's okay," Tate said. "That's good, Mom." Tate *did* think it was good. Her mother was in love, she was feeling things. Her mother was a woman, a human being: Had Tate ever really considered this? Does anyone think this way about her own mother—that she's a person with desires and longings and tender, aching spots? Tate had always fiercely loved her mother, but had she ever known her?

Tate walked to the waterline. Birdie followed. Tate picked up a rock and threw it the way she'd seen Chess do.

"Barrett Lee," she said.

Birdie bent down and picked up a rock the size and shape of an egg. She threw it, and it plunked a few yards offshore.

"Hank," she said.

Were they getting rid of the men? Tate wondered. Or beckoning them?

Birdie said, "I should have thrown my phone."

* * *

Birdie headed back to the house; she didn't want Chess and India to worry, she said. Neither of them knew where she was.

"Your secret is safe with me," Tate said.

"And yours with me," Birdie said. "If it makes you feel any better, I had a terrific crush on Chuck Lee when I was a girl."

"On Chuck?" Tate said. "Really? You did?"

"And so did India," Birdie said. "It's like everything cycles through: Tate women with crushes on Lee men, generation after generation."

After Birdie was gone, Tate lay on her towel in the sun. Her mother was in love with Hank. This felt like something she and Chess could whisper about in the dark nighttime attic—but Tate didn't want to share her mother's confidence. As Tate drifted off to sleep, she thought back to when her mother had lost those two pregnancies. She remembered her mother in the hospital at least once; what she remembered was that their father had given them chocolate ice cream for dinner, and when Tate told her mother, in the hospital, that Daddy had given them chocolate ice cream for dinner, her mother had cried. Tate hadn't eaten chocolate ice cream since. Tate had been pretty young, four or five, and she didn't remember anyone explaining what had happened, although perhaps her father or Aunt India had tried, because it was right around that time that Tate began to pray fervently for another brother or sister. She had even asked Santa to bring one on Christmas Eve. And then, when no new sibling appeared, Tate invented one—she alternated between a brother named Jaysen (spelled just that way) and a sister named Molly. Tate marveled: she hadn't thought about Jaysen or Molly in a long, long time. The important thing, Tate remembered, was that Jaysen and/or Molly was her very best friend, devoted solely to her. The Jaysen and Molly of Tate's imagination didn't even know Chess existed.

Tate awoke to the sound of a boat motor. She opened her eyes and propped herself on her elbows. Barrett Lee's boat had come up the gut into the pond. She heard a second noise, small music, a faraway tune, something familiar. Her iPod was on at her feet. It was playing "Glory Days."

She grabbed the iPod and shut it off, grateful for the distraction from the main event: Barrett Lee in his boat. Here? She looked out to where her stone had finally submerged; he was closer than that now.

She had to wake up.

She drank what was left of her lemonade. It was warm and sour. She was awake; this was real. Barrett anchored the boat, jumped over the side, and waded in. Tate stared at him.

He said, "They told me you were here."

She couldn't risk saying the wrong thing. She waited.

"Listen, I have this thing tomorrow night. It's a dinner party thrown by that client of mine I told you about. The party is at her house in Brant Point. It'll be pretty fancy. Would you like to go with me?"

"Yes," Tate said. The word slipped out on its own, without her permission. The mind was the world's fastest computer. So many thoughts in an instant, overlapping, colliding thoughts, thoughts without words. A dinner party with Barrett. Yes. Anywhere with Barrett. Did it matter that he had asked Chess first? That Tate was his second choice and everyone would know it? It *did* matter, but not enough to turn him down. She would never turn Barrett Lee down.

"Yes?" he said. He sounded surprised. He had expected, maybe, to strike out with both Cousins girls.

"I'd love to," she said. "You'll come get me?"

"At six," he said. "Tomorrow night at six. The thing is..."

"What?" Tate said.

"I can't bring you back until morning," he said. "By the time the dinner party is over, it will be too late. So you'll have to stay with me. I'll bring you back Sunday morning. Early, in time for you to run, I promise."

In time for her to run. Okay, that was sweet. That was thoughtful. He knew who he was asking out.

"I'll stay at your house?" she said.

"My house," he said. "Is that okay?"

"It's okay," she said.

"That's the only thing about dating a Tuckernuck girl," he said. "No way to get her home at night."

A Tuckernuck girl.

They said other things, small talk: *Good-bye. See you tomorrow. It's dressy, I think. I'm wearing a sport coat.* Tate didn't remember exactly. Her thoughts were with the God of Tuckernuck. She was before him, clasping his hands in thanks. Kissing his feet.

INDIA

When Barrett appeared in the afternoon, he had a letter for India.

"Mail call," he said.

This was highly unusual. Grant used to receive mail, of course, documents that needed his signature; these were FedExed to Chuck Lee, and then Chuck Lee would bring them over on his boat and hand them to Grant with a withering look. Receiving mail was understood to be an infraction against the Tuckernuck lifestyle. There was supposed to be no mail, no phone calls, no communication with the outside world. India had been raised in this tradition. And yet, she couldn't just fall off the face of the earth for thirty days. She had left the address of Barrett's caretaking business with her three sons and with her assistant, Ainslie. She had been clear: *Use the address only in case of emergency.* The sight of Barrett waggling the envelope, therefore, inspired worry, which quickly morphed into fear.

Her first thought was, *The baby.*

Billy's baby. Heidi, Billy's wife, was twenty-nine weeks along. Everything was going smoothly; the pregnancy had been closely monitored. Heidi was an obstetrician herself; she had a sonogram machine right there in her office and she used it on herself the last day of every month. Heidi felt a heavy responsibility in carrying Bill Bishop's grandson, the heir to that famous name, but Heidi was equal to it. She was a medical professional who followed her own advice: she took vitamins, she ate leafy greens and bananas, she had stopped drinking. Still, things could go wrong, so many goddamned things could go wrong during pregnancy or delivery—not to mention a whole wide world of disease and birth defects. Had it been this way when India was pregnant? Probably so, though not everything had a diagnosis like it did now. When India looked at the white of the envelope in Barrett's hand, she thought, *Heidi has gone into preterm labor. She will deliver before the baby's lungs are mature. If the baby lives, there will be weeks in the NICU, respirators, and even then, possible brain damage.* Oh, Billy. He and Heidi were perfectionists and overachievers. They would not handle this well.

Or, India thought, the letter could be in regard to Teddy. Of her three sons, Teddy worried her the most because he was the most like Bill. He liked to work with his hands; he had started a roofing company in the northwest suburbs of Philadelphia—Harleysville, Gilbertsville, Oaks—former farmland that now sprouted headquarters for pharmaceutical companies and McMansions for the executives. Teddy had had a longtime girlfriend named Kimberly, but they were always breaking up and getting back together. Teddy was emotionally unstable; he'd had one episode that landed him in the psych ward of Quakertown Hospital. The doctors put him on Zoloft, but he drank too much. He was, India had to admit, a time bomb. So the envelope said what? That he had killed Kimberly? Killed himself?

The letter would not be about Ethan. Ethan, at twenty-seven, was the happiest person India had ever known. He was an anchorman on a Philadelphia sports-news channel, which afforded him a bit of minor celebrity, enough to get him laid whenever he was out at the bars. Ethan had a golden retriever named Dr. J. He lived in a loft in Manayunk. He had been only twelve years old when Bill died, but he was free of anxiety, which just went to show that things didn't always turn out the way one expected.

India took the envelope from Barrett. The front said, *India Bishop, Tuckernuck Island.* That was all it said; it didn't list the address for the caretaking company that India had given the boys and Ainslie. The letter was postmarked from Philadelphia.

India Bishop, Tuckernuck Island.

"I can't believe this reached me," India said.

"It helps that my father knows everyone on Nantucket, including the postmaster," Barrett said. "They're in Rotary together. When the letter came through, the postmaster gave it to my dad and my dad gave it to me."

"Well," said India, trying to smile, "thank you."

"You're welcome," Barrett said. "Hey, do you know where Tate is?"

"North Pond," India said.

"Great," Barrett said. He dropped two bags of groceries, a bag of ice, and another case of wine in the kitchen, and then looked like he was anxious to get back to the boat. India thought to mention that Tate had specifically said she wanted to be alone, but India selfishly wanted Barrett to leave so she could have some privacy for her letter. Birdie was off on a walk somewhere, and Chess was asleep on the living room sofa. Chess had napped on the beach for nearly two hours, then come up to the house because the beach was too hot, and she had fallen asleep again. She hadn't eaten a bite of lunch. Birdie was worried about her; before she left for her walk, she told India how worried she was, and she implored India to talk to Chess. With Tate gone for the day, this would be the perfect opportunity. *Right, okay,* India said. *I intend to, I will.* But India wasn't sure what to say. She could tell Chess about her own experiences, but who knew if they would resonate? In India's opinion, every woman had to go through the fire alone.

And now, India was distracted. The letter! As soon as Barrett disappeared down the beach steps, she put on Bill's reading glasses and slit the letter open with a butter knife.

A piece of white copy paper, folded in thirds. At the top, in red felt-tip pen, it said: *Was I wrong about you?*

India read the line twice, then a third time. Then she sighed, folded the letter up, and slid it back into the envelope. She let Bill's reading glasses fall to her chest.

The letter was from Lula.

On the one hand, India felt relieved. A letter from her sons would only have contained tragic news. On the other hand, India felt oddly exposed. Lula had found her, here on Tuckernuck, with an envelope that had been addressed for the pony express.

Lula might have called Ainslie to figure out where India was; perhaps Ainslie had given up the name of the island (but not the caretaker's address). Or Lula remembered India mentioning that her ancestral summer home was on this sandbar called Tuckernuck. India felt relieved that the letter wasn't harsher; if Lula was angry enough to leave PAFA, then she was angry enough to write more than that one little line. Lula had censored herself; she had shown restraint. She had, almost, accepted the blame.

India didn't know how to answer the question.

She lit a cigarette, then she repaired to the kitchen to pour herself a glass of wine. It was only three o'clock, but what the hell, Barrett had delivered a new case of Sancerre. It was chilled, and India had suffered a shock. She would have a drink.

She sat back down at the picnic table and ran her hand through her spiky, salt-stiffened hair, feeling newly self-conscious, as if someone were watching her. She smoked her cigarette down to the filter, sipped her wine, raised her face to the sun, wrinkles be damned, regarded the envelope, and shook her head. Jesus.

Was Lula wrong about her?

Yes, Lula, you were probably wrong, you took the things I said and did the wrong way, you invested them with too much meaning. Was that the answer? *I misled you, I vacillated, I didn't know what I wanted or what I was feeling. I was out of my comfort zone.*

India finished her glass of wine and poured another. It was cold and it was good—Birdie knew her Sancerres—and India thought, *Goddamn it!* She had made it through an entire week without thinking about PAFA in general and Lula in particular, and now this.

* * *

Tallulah Simpson. Lula had come to PAFA late in life, which is to say, at the age of twenty-six. She already had a degree in Romance languages from McGill University. She spoke French, Italian, Spanish, Portuguese, Arabic, and Hindi. The languages were a gift, more of a gift, perhaps, than her art; ever since Lula was a little girl, she had wanted to be an interpreter for an important organization—Unicef, the World Bank, the Red Cross. She had worked for a few years as a translator for big tobacco; she traveled between Montreal, Paris, and India. She hadn't painted anything in her life until she contracted dengue fever in India and was hotel-bound on big tobacco's dime. She recovered from the fever in three weeks and took another three weeks to regain her strength. This was when she started to paint—out of boredom, she said, and weakness. She had wanted to write a novel, but thinking hurt her brain. Painting was easier; she started with watercolors and tempera on heavy, expensive paper from the hotel's business center. She already knew what she wanted to paint; the images had been with her since birth.

Lula had told India this much during their first meeting over lattes at the White Dog Cafe, on the first October day that it was chilly enough to enjoy an afternoon coffee. The meeting was official. India was Lula's second-year adviser. India's position at the academy was such that she handpicked all of her advisees; it was a condition of her serving as an adviser at all. (She was such a bitch.) India chose the second-year students who had proved during their first year to be the most interesting, the most talented, the most attractive—and Tallulah Simpson was at the top of each category. She was stunning—with long, straight black hair, clear green eyes, and golden skin. Her mouth was wide; there was a gap between her front teeth. She had an unplaceable accent. She smoked and drank and used foreign phrases; she wore expensive, stylish clothes—flaring tops, tight jeans, impossibly high heels. (India ended up emulating her fashion sense; she had, with certain purchases, downright plagiarized it.) Lula's father, now dead, had been an Iranian businessman who had immigrated to Canada in the late seventies, and Lula's mother was from a prominent family in Bangalore. Lula's life had been one of privilege, though she had been marginalized, even among the tolerant Canadians, because of her race. She understood the pain of being an outsider, and from this pain came the inspiration for her paintings.

What India had thought was, *Oh, come on.*

The story sounded worn out and typical; India had hoped for more. But most of PAFA's students—aspiring artists in their late teens and early twenties—held an overly romanticized vision of themselves. They liked to talk about their *pain,* their *inspiration.* They didn't realize yet that their currency would be hard work and ambition.

Lula had been a little moony at that first coffee, but she was a fiercely talented painter. She was always in the studio, always experimenting with different canvases and paints and techniques. She brought gesso back into fashion, then gouache. She did studies of color and texture, underpainting and overpainting. She studied her history—Matisse, Modigliani, O'Keeffe, Pollock, Rothko. She loved Rothko; she single-handedly started a Rothko renaissance. Suddenly, references to Rothko's paintings were appearing in everyone's work, and the faculty were shaking their heads. It was because of Tallulah. She set trends.

Lula never slept; that was the rumor. Her insomnia had been inherited from her Iranian father, who had also never slept. Lula mentioned her insomnia to India when they met again for coffee at the White Dog. India admitted to Lula that she didn't sleep either, though her insomnia was situational and not inherited. It had been caused by her husband's suicide.

India spent her insomniac hours drinking chamomile tea and paging through fashion magazines. She listened to John Coltrane; she watched *Love Story* on TNT. Lula went to Tattooed Mom and 105 Social; she drank champagne bought for her by men with expense accounts; she did recreational drugs. At dawn, she went home, washed her hair, ate a hard-boiled egg, and was in her studio by 7 A.M.

During that second year, Lula discovered the female nude. She spent long hours in Cast Hall, sketching the plaster forms of the human body; she would spend an hour on an ear, an entire day on a hand. She wanted to be technically perfect. The most famous of PAFA's instructors, Thomas Eakins, had encouraged his students to dissect dead bodies. In this tradition, Lula hounded someone at UPenn's medical school, and she spent a week sketching cadavers. News of this over-the-top effort in the name of authenticity traveled through the halls of the school; Lula quickly became the It Girl with the untouchable talent, the sick work ethic. India and the other professors knew that a burnished reputation in only her second year could be a good thing or a bad thing. But the work spoke for itself: One entire wall of Lula's studio was dedicated to a study done in pink, of a woman dancing. The woman was six feet tall and had her arms extended over her head; Lula had rendered her sixteen times in succession, so that to look at the wall from left to right was to sense the woman twirling.

At the end of the year, Lula won the cash award for the Most Promising Student. This was the subject of much controversy and conversation because she was the only student who hadn't completed a single canvas. Her entire oeuvre, at that point, was studies. But the studies showed brilliance, and as India—who held the most influential vote where this award was concerned—pointed out, not one of the other students' finished canvases held the promise of Tallulah's studies.

In Lula's third year, the coffees at the White Dog turned into dinners at places like Susanna Foo and Morimoto. People whispered that this was unethical (there wasn't a single whisper that didn't make it, eventually, to India's ear). But there was nothing unethical about the dinners. Lula and India were friends, with a shared taste for exotic food and exquisite wine. Always, they split the bill.

And then, one night, India offered to entertain Lula at home. She would cook. Lula borrowed somebody's car and drove out to India's heavily wooded suburb. Lula, the city mouse, seemed intimidated by the Main Line. It was so old and storied. So Waspy. Nothing like the city, she said. She could work the city. But covered bridges and massive estates, country clubs with gates, and hundred-year-old trees—these put her out.

Just look at this house, Lula said.

She was referring to the fact that it was built from stones that had been dredged out of the Delaware River in the eighteenth century. The foyer had a vaulted ceiling and a brick floor. It seemed imposing to Lula, who lived in an apartment that was modern and minimalist.

India invited Lula into the kitchen, a massive, magnificent room with marble countertops, an acre of butcher block, gleaming copper cookware, walnut cabinets whose fixtures had been smoothed with use. When the boys were still at home, and when Bill was working, India's only job had been to keep things happy and humming. She had cooked large, elaborate meals, doubling and tripling recipes to meet the boys' appetites. She told Tallulah this. She said, "And now, I hardly ever use it. So I'm glad you're here."

Lula kissed India flush on the mouth, which took India by surprise but didn't alarm her. Lula had brought her a pink gerbera daisy in a pot wrapped in pink foil, a very un-Lula-like present, but Lula said, "The suburbs, I just wasn't sure." She had also brought two skinny joints in a sandwich bag. "One for now," she said. "One for later, in case you can't sleep."

India poured wine; they lit up the first joint. It had been a while since India had smoked dope, and she had certainly never smoked with a student. But she was lulled by the safety of her own kitchen, and the dope was good. India got very high; any qualms she had floated to the ceiling with the smoke. She stirred the pasta sauce on the stove. Lula asked if she might have a peek at the rest of the house. India felt a stab of some old, forgotten jealousy. This was, after all, Bill Bishop's house, and out back was Bill's studio. Lula would want to see it; that was, quite possibly, the reason she'd agreed to come at all.

"You can look around," India said. "But I am not giving a tour. I don't mean to be rude, but I find pointing out all of Bill's *objets* tiresome."

"Yes," Lula said. "I'll bet."

She poked around anyway. She opened the back door, activating the motion-detector lights, and slipped across the back lawn to Bill's studio, which was locked. Lula hurried back into the house, and India decided not to say anything.

They had a lovely dinner: A salad of greens, figs, toasted pine nuts, and herbed goat cheese, tossed with India's famous vinaigrette. Fettuccine with truffle butter, cream, and pecorino cheese. Homemade bread.

"Homemade *bread?*" Lula said. She was stuffing her face with food, the way India had never seen her do in public. It was the pot, maybe. Or she felt at ease here. Or she was simply hungry: Like all workaholic insomniacs, Lula barely ate. She lived on coffee and cigarettes and nibbled at sad, shriveled pieces of cheese naan. Now, Lula slathered the homemade bread with butter. India was delighted.

Over dessert—a plum crumble with amaretto ice cream—Lula told India that the female nudes were no accident. They had been born out of a discovery she had made a year earlier: the sexual discovery of women.

"You mean," India said, "you're a lesbian?"

"Bisexual," Lula said. "I've been with too many men to consider myself a lesbian. I like men, but I'm done with them sexually, for the time being."

"Are you?" India said.

"I'm into women," Lula said.

"Is there anyone special?" India asked.

"No," Lula said. "Not really. Do you ever think about women?"

"No," India said. "Never." When she said this, she felt immature, provincial.

"Let me ask you another question," Lula said. She had devoured her dessert and was pressing the tines of her fork against the remaining crumbs. "Would you ever consider modeling for me?"

India had smoked the second joint late that night, blowing the smoke out her open bedroom window. Insomnia, her own personal Satan, had her by the neck. Her mind was a bloodred room, alarms sounding. She had known, the second she agreed to model for Lula, that she wouldn't be able to sleep. She feared she would never sleep again.

Initially, she had turned Lula down. *No, heavens, no, there is nothing about my body that deserves to be reproduced in any medium.*

Lula had been persistent. *I'm trying to get at something inside the body. To show inner strength, resilience. Surely you've picked up on that?*

Yes, India had picked up on it. It was what made the nudes distinctive. You looked at Lula's figures and saw the iron and the elasticity.

Who have you used before? India asked.

Lula shrugged. *The sylphs from the stable.* She meant the aspiring actresses and waitresses who got paid thirty dollars an hour to pose for PAFA students. *Also, a friend of mine from over the summer. And once, a black high school girl I picked up off the street.*

Jesus, India thought. Lula was out there, inviting lawsuits. And yet, India had seen the studies of the black teenager and found them brilliant.

No one can know, India said. *No one can know I'm doing it and no one can know it's me when they see the paintings. You can imagine the imbroglio that would ensue?*

I can imagine, Lula said.

So, India said, feeling both honored and supremely uncomfortable. Feeling, in fact, like she was being propositioned. This was a chance to be a part of something new and alive. There was no doubt in India's mind that Lula was going to become a major artist of the new millennium—as big someday as Rothko himself, or Pollock, or O'Keeffe—and how could India, mere mortal that she was, give up the opportunity to be a part of that? India did possess inner strength and she did possess resilience and she was sinfully proud of both. She was a phoenix, risen from the ashes. She should be painted! If not her, then whom? Lula might ask Ainslie next, or Spencer Frost's sultry wife, Aversa. India would have been offered her chance and blown it. So she said yes. She would pose.

Lula had left the house shortly after getting the answer she was looking for, taking with her a generous piece of plum crumble on a paper plate sealed with Saran Wrap. Lula was drunk and high and driving a borrowed car on unfamiliar, winding roads; it was unethical, indeed criminal, to send her home. India should have invited Lula to spend the night. *You can follow me in tomorrow morning.* But India's sense of decorum told her to *get the girl out of the house* before any other boundaries were crossed.

India smoked the joint, which led her downstairs to the kitchen to finish both the plum crumble and the amaretto ice cream. She fell asleep around five and awoke at seven with her teeth unbrushed and a vague sense of shame in her heart.

At the picnic table, India polished off the second glass of wine. It was quarter to four and she was still alone. It was a gift, she supposed, to have time to think about the letter, and about Lula, without other people around. If Birdie were here, she would want to know who the letter was from and what it said. India's head was floating. It was a singular experience, getting drunk on a sunny afternoon. She had reached the point where she either had to rein herself in—figure out how to work the ancient French press and make herself a cup of coffee—or keep going with wine. What the hell, she thought. She was on Tuckernuck, where nothing was expected of her.

In the kitchen, she poured herself another glass of wine. She checked to make sure Chess was still breathing. Yes? Okay.

* * *

Posing for Lula was as secret as a love affair. India refused to pose in Lula's studio or in any other PAFA-owned space. And so they decided on Lula's apartment.

India checked in with the doorman under an assumed name, Elizabeth Tate, which was, India told Lula, a family name. Lula didn't understand the need for aliases—the doorman was discreet, India could use her own name. But no, she wouldn't.

Lula met India at the apartment door. She had Schubert playing, which was a balm for India's sensibilities; in her studio at school, Lula listened to the Smashing Pumpkins and the Sex Pistols and the Ramones at ludicrous volume. (The other students would have complained if it had been anyone but Lula.) Lula greeted India in a businesslike manner—a crisp hello, no kiss—and handed India a waffled white robe.

"You can change in the bathroom," she said.

Lula's bathroom was sleek and modern like the rest of the apartment, and as impersonal as a bathroom at a hotel. All of Lula's personal effects were secreted away behind mirrored cabinets. So many mirrors, doubling and quadrupling India's form in its dishabille. She tried not to look at herself. Her mission here today was *not* one of personal vanity. It wasn't about the body and what had happened to her once-magnificent ass (too much plum crumble, too many sweet cosmopolitans, age). It was about art.

She entered the living room in her robe. "Where would you like me?" she asked.

"I'm not sure," Lula said. She wore a white ruffled tunic over some electric green leggings. She was barefoot, she was smoking. Her hair was half-up, half-down; she had kohl smudged around her eyes. "I've been thinking about it. Let's start on the sofa."

The sofa was white suede. India was afraid of it. Or

rather, what she was afraid of was this moment, the moment she was to remove her robe. It wasn't like India to be nervous; it wasn't like India to feel vulnerable. She tried to concentrate on other things. The Schubert was nice. There was a vase of crimson dahlias on the table next to the sofa.

She slipped off her robe, exposing her backside to Lula. She lay down on the sofa. "Like this?" she said. Her voice sounded strange.

Lula barely nodded her assent. Her pencil made a frantic scratching sound against the paper. India was electrified. She was instantly aroused, as sexually turned on as she had ever been in her life. She was nothing at that moment but a naked body stretched out on skin-soft suede. She was a woman with another woman's eyes all over her. It was obscene and exhilarating. Lula's pencil was moving faster and faster. India felt as if the pencil was touching her, as if the eraser of the pencil were teasing at her nipples, which were now erect. Did Lula see? Did she see what she was *doing* to India?

Lula said, "Pivot your hips, a little, toward me."

India had heard all the jokes, of course, about the sylphs from the stable. The girls who modeled at PAFA were, when class was over, the easiest lays in the Delaware Valley. It only depended on which student offered to buy her a drink first. Now, India understood why. It was an incredibly sensual experience to bare your body and let another person render you.

India closed her eyes. She was wet between the legs. She was pulsing with heat and light.

"Eyes open!" Lula snapped.

India opened her eyes.

She had managed to get out of the apartment an hour later without incident, a fact that had dismayed her at the time and came as an enormous relief once she was out on the cold city street.

What had happened in there? India wondered. What kind of witchcraft?

She decided she wouldn't go back.

But go back she did, every Tuesday at five o'clock, for eight weeks. The posing took the place of their weekly dinners. India couldn't sit with Lula and have a meal; something had shifted between them. The posing was serious business; during the sessions, they barely spoke. India didn't know how to process the sexual energy. Did Lula sense it? Did she feel it, too? She didn't let on.

During those eight weeks, India started to take care of her body again. She joined a gym in King of Prussia; it wasn't a place where India would bump into anyone she knew, so the business of building her strength and endurance was her only focus. She hired a personal trainer named Robbie, who was a transvestite and worked her like an ox through the machines and the free weights. She ate chicken and fish and vegetables. She cut down on cigarettes and stopped drinking at home. She invested in creams and lotions for her skin; she booked manicures and pedicures and massages on the weekends. (Taking care of herself, India realized, could take up every spare hour if she let it. Did other people do this?) She flossed every time she brushed. She took vitamins. She soaked in lavender baths. She considered getting a risqué wax on her pubic hair, but she didn't want to call attention to herself.

Lula didn't seem to notice any change, until one day when India slipped off the robe, Lula said, "Are you getting skinny on me, Indie?"

India was quick to deny it.

"Really?" Lula said. "You look positively svelte. And you're glowing. What's that about?"

India shrugged.

"Lie down," Lula said.

Then, the posing ended. It was spring break, which was two weeks long. India went to Greece with her college roommate Paula Dore-Duffy, who was now a professor of neurology at Wayne State University. Paula did research on the blood-brain barrier; she wasn't interested in the art world or PAFA or late-emerging lesbian feelings, and India didn't speak of these things. Paula wanted to shed her white lab coat, drink ouzo, and dance in the hotel discos, which overlooked the Aegean Sea, and India joined her in these pursuits. The one morning at breakfast when Paula did ask India about work, India joked that thinking about PAFA made her worry for her own blood-brain barrier, and she dove into her honey and yogurt. The subject didn't come up again. It was a relief.

When India got back to the academy, things progressed into end-of-the-year mode. Third- and fourth-year students were preparing for the Annual Student Exhibition. India checked in with all of her advisees, including Lula. Lula was busy painting. She was back to her obsessive ways—in her studio from seven in the morning until midnight, smoking two packs a day, drinking ten lattes, ordering Indian food from Mumbai Palace that sat, untouched, in the cartons.

Everyone's expecting big things, India told her.

Fuck you, Lula said. But she was smiling when she said it.

The ASE was always the biggest night of the academic year; it was, in many ways, more important than graduation. Graduation was a ceremony, a passing on of a (basically useless) degree in fine arts. But the ASE was the meat; it was the money. Art dealers from all over the city and from New York and Boston and Chicago attended—as well as family, friends, previous graduates, colleagues from other schools, other museum curators, serious collectors, novice collectors, and society matrons who couldn't tell Winslow Homer from Homer Simpson but who wanted to see and be seen. The ASE was the premier evening in the Philadelphia art world; there was a line at the gates hours before.

India always wore something new and fabulous to the ASE because inevitably her photograph appeared on the society page of the *Philadelphia Inquirer* and the glossy center pages of *Philadelphia* magazine. She was, in so many ways, the face of PAFA; hers was the name people recognized. India Bishop, widow of the famous sculptor. And this year she knew her involvement would be deeper and more nuanced than it had been in years past. The paintings everyone would be talking about would be of her.

Because the ASE was student curated (which was part of the buzz: not even the administration knew what to expect), India hadn't seen the paintings. A hundred times, India had been tempted to ask to see the paintings so she could confirm that the nude body would not be recognizable as *her* nude body—but she couldn't risk insulting Lula this way. She and Lula had an understanding: her one condition would be honored.

India wore a flowing white one-shouldered Elie Tahari dress that, while quite lovely, most closely resembled a paint-splattered sheet thrown over her body. Before India even made it through the back entrance, before she lifted a glass of champagne from the tray, she was receiving compliments on it. *Beautiful dress, so elegant, so fitting, where did you get it?* People were everywhere, they were a flock of birds descending on her, seagulls at the beach where she had the only sandwich. Everyone wanted to talk to her; everyone wanted her attention. A reporter from the *Inquirer* snapped her picture while she still had her sunglasses on. India was overwhelmed. She needed the tiniest bit of personal space, a few moments to set down her purse, taste the champagne, get into the exhibit rooms. Had her entrance always caused such a buzz? Or was this interest caused by something else? Did they know? Was it obvious, or just a rumor?

India forced out a breath. She had to relax. The ASE was this overwhelming every year, she reassured herself, because she knew nearly everyone in the room, and those few people she didn't know wanted an introduction. Still, scenes from her waking nightmares spooled through her head—her body hideous and lumpy, her face twisted and ugly, her form revealing what an evil bitch she really was—as she made her way through the crowd.

The president of the board of directors, Spencer Frost, was waiting for her just outside the exhibit rooms. He was flushed and sweating, as if experiencing his own private ecstasy. "My God, India, it's fantastic. The girl is a superstar. I want to buy them all. I've already bought two for myself and one for the school. They are…well, go, woman, see for yourself."

India entered the front room, which held huge, soaring canvases—like Delacroix at the Louvre—they were all Lula's and they were all of India. It was India deconstructed and reconstructed—India in Rothko's smudged planes of color—India's breasts and legs and once-magnificent ass resplendent in a way that suggested fluid motion. Her skin was luminescent, the lines flawless. India had to jockey for position—the room was packed, and India's heart momentarily went out to the students whose work would receive one-tenth of this attention—because she wanted to *see* them. When she viewed them properly, she was triumphant. Not for herself (well, maybe a little bit for herself) but for Lula.

What she thought was, *She did it.*

India rose from the picnic table with the letter. She poured herself another glass of wine and carried the letter upstairs to her bedroom. Roger was perched on the dresser; in the humidity his seaweed hair had gone limp. She tucked the letter from Lula into her dresser drawer and contemplated taking a nap on her jelly-filled mattress, but that would lead to her waking in an hour or two with a flannel mouth and a pounding headache. No, thank you.

Downstairs, she thought she heard Chess stirring. She shut the dresser drawer tight.

Was I wrong about you?

The 108th ASE was a success such as neither Lula nor India could have imagined. Lula sold every painting. She sold two to Spencer Frost for his private collection (and it was well known that he only collected *dead painters*), and one to the school through Spencer Frost. She sold her largest canvas to Mary Rose Garth, rubber heiress, who was the most flamboyant presence at the ASE (she had been known to come to the show with a sheet of red dot stickers in her purse so she could claim the best paintings before anyone else even saw them). Lula sold one canvas to a collector in Seattle (it was unconfirmed, but rumor had it, it was Bill Gates), and one to the most prestigious all-female law firm in Philadelphia. Every gallery owner present had offered to represent her. Lula was going to be rich, and she was going to be famous.

"But I'm not dropping out of school," she told India. "I'm going to finish. Get my goddamned certificate."

"Of course you are, silly girl," India said. "Silly goose."

She was quite drunk. It was late—twenty minutes past three. Lula and India had survived the show and the after-show reception, and the dinner at Tria after the reception, and drinks at Valanni after dinner, and dancing at 105 Social after those drinks. They smoked a joint on their way back to North Broad Street. Lula wanted to see the paintings one more time—some of them would be whisked away by their new owners in the morning—and India did, too.

It was as they stood in front of the paintings and Lula announced her promise to stay in school that Lula wound her arms around India's waist and India felt Lula's mouth on her neck. India was drunk and high and shimmying with the aftershocks of the most extraordinary night of her life. She might well have submitted to Lula, slipped underwater and drowned in the girl.

But instead, India pulled away. "No," she said. "I'm sorry."

Lula tried again. She was gentle and her voice was calm. "I saw it in you when you posed for me. I saw it in you, but I waited."

What could India say? The hours that she had posed for Lula were the most erotic hours of her life. India couldn't deny that. Had Lula made her advances when India was prone on the suede sofa, India would never have been able to rebuff her.

"I'm sorry," India said.

"I love you," Lula said. "I mean it. I love you, India."

India shivered. For the first time that night, she thought of Bill and how frenzied and full her life with him had been. Even when the kids were sick and the weather was gray, even when he was manic or depressed, India felt alive. She felt engaged, interested, challenged. Such was life with a genius.

But she couldn't do it again.

"Lula," India said. She touched Lula's chin and turned her face so Lula would look at her. "I'm sorry."

Lula slapped her, hard, across the face.

India cried out. In the cavernous room, the cry echoed. Again, Bill: He had slapped her once in public, on a subway platform in Stockholm. She had promised to divorce him. But she hadn't.

Should she slap Lula now? Did Lula want a catfight, with pulled hair and torn clothes? Would it end with the two of them intertwined in a writhing pile on the floor?

India turned. She picked her clutch off the waiter's tray and walked out of the room.

"India!" Lula called. "INDIA!"

India didn't stop. She drove all the way home and slept like a baby until noon the next day.

It was Memorial Day weekend. India spent it quietly at home, tending to her garden. By Tuesday morning, the news had spread like an epidemic: Tallulah Simpson was withdrawing. Transferring to Parsons.

When India got downstairs, Chess was blinking, her eyes wide and dazed like the eyes of someone who had just been born.

"What time is it?" Chess asked.

"Nearly five," India said, though it was only quarter past four. "Would you like a glass of wine?"

"Yes," Chess said. "Where's my mother?"

"She's out on a walk," India said.

Chess nodded. "I've been asleep forever."

"Do you sleep at night?" India asked.

"Like a rock."

"Lucky you," India said, though there was nothing

lucky about it. The girl was depressed. India filled with guilt. She was supposed to talk to Chess. She was supposed to help. That was why she'd been invited along.

India poured Chess a glass of wine and refilled her own. She was drunk or nearly so, which was not a bad state to be in when embarking on a frank conversation.

"Sit with me," India said.

Chess accepted the wine gratefully and sat at the picnic table. India rummaged through the kitchen for snacks—she found half a tin of Spanish peanuts and a box of Bremner wafers that had gone stale and tasted like wet cardboard.

India had an opening line on her tongue. *Your mother wanted me to talk to you.* But how awkward, how schoolmarmish. She would sound like a scold. The idea, India knew, was for her to talk to Chess about Bill—how Bill had died and what that had felt like and how she had recovered. But India didn't want to talk about Bill. Her mind was elsewhere.

India pondered for a second as she studied Chess's face. Without the frame of her hair, Chess's face was even more striking than usual. She had light blue eyes with a dark ring around the iris, the effect of which was quite arresting. There were pink, crosshatched marks on her face where her cheek had met with the ass-scratching material of the living room sofa. The poor girl was dying for something—a scrap, a hint, some direction about what to do. She had broken her engagement; her fiancé had died. There were other things that she wasn't telling. She wasn't ready to talk, but looking at her now, India wondered if she might be ready to listen.

Would she be able to handle the story about Lula and her dear old aunt?

Oh, hell, India, she told herself. *Get on with it!*

"I received a letter today," she said.

CHESS

Her depression was a place to hide. Birdie had knocked and Chess had ignored her. Barrett Lee had knocked and Chess had told him to go away. India had knocked and Chess—mostly because she couldn't bring herself to be rude to her aunt—had agreed to listen. Aunt India talked about a student at PAFA, and a connection between them that couldn't be reduced. The story was engrossing. For the first time since she'd arrived, Chess thought about something other than herself.

"Do you love her?" Chess asked.

India put her fingers to her temples and rolled her eyes back in her head, like a swami trying to see the future. "I don't know," she said. She smiled at Chess, then lit a cigarette. "The thing is, my darling, human emotions present themselves in any number of shocking ways. Do you know what I'm telling you?"

"What?" Chess said.

"I'm telling you that you aren't alone."

Day seven.

Human emotions present themselves in any number of shocking ways.

—India Bishop

Nick had kissed me. I thought about that kiss a hundred times a day, a thousand times. I tried to remember how I had acted or reacted, but it had happened so quickly that I couldn't remember myself. I could only remember him. I wondered if I should have said something different or done something different, because after that one kiss, there was nothing for a long time. I should have said something to let him know how I felt about him, I should have kept him there longer, kissed him some more, done more than kiss him.

I continued to date Michael. I saw Nick infrequently—once a month we would go watch him play at the Bowery Ballroom or at Roseland and he would look upon me with intense longing, but only once, and then he wouldn't look again. He always had women around him—skinny, long-haired girls in jeans and tank tops and handmade jewelry, beautiful, underfed girls who were the band's groupies—but I never saw the same girl twice, and the one time I asked Michael if he thought Nick was dating, he said, "What, exactly, qualifies as dating?"

We attended family dinners with Cy and Evelyn, but Nick never came.

Michael saw Nick on Wednesday nights at his poker game. The game was hosted by Christo Snow, who had gone to Englewood High with Michael and Nick. The games were high stakes, the food was catered, and Christo hired not only a dealer from Atlantic City but a security guard as well. Michael made money or lost money. Nick always made money; it was his primary source of income. One night, after the game, Michael came home with a rosy, swollen eye. Nick had punched him.

I gasped, "Why?"

"We had a fight."

"About what?"

As was usual after these poker games, Michael was drunk. Otherwise, he would never have told me.

"About you."

"Me?"

"He said I wasn't right for you."

"Not right for me?"

"Not good enough for you."

My head swam. I remembered that Michael had long ago broken Nick's nose, over a girl. I should have felt some sympathy for Michael, but instead my heart felt like it was being carried away by bluebirds. Nick had feelings for me.

"Well, that's silly," I said.

* * *

I saw Nick again the week before Christmas. He was sitting on a bench in the lobby of my office building. I was leaving for the day; we had just put the February issue to bed with its comforting soups and stews and a menu for a snow-day sledding party. I felt the same massive relief I always felt when I put an issue to bed and the issue was good, and in addition, it was Christmas, I had twelve days off from work, and there was a fancy Christmas party that night for Michael's company, which was being held at the Morgan Library. I was in a singular mood. I didn't love Christmas the way Birdie or Tate loved Christmas; Christmas was for children and I didn't have any children and I was no longer a child myself—but on that day, I was in the spirit.

And then I saw someone who looked like Nick but would never be Nick, sitting on a vinyl bench by the revolving door of our office building. I got closer and saw his face, his hair, those eyes. He was wearing a black wool coat and jeans, and the security guards that manned the entrance eyed him suspiciously.

I said, "Nick?"

He gave me the look. My head buzzed. They played carols in the lobby, and the song at that moment was Burl Ives singing "Have a Holly Jolly Christmas."

He said, "I was in the neighborhood."

That was a lie. I worked in Midtown. Nick Morgan would never have had any reason to be in Midtown.

I didn't know what to say. I couldn't take my eyes off him and I didn't want him to take his eyes off me. We stood in the marble lobby of my building with people going past in both directions and Burl Ives crooning, locked in some kind of silvery force field.

Finally, he said, "Let's get out of here."

We walked. He led, I followed at his elbow. We walked up Fifth Avenue amid the throngs of people. So many people, so much Christmas cheer—tinsel on lampposts and wrapping paper covering the Louis Vuitton store and sugar-plum visions in the window at Henri Bendel. We walked in front of the Plaza Hotel; across the street, the line at FAO Schwarz was five hundred people long. When I walked in the city with Michael, these details interested me. With Nick, I cared only about Nick.

We walked into the park, we took the first footpath. It was cold, but I didn't care. Nick guided me toward a tree—bare-branched, majestic, sheltering. It instantly became our tree. I turned around to face Nick and he kissed me. He really kissed me, we were kissing, and God, he was the best kisser I had ever known. More sensual than Michael—more careful, less careful. He said, "I am obsessed with you."

This should have come as a surprise to me, but it didn't. Although I was dating Michael, I thought of Nick every hour of every day. I dreamed about him. I fixated on the poster in Michael's kitchen and on the pictures of Nick and Michael as children in Cy and Evelyn's house. I created excuses to say his name.

I said, "What are we going to do?"

He didn't answer.

I thought about what would happen if I just told Michael, Listen, I'm in love with your brother. *It would be bad, certainly; there would be another swollen eye or broken nose, or worse. Cy and Evelyn would be stymied, but would they let it destroy their world? Would they disown Nick, and if they did disown him, would it destroy our world?*

Nick was shaking his head. He said, "I hate the guy, I really hate him, but I love him, too, and I just can't do *that to him."*

I said, "No, me either."

Nick said, "But I couldn't wait any longer. I had to come to you. I had to kiss you today."

"Okay," I said. "Yes," I said. We kissed some more—I could not get enough *of him—and then he pulled away and turned and left—left me there in the dark park, which was something his brother, the gentleman, would never have done.*

A week later, Christmas Day, I went to the Morgans' house in New Jersey, trembling with anticipation. That morning, Birdie had made our usual holiday brunch of eggs Benedict and sticky buns, and I hadn't been able to eat a bite. Michael and I drove south to his parents' house, and I pretended to be napping so I didn't have to speak. We walked into the Morgan house, which, just like Birdie's house, was festooned with evergreen garland and smelled like cinnamon. Evelyn popped out of the living room, where there was a roaring fire and a towering tree with dozens of presents piled under it. Evelyn was wearing an embroidered Christmas sweater and red velvet pants. She said, "I'm so glad you made it. Dora's here, but your brother's not coming."

"Not coming?"

"He called this morning. He doesn't feel well, he said." Evelyn frowned. "Though he sounded perfectly fine to me."

Tate came home from her day of solitude at North Pond sunburned and twitching with excitement. Her joy was off-putting. How could Chess confide in her sister about "all that had happened" when her sister was so happy?

Tate said, "Come up to the attic with me. I want to tell you something."

Chess said, "I can't. I'm helping Birdie with dinner." This was true: she was shucking corn. But she had only one ear left.

"I need you now," Tate said.

Chess sighed. "One second. Let me finish."

The attic was a hotbox. The tiny window in the eaves

was open, but no air passed through it. Tate pulled Chess next to her on the bed.

"Guess what happened?" Tate said.

"What?" Chess said.

"Barrett asked me on a date. To a dinner party on Nantucket tomorrow night."

Chess was silent. What to say?

"I know he asked you first," Tate said.

Chess wiggled her toes. "He asked me this morning. He was only doing it to be nice. To prove that he's not mad anymore."

"Why would he be mad at you?" Tate asked.

"Oh," Chess said. She wasn't sure she could switch gears and talk about Barrett. "Because of something that happened a long time ago."

Tate crossed her eyes and stuck out her tongue. She was so childish sometimes, as emotionally crippled as a teenage boy. Tate was her sister, her love was unconditional, but the reality was tough: Tate didn't possess the maturity or understanding to handle the things that Chess wanted to tell her. Tate was a computer person, not a literary person; for Tate, something either worked or it didn't. She wasn't interested in situations that were complex or morally ambiguous. She didn't want to hear what had happened between Barrett and Chess thirteen years earlier; for Tate, the past was the past, and what was the point of revisiting it? Tate wasn't evolved enough to understand how, in many ways, the past revealed things. Tate was only concerned with the past few hours, today, tomorrow, her and Barrett Lee together. She was floating, and Chess didn't want to wield the needle that would pop her balloon.

"You're going to have fun," Chess said. "I think you and Barrett will be a much better match."

"Yes," Tate said. "We will be."

BIRDIE

At two o'clock in the morning, she found herself awake.

She had gone to bed at ten o'clock as usual, after dinner and several glasses of wine and an hour or two spent needlepointing a stocking for India's grandson.

She had asked India, "Are you excited about becoming a grandmother?"

They were sitting together on the screened-in porch. India was smoking her hundredth cigarette and drinking, she claimed, her eleventh glass of wine. She was drunk and waxing poetic. "I don't think anyone is *excited* to become a grandmother, heralding as it does the fact that one is officially old. It's hard to think of one's self as a sex symbol when one is a grandmother, right? I mean, where did our lives go? It seemed like we were teenagers forever, and then we were young wives and then we were mothers, and then there was that interminable time when the kids were growing up and Bill and I were focused on building his career and taking care of the house and making it all work, and then Bill died, and there was a long stretch of mourning and then me picking myself up and getting on with my life, and for about five minutes, it seemed, I was free and independent and insanely productive, and now all of a sudden, it's over. I'm going to be a *grandmother*." She blew out a stream of smoke. "But yes, I think once it happens, I'll be excited."

Birdie said, "Well, I'm excited to become a grandparent someday."

India said, not unkindly, "Oh, Birdie, of course you are."

Hank was a grandparent, Birdie thought, and he loved it. He was involved in his grandchildren's lives. He took them on outings to the Stew Leonard dairy and the children's museum in Norwalk. He picked them up from school every Tuesday.

Birdie sighed. She would like to go just ten minutes, just five minutes, without thinking about Hank. This would only happen, she realized, once she had a nice, long, meaningful conversation with the man. She craved this conversation physically, the way she craved food or nicotine. Tate had made a good point that afternoon: Birdie was calling Hank at a consistently bad time. And so, Birdie thought, she would ambush him. If she woke up in the middle of the night, she would get out of bed, walk to Bigelow Point with the aid of a flashlight, and call Hank then. The idea had wormed its way into Birdie's subconscious, and voilà!—she woke up.

She felt her way down the stairs. She had left her cell phone and a flashlight next to each other on the counter. She gripped them both. She found her sandals. She slipped outside.

Okay, she thought, as she headed down the dirt path, she was certifiable. Here she was at two o'clock in the morning walking across Tuckernuck to Bigelow Point. She should have taken the Scout, but she was afraid the sound of the engine would wake India and the girls.

There was a waxing gibbous moon, which brightened her way considerably. Birdie shined the flashlight beam at the trail. She wasn't afraid of wild animals, but she was afraid of tripping on a root or a stone and breaking her leg, or stepping into an unexpected hole and twisting her ankle. She proceeded cautiously, stopping every once in a while to look at Tuckernuck Island in the depths of night. It was starkly beautiful—the trail and surrounding low brush shone in the moonlight.

A simple world. Her complicated heart. She kept going.

It seemed a long way, and at one point, Birdie feared she was lost. Then she approached Adeliza Coffin's house—even in the moonlight, it was dark and sinister. Her grandparents had told stories about Adeliza standing on her doorstep with a shotgun, scaring away those who dared to trespass on Tuckernuck's hallowed acres. "She was a formidable woman," Birdie's grandfather had said, though it was unclear if he'd known her personally or was simply recounting legend. Birdie hurried past Adeliza's house—as children, she and India had held their breath and plugged their noses. The good news about Adeliza Coffin's house was that it was the last landmark before the water. Birdie kept going, and soon she heard waves and saw water sparkling in front of her like a smooth silk sheet. She stepped onto the slender spit of land that contained North Pond: Bigelow Point.

The tide was high. The tip of the point was covered by water. How high was the water? Birdie was in her nightgown, a simple white cotton affair that came to her knees. And she was wearing underwear. India slept in the nude; when she wandered the house, she put on a silk kimono but wore nothing underneath. India couldn't cross Tuckernuck at night.

Birdie stepped into the water on the ocean side. It was warm, warmer than the air. She waded out toward the tip of the point, and when the water encroached, she lifted her nightgown. The water was at midthigh. The water was so warm, Birdie felt the urge to pee. She would satisfy her urges one at a time, starting with the most important. The most important was Hank.

She called Hank at home. He would be sleeping, but he kept a phone right by his bed in case someone from the facility called about Caroline. Hank was a light sleeper. In the times that they had spent the night together, Birdie never failed to wake him when she rose to use the bathroom or startled from a dream. When the phone rang, Hank would hear it. Hank would answer it.

The phone rang. Four times, five, six, seven. Then there was a clicking noise. It was Hank's voice on the answering machine. Birdie hung up.

She called right back, praying, *Please, Hank, wake up, pick up.*

Again, the machine. Birdie called back again. It was the middle of the night. He might be fast, fast asleep, in the deep REM stage, where he heard the phone but thought it was part of his dream.

Again. Again. Again.

Birdie tried his cell phone next. It was quarter past three. There was no reason for Hank to be *out* at this hour, no way, but he might have been doing sleepover babysitting duty for Nathan or Cassandra.

Hank didn't answer his cell phone. Birdie called four times. Then, she called his house again, and when the machine picked up she left a message. She said, "Goddamn it, Hank." And then she hung up.

Goddamn it, Hank: not very eloquent, but it got her point across. She was tired of this. She wanted to talk to him.

She realized the water was getting higher, and in her frenzy to get ahold of Hank she had dropped the hem of her nightgown and now it was soaked. And her underwear was wet; the water was that high. This being the case, Birdie peed, sweet release, then wondered if her urine would draw sharks. The beach looked far away; she might have to swim, which would leave her drenched from head to toe in the middle of the night two miles from home. And in swimming to shore, she would ruin her cell phone. She started to cry—not because she was wet or afraid of sharks, not even because she was bone-crushingly tired. She cried because of Hank.

As she waded back to shore, she once again did the unthinkable and called Grant. He answered on the third ring in his middle-of-the-night voice, a voice that sounded alert and awake but that was, in fact, buried.

"Hello?" he said.

"Grant?"

"Bird?" he said. She was grateful that he knew it was her. The day might come, she realized, when that would not be the case. "Are you okay?"

"Hank doesn't love me," she said.

"Hank?" he said. "Who's Hank?"

"My boyfriend," she said. "The man I've been seeing."

"Oh," Grant said. "Where are you?"

"Tuckernuck," she said. "Bigelow Point."

"It's the middle of the night," he said.

"I know," Birdie said. "Hank doesn't love me."

There was a long pause. Long enough that Birdie wondered if Grant had fallen back to sleep.

"Grant?" she said.

He started. Yes, she'd caught him trying to sneak back to sleep. He had done this often in their life together. "What do you want me to do?" Grant said. "Beat the guy up? Call him and tell him he's an idiot?"

Birdie reached the shore. She found the flashlight in the sand and poked the beam into the dark sky. "Would you?" she said.

TATE

She had nothing to wear. She hadn't, in her wildest dreams, been expecting to attend a fancy dinner party at some flashy house on Nantucket. She had running clothes, bathing suits, shorts, and T-shirts. But Chess, thankfully, had carted along her entire closet.

Tate said, "Is it okay if I borrow something? If you say no, I don't know what I'll do."

Chess said, "Take whatever you want."

Tate said, "Will you help me?"

Chess huffed, but Tate wasn't fooled. Chess considered herself to be too *depressed* to help with something as frivolous as outfit selection, but Tate knew that secretly she was flattered and welcomed the distraction. And in this case, outfit selection was everything. If Tate wore the right outfit, she would feel sexy and confident, and if she felt sexy and confident, Barrett Lee would fall in love with her. Tate had been worried that perhaps Chess harbored feelings for Barrett herself, but that didn't seem to be the case. Barrett Lee fell into the same category with everyone else: Chess was too self-absorbed to give him a second thought.

Chess's dresses hung from a wooden pole in the makeshift attic closet. Tate selected a white sundress with blue flowers. She slipped it on. Pretty, but maybe a little prim? Chess lay on the bed.

She said, "I wore that dress the first time I met Michael's parents. Family dinner at the house. Nick was there, and Cy and Evelyn, of course."

Tate's arms hung at her sides. Was this how it was going to be? Tate shucked off the dress. She reached for an orange halter dress with white polka dots.

"I bought that for the rehearsal dinner," Chess said. "Try it on."

Tate hesitated. Chess had bought this one for the rehearsal dinner? Tate tried it on. It was adorable, cute and flirty, and Tate loved the idea of wearing orange. What a statement; she would liven up the party with a juicy sunburst. But something about the dress screamed, *Chess!* It was the polka dots, maybe, or the ruffle across the top. Chess had bought this dress for her rehearsal dinner. It was off-limits.

"I don't think so," Tate said.

Chess said, "I'll never wear it."

"You'll wear it," Tate said. She regarded the riches in the closet. There were so many dresses! Chess's life with Michael Morgan had been…what? One cocktail party after another?

"I will never get dressed up and go out again," Chess said.

"You will so," Tate said. "Your hair will grow back." Already a blond fuzz was coming in; Chess's head looked like a peach.

"I'm not saying that to evoke pity," Chess said. "I just want you to know you can borrow whatever you want."

"Okay," Tate said. Even at home in her own closet, Tate didn't have one single appropriate outfit for an evening like tonight. She didn't own summer dresses meant for dinner parties because she didn't get invited to dinner parties. She didn't have dinner with her boyfriends' parents. She was, she realized at that second, socially retarded. All she did was work, and occasionally she spent a whoop-de-do night performing karaoke in a hotel bar with clients and their much more spirited secretaries. Just as Tate was about to wallow in self-pity over this and move from there into panic—would she know how to *act* at this dinner party?—Chess said, "Try on the red one."

Tate pulled a red dress out of the closet. It was a simple silk sheath. "This doesn't come with some devastating memory attached?"

"Well, sort of," Chess said. "That was what I wore to Bungalow Eight the night I broke up with Michael."

"Jesus, Chess," Tate said. This was the dumping dress?

"Try it on," Chess said. "For a while there, I considered that my lucky dress. And I have killer red Jimmy Choo heels to match."

Tate tried the red dress on. It was a stunner. She tried on the killer heels. They were red suede peep toes with red snakeskin uppers. Tate felt like a woman, perhaps for the first time ever. What did that say about her? She didn't want to think about it. She just wanted to stay in this dress forever, despite the fact that it had a backstory even more lurid than the orange polka-dot dress. "This is it," Tate said. "This is the one."

"That's it," Chess agreed. "Your lucky dress. Your break-somebody's-heart dress."

Tate had the dress and the shoes, and she had her tan. She worked on the rest, but it was tricky. She filed and polished her nails—perfect except for the sand scattered across the polish. She washed and conditioned her hair in the bracing shower, then brushed it out. A hair dryer would have been nice; as it was, she had to hope for the best. She allowed India to apply makeup to her eyes and lips. Tate never wore anything more than Chap Stick, but India insisted on mascara, eyeliner, a little lip gloss. Birdie lent Tate a silver clutch that she claimed had belonged to Tate's great-grandmother in the 1930s and was a denizen of the top drawer of the dresser in Birdie's room. (Was she making this up?) India lent her a gold wrap (pedigree: Wanamaker's, 1994). Why India had brought a gold wrap to Tuckernuck was beyond Tate, but she didn't question. She was Cinderella today; it was okay if things just appeared.

"How do I look?" Tate asked. There wasn't a mirror in the house where she could get a fair read. She was worried about her hair.

"Oh, honey," Birdie said, "you look just beautiful."

"I'm going to take your picture," India said. She had brought one of those disposable cameras that came in a cardboard box. This was, to Tate's knowledge, the first time she'd used it. It had been an uneventful trip.

Tate was embarrassed as she mugged for the camera. She felt guilty getting all dressed up and going out for a dinner party on the big island—the real world, with electricity and hot water and other people engaging her in conversation. Shouldn't she stay home and eat corn on the cob and blueberry pie and play solitaire while everyone else read or needlepointed or sunk deeper into their interior lives? No, that was silly. She was going.

This was, in so many ways, all she'd ever wanted.

She was standing on the beach in her red silk dress with India's wrap and her great-grandmother's clutch purse and Chess's shoes in her hand when Barrett pulled the boat in at six o'clock. There was also a backpack at her feet, containing a nightgown (borrowed from Chess), her toothbrush, and her running clothes. Up on the bluff, Tate had kissed and hugged everyone good-bye as though she were leaving on a long journey.

"I'll be back in the morning," she said. It was funny how Tuckernuck, one of the most remote places on the eastern seaboard, now felt like the center of the universe.

Barrett cut the engine. He was staring at her in a way that Tate had been waiting for all her life. Staring! He said, "Man, do you look good."

Tate bowed her head so he wouldn't see the stupid expression on her face. The dress had worked. And the makeup. And whatever else he was reacting to. Barrett hopped out of the boat and dragged it to shore, just as he always did. But this time was so different: He was wearing a white oxford shirt, a kelly green tie printed with sailboats, a navy blazer, and khaki shorts. He approached Tate and said, "I'm going to get this out of the way." And he kissed her. He tasted like beer. His mouth was warm and soft, and Tate felt a jolt, blood flowing to all the right places. Her stomach dropped, her eyelids fluttered. Ka-bam!

Oh, God, she thought. *Kiss me again.*

He kissed her again. It was like a scene straight from her seventeen-year-old fantasies. Then she heard a noise, a wolf whistle, and cheering, and when she glanced up at the bluff, she saw Aunt India and Birdie watching. Barrett laughed, and in one smooth movement, he scooped Tate up and deposited her gently in the boat named *Girlfriend.* Tate accepted her accoutrements and her backpack. Barrett hopped in and pulled the anchor, and they were off. Tate waved good-bye.

It was, Tate knew, a very big night for Barrett. The people who were having the party, the Fullins, were his most important caretaking clients. By "most important," Barrett meant that they were high maintenance; Anita Fullin was the woman who had called Barrett in from fishing because her pipes were making noise. Anita Fullin needed him to do everything for her, he said, right down to replacing the paper towels in the kitchen.

"You're kidding about that, right?" Tate said.

"Right," he said.

The Fullins had money to burn, and they paid premium rates; the boat, *Girlfriend,* had been their boat. They had given it to Barrett as a bonus at the end of last summer. He had to take good care of these people; they were his patrons.

The Fullins threw this party each year, inviting everyone they knew on the island—which meant friends from Manhattan who were renting on the Cliff, as well as Barrett, Mrs. Fullin's masseuse, the manager of their beach club, Mr. Fullin's favorite golf caddy, the maître d' from LoLa 41. It was a nice mix of summer people and locals, Barrett said. It was a nice party, though he'd missed it the past two years because—well, he said, because of Stephanie.

"This is the first time I've been out," he said. "Like this, you know, since she died."

Tate nodded. She wanted to know everything. And in addition to knowing everything, she wanted to kiss Barrett some more, loosen that tie, unbutton that shirt... she was a racehorse bucking at the gate. But this had always been her problem with men, right? She came on too strong, too soon. She had dry spells that lasted years (the last man she'd slept with had been Andre Clairfield, who was on the practice squad for the Carolina Panthers, but that had been a drunk, late-night sex thing and should probably not be counted), and then when she found someone she really liked, she was out of practice with ladylike restraint. She was too hungry, too eager, and she frightened men away.

She would not frighten Barrett away. He was, she realized, a man of few words. (Had this always been the case, she wondered, or was it a result of losing his wife?) He was trying hard now, she could tell, to talk about the evening ahead so she would be prepared.

"Where are your kids?" she said.

"With my parents," Barrett said. "And they're spending the night."

Tate had wondered if she would wake up in the morning to find two little boys staring at her as though she were a visitor from another planet, the way it always seemed to happen in the movies. Tate, naked or nearly so, in their father's bed. The older one proclaiming, "You're not my mommy."

"Okay," Tate said. They were now in Barrett's car—a black Toyota pickup—barreling down Madaket Road. After a week on a deserted island, with its rutted dirt paths, the sensation of driving this fast seemed foreign. They passed the dump, which smelled like a rotten-egg omelet, but Tate pretended not to notice. Barrett hummed along with the radio, Fleetwood Mac singing "You Make Loving Fun." Then the DJ came on with the weather report: clouds overnight, rain tomorrow, wind from the southwest at fifteen to twenty knots.

They drove into town. When Tate was young, her father would bring her and Chess over for one day trip per summer. He would use the phone at his insurance agent, Congdon and Coleman, to call his office while she and Chess were set free in town with spending money. They went to the pharmacy lunch counter for peppermint-stick ice cream at 10 A.M. They browsed Mitchell's Book Corner (though this was mostly Chess; what Tate remembered about the bookstore was begging Chess to leave). They went to the Hub to ogle *Seventeen* magazine and buy candy. Then they reunited with their father for lunch at the Brotherhood of Thieves; in the dark, subterranean dining room, they ate chowder and thick burgers and curly fries. Tate remembered using the hot water tap in the bathroom, letting it run over her hands; she remembered looking in the clear silver of the mirror. Everything was a novelty after being on Tuckernuck; the soap dispenser hanging from the wall was a novelty. In the afternoon, their father took them to the Whaling Museum or to the Jetties to play tennis. Or they rented bikes and rode out to Sconset to see the Sankaty Lighthouse and get yet another ice cream from the Sconset Market. The Nantucket days had always been fun, and before they left they always paid homage to the yellow clapboard house with the wraparound porch on Gay Street that had, decades earlier, belonged to their great-grandparents, Arthur and Emilie Tate. Nantucket had never been home for Tate, however. It had never been more than a gateway to Tuckernuck. Tuckernuck was the real thing. It was an island for purists.

Tate wanted to share her memories with Barrett, but

Barrett was preoccupied with pulling in behind a long line of cars parked on the street. They had arrived. Barrett looked in the rearview mirror and straightened his tie. He smiled at Tate. She was still worried about her hair, especially after the boat ride.

I can look even better than this, she wanted to tell him. *Really, I can.*

He said, "You are so beautiful, Tate. Honestly, I could eat you."

She inched toward him. She didn't want to be pushy, she didn't even want to be easy, but the man was a magnet. They started kissing again. Tate thought, *Let's forgo this party and go back to your house and eat each other up.* But then she remembered herself and pulled away. She sensed this was what Chess would do.

"Please?" he said. "Don't stop?"

Tate said, "Let's go. We're expected."

The party, in Tate's mind, was just something to be survived before she and Barrett could be alone. But as they approached the house, she rearranged her expectations. The house they were going to, Tate could see, was gargantuan, with massive windows and multilayered decks. Barrett led Tate through a white latticed archway dripping with 'New Dawn' roses (Birdie's favorite; Tate would have to remember to tell her). There were people all over the lawn holding drinks, there were wait staff in white shirts and black vests offering things on silver trays, there was live music coming from somewhere. Tate scanned the property: a jazz trio played on one of the decks. Tate was dumbfounded. She felt like she was stepping onto a Broadway stage and didn't know any of her lines. India could handle this kind of glittering social scene, and Chess in her former state could handle this, even Birdie could handle this—but Tate could not.

Her heels sunk into the grass. She had to unplug herself with every step. She looked around. Other women were wearing heels and they didn't seem to be sinking. Was there something wrong with the way she was walking? Oh, probably. Tate was most comfortable in sneakers. To work, she wore loafers or ballet flats. She should have asked Chess for a heels tutorial.

"Hold on to me," Barrett said, offering his arm. "I want to get a drink and then we'll find Anita to say hello."

Yes, thought Tate. What you needed when you attended a party like this was a plan, at least to start with. If left to her own devices, Tate would wander around, accept a tequila drink, eat something from a tray that she was allergic to, and trip in her heels, ending up on her knees in the flower bed.

Barrett handed her a glass of champagne. She guzzled it—straight down the hatch—and then quietly burped. This was exactly what she meant by too eager.

Barrett laughed. "You don't have to be nervous," he said.

"I'm not nervous," she said.

She lassoed a server with more champagne and took a second glass, placing her first glass on the tray. All this without spilling or breaking anything.

"I'm going to sip this one," she promised.

They weaved through the crowd. They had a mission: find the hostess. The rear of the house, Tate soon discovered, fronted Nantucket Harbor.

"Look at this view," she said.

"It's no better than the view from your house," Barrett said.

This was true. The Tuckernuck house looked out over the water. Still, there was something breathtaking about the manicured lawn and the pale strip of private beach and the expanse of Nantucket Harbor with Brant Point Lighthouse, sailboats, the descending sun.

Barrett was stopped in his tracks by a middle-aged couple. The man had gray hair and broken capillaries across his cheeks. The woman had frosted hair in a bob; she was wearing Birdie's perfume, Coco by Chanel. Tate tried to focus, look them in the eye, smile, sparkle. She loved Barrett; she wanted to do a good job for him.

"Tate Cousins," Barrett said, "I'd like you to meet Eugene and Beatrice AuClaire. The AuClaires are clients of mine on Hinckley Lane."

Mrs. AuClaire (Tate had already lost her first name. Beverly?) smiled at Tate with a certain look on her face. What was that look? "Lovely to meet you," Mrs. AuClaire said. She and Tate shook hands. Tate's grip was too firm; Mrs. AuClaire flinched and Tate thought, *Oh, shit.* She was gentler with Mr. AuClaire, but Mr. AuClaire wasn't interested in Tate; he was interested in Barrett. He wanted to know where the fish were jumping. This left Tate to think of something to say to Mrs. AuClaire. Mrs. AuClaire smelled like Birdie; it was distracting. Mrs. AuClaire was examining her. Tate feared for her hair, she feared for her makeup; it felt like she had crumbs in her eyes. Mrs. AuClaire said, "You're a friend of Barrett's, then?" And Tate, all of a sudden, recognized the certain look. *You're not my mommy.* Mrs. AuClaire must have known Barrett's wife, Stephanie. For all Tate knew, Stephanie had been Mrs. AuClaire's niece, or her daughter's best friend.

"That's right," Tate said. "Barrett caretakes for my family as well."

"Oh, really?" Mrs. AuClaire said. This information seemed to take her by surprise. She had probably thought Barrett met Tate at a strip club on the Cape. "Where do you live?"

Tate took a breath. The glass of champagne she'd inhaled was taking its revenge; the gases were threatening to come out her nose. Her face was warm and she felt dizzy. She was unsteady in her shoes and Barrett had let go and she didn't want to take his arm for fear of seeming clingy or seeming, to Mrs. AuClaire, like she was anything more than a client, just like them.

"We have a house on Tuckernuck," Tate said.

Mrs. AuClaire's eyes popped open—a facial expression her plastic surgeon had not anticipated. It looked like her face was going to break and fall to pieces in the grass. "Tuckernuck!" she said. "I love Tuckernuck! Oh, we adore it, but of course it's private and you have to be invited. We used to take the kids to Whale Shoal on our boat when they were little because Whale Shoal is open to everyone, and they would collect those whelk shells. Oh, my darling girl, you don't know how lucky you are. Eugene, this girl"—Mrs. AuClaire had clearly forgotten her name, too—"lives on Tuckernuck!"

The news was intriguing enough to tear Mr. AuClaire away from his discussion of striped bass off Sankaty Head. "You *live* there?" he said. "How does that work, exactly?"

"Well," Tate said, "our house has a well and a generator. The generator runs the pump so we have running water—cold only, there's no water heater—and we have electricity for a few small things. A half-size refrigerator, a few lamps. We cook on a grill and on a gas camp stove. And Barrett"—here, Tate did take his arm because her enthusiasm had set her teetering and she was afraid she would fall—"brings our groceries each day and bags of ice and my mother's wine." Mrs. AuClaire smiled. "He brings us the newspaper and takes away our trash and our laundry. We live very simply. We go to the beach, mostly. We read and play cards." She paused. The

AuClaires were looking at her eagerly. "And we talk. We tell each other things."

"Marvelous," Mrs. AuClaire whispered.

Barrett excused them from the AuClaires' company in order to search out the Fullins. They found Mrs. Fullin standing on the edge of the lawn, surrounded by women friends. Mrs. Fullin had long, wavy black hair with a brightly colored scarf weaved through it. She was deeply, glamorously tanned, like a woman stepping off a yacht in the Mediterranean. She wore—Tate blinked—an orange halter dress with white polka dots. It was Chess's rehearsal dinner dress, exactly. Mrs. Fullin was on fire in it. She had a curvy body and beautiful, slender legs; she wore very high orange patent leather sandals, which didn't seem to be giving her one iota of trouble. When Mrs. Fullin saw Barrett, she let go a scream like teenage girls did for the Jonas Brothers.

"Barrett, you did it! You wore a jacket! God, are you *gorgeous!*" She hugged Barrett and kissed him, leaving a coral smudge on his cheek. Her eyes were very dark, rimmed by electric blue liner. She was probably forty-five, Tate guessed, but she had the va-va-voom factor of a twenty-one-year-old supermodel. She beamed at Tate. "And you—you're the girl from Tuckernuck?"

Tate smiled. She felt dowdy and tongue-tied; she felt like her teeth were coated with moss. "Tate Cousins," she said.

"So, ladies," Mrs. Fullin said to her entourage, "Tate lives on Tuckernuck."

"Where's Tuckernuck?" one of the women asked.

"Is that the place with the seals?" another asked.

"No," Tate said before she realized she had even spoken. "That's Muskeget. Tuckernuck is closer in. It's half a mile off Eel Point." The women stared at her blankly, and Tate realized that although they all probably owned humongous summer homes, they might not know the island well enough to know where Eel Point was.

Mrs. Fullin said, "I am very jealous of you, having Barrett come over there twice a day. In fact, I can hardly stand it. If I could, I would have him live here with us." She winked. "Of course, Roman would begin to wonder."

"For good reason," one of the women said.

Mrs. Fullin said, "Isn't Barrett the most gorgeous creature you have ever laid eyes on?"

Barrett said, "Anita, please."

Mrs. Fullin looked at Tate. "I hate you for stealing him away from me. I hate you, your sister, your mother, and your aunt."

Tate was thunderstruck. She could survive the attack—it was delivered tongue in cheek, meant to be a joke. But Tate felt violated. The only way this woman could have known about Tate's mother and sister and aunt was if Barrett had talked about them. Did he talk about them with Anita Fullin? What did he say? *They* didn't make him change the paper towel roll! Tate tried to smile, though she was sure she looked like she was in pain. What she wanted to say was, *I heard you ruined Barrett's fishing trip the other night.* When Barrett told her that story, Tate had pictured someone older, perhaps even elderly, fragile, helpless. The reality was that Anita Fullin was a bombshell and it sounded like she had a crush on Barrett.

Barrett intervened, to change the subject. "This is a great party," he said.

"It is great, isn't it?" Mrs. Fullin said. She reached for his hand. "I am so glad you're here. Last year wasn't the same without you."

They looked at each other, and something passed

between them. Tate guzzled the rest of her champagne. She checked the faces of the other women, all of whom were watching Barrett and Mrs. Fullin like it was something being shown on TV.

Barrett said, "I just couldn't do it last year." He took a sip of his drink.

"Of course not," Mrs. Fullin said. She beamed at him and then at Tate. "But look, life goes on!"

The interaction with Anita Fullin left Tate feeling threatened and uncomfortable. She had half a mind to sneak into the house, find the computer, and lose herself in the electronic world. (This temptation was very real. It was, Tate imagined, the same urge her father felt when he passed a golf course.) But Barrett hung on to Tate, and sensing that her shoes were driving her insane (they weren't called killer heels for nothing), he directed her to the seawall, where they sat side by side and admired the harbor. Tate was happier. She drank her champagne and Barrett flagged down servers and they ate mini crab cakes and sticky Chinese ribs and cheddar tartlets.

Tate said, "Mrs. Fullin loves you."

"Yeah," Barrett said. "It's a problem."

"She's beautiful," Tate said.

"You're beautiful," he said.

Dinner was served in the side yard under a tent. There were ten round tables of ten and a rectangular head table of sixteen, which was where Barrett and Tate were seated. Barrett was placed at one end of the table, to Anita Fullin's left, and Tate was all the way at the opposite end, to Mr. Fullin's left. This was, in Tate's mind, the worst possible scenario, and she thought that Barrett might do something about it—switch the place cards?—but he just licked his bottom lip.

"Are you going to be okay down here by yourself?" he asked.

No, she thought. But she said, "Yes. Absolutely."

It was an honor to be seated at the head table, Tate recognized, even as she wished that they'd been stuck in Siberia with the middle-aged AuClaires. Barrett and Tate moved through the buffet line together. The food was amazing and Tate didn't hold back. She piled her plate with grilled lamb, green beans, a beautiful potato salad, and sautéed cherry tomatoes, as well as a lobster tail, six jumbo shrimp, and four raw oysters, which she drowned with mignonette. She plucked another glass of champagne off a passing tray. Then she sat in her assigned seat and watched as Barrett journeyed to the other side of the world.

Roman Fullin was bald and wore square glasses. He had the distracted manner of a very important man who made lots of money. He sat down, flagged a server, and asked for a glass of red wine from one of the bottles he had set aside. For this table only, he said. He inspected his plate of food as though he didn't recognize anything on it; then he shifted his eyes to Tate's loaded plate; then his eyes swept up to Tate's face. Who was this woman sitting next to him at the head table? Tate felt like she was encroaching on his personal territory; she felt like he had just discovered her in his master bedroom.

"Hi," he said, offering a hand. "Roman Fullin."

"Hi," she said. "I'm Tate Cousins."

"Tate Cousins," he said, repeating it loudly, perhaps to see if it rang a bell.

She said, "I'm Barrett Lee's date."

"Ah," Roman said, though he still seemed nonplussed. He considered the people to his right and Tate's left, whom he clearly knew a lot better. "Betsy, Bernie, Joyce, Whitney, Monk—this is Tate Cousins."

"Cousins?" one of the men said. All of the men at the table looked alike, and Tate hadn't been able to pin down any names. "You aren't by any chance related to Grant Cousins?"

Tate was sucking down an oyster, which gave her a second to think. People either loved her father or they hated him. She was feeling too vulnerable to lie. "He's my father," she said.

"Whoa!" the man said. "What are the chances? He's my lawyer."

Roman Fullin's eyebrows shot up. "What are the chances, indeed! He's not the guy who..."

And the other man said, "Yep, the very same one." To Tate, he said, "Your father is a genius. He really saved my tail. Does he ever mention the name Whit Vargas? I send him Yankees tickets every time they cross my desk."

Tate sucked down another oyster, and some of the mignonette dripped onto her silk sheath. She forgot her manners when she was nervous, and she was very nervous now, though things had taken a turn for the better. At least she had an agreeable pedigree. She checked on Barrett at the other end of the table; he was locked into conversation with Anita Fullin.

She shook her head at Whit Vargas. "He rarely talks about his clients," she said. "He likes to respect their privacy."

Whit Vargas held a dripping piece of tenderloin in front of his mouth. "I should be grateful for that!" he said.

Roman Fullin was filled with new interest where Tate was concerned. "So wait," he said. "Who did you say you came with?"

"Barrett," she said. "Barrett Lee."

"And how do you know Barrett?"

"He caretakes our house on Tuckernuck."

"Ahhhhh," Roman said, as though it were all so clear to him now. "You're part of the Tuckernuck family. The bane of my wife's existence."

"Apparently," Tate said.

"So you *live* on Tuckernuck?" Roman said. "You spend the night there?"

Did people know how asinine they sounded when they asked these questions? "Live there, spend the night there," Tate confirmed.

"Wait a minute," Whit Vargas said. "Where is Tuckernuck again?"

"It's an island, Whit," Roman said. "Another island."

"Half a mile off the west coast," Tate said.

"What do you do about electricity?" Roman said.

By the time Tate finished her dinner, she was the star of the eastern half of the table. She was, more truthfully, a museum exhibit, an anthropological study: Tate Cousins of Tuckernuck, a woman from a respectable family, who was living for a month without hot water (the women couldn't believe it) and without a phone, Internet, or TV (the men couldn't believe it). Tate decided to take this particular ball and run with it. She was funny and charming, smart and self-effacing. She checked on Barrett at the other end of the table. Was he watching her? Did he see that she had turned a potentially disastrous social situation on its head and now had all of these Upper East Siders eating out of her hand? Was he impressed? Did he love her?

When the plates were cleared and the band started playing, Roman Fullin stood up and asked Tate to dance.

Tate took his hand. She couldn't very well turn him down, could she? And yet they would be the first people dancing. Shouldn't he be asking his wife to dance? Her shoes were another problem; it felt like her feet were caught in a couple of mousetraps.

Tate said, "This is a beautiful party. It's like a wedding."

"Every year a wedding," he said. "Anita has to have it. She lives for this night."

Other couples joined them on the dance floor, including Barrett and Anita Fullin. Anita was glowing in her orange dress. (Thank God Tate had not worn that dress!) Anita shrieked as Barrett spun her around.

Roman said, "Anita is loaded. I'd better go rescue her."

They separated and Tate found herself in Barrett's arms.

He said, "Let's get out of here."

Tate said, "You read my mind."

As Tate buckled herself into Barrett's truck, she was sober enough to realize that she was drunk, but she wasn't sober enough to do anything about it. She felt like she was standing at the top of a ski run and had just been pushed. She was headed downhill without her poles. She pried off her shoes and the blood rushed back into her feet. The relief was nearly erotic.

She said, "Anita Fullin doesn't like me."

"Anita Fullin doesn't know you," Barrett said. "Plus, she's very insecure."

"That doesn't make any sense," Tate said. "She has no reason to be insecure."

"Trust me," Barrett said.

Tate said, "I was so stupid. I had this crazy idea that we were your only clients."

"You haven't been here in thirteen years," Barrett said. "If you were my only clients, I'd be in pretty sad shape."

"I knew you had other clients," Tate said. "But I didn't think about them. I didn't have to meet them. And Anita is so... possessive."

"You don't know the half of it," Barrett said. He fiddled

with the radio, then popped in a CD. It was Bruce Springsteen's *18 Tracks.* Tate couldn't believe it. She said, "Wait a minute, this is Bruce. This is *Eighteen Tracks.*"

"It is."

Tate said, "Do you like him? Do you love him? This album is only owned by people who love him."

Barrett grinned. He said, "I like him. A lot. But I don't love him as much as you do. Full disclosure is I asked your mother what kind of music you liked and she said there was only one answer. So I went out this afternoon and borrowed this disc from a friend of mine."

"You didn't!" she said.

"I did."

"You asked my mother?"

"I did. I wanted to make sure I had things you liked. I want you to be happy."

He wanted her to be happy. He didn't realize he didn't have to try. He didn't realize that she was delirious just sitting in the cab of his truck, just gazing upon his face.

The song was "Thundercrack." Tate sang along.

Barrett's house was way out in Tom Nevers, down one dirt road and then another. It was dark, but Tate could see that his house was tall and skinny, with a deck off the second story. The yard was cluttered with things—a boat trailer, buoys clustered like grapes, lengths of rope, plastic buckets and shovels, a spade, a rake, a toy car big enough for two kids to sit in. There was a clothesline with beach towels flapping; the wind had picked up. Barrett led Tate by the hand, and she was taking gulps of chilly night air, trying to sober up. Barrett pointed to a dark square. "There is my pathetic attempt at keeping the garden going," he said.

The wife's garden, Tate thought.

He stopped at the clothesline, unpinned the towels,

and folded them in neat squares. "It's supposed to rain," he said.

He led her up a flight of stairs to a side door, and they entered the house. They were suddenly in the kitchen, which was cluttered and homey. Tate blinked. There were children's storybooks and coloring books and crayons and empty juice boxes on the counter, a plate with pieces of hot dog and a smear of ketchup, the core of a pear. There was mail in a pile next to a dying houseplant. A stack of old *Sports Illustrateds*.

Barrett grabbed the dirty dinner plate and the empty juice boxes and said, "I meant to clean up before. The day got away from me."

Tate said, "Please don't worry about it." She liked the mess; she liked the story it told. She could imagine Barrett trying to get his kids dinner so he could drop them off at his parents' house, while at the same time trying to get dressed up, while at the same time trying to get to Madaket Harbor to get the boat to Tuckernuck for Tate at six. If Barrett were to see the space that Tate called home—the white condo empty and clean except for the mattress on the floor in front of the big-screen TV—he would think what? That she was lonely and worked too hard.

She stepped into the living room. It was an upside-down house with all of the common space on the second floor. There were big windows overlooking the moors of Tom Nevers and the southeast coast. There was a door that led to the deck. Tate peeked out: there was a gas grill, a potted pink geranium that seemed to be faring better than the garden or the houseplant, and two white Adirondack chairs.

"This is nice," Tate said.

Barrett was busy in the kitchen. Tate noted the TV (a fifty-two-inch flat-screen Aquos, just like her own) and the furniture—some of it newish looking from

Restoration Hardware (a leather sofa, a pine coffee table) and some of it thrift-store-esque, perhaps borrowed or inherited from caretaking clients or his parents (a green easy chair that may have been a recliner, a cabinet for the big TV). There was only one thing Tate was interested in, and that was a picture of his wife. She found what she was looking for on a long, narrow table under the biggest picture window. On this table was a glass lamp and a slew of framed photographs.

The first one Tate picked up was a wedding picture: Barrett and Stephanie in a horse-drawn carriage. Stephanie was lovely. She had the kind of red hair that people commented on, and milk glass skin. And lots of freckles. She had a cracking, mischievous smile. Tate was so taken with this picture that she cooed. She hadn't known what to expect, but she had *not* been expecting red hair; she had been picturing someone cool and blond like Chess, or maybe someone dark like Anita Fullin. Tate picked up another picture—Stephanie holding one of the babies. This gave Tate a closer look at her face. That milky skin, the pale blue shadows under her green eyes. Her freckles were remarkable. In the picture, she looked exhausted but luminous. Tate reached for another picture—Stephanie sitting in Barrett's boat. She was wearing a yellow bikini. She was very thin.

"Hey." Tate felt Barrett's hand on her back. She fumbled the picture; it fell and knocked over other pictures.

"Oh, God," Tate said, trying to set everything upright. "Sorry. I was just worshipping at the temple."

"Come with me," he said.

She thought they were going to the bedroom, but instead he led her out onto the deck. He had a bottle of champagne in his hands.

"Do you like Veuve Clicquot?" he asked.

She recognized the bottle as the champagne that

Chess had ordered once at a restaurant when Tate was in New York on business, but Tate didn't drink champagne except for at weddings and at very fancy parties like the one they had just attended. She drank wine, but only with her mother. If left to her own devices, Tate drank beer; at home in her sadly stocked fridge, she kept a six-pack of Miller Genuine Draft. This was pathetic. It was unworldly and unladylike.

She took the bottle from him and stuck it in the dirt of the potted geranium. "I don't want it right now. It would be wasted on me."

"Okay," he said. He gathered her up and they leaned against the railing of the deck. She buried her face in his shirt; he'd taken off his tie and his shirt was open at the neck. She kissed his neck, she tasted him—sweat and charcoal smoke. He made a noise. He raised her chin and they kissed gently for a second, one second, two; then the switch was flipped, the power surged. There was no point holding back. He was a lonely single dad; she was just plain desperate. She'd wanted him since she was seventeen. They kissed madly, they tore at each other's clothes. Tate popped one of Barrett's shirt buttons and he yanked at her dress, and it occurred to her that he should be careful with the dress because it was Chess's, but who cared? She struggled to get the dress over her head. She would replace the dress for Chess a hundred times. She unhooked her bra and set her breasts free in the misty night air and Barrett roared like a lion and led her back inside. She was wearing only her lace thong, but he had on pants and a belt.

"Goddamn it," he said. "I want you so badly."

She fell back on the sofa and offered up a prayer of thanks. *Thank you thank you thank you.* This was all she'd ever dreamed about.

He knelt before her. There were tears in his eyes.

* * *

So that, Tate thought later, was what sex was supposed to feel like. Heady, electric, immediate. Thrilling like a bungee jump, satisfying like a deep drink of cold water. Now Barrett was asleep, snoring softly next to her on the bed. They had moved downstairs to his bedroom, which was, surprisingly, Stephanie-free. There was a pencil-post bed covered with a sumptuous down comforter and some awesome pillows. There was a dresser with a large mirror attached. A painting by Illya Kagan hung over the bed; it was the view across North Pond on Tuckernuck.

Tate couldn't sleep, would not sleep at all this night, she knew. She climbed out of bed to pee, then tiptoed upstairs. She retrieved the bottle of champagne from the planter on the deck and put it in the fridge. There was Heineken in the fridge and juice boxes, a package of Ball Park franks, a gallon of whole milk. There was a carton of Minute Maid no-pulp and a jar of garlic dill pickles, some nice-looking lettuce, half a cucumber wrapped in plastic, and a pound of Italian roast beef in the deli drawer. *Okay,* Tate thought. Barrett's fridge held nothing gourmet or intimidating. The freezer contained chicken nuggets, Ziploc bags of striped bass filets with the date marked on them in black Sharpie, and a bottle of vodka.

Tate poured herself a glass of ice water. She walked back over to the pictures.

In the morning, Barrett found her asleep on the sofa.

"What are you doing up here?" he said.

She was confused. She didn't remember lying down, but her head was on a throw pillow and she had covered herself with the fleece blanket. She checked surreptitiously to see if she'd brought over any of the photographs. She had studied them all. They were all neat and upright on their home table, thank God.

"I'm not sure," she said.

He squeezed onto the sofa next to her. "It's raining," he said.

"Is it?"

"Do you just want to stay here today? We could drink that champagne. Eat strawberries in bed, listen to Springsteen, stay under the covers."

Tate thought, *Yes!* But then she thought for a minute. "What about your kids?" she said.

"I could ask my mother to keep them."

"It's Sunday," Tate said. "I'm sure they want to see you."

"They do," he said. "For sure they do. We could hang out with them together. Go to lunch, take them to the movies."

"That sounds great...," Tate said.

"But?"

"But not today," Tate said.

"It's too soon?" he said. He sounded worried.

What she wanted to say was that it was *not* too soon; it couldn't be too soon since she had waited thirteen years for this. She would marry him tomorrow and adopt the kids on Tuesday. She would quit her job, sell her condo, and learn everything there was to know about Thomas the Tank Engine. But this, she sensed, fell under the category of Too Eager. Staying here even one more hour would be pushing some kind of invisible envelope.

"It's too soon," she said. "Do you mind taking me home?"

He was crushed. She was crushed, too, while simultaneously being thrilled that he was crushed. He kissed her. Under the blanket, she was naked.

She would stay one more hour.

CHESS

Day nine.

The next time Michael and I went to see Nick play, it was at Irving Plaza: Diplomatic Immunity was opening for the Strokes, and it was a very big deal. We couldn't just stroll backstage; we had to get passes. It was April. I hadn't seen or spoken to Nick since the week before Christmas in Central Park, and as far as I knew, Michael hadn't either. Nick had stopped going to Christo's poker game, which surprised Michael. It was his main source of income.

What had passed between Nick and me in the park was so intense that I had been emotionally hobbled for days afterward. I had been high as a kite at Michael's company's holiday party, and then mute and depressed with the hangover. It was a hangover, also, from being with Nick. But when Nick bagged on Christmas and then again on New Year's, and then when I didn't see him throughout the cold winter months, my feelings went into hibernation. To long for the impossible was counterproductive. My heart and body ached for Nick, but Michael was my better match: he had money, we did lovely things together at night and on the weekends. I was content.

And then, news arrived—via a text message to Michael—about the show at Irving Plaza. Backstage passes arrived.

As we walked into the show, Michael said, "So tonight we're going to meet the girl Nick is dating."

My jaw ached. "He's dating someone?"

"I guess so. She's a student. She goes to the New School."

I got a bad feeling. Was there any way that... but I talked myself out of it.

I could barely stand to watch the show, though the band was better than ever. Opening for the Strokes had raised Diplomatic Immunity to a new level. Seeing Nick in person up onstage was both intoxicating and incredibly painful. I loved him, I desired him, it was so wrong, *but it was the only right thing. My feelings were so overwhelming that I had tears standing in my eyes, and I thought,* I have to tell Michael.

I would tell him that night, I decided, once we were home.

After Diplomatic Immunity had finished their set, Michael and I fought our way backstage. We saw Nick first, toweling off, still glowing, high from the energy of the crowd. I hated him in that moment; I wanted him to be a musician, sweet and pure, and not a smug and cocky showman. I wanted the glory of it not to matter to him. But he was a human being like the rest of us, and whereas Michael and I experienced a certain kind of glory on a daily basis, Nick didn't, and so I forgave him his self-satisfied mugging. And then, in a fleeting second, I hated him again because there was someone in his arms, it was a girl, and it was not just a girl but Rhonda.

No, I thought. But yes. Rhonda was the girl, the girlfriend, she was a student at the New School, getting a quasi-graduate degree in urban studies, which had seemed a fanciful way to spend her father's money and avoid the workforce. I hadn't seen Rhonda much since that first night at the Bowery Ballroom: I spent so many nights at Michael's that there were weeks when I returned to my own apartment only on Sunday and Monday nights. I hadn't nourished the friendship. I felt guilty about this, especially when I saw Rhonda in the lobby of the building and we promised to get together, which I knew would never happen because I was always with Michael—but I reasoned that Rhonda was a big girl with her own life and other friends and she would be fine without me. She would understand. That she was now dating my boyfriend's brother shouldn't have felt like an offense, but of course, it did. Why the hell hadn't she told *me? Why hadn't she sent me a text or an e-mail that said,*

Hey, heads up, I'm meeting Nick out tonight. *Had she bumped into him somewhere? Or had he sought her out? I had to know but I couldn't stand to hear the answer.*

Michael held my hand. He pulled me toward the spectacle of Nick and Rhonda intertwined. Her boobs were fake, I thought. Did Nick know this?

Rhonda turned and saw me, and her face came alive with irrepressible joy(!). Rhonda didn't have a deceptive or mean bone in her body, which was one of the reasons I had befriended her. She would only have been thinking of how excited I would be that she was dating Nick. We had been estranged, and now we were reunited. We would be like sisters!

"Hey!" she said, and she kissed me on the mouth. "Did you see the show? Wasn't it amazing?"

"It was amazing," I agreed. "The best they've ever played." How I found it within myself to be so generous, I had no idea. Because my anger at Nick was bowling me over like a mighty wind. This, I suspected, had been all his doing. He had started dating, not just any girl—not the girl who worked at the New York Public Library where he liked to write his lyrics, and not the Thai girl who worked the Tom Yum cart on Saint Mark's Place—but my friend Rhonda. My closest friend.

Nick looked at me, and it was the same look that reached right inside me and turned my heart like a knob, but it was different, too. He was angry, angrier than I was. He was saying, Now you know how it feels. You're sleeping with my brother, who has always gotten the best of everything. You are practically living with him. So now there's Rhonda. We're even.

I had to leave the greenroom. There was talk of the four of us going to the Spotted Pig for drinks after the show, and I smiled and said, "Yep, that sounds great!" Nick was staring at me. He said, "Do you feel okay, Chess? You look kind of sick." I wanted to sock him. I excused myself for the ladies' room. I stood in front of the mirror until another girl jostled me with her oversize Tory Burch bag. Instead of going back to the greenroom, I rejoined the throngs of people on the dance floor. The Strokes were playing "Last Nite," which was my favorite of their songs. I was lost in a tangle of strangers, a mob of unfamiliar bodies. Rhonda. It had been a stroke of genius on his part. When the song was over and everyone around me was cheering and screaming for another song, I headed for the Exit sign and I was dumped out onto the cool street. Ha! I had been part of a couple for so long, I never acted with a solo conscience. I thought of Michael, who by now would be hovering by the ladies' room door, enlisting Rhonda to go in and collect me. He would be worried. I didn't want him *to worry, I wanted Nick to worry. I hailed a taxi and headed home. My phone was ringing—three times it was Michael and three times I didn't answer, even though I knew this was cruel. The fourth time my phone rang I was going to answer it, but it was Nick calling, and I didn't pick up. Nick knew why I'd left.*

When I reached my apartment, I dead-bolted my door and sent Michael a text that said: Got home safely. Good night.

He wrote back, saying: WTF?

And then the phone in my apartment rang and it was Michael. He was ranting. "How could you just leave? What the hell were you thinking? I thought something had happened to you! This is New York, babe. Men are out there with date-rape drugs. I thought someone had hurt you! It was so unlike you, leaving like that—you are not that thoughtless, just walking out, leaving me there. What the hell were you thinking, Chess?"

Tell him? I couldn't tell him. And I couldn't ask: Was Nick worried? Did he care?

I said, "I wasn't thinking, Michael. I'm sorry."

Michael said, "What the hell, Chess?" His voice was sad and defeated, as though I were always letting him down like this, which was unfair because I had never disappointed him before. I had been a good girl, a good girlfriend. But Michael was no dummy; he dealt in human resources. Maybe he had guessed. There had been isolated moments when he would look deeply into my eyes, brush a hair off my face, kiss the back of my neck, or make some other intimate gesture, and I would flinch. Swat him away.

"What?" he'd say. "What?"

And I would think, I don't love you enough. I don't love you *that way.*

Something had to give, I thought.

She would never have admitted it to anyone, she wouldn't even write the words down in her journal, but she was anxious for Tate to get home.

It didn't help that it was raining. Rain in the Tuckernuck house was never good. It started out as a novel and quasi-exciting development. *It's raining! Quick—put the top up on the Scout, close the windows, hunker down!* These were the traditional steps, and woe to the person who was outside in a downpour grappling with the Scout. This morning, because she decided that her mother and aunt should be spared the indignity, that person was Chess.

She ran back into the house, soaking wet. Her mother had breakfast going—bacon and scrambled eggs and the sticky buns that she'd been saving for a special occasion. (The rain qualified.) She was making a second pot of coffee and had gone to the trouble of heating up milk on the stovetop. India, meanwhile, was stuffing newspaper, kindling, and sticks into the woodstove.

"She was a Girl Scout," Birdie said.

"Who are we kidding?" India said. "Birdie was the Girl Scout."

Chess shivered. She accepted a hot, milky mug of coffee from her mother and she bundled up in the scratchy afghan in the traditional starburst pattern that her grandmother had knitted. India got the woodstove raging and the three of them huddled around it with their breakfasts while the rain came down.

"Do you think Barrett will bring Tate home in this weather?" Birdie said.

"Never," India said. "He'll hold on to her."

Chess felt jealous—not because Tate was with Barrett, but rather because Barrett was with Tate. Tate had been gone for fourteen hours and Chess wanted her back. They had lived together on Tuckernuck for more than a week, and Chess had grown used to Tate's indefatigable optimism; she took a dose of it every day like a vitamin.

She could see from here how the rest of the day would go: Birdie and India would resort to all of the usual rainy-day amusements—cards, books, Monopoly—and they would smoke and try to guess when the rain would stop. Birdie would make too much food and they would start drinking at noon. All of this would be done without Tate, and so no matter how much fun was to be had (drunk Monopoly?), the day would wobble like a three-legged table. The numbers would be uneven; Chess would be the odd man out. They would all resort to wondering aloud about Tate: Was she having fun? What were she and Barrett doing together? Would this become a bona fide romance? What kind of future did it have? And this would make Chess feel Tate's absence more keenly. She hated missing people. It was like a disease.

Chess drank her coffee, ate one-quarter of a sticky

bun to appease her mother, and retreated to the attic to work on her confession. The rain clattered against the roof. Chess could hear the waves pounding against their little beach. If Tate hadn't come to Tuckernuck, Chess realized, every hour of every day would be like this.

It was ten o'clock, eleven o'clock. Chess wondered if Barrett and Tate were having sex. Chess's own sexual desire had wilted like an unwatered flower. She was too depressed to touch herself.

Tate and Barrett. Barrett Lee: one more person for Chess to feel bad about.

Everyone knew about Chess's ill-fated date with Barrett Lee the summer after Chess's freshman year of college—Barrett took Chess on a picnic, Chess puked off the back of the boat. Everyone thought that was it. The end. Chess's feelings for Barrett Lee hadn't been clear that summer. If pressed, she would have said she felt nothing for him; she could see he was attractive, certainly, but he wasn't headed to college, and that turned her off immediately. He would become a fisherman or a carpenter and live on Nantucket his whole life, never leaving except to go to Hyannis to Christmas shop and to Aruba for a week in February. He was his father in the making. Chuck Lee was a lovely man, but he was an old salt, and Barrett Lee was an old salt in training. Chess wanted nothing to do with him.

When Barrett asked her out that summer, however, for a picnic, she said yes without hesitating. Her main impetus, she had to admit, was that Tate so ardently loved Barrett. It was irresistible, at nineteen, to go on a date just to upset Tate. And, too, Chess was bored. There was nothing to do on Tuckernuck but read and play backgammon with her parents. Going on a picnic with Barrett was, at least, something different.

She drank too much; this was accidental. It was hot

out on the water, Chess was thirsty, the beer was icy cold, and one beer begat the desire for another beer. The sickness caught her off-guard. It rolled over her like a wave. The ham sandwich Barrett had offered her had tasted funny, but she had eaten it to be polite. The spoiled sandwich and the diesel fumes and the motion of the boat and the beer had a cumulative effect: the nausea slapped her and she puked off the back of the boat. Barrett gave her a bottle of water to rinse her mouth and offered her a Life Saver. He initially seemed grossed out, though he quickly recovered and said something to the effect of, "Happens to the best of us." But this didn't help. Chess was ashamed. She had put on a mortifying show when all along she had considered herself superior to Barrett Lee. It was awful. She wanted off that boat.

Chess and her family departed from Tuckernuck when their two weeks were up, and at the end of August, Chess returned to Colchester. She would never forget the day that Barrett showed up out of the blue: October 18. It was the Platonic ideal of a Saturday in October in the state of Vermont. The sun was out, and the sky was a clear, piercing blue. It was sweater and apple-cider weather. Chess and her sorority sisters were selling beers and brats at the Colchester versus Colgate football tailgate. The tailgate was held on the field outside the stadium, which was ringed by maples and oaks that were ablaze with color. The field was swarming with drunk alumni and students from both universities, and young families from Burlington with their golden retrievers and towheaded toddlers.

Chad Miner, a minor god in SigEp, was the first one to tell Chess. "Somebody's looking for you," he said. "Some dude."

"Really?" Chess said. She wanted Chad Miner to be the one looking for her. "Who is it?"

"Don't know him," Chad said. "He doesn't go here."

Next was Marcy Mills, from Chess's expository writing class. She bought a sausage from Chess, then said, "Oh, by the way, there's a guy wandering around here looking for you."

"Who?" Chess said.

Marcy shrugged and zigzagged her brat with bright yellow mustard. "I didn't know him. But I heard him asking someone else if he knew Chess Cousins. So I told him I knew you, and he asked if I knew where you were, and I said no. Because look at all these people!"

"Yeah," Chess said. She moved the sausages perfunctorily along the grill, making sure they were browned. "What did he look like?"

"Blond," Marcy said. "Cute."

"Send him my way!" said Alison Bellafaqua, who was standing next to Chess at the keg, filling plastic cups with foamy Budweiser.

Chess still didn't think that much about it. If she was thinking at all, it was of Luke Arvey, a guy she'd gone to high school with who now went to Colgate—but Luke was neither blond nor cute. Chess also had a second cousin on her father's side—a Cousins cousin—who went to Colgate, but she hadn't seen him since a family reunion the summer she was nine years old. She wouldn't be able to pick him out of a crowd of two.

Then Ellie Grumbel and Veronica Upton approached Chess—they were both drunk already—and they said, in singsongy chorus, "Someone is *looking* for you!"

Now Chess was annoyed. "Who is it? Did he tell you his name?"

Alison Bellafaqua said, "Pull those babies off." Meaning the brats. "The game starts in ten minutes and we have to get the cash box back..."

Her voice was drowned out by the marching band

passing through the middle of the field, on its way to the stadium. The students from both schools were meant to follow it into the stands. Although it was hokey, Chess loved following the band into the game. She, like her mother, was a helpless rah-rah and a sucker for any kind of tradition. But she couldn't follow the band today because of her beer-and-brat duties. Alison was right: They needed to shut the stand down and take the cash box back to the sorority house. They needed to *hurry* or they were going to miss kickoff.

Ellie Grumbel, Chess realized, was still standing there, swaying, threatening to fall over. She said, "I think he said his name was Bennett."

Chess looked up in alarm. She got a bad feeling.

"He said he was from Nantucket," Veronica said. "A friend of yours from Nantucket?"

"Is it Barrett?" Chess said. "Barrett Lee?"

She didn't have to wait for a response because at the instant Chess said his name, she saw him through an opening in the crowd. Barrett Lee. Chess's heart plummeted. He was wearing a navy turtleneck and a striped cotton sweater and jeans—it was weird, she thought, to see him in real clothes instead of a bathing suit and a T-shirt. He was alone as far as Chess could tell. He was scanning the crowd—for her—and what struck Chess was how utterly out of place he looked, despite his attempt at preppy college attire. What struck Chess was how pathetic it was that he had shown up—here, at her college!—without warning. She wanted to hide. She felt threatened. Not physically threatened, certainly; it was her way of life that seemed to be in danger. She wanted to watch the game; she wanted to participate in some postgame tailgating and catch up on the fun she had missed while stuck at the sorority sausage station. She wanted to change into her new jeans and her new top from J.Crew (purchased with a surprise hundred-dollar check from her father) and try again with Chad Miner at the twelve-keg SigEp party later. And she had a shitload of studying to do the next day and a paper to write, not to mention her standing Sunday night pizza date with her best friends, the two Kathleens. That was her weekend; it was perfect in its symmetry and balance between the social and the studious. She didn't want—indeed, couldn't handle—a disruption by the surprise appearance of Barrett Lee from Nantucket.

Her mother would be horrified; Chess knew this even as she was acting, and she prayed (a) for forgiveness and (b) that the heinous act she was about to commit would never be discovered.

She grabbed the cash box. "I'll take this back to the house," she told Alison.

"But wait," Alison said. Alison was heavy and had long, thick black hair and fearsome eyebrows. "You're leaving me to clean all this up?"

Chess was already yards away. "Can you?" she called over her shoulder. And with that, she was gone. She weaved and bobbed. There were too many people to flat-out run, but she was hurrying. Then she spied an opening. She ran with the cash box under her arm, around parked cars, over spread-out blankets weighted down with potato salad and six-foot subs. She thought of Jim Cross, the star running back for Colchester's football team. She was Jim Cross! She thought, *Barrett Lee! Why? What for? How?* It was a glorious autumn Saturday. Summertime—Tuckernuck, the beach, bonfires, the fateful picnic—was long forgotten. Those things belonged in another season.

What was he *doing* here?

Soon, Chess was on the street. She was making her way to the Delta Gamma house. She would drop off the cash box, then sneak through the backstreets to the stadium. She would avoid Barrett Lee until the game was over, by which point, she was sure, he would have given up and left.

She marched up the steps of the sorority house. It was a delft blue Victorian with white trim like icing on a cake. They had a house mother, Carla Bye, who kept the girls on-task with cleaning and straightening, and Chess was glad. She had moved from the dorms into the house that year and she appreciated the quiet, feminine order. The dorms had been loud and lawless; there were boys in Chess's dorm who chewed tobacco and left plastic cups half-filled with brown spit on the windowsills. They played Frisbee in the halls at two in the morning, drunk, blaring Guns N' Roses. The Delta Gamma house was more like Chess's mother's house in its civility, except that it was college and Chess was free to do exactly as she liked.

She just had to drop the cash box—give it to Carla if she was around, or exercise due diligence and lock it up in the house safe. From the front porch, Chess heard a tremendous, distant roar and knew that the Colchester team had stormed the field. Shit. She was going to miss kickoff.

She heard Carla Bye chatting away in the front room. Some of Chess's sorority sisters found Carla Bye annoying and pathetic; others blatantly disregarded the house rule about overnight guests, claiming that Carla didn't mind. *Carla Bye* wants *us to get laid!* was an oft-repeated battle cry, one with which Chess couldn't disagree. On mornings when a young man descended the stairs, Carla often volunteered to make him an omelet.

On football weekends, Carla kept hours in the front parlor, where she was available to welcome alumnae Delta Gammas or DGs from other chapters. Carla had the gift of gab; she thrived on this kind of interaction.

She was chatting with someone now, and all Chess thought was, *Good, give her the cash box and bolt!*

Chess rushed into the parlor. Carla Bye said, "What luck! Here she is!"

Chess was confused. Then she looked at the occupant of the chintz wingback chair: Barrett Lee.

Chess gasped in horror, which was mistaken for surprise by Barrett Lee and Carla Bye. Meanwhile, Chess was thinking, *Shit! This is not happening!* She felt the walls of her perfectly constructed weekend caving in.

Carla Bye was staring at her. Manners!

"Barrett?" Chess said. "Barrett Lee?"

He stood up. Carla Bye had already plied him with cider and pumpkin muffins. There was a white and blue duffel bag that smelled vaguely of locker room next to his chair.

"Hey, Chess," he said. "How are you?" He bent in to—what? Kiss her? She bypassed his lips and gave him a chaste, sisterly hug.

"He came all the way from Nantucket this morning!" Carla proclaimed.

"Took the first plane," Barrett said. "And drove six hours."

Why? Chess thought. *Why are you here?*

Carla said, "I invited Barrett to leave his duffel bag in your room," she said. "He wanted to wait until you arrived. Such a gentleman."

Chess said, "I'm on my way to the game. I'm sorry, I don't have a guest ticket..."

He said, "Would you like to go for a walk? Or get some lunch?"

Chess felt hot and panicky. Her heart was still racing from her gallop across town. She said, "Let's talk out on the porch."

Carla took her cue. "Yes, let me give you young people

some privacy. I'll just take Barrett's bag up to your room, Chess."

Carla Bye wants *us to get laid!*

No! Chess thought. But she was too polite to shout it out. It didn't matter. They could get his bag later; Barrett Lee wasn't staying.

Barrett followed Chess out the front door onto the porch. She leaned against the railing and he sat on the swing. She heard another cheer from the stadium. The game!

Chess said, "What are you doing here, Barrett?"

He shrugged, grinned. "I had island fever. I needed a road trip."

"So you came *here* to see *me?* Why?"

"I don't know," he said. "I've been thinking about you. We never really got together."

"That's right," Chess said. "We never really got together."

"So I thought, maybe now..."

"Maybe now what?"

"Maybe now we could get together. So I drove up here."

"You didn't call," Chess said. "You gave me no warning. I have plans this weekend."

"You do?"

"Yes! For starters, I'm supposed to be at that football game. My friends are waiting for me."

"I'll go with you. I'd like to meet your friends."

"I don't have a guest ticket," she said. "Because I had no idea you were coming. And the game is sold out."

"Is it a big game?" he asked.

"They're all big games," Chess said. "There are only six home games, and they're all big." She tried to calm down; she was squeaking like a child. "I have tailgating plans after the game and then dinner plans and then a party tonight, which is invitation only." This wasn't strictly true, though the SigEps would not be thrilled about a strange guy in their fraternity house; they liked to keep the male-female ratio in their distinct favor. "And tomorrow I have to study. I have a paper due."

"A paper?" he said.

"Yes," she said. "A paper. A college paper. Fifteen pages on *The Birth of Venus.*"

He stared at her. She said, "It's a painting. By Botticelli."

He stood up. "I'm starving. Do you want to get lunch? I saw a place in town that looked good."

Chess felt her eyes cross. "Are you not listening to me? I'm supposed to be at the game."

"Skip it."

"I don't *want* to skip it," Chess said. She was officially acting like a petulant child. She wondered for a minute what Birdie would have her do. Drop everything to spend the weekend with Barrett Lee? *Make a compromise,* Birdie would say. *Go to lunch with him, then bid him good-bye.* But Chess couldn't even bring herself to do that. "Listen, I appreciate that you got up at dawn and took the first flight and drove all the way here to see me. But I didn't know you were coming. And I'm sorry, Barrett, but I have plans already. I have plans all weekend and I can't include you in them."

"You can't?" he said.

He was making her feel like a complete ogre, ungenerous, ungracious, inflexible. And she hated him for making her feel that way. It wasn't fair. His showing up here *was not fair;* it was manipulative. She checked her watch: it was one thirty. The first quarter would be nearly over.

She said, "I have to go."

He said, "Should I just wait for you here, then?"

Island fever. I needed a road trip. What he needed, Chess thought, was to be going to college himself. In a flash of empathy she realized that this was the first fall that Barrett had no school. The fishing and the carpentry and the partying weren't fulfilling him.

"You should go," Chess said.

"Go?"

"Or stay. Stay here in town if you want. But you can't stay with me here. If you had called me, I might have been able to make arrangements, but you didn't call. You just showed up and expected me to drop everything."

"It's a weekend," he said.

"My weekends are *busy.* I have a *life.*"

"Okay," he said. "Don't get upset. I'll go."

"Great," Chess said. "So now I feel terrible that you drove six hours to get here and I'm turning you away. But why should I feel terrible? I did nothing wrong."

"You did nothing wrong," he said. "I thought maybe we could hang out. But whatever . . . I'll get my bag."

"I'll get your bag," Chess said. "You don't know where my room is." She bounded inside and upstairs and grabbed his duffel bag off her rocking chair. *I'm sorry, Birdie!* she thought. Her mother would be horrified, she was sure. Downstairs, the front parlor was deserted. Chess snatched two of the pumpkin muffins and wrapped them in a paper napkin for Barrett. See? She wasn't completely thoughtless.

Barrett was standing on the top step, looking down on the street.

"Where did you park?" Chess asked. As a tiny concession, she figured she would walk Barrett to his car on her way to the stadium. But even this was mostly so she could be sure he got into his car and drove away.

"Right there." He pointed to a battered blue Jeep with a black vinyl top. Tate, Chess thought, would love that car. If Barrett had been smarter, he would have headed south instead of north. He would have gone to New Canaan to surprise Tate. She would have been as fantastically happy as Chess was agitated and disturbed.

"Okay," she said. She handed him his duffel bag and the muffins, which he accepted without comment, and she led him down the stairs and stood by the door of the Jeep. If she hurried, she would make it to the stadium by halftime.

"I'm sorry this didn't work out," she said.

"Yeah," he said. "Me, too."

"I'm sorry," she said again. Why was *she* apologizing? This wasn't her fault, but somehow it was.

She wanted him to say, *It's okay.* She wanted him to exonerate her, set her free. But he just stared at her and then his face got closer and closer to hers, and he kissed her.

The kiss was nice, really nice, but that may have been because Chess knew that was it, the end.

The end, until this summer. Chess had thought squeamishly about that October 18 and the surprise appearance of Barrett Lee over the years, and what she thought was that she should have skipped the game and gone to lunch with him. She could have brought him along to the tailgating and the party. He might even have slept on the floor of her room. But Chess wanted him out of there. It was kind of a class thing, on top of everything else. Chess was sure he wouldn't fit in.

Birdie had not found out. All that was left was Chess's shame, which was old and weak now, compared to her more recent shame.

It could be her on Nantucket this morning with Barrett Lee. He *had* asked her first. He had led her out to where the Scout was parked, and said, "I have a dinner party to attend tomorrow night. Very fancy, and I need a date. Would you like to go with me?"

Upon his asking, the whole botched road trip came back to Chess in a flash. Here was her chance to atone for the wrong she'd done him. But she couldn't say yes. The idea of attending a dinner party paralyzed her, and it had nothing to do with the fact that she would be fielding sympathetic glances from people who thought she had cancer. She wasn't strong enough to meet people, make chitchat, eat a meal, pretend to be fine. And, too, she didn't want to lead Barrett Lee on; she didn't want to give him hope. The fact that a dozen years had passed and Barrett Lee was now a widower and Chess was also a kind of widow did seem an incredible irony, but it wasn't strong enough to bring them together. She loved someone else.

"I can't," Chess said.

"You have other plans?" he said, with an ironic half smile.

She adjusted her blue crocheted cap. "I'm not in a good place."

"Yeah," he said. "I can see that. I thought maybe getting out would help."

"It won't. I'm sorry. I can't explain it."

"Hey," he said, holding up his palms, "no one's asking you to."

She said, "Ask Tate to the party."

And he said, "I will. She was my first choice anyway."

He had said this, maybe, to hurt her. But Chess was beyond being able to be hurt by Barrett Lee, and, too, she knew she deserved it.

"She should be," Chess said.

"She is," Barrett said.

You were his first choice, Chess thought. She should have told Tate this before Tate left for the party. Why hadn't she?

Eleven o'clock. Noon. No Tate.

At twelve thirty, Birdie called up the stairs: the chowder was ready. Chess was actually engrossed in her book—it was one of the good parts with Natasha in the court—but there was no hurry, so Chess set the book down.

Birdie and India had poured themselves glasses of wine. Three bowls of chowder steamed. There was a box of oyster crackers.

India said, "Chess, do you want a glass of Sancerre?"

Chess said no. She sat at the table. She was sad enough to cry, though she couldn't say why, which made things worse. Her mother brought her a glass of iced tea with a wedge of lemon, just how she liked it. Chess's eyes welled, but she didn't want her mother or India to see; if they saw her crying, they would ask why, and she couldn't explain.

The door flew open. Tate burst in, wearing an army green rain poncho. She was soaking wet.

"I'm home!" she said. "Did you miss me?"

Tate had brought back a portable DVD player and a copy of *Ghost,* which had been her and Chess's favorite movie growing up. The DVD player was contraband—against one of the long-standing Tuckernuck rules—but Barrett had insisted Tate borrow it, because what else were they going to do in the Tuckernuck house in the rain?

Chess had missed her sister, but now that Tate was back, Chess became consumed with anger. Tate was giddy and glowing with the effects of sex and new love, she was Tate in extremis, Tate times one hundred, and Chess couldn't handle it. Tate could watch the movie, Tate could enjoy the movie, Tate could cry over the movie (she always did), but Chess wouldn't join her. She was being mean and petty, she knew this, but she couldn't move past her anger. It would feel good to hunker under the covers with Tate and watch the movie, it would feel as good as a hot bath, but Chess couldn't cross the chasm that would take her to happiness, however fleeting. She was stuck in her misery. Stuck!

Chess said, "I'm not watching it."

Tate said, "What? Come on! It's our favorite movie."

Chess said, "It *was* our favorite movie."

Tate said, "So, what, you've grown up now, you have another favorite movie? Fine. That doesn't mean you can't watch it. It'll be fun."

"No," Chess said.

Tate said, "Fine, I'll watch it myself."

Chess said, "Knock yourself out."

Tate said, "So I guess you're not going to ask me how my date was."

"That's right."

Tate said, "It was amazing." She paused, waiting for Chess to comment or look at her, but Chess did neither. "I'm in love. So you can tell me anything and I'll understand. I'll understand because I'm in love now, too."

Chess gazed at her sister's earnest face. It was as always: Tate trying to keep up with Chess. The roles they would never abandon.

"You know something?" Chess said. "It was really nice here without you."

Tate flinched. She still had the remains of last night's makeup shadowing her eyes.

"Was it?" Tate said.

"It was."

Tate rummaged through her overnight bag and pulled out a bottle of Veuve Clicquot. She wielded it like a club, and for a second, Chess thought Tate was going to slug her with it.

"I brought you this," Tate said. She tossed it on the bed. "Enjoy."

TATE

When she woke up on Monday morning, the sky was blue, the sun was out, and all of Tuckernuck was green and sparkling. Tate went downstairs for coffee, and there was Birdie, squeezing oranges for juice.

"Good morning," Birdie whispered.

Tate kissed her mother's soft cheek. God, life was hard. Chess had been such a bitch yesterday, so cruel and cutting; it was like they were teenagers again. She had practically brought Tate to tears. Tate had been on the verge of saying, *Fuck you, I'm not sitting around for this, I'm leaving.* The experiment had failed. Tuckernuck wasn't bringing them closer; it wasn't healing them. Chess hadn't told Tate the first thing about what happened between her and Michael Morgan; she hadn't pulled back the covers to reveal an inch. It was just like always: Chess didn't think Tate was smart enough or *emotionally evolved* enough to understand.

You know, it was really nice here without you.

Tate would be leaving today with her duffel bag packed and the volume on her iPod turned all the way up—if it weren't for the fact that she was in love with Barrett Lee. And really, she couldn't leave Birdie. Birdie, who squeezed Tate's juice and pressed her coffee; Birdie, who provided exactly the kind of love that Tate needed.

Chess is such a miserable bitch! Tate nearly said it out loud. She would have, except the words would destroy Birdie. And Tate *was* emotionally evolved enough to realize that Chess was hurting and she wanted others to hurt. Tate thought Chess might try to climb into bed with her, and if she had, Tate would have welcomed her and all would have been forgiven. But she hadn't. For the first time since they'd landed on Tuckernuck, Chess had slept in her own bed.

Tate stretched, using the picnic table. She finished her coffee. She said to Birdie, "Okay, I'll be back."

Birdie said, "Be careful!"

As Tate ran, her thoughts switched to Barrett. She didn't know what to expect. She was in love with Barrett wholly and completely, but her feelings had had a thirteen-year head start. She couldn't expect Barrett to feel the same way. He felt something, she knew that. He liked her, he wanted to spend time with her. But what did that mean? What would that look like day-to-day? She had no idea how to conduct a relationship, but she didn't tell Barrett this. She was afraid he'd find out on his own.

She finished her run, and before she headed back up the stairs, she scanned the horizon. No boats.

She hung by the tree branch from her knees. She was distracted. He was coming, right? He had to come—not for her, but because it was his job. A watched pot never boils. Never? She did twenty-five ups and had decided she would do ten more, when she heard him say, "Hey, Monkey Girl."

He was walking toward the house with groceries in one hand and a bag of ice in the other. He was grinning.

Her heart was hanging upside down. What to do? She did ten extra ups while Barrett was in the kitchen talking to Birdie, and then she flipped to the ground. This was excruciating. She loved him, she wanted to scream it, she wanted to tackle him. She didn't know how to act or how to arrange her face. They hadn't talked about another date. They hadn't talked about how things would be.

She was hot and sweaty. Should she get in the shower and let him head on his way? She didn't know. She was confused. He was still in the kitchen with Birdie. He was saying, "Yeah, she had them all eating out of her hand. They loved her." Did he mean Tate, on Saturday night? Of course he did. But he may have been playing it up for Birdie's sake. Tate wanted to grab him, but she reined herself in. Stop. Be quiet. Be still. Let him come to you. She stretched out against the picnic table.

She heard Birdie say, "Okay, then, we'll see you this afternoon."

She heard his footsteps coming out of the house. She didn't turn. He would leave, then, without another word? She sang the beginning of "Hungry Heart" to herself, softly, to calm her nerves. She heard him whisper, "Pssst."

Was she imagining that?

"Psssst."

She turned. He was nodding his head. *Follow me.* The anxiety cleared; she was empty, light, expectant.

She followed him to the front of the house. He said, "You *cannot* ignore me like that. You will make me crazy." He pushed her up against the wall and kissed her. The kissing was so new, so passionate, she could have kissed him for hours. His tongue, his face, his hair, his shoulders. She would never tire of him, never get enough. And there he was, feeling the same way, she could tell. He didn't pull away, he didn't look at his watch or check over her shoulder. He was focused on her. For ten minutes, fifteen minutes. When they did stop kissing long enough to speak, he said, "God, I missed you after you left."

"I know," she said.

"I thought about you all day, all night, every second this morning. The anticipation of seeing you made me buzz, you know?" He shook his head. "I never thought I'd feel this way again."

She said, "What do you have to do today?"

He said, "I have five places to be right now."

She said, "So you have to go?"

"And leave you? No way."

He did pull himself away. Anita Fullin needed him at ten, and he had clients out in Sconset with a wasp's nest in the eaves. That had to be dealt with this morning.

He said, "I'll be back this afternoon, okay?"

They kissed, they couldn't pull apart, but then, yes, he went, she pushed him. He turned and waved three times between the house and the bluff.

Tate walked around in a daze. She showered, ate breakfast, put on her bathing suit, headed down to the beach. Chess came down to the beach, too, but Tate ignored her. It was surprisingly easy. Birdie and India came down with their upright chairs and the cooler of lunch; India carried the Frisbee. She said to Tate, "You forgot this."

Tate said, "I don't want to play." She was distracted. All she wanted to do was think about Barrett.

Chess said, "You're awfully quiet."

Tate snorted. "That's the pot calling the kettle black."

Chess said, "Do you want to go for a walk?"

Tate said, "Not with you."

Chess said, "Suit yourself."

There was a note in Chess's voice that snapped at Tate like a rubber band hitting her in the face. "Okay," she said. "You want to walk? We'll walk."

Chess looked back at Birdie and India. "We're going for a walk."

Birdie smiled. "That will be nice."

Tate shook her head. Her mother was wonderfully naive. She thought this was it, the breakthrough. Well, it was a breakthrough of sorts because Tate was done trying.

They walked for a long time without talking. Tate thought that Chess might apologize for what she'd said the day before. And then Tate decided that she wouldn't speak at all unless Chess apologized. So there was silence. Chess didn't apologize and Tate didn't speak. It was a test of wills, and as with any kind of competition with Chess, Tate knew she would lose. They walked all the way down to Whale Shoal, where Tate had seen the sister seagulls squawking at each other.

Chess said, "I hate you because you're happy."

Tate felt a small sense of accomplishment. Finally, Chess was telling her the truth.

That afternoon, Barrett showed up earlier than normal. They were all lying on the beach when his boat pulled in.

Birdie said, "My word, Barrett is early."

India said, "I wonder why?"

Tate sat up on her blanket. There was a woman inside her, jumping up and down like a contestant on a game show.

Barrett anchored the boat and waded to shore. He had a bag of groceries in one hand and a bouquet of flowers in the other hand—blue hydrangeas, pink lilies, white irises. Tate sucked in her breath. He presented the flowers to her with a flourish.

"For you," he said.

"For me?" she said. She couldn't believe it. Tears stung her eyes. She was thirty years old and she hadn't been given flowers by a man since Lincoln Brown picked her up for the prom and brought a wrist corsage.

He held out the other bag. "And four rib-eye steaks, a head of butter lettuce, champagne vinegar, a wedge of Maytag blue cheese, and a book of crossword puzzles."

"God bless you," India said.

Barrett said, "I'll take it all up. Madame, can I put your flowers in water?"

Tate hopped to her feet. "I'll come with you."

Chess, who Tate thought was napping, raised her head off her towel and said, "I think I'm going to puke."

Tate couldn't stop thanking him. "They're beautiful," she said. "They're gorgeous. You didn't have to do this."

"I wanted to."

She buried her face in the flowers and inhaled their scent. Did it get any better than this? Did it? The man she was newly in love with had just brought her flowers. They could get married, she supposed, and have children together, but would she be any happier then than she was right this second?

"I want you to look at them and think of me. And know I'm thinking of you. Even when I'm changing Anita Fullin's lightbulbs."

In the kitchen, he put the groceries away and she unwrapped the flowers, cut their stems, and placed them in a jug filled with water. He grabbed her. They were in the house alone.

"Do you want to go upstairs?" Tate asked. She filled with a nervous kind of daring. Never in a million years did she think she would be having clandestine sex in the Tuckernuck house. No doubt the house had seen its share of conjugal relations—her mother and father's, Aunt India and Uncle Bill's, her grandparents', her great-grandparents', for God's sake. That kind of sex was necessary and sustaining, the kind that created future generations who would then enjoy the house themselves. But the Tuckernuck house wasn't built for sex that was wild and secret; the walls were thin and the floors unsteady. If a bed started to rock, it might crash through the floor.

Barrett said, "I have a better idea."

* * *

He took her for a ride in his boat. Tate had feared he would invite Chess along, or even Birdie and India, but what he said was, "I'm going to steal Tate away for a little while." And they hopped in and sped off. Chess, India, and Birdie stared after them with naked longing.

Tate felt guilty for about thirty seconds; then exhilaration kicked in. She loved being out on the water, in the sun, with the wind in her face. They zipped around Tuckernuck, waving to the people they saw on the shore. *Life is good!* They cruised over to Muskeget, an island even smaller than Tuckernuck that had only two houses. Muskeget was home to a colony of seals; there were some lounging on the rocky shores, and Barrett pulled in close enough that Tate could practically touch them. She was excited to see the seals, more excited than she would be under other circumstances. (In fact, she remembered Barrett's father taking them on a "seal cruise" when Tate was twelve or thirteen. She had been unimpressed then, filled with adolescent ennui and a touch of disgust—the seals smelled!)

Barrett motored back to Tuckernuck, to the remote northeast coast, to a tiny crescent of beach at the top of East Pond that Tate didn't even know existed, and he cut the engine. He anchored. He took off his shirt.

"Come on," he said. "We're swimming in."

And they did. They raced. Tate loved this kind of companionship, this playfulness. She nearly beat him, she was a good swimmer, but he flopped onto shore a second before her, and before she could even catch her breath, he was on top of her. They made love in the sand.

They rinsed off in the water—sand was *everywhere*—and lay back in the sun.

Tate said, "There are all these things I want to know."

Barrett said, "Take it easy on me."

Tate said, "How did you meet Stephanie?"

Barrett sighed. "I'm not a good talker. Especially not about Steph."

"Just answer the question," Tate said. "Please?"

"We worked together at the Boarding House," he said. "Waiting tables."

"You waited tables?"

"Three summers. The first two summers were uneventful. The third summer was Stephanie."

"She grew up on Nantucket?"

"Quincy, Mass. Irish Catholic. Five brothers and her. Her parents have a cottage in Chatham. She used to work summers in Chatham, at the Squire, but she came to Nantucket one year because the money was better." He reached out and touched Tate's face. "Can I be done?"

"I want to know you," she said.

He pressed his lips together, and Tate feared she'd messed up. He whispered in her ear. "Will you come back with me tonight? Spend the night at my house? Please?"

She swooned. *Yes!* But no, she couldn't. She couldn't abandon her mother and Aunt India. She couldn't abandon Chess; they had just moved one baby step forward.

"I want to," she said. "But I can't. I have to stay with my family. They need me."

"I need you."

"They need me more."

"More than me?"

"I think so."

INDIA

India was sleeping at night.

It was a miracle. The first night she had been exhausted from traveling, but then she slept just as soundly the second night, then the third night, the fourth, the fifth, the sixth. She lay down on her gelatinous mattress, surrounded herself with the new, firm pillows Birdie had ordered from a catalog, and let the angels carry her away, just as she had when she was a child in this house, then a teenager (she'd slept until noon in those days), then a young wife and mother alongside Bill. She slept for long, luxurious, uninterrupted hours and awoke with the sun streaming in the windows and dust motes dancing in the air and the smell of bacon and the sound of Birdie downstairs humming Linda Ronstadt. And India felt triumphant, as proud of herself as if she'd run a sub-four-hour marathon.

Was I wrong about you?

The letter from Lula hadn't disrupted India's sleep. She had feared it might; she feared she would toss and turn, rolling the stupid question around in her mind like an obsidian marble, black and impenetrable. But India lay down, prepared for the worst, and was escorted to the twilight blue waiting room where she loitered in half consciousness until she was whisked to the inner chamber of sleep.

During the day, however, India was restless. She picked at the meaning of the question, she composed possible responses, she revisited the events of the spring until she feared for their veracity. Had all that really happened, or was India embellishing it? She was preoccupied; she couldn't relax.

Which left her on an equal footing with everybody else.

India took a walk, not to the northwest, where Birdie and Tate liked to go, but to the northeast, past East Pond. This was India's first venture off the property since they'd been here; she was lazy when it came to exercise, always had been, and the cigarettes punished her lungs with a creeping burn. But India used to be fond of this walk—it was sweet with lilac and honeysuckle. She passed the house owned by the pilot, who kept a Cessna parked in his yard like a car. There was a woman of a certain age in the yard, deadheading daylilies. She waved to India and said, "Life is good!"

"Life is good!" India called back, cringing internally. She and Birdie had been taught as children to always use the proper Tuckernuck greeting, but it made India feel like a dipshit. India picked up her pace so as not to get caught up in an unexpected visit.

She was on a mission, of sorts.

She passed the old schoolhouse, with its white clapboard siding. India could almost hear the schoolmarm slapping her ruler down on the desks. It had been refurbished as a private home, but for a long while it had stood abandoned, and once, years earlier, India and Bill had broken in and made love in the classroom. The room had smelled like chalk dust.

Bill had said, "I'm going to teach you a thing or two."

Then, India had been an eager student. She and Bill had had a rousing sex life—every night for days at a stretch, replete with moaning, heavy breathing, and whispering dirty, lascivious things in each other's ear. Birdie had caught them once, buck naked, in the back of the Scout.

Now, India thought, *Bill, will you please leave me alone?*

Over the past few days, India had watched Tate and Barrett together, and she had seen that spark of raw sexual energy. It was present in the way he looked at her, the way she touched him. It was electrifying. Just the night before, India had had a dream in which she was lying on the beach, facedown in the sand with the sun on her back. She knew someone was watching her, but when she checked to the left and the right, there was no one. Then she realized there was a man gazing down at her from the lighthouse. (This was odd and dreamlike; Tuckernuck didn't have a lighthouse.) This man appeared on the bluff. It was Bill. No, it wasn't Bill. It was Barrett Lee. India didn't move; she pretended to be asleep. She heard Barrett approaching. His feet crunched in the sand. She felt something icy drag along her spine. She shivered and raised her head. It wasn't Barrett Lee at all—it was Chuck Lee, with two bottles of beer dangling from his fingers.

In the dream, Chuck Lee was gruff and sexy, as he had been when India, who was way underage, had a terrible crush on him.

India said to him, *I met your son.*

He took a drag off his cigarette. *My son?*

India had woken up at that point, on fire. Turned on by her ancient memories of Chuck Lee? She was confused.

Was I wrong about you?

India approached East Pond. It was surrounded by thick *Rosa rugosa* bushes, but she found a narrow path that led to the water. Her boys used to come out here to sail the simple boats that Bill made for them—long, flat pieces of wood, they may even have been paint stirrers, with a hole drilled in one end and a piece of string attached. Today, there were canvasback ducks on the pond, which made India feel less alone. She had witnesses.

She took Lula's letter out of the pocket of her beach cover-up and tore it into even strips, and then she tore the strips into squares. She threw the squares into the air like confetti, and they fluttered to the surface of the pond. The ducks swam right over, thinking it was bread. But when they discovered it was paper, they paddled away.

Such ceremony was unnecessary, even silly, India knew; she could just have crumpled the note and left it in the kitchen trash. But allowing the note to float away seemed like the proper thing. India didn't need drama or romance; she had seen her share and survived. She was beyond all that now. She was, after all, practically a grandmother.

CHESS

Day twelve.

A few days after my solo exodus from Irving Plaza, Nick called me at work.

He said, "You were upset about Rhonda?"

I didn't respond.

He said, "You were upset about Rhonda."

I said, "You deserve someone. And Rhonda is hot. I can see why you like her."

He said, "She is hot. But she's not you."

I said, "Do you love me?"

He said, "I don't even allow myself to think in those terms. You're my brother's girlfriend. But since you're asking, I will say that I have feelings for you that seem to own me. I'm not sure if it's love, but it's something big and I can't shake it."

I said, "I feel the same way."

There was a long pause. Finally, I said, "So we tell him."

"We can't," Nick said. "It won't work. It will be ugly and you'll be miserable. We'll both be miserable. I am not Michael, Chess. Michael is the legit brother. I am not legit. I am a musician with a halfway-decent band. I don't make any money. Michael's out climbing the corporate ladder, and I'm out climbing the face of a mountain." He paused. "And I'm a gambler."

"That's what I like about you," I said. "Free spirit."

"You're romanticizing the situation. The fact is I live in a hovel, and if I hit a bad streak at cards, I'm going to be back in Bergen County living with Cy and Evelyn. You deserve more, Chess—that's what I tell myself when I'm thinking about stealing you away. You deserve Michael."

"But I want you," I said.

"Well, the feeling's mutual," Nick said. "I've never wanted anything so badly in my life."

We sat with that awhile. I said, "I keep wishing that Michael would fall in love with someone else."

Nick said, "I keep wishing Michael would die."

He might have expected me to be shocked, but I wasn't.

He said, "Will you meet me in thirty minutes? At the tree?"

I said I would.

Summer came, and Michael and I took a trip to Bar Harbor. It was so perfectly us: the lobsters, the blueberries, the pine trees and clear, cold water. We rode our bikes around Acadia National Park. We got up early in the morning to run; we saw deer. We got along perfectly; we didn't argue. Everything that I wanted to do, he wanted to do, and vice versa. We sat in Adirondack chairs and read our books in the sun, and although that was pleasant, I couldn't help the sinking feeling that we might as well have been eighty years old.

We took a hike to the summit of Champlain Mountain. It was a strenuous hike and I was in a bad mood. The night before, we'd met a Princeton friend of Michael's and his fiancée for dinner at the Bayview Hotel. Their names were Carter and Kate. Kate was lovely, but she was dull; she talked only about her wedding, which was to be held that fall at the Pierre Hotel. Carter talked about the house they were buying in Ridgewood, New Jersey. He talked about mortgages and closing costs, and how good the public schools were. He looked right at me and said, "Because, you know, in the not-too-distant future, all our Saturdays are going to be spent watching our kids play soccer."

I smiled at Carter, but my heart faltered. Was he right? My life, certainly, had unfolded in a certain way, but was I automatically destined for a life in the wealthy suburbs with a husband and kids and a Range Rover and a seat on the board of a worthy charity to keep my mind occupied? That was the life Michael wanted, but I wasn't ready to surrender. I wanted something less prescribed, *something edgier, deeper, more meaningful. I wanted to travel through India, I wanted to write a novel, I wanted true love, the kind of love that left me agitated and breathless.*

When we reached the top of Champlain Mountain and looked out over the misty, blue green trees below us, I wanted to call out Nick's name. I wanted to shout it. I wanted to tell Michael then and there.

He would have to understand that I couldn't help how I felt.

But, also, I couldn't help who I was. I wasn't a rebel. I didn't rock the boat.

I said nothing.

* * *

It killed Chess to watch Tate and Barrett. And yet they were on Tuckernuck; there was nothing to do *but* watch.

Barrett brought Tate flowers. He took her for rides in the boat. They went to the remote beaches of Tuckernuck, and they went to Muskeget. They made love either on the boat itself or on the beach. Chess didn't ask about this and Tate didn't tell, but Chess noticed the way that Tate glowed.

Barrett and Tate surf cast on the beach. There was a joke between them—an old joke about the time their father had paid Barrett to take Tate fishing (*He had to pay you to spend time with me alone!*) and she'd cast her line out all by herself (*She was a natural!*) and she caught the biggest fish he'd ever seen without a lick of help from him (*A forty-two-inch striper!*). Chess didn't want to be party to the inside jokes of their past or their present. She buried her face in her arms and wished that their beach was just a little bit bigger.

Tate called over to Chess, "Come on! Do you want to try?"

"No," Chess said.

After two or three dozen casts, Tate got a bite, and she reeled the line in. She had a bluefish; its steely scales glistened in the sun. The fish flopped and struggled, fighting to be free, and Tate said, "Look!"

When Chess looked at the fish, she saw herself.

Barrett took over, cutting the line, pulling the hook, carefully, from the fish's mouth with pliers. The fish flailed desperately on the sand; Chess couldn't stand to watch. She thought, *Oh, God, please throw it back.*

Barrett and Tate started kissing. She was thrilled at her accomplishment and he was proud of her, but really, it was just an excuse for them to be all over each other.

Birdie walked over to inspect the fish. "Do you want me to cook it tonight for dinner?"

Tate said, "No, I don't think so."

Barrett threw the fish back into the ocean. Chess closed her eyes.

Tate went to Nantucket to spend another night with Barrett. Barrett was taking Tate to the Company of the Cauldron for dinner; he had booked the private table in the back garden. Chess bristled at this kind of information. She was, childishly, writing down the phrases that bothered her in her journal. *Private table in the back garden.* Chess reminded herself that she had been romanced in this same way. Michael used to send Chess flowers at work. The delivery man would walk into the magazine's offices with an armload of sunflowers or long-stemmed roses and everyone would say, "They're for Chess." Michael used to take her out for romantic dinners all the time, for the heck of it. Babbo because she'd put an issue to bed; Café des Artistes because it was a Wednesday and raining.

Tate didn't get home until late the following afternoon. Again, Chess missed her keenly and found herself waiting around for Tate to return—but then, when Tate did return, Chess was sullen and resentful.

Tate said, "Tomorrow, the kids are coming."

Birdie and India were over the moon about this prospect. Kids! Birdie asked Barrett to bring the fixings for a clambake. They would eat lobsters on the beach and have a bonfire—with marshmallows to roast for Cameron and Tucker. Birdie and India wanted to relive the days when they were young mothers. Tate wanted to be with Barrett. Chess wanted only to survive.

Barrett dug a hole in the sand, and Tate collected driftwood for the fire. Barrett brought sticks for the marshmallow roast, and fishing poles so that he and Tate and Cameron could surf cast. Birdie went crazy chilling wine, mixing up potato salad, melting butter over the camp stove. There was a sense of anticipation. It would be a party. Chess wanted to hole up in the attic and cry.

Tate left with Barrett to go get the kids. Chess got roped into helping India haul the coolers and the bags of food down to the beach. Chess laid down the blankets and stuffed wadded-up newspaper under the driftwood. This clambake-bonfire was taking an enormous amount of effort, Chess thought, from matches to trash bags to little dishes for the melted butter and silver claw crackers for the lobsters.

India said, "Bill used to love the nights we had bonfires."

Yes, Chess remembered. Uncle Bill had been the fire man, the marshmallow man. All the kids would roast their marshmallows and then present them to Uncle Bill for inspection. The Bishop boys always stuck theirs right into the flame, where they would catch fire like a torch and then turn gray and ashy. Chess was careful with her marshmallows; she kept her stick inches from the low burn. She took her time achieving a golden brown skin that caramelized over the gooey white middle. *Now* that's *a perfectly roasted marshmallow,* Uncle Bill would say. Chess remembered him smiling at her. *You know how to wait. You, my dear, are a master craftsperson.*

Chess had been embarrassed and delighted by this praise. When Uncle Bill said those things, they seemed important and true.

The boat pulled in, and Chess saw them: two strawberry blond, freckled little boys who were so cute it was like they had been ordered from a catalog. Chess didn't know anything about kids beyond having been one herself. She hadn't babysat growing up; she had never been a camp counselor or a youth-group leader. When Michael talked about getting married and "having kids," Chess nodded blithely along, although the phrase "having kids" meant nothing to her. When she saw Tate, however, she felt bizarrely jealous, like Tate had gone away for an hour and returned with an instant family. The boys were nearly identical, one a smaller version of the other. They were wearing orange life preservers, the same kind that Chess and Tate used to wear. Chess stood up. For the first time all day, she felt interested in what was going on.

Barrett carried the older boy, and Tate carried the younger. Tate was a natural, which was surprising, because as far as Chess knew, Tate didn't have any more experience with kids than she did. But the little boy clung to her neck, and she looked at ease.

"Hi!" Chess said. Her voice, to her surprise, sounded almost friendly.

They all waded in, and Barrett and Tate set the boys down onshore.

"This is Cameron," Barrett said. "And this is Tucker."

They were struggling to get the life preservers *off,* and Chess remembered the feel of the cumbersome, restrictive weight around her neck. She helped Cameron unbuckle his.

"Welcome to Tuckernuck," she said.

He said, "What happened to your hair?"

Chess touched her head. She was wearing the blue crocheted cap even though her hair had started growing in. But to the kids, she would still look bald.

"Cameron," Barrett said sternly.

"I cut it," Chess said.

"Oh," he said. "How come?"

"Cameron, stop," Barrett said. "This is Tate's sister, Chess."

"Because I felt like it," Chess said.

This answer worked—of course it worked, it was a five-year-old's answer for a five-year-old. Cameron nodded and stuck out his hand. Chess shook it.

Barrett said, "And this is Miss Birdie and Miss India."

Birdie and India bowed to Cameron like he was a little prince. Chess smiled. He embodied the royalty of youth, which had been missing from the Tuckernuck compound for nearly two decades. Cameron stared at the two older ladies and decided that they weren't harboring anything that interested him (they didn't have candy or money), so he wandered off down the beach. Tucker, meanwhile, darted into the water.

"Whoa, little dude!" Tate called out. "You've got to put your suit on!" She looked at Barrett. "Where's his suit?"

"In the canvas bag," Barrett said.

"The children are darling!" Birdie said. She looked happier than she had in days. "They look just like you."

"They look like their mother," Barrett said. "The hair, the freckles."

"Take some of the credit," Birdie said. "They are absolute angels."

"They are *not* angels, I assure you," Barrett said. "Cameron!" he called out. "Don't go too far, okay, buddy?"

"Okay," Cameron echoed. Already he was down the beach, putting shells in a bucket. Tate was expertly changing Tucker into his bathing suit. Chess was blown away. It looked like Tate had done an internship at a day care, she was so practiced and efficient.

The kids made things better, lighter, happier. It was weird, the way they stole the spotlight and alleviated tension. There was no time to worry about yourself when you had to worry about the children: Were they safe in the water? Was their corn buttered? *Be careful not to spill your drink!* Chess pitched in, helping to assemble plates of food and pour wine; she pulled the meat out of Tate's lobster because Tate had Tucker on her lap. Once the sun set, Barrett lit the fire. Cameron and Chess had a rock-throwing contest. Chess would throw a rock, and Cameron would try to throw a rock farther. Or he would throw a bigger, heavier rock. Or a smoother, shinier rock. Chess felt touched that he had joined in her private game (*Get rid of the heavy stuff*); she was keenly aware that he had no mother, and so any woman in the right age range might do. She tried to appreciate the wonder he felt about something as simple as an egg-shaped marble white rock with an orange spot on it.

Yes, she said. *That one will go far.* Cameron threw it with a grunt. Chess smiled.

India took pictures with her disposable camera. She took the boys individually and together, and she took a picture of Barrett with the boys and she took a picture of Barrett, Tate, and the boys.

"Now there's one for the Christmas card!" India said.

Tate said, "Whoa, you're moving a little fast," but Chess could tell she liked the idea of it.

India tried to take a picture of Chess with Cameron, but Chess held her hand out in front of the lens like she was fending off the paparazzi. "Please don't," she said. "The camera will break."

"Why?" Cameron said.

"Because I'm ugly."

India lowered the camera and gave Chess an admonishing look. Cameron said, "You're not ugly. You're just bald, like Grandpa Chuck."

India barked out a laugh. "Out of the mouths of babes."

The fire raged, hot and elemental in the dark night. India and Birdie collapsed into beach chairs and swaddled their bare legs with beach towels. Their faces were warm and orange with the flames. India looked contented and Birdie looked wistful, which was the exact combination of how Chess was feeling.

No one had touched the marshmallows. Chess pulled the sticks out and offered one to Cameron. She said, "It's a stick. For roasting marshmallows."

He said, "No, thank you." He was busy lining up the rocks he'd found along the edge of the blanket.

Tate and Barrett were huddled together with Tucker lying across their laps. Chess said, "Marshmallow stick?"

Barrett shook his head and Tate put a finger to her lips. Tucker was almost asleep.

Chess said, "All right. I guess I'll make one."

She impaled a marshmallow on a stick and settled on the blanket next to Cameron and held the marshmallow inches away from the low, glowing embers. India started singing "Songbird" by Fleetwood Mac, the favorite campfire song of their youth—and Chess shivered. She hadn't heard "Songbird" in years and years, perhaps not since the last time she had roasted a marshmallow on this beach. India's voice was thin and smooth; she couldn't sing an aria, but she could sing a lullaby.

The fire crackled. Tucker's eyes drifted closed. Chess checked her marshmallow. It was a light caramel color. She let it cool for a few seconds. She felt the buoyancy of childhood, the lightness, the freedom from the weight she carried around. Just for a second.

Chess showed Cameron the marshmallow.

"Want a bite?" she asked.

He nodded. She let him taste. It was perfect—crisp and gooey.

He said, "It's good."

India sang, "*And I love you, I love you, I love you, like never before.*"

It was a major production carrying everything back up to the house, including two sleeping kids, but they got it done, finally—they extinguished the fire, they folded the blankets, they put the leftover potato salad in the fridge. Chess was sleeping in the other twin bed in Birdie's room so that Barrett and Tate and the kids could have the attic. Out of habit, however, Chess and Tate used the bathroom together. They brushed their teeth together and peed in front of each other, saving the poor toilet a flush. Before they finished up, Chess caught Tate's eye in the grainy mirror.

"You're really lucky," Chess said.

BIRDIE

Tate was in love for the first time ever. Birdie wanted to be happy for her, but she found herself thinking like a cynic and a realist. Tate and Barrett were very public with their displays of affection, which Birdie found disquieting, not because it offended her sensibilities (although it did, to a degree; she had always been a little conservative that way), but because she was envious.

Hank!

It was difficult for Birdie to be around Barrett and Tate and their delirious happiness, which now included Barrett's children, Cameron and Tucker, who were the cutest, sweetest boys on earth (the freckles, the chubby hands, the practiced manners), because Birdie's own heart was bleeding.

She had moments of clarity, like the sun breaking through the clouds. She had known Hank less than six months, she wouldn't let herself pine for him another second, she wouldn't let herself wonder what he was doing or why he didn't answer her afternoon phone calls; she tried not to wonder why he hadn't answered her calls in the middle of the night. Where had he been? What had he been doing? It didn't matter, it was none of her business, he owed her nothing, they had taken no vows and made no promises. She wouldn't allow his silence to ruin her vacation.

But then something would remind her of him, something as simple as the climbing 'New Dawn' roses on the Constable house or a glass of Sancerre, and she would be angry again, and hurt. Theirs could have been the romantic story here: the love she had found after a difficult and ultimately unsatisfying thirty-year marriage. It could have been Hank and Birdie that everyone watched with envy: the two of them holding hands and kissing and feeding each other bites of butter-soaked lobster meat, the two of them taking trips to Iceland and Rio de Janeiro, hosting gatherings of their blended families, children, grandchildren, the two of them with their mature IRAs, their matched set of interests, going to the Chagall exhibit on Tuesday, puttering in the garden on Thursday, commingling their soprano and baritone for the hymns on Sunday. Why couldn't it be them?

Morning arrived, and after one night of Tate being away on Nantucket with Barrett and another night of hosting Barrett and his children here, things were back to normal. Tate had slept in the attic and had gotten up to go for her run. Birdie had made the coffee and she was cutting up strawberries and kiwi for the fruit salad. Tate kissed her mother on the cheek as she always did. Tate had always been very generous with her affections, very appreciative of Birdie and her efforts.

Tate took her coffee out to the picnic table and started stretching her hamstrings. She had a beautiful figure, and she was very tan from the sun. It was possible she had never looked better. Birdie put down her paring knife, abandoned the fruit salad, and stood outside in the sun, watching Tate.

An hour or so later, India descended the stairs wearing her kimono.

"Sleep okay?" Birdie asked.

"Slept great," India said. She accepted a cup of coffee from Birdie, and a dish of strawberries and kiwi fruit. "Kiwi," she said. "Can you imagine what Mother would say if she saw us eating kiwi on Tuckernuck?"

Birdie bleated out a laugh.

"Remember how she used to read our grocery list over the CB radio to Chuck?" India said. "Remember the dog Chuck used to have when we were little girls? The one who used to ride on the bow of the boat? God, what was that dog's name?"

"Queenie," Birdie said.

"Queenie!" India said. She looked at Birdie. "Where is the delight in unearthing a golden nugget from our shared childhood? Is something wrong?"

Birdie dropped four circles of batter on the heated skillet. She had considered telling India about her troubles with Hank, but India knew Hank, India had *dated* Hank, and thus it wasn't a topic she wanted to get into.

Instead, she said, "I'm worried about Tate and Barrett."

"Worried?" India said. "What is there to be worried about? Those two are positively beautiful together. They're like movie stars."

Birdie flipped the pancakes. The tops were smooth and golden brown.

"Their relationship is moving awfully fast, it seems. And, well, you know, it's a little bit make-believe. We're leaving in two weeks. Tate will go back to her life and Barrett will go back to his. What's happening now is a fantasy."

"I'll tell you what," India said. "Barrett Lee is one hell of a fantasy."

"And you know how Tate is," Birdie said. "She's as naive as a child. She doesn't see that this thing with Barrett is just a summer romance. It's not meant to last."

This sounded harsh, even to Birdie's own ears, but she meant it. Nothing lasted. The giddy, head-over-heels infatuation faded; it mellowed into something else. You got married, then divorced. Or your husband killed himself. Or your brain synapses became encased in gooey plaque and you started putting the frying pan in the icebox instead of in the cabinet where it belonged. "I'm afraid she's going to get hurt," Birdie said. "She has no idea what she's doing."

At that moment, Tate walked into the kitchen. Her face was red and sweaty from the exertion of the run, but then Birdie noticed her eyes were watering.

"Thanks a lot, Mom," she said.

"Oh, honey, I...," Birdie said. She scrambled mentally backward, wondering how much Tate had overheard. The pancakes started to smoke.

Tate said, "You're just like Chess."

Now it was Birdie's turn to be astonished. She had never been likened to Chess, ever. "What?" she said.

"You don't want me to be happy," Tate said, and she bounded up the stairs.

That afternoon, Birdie returned to Bigelow Point with her cell phone. She told herself she wanted the walk; the exercise would be good for her, and the me-myself time would be good for her. When she reached the point, she called Hank. She had no expectations. He wouldn't answer, she wouldn't leave a message. Calling was fruitless. But she couldn't not call. Not calling was, somehow, beyond her.

She dialed the number, then waited. The tide was low; the water was ankle deep. She was wearing her father's hat, which protected her face from the beating sun. Could it protect her in other ways? She wondered if her father would approve of Hank. She decided the answer was no; he would not approve on principle. Her father had been a traditionalist; he had adored Grant.

The phone rang twice, three times, four. Predictable. Birdie waited for the sound of Hank's voice on the voice mail. To hear his voice, even in the five-second recording, was worth the hour-long walk.

This is Hank. I'm not available. Leave a message.

The man spoke the truth, Birdie thought. He wasn't available. She would not leave a message. She hung up. She gazed out at the water and thought what she always thought: *Enough of this, Birdie! Move on!*

She wished she hadn't said anything to India about Tate that morning. She had been a mother for thirty-two years, and she was still making regrettable mistakes.

The phone sprang to life in her hand. It vibrated, it sang out its electric tune. She held it at arm's length so she could read the display. It was Hank, calling her back.

She opened the phone. "Hello?"

"Hello, Birdie," he said.

"Hello, Hank," she said. The hand she held the phone in was shaking. This was a case of "Be careful what you wish for." She had Hank on the phone, but she didn't know what to say. She should have prepared something.

He said, "How are you?"

How are you? Was she supposed to answer that?

What if she *did* answer that? What if she told him the truth? Would the world end?

"I've had an emotional couple of weeks," she said. "It's tough, you know, living with India and the girls out here in the middle of nowhere. Well, what's tough is that we talk all the time, we have nothing to do but talk, and we strike nerves every once in a while and we backpedal, and...oh, jeez, you can imagine."

Hank didn't respond. Maybe he couldn't imagine. What, after all, did he know of mothers with daughters, or sisters with sisters?

"And I've been missing you," Birdie said. "I think about you far too often. I feel this longing, this aching—made worse by the fact that you don't seem to miss me at all. When I called last week, you sounded uninterested. And then when I called you in the middle of the night, you didn't answer. I left a message. Did you get that message?"

"I did," he said.

"Where were you?" Birdie asked. "Why didn't you answer the phone? I called four or five times."

"I wasn't at home," Hank said. "I heard my cell phone ringing but I wasn't in a place where I was free to answer it."

"Are you seeing someone else?" Birdie asked. This was her biggest concern: that someone would steal Hank away. The world was filled with single women, and Hank was a desirable catch. Birdie pictured her rival as someone like Ondine Morris, the redheaded siren who had been after Grant all those years ago. Ondine Morris was both a golfer and a socialite, and when her husband lost all his money in the stock market crash of 1987, Ondine had pursued Grant shamelessly, despite the fact that she and Birdie were friends. Grant couldn't have cared less about Ondine Morris; all women were extraneous to Grant, even those women with an eight handicap. But the threat of Ondine Morris or someone like her remained a specter to Birdie, always lurking.

"No," Hank said.

"You can tell me if you are," Birdie said. "I'll understand."

"I'm not seeing anyone else, Birdie," Hank said. "But I have been preoccupied, and not very forthcoming, for which I apologize."

"Well, be forthcoming now, please," Birdie said. "Explain yourself."

"It's Caroline," Hank said. He gave off a huge, heavy sigh. "She's dead."

Birdie gasped. "She's dead? She died?"

"When you called that night, I was with her at the facility. They had moved her upstairs. I was asleep in a chair next to her bed, holding her hand. She had a massive stroke, they told me it was bad and I went, and she died on Sunday morning."

"Oh, Hank," Birdie said.

"We held the funeral on Wednesday," he said. "The church was packed. I have enough casseroles to last me the rest of my life."

"I'm sorry," Birdie said. "I had no idea." Never once had it occurred to her that something had happened to Caroline. Caroline had Alzheimer's, and Birdie had assumed she would decline incrementally for years and years. For her to fall so dramatically wasn't something Birdie had expected. Caroline's death was certainly sad news, but her quality of life had been poor, and now Hank was free. There would be a period of mourning, maybe as long as a year, before Birdie would be officially introduced around, until she would meet Hank's children and grandchildren, but it would be worth the wait.

Birdie said, "Oh, Hank, I didn't say this before I left,

but I wanted to, and so I'll say it now: I love you. I love you, Hank Dunlap."

Hank coughed, or cleared his throat. "You are such a wonderful woman, Birdie."

And Birdie thought, *Oh, God, no.*

She said, "Hank..."

He said, "I can't see you anymore. I am... well, I'm taking Caroline's death badly. I can't sleep, I can't eat, I'm filled with sadness, but I'm also plagued with guilt. It haunts me that I was out enjoying life with you—I was at the theater with you, I was in hotel rooms with you—while she was trapped in an institution. I should have waited until she was gone."

Birdie was trying to process what he was saying, but it was coming together slowly. He *regretted* the theater? He *regretted* their night at the Sherry-Netherland? "Well, why didn't you, then? Why didn't you wait?"

"I was so lonely...," he said.

"Hank," Birdie said, "it's *okay.* Caroline was very sick, Hank. Why, one of the first things you told me was that she didn't recognize you or the kids. She thought you were a kind stranger, bringing her chocolates every week. You had every right to continue to live your life."

"There was more than just you," Hank said. "I was unfaithful before Caroline got sick. I never deserved her love. I see that now and I feel I owe her something, an atonement, a penance. And my penance is going to be giving you up."

"Giving me up?" Birdie said. "But why?"

"I was conducting a relationship with you while I was married."

"But Caroline could have hung on for fifteen or twenty more years, and what were you supposed to do? Squander those years? I thought you... well, I thought you'd come to terms with your actions within yourself."

"I thought so, too."

"You just need time," Birdie said. Because Hank's reasoning was so strange and convoluted, it sounded like a case of temporary insanity.

"Birdie," he said.

And with that word, her name, she knew. He was gone. It was stupid, it was a sham, his offering her up as an atonement to his dead wife like some sacrificial lamb. He had been unfaithful throughout his marriage: this was news to Birdie, big news. They had talked for hours about their respective marriages, they had dissected them and labeled the good and the bad, but Hank had never confessed to having been unfaithful. He was a liar, Birdie thought. Caroline might not even be dead. This whole thing might be an elaborate story concocted to end their relationship. But it didn't matter. The story's ending was the same no matter what the circumstances: He didn't love her. It was over.

She said, "We were so perfect together."

He said, "You're a wonderful woman, Birdie."

She could stand many things, but she would not be patronized. She hung up the phone without saying good-bye.

He called back a second later, and Birdie didn't answer. Now *that* felt good.

Standing there, she was both fuming and incredulous. Damn Hank Dunlap! (She couldn't stand the thought of him arriving at her front door with the bouquet of hyacinths, wearing his little glasses; he was like a demon sent to trick her.) She thought Hank was one person, but he was someone else. It was okay. It happened to the best of us.

Birdie called Grant at work. His secretary, Alice, put her right through, and when he answered, "Hey, Bird," so casual and familiar, she burst into tears. He shushed her; he'd always been a good, soothing shusher, since it required no language or expression of actual sentiment.

He said, "Is it Hank again?"

"We broke up."

"For good?"

"For good."

"What happened?"

She told him: Caroline dead, Hank guilty, Birdie gone.

"So if you'd met him in six months, after his wife was already dead, it would have been fine?"

"Yeah," Birdie said. "It makes no sense."

"Well, Birdie, what can I say? The guy's an idiot."

"You don't even know him."

"He let you go. He's an idiot."

"You let me go," Birdie said.

"And I'm an idiot," Grant said.

Despite herself, Birdie smiled. This was as sweet as Grant got.

"You're not an idiot," she said.

TATE

They had officially been "together" for only nine days, but every day on Tuckernuck was a lifetime, and so it felt like forever. They had made love sixteen times, they had shared eleven meals, they had watched three movies, gone to two restaurants, taken five boat rides, caught two fish. She had loved his children immediately and not only because they were his children. She had comforted Cameron from a bad dream and changed Tucker's pajamas and sheets after he wet the bed.

Barrett said he didn't like to talk about Steph, but he was actually quite eloquent on the topic of his late wife, especially late at night as he and Tate lay in bed. He told her pieces of the story that together formed a cohesive whole. It wasn't exactly the fairy tale Tate had imagined.

Barrett met Stephanie the summer they both waited tables at the Boarding House. Barrett didn't think she was pretty right away, but she was friendly and she had a sweet voice. They fell into a predictable routine of closing up the restaurant together after a few postshift drinks; sometimes, they went dancing at the Chicken Box, and sometimes they drove to the beach. He kissed her for the first time at Henry's sandwich shop. It was morning, and they were headed out to Great Point with a cooler full of beer. At the counter, Stephanie ordered roast beef with horseradish mayonnaise and cucumber, and Barrett kissed her because that was the exact sandwich he was about to order for himself.

They dated for three years. Steph finished up her nursing degree at Simmons College in Boston. Her job waiting tables turned into a job in labor and delivery at the Nantucket Cottage Hospital. Barrett asked his parents for a loan and he bought the house in Tom Nevers, which at the time was just a shell abandoned by another builder, so he got it for a steal and was able to finish it up the way he wanted. Steph moved in with him, and their crazy life settled down. She had a real job; he had a mortgage payment. They got married, and he took over his father's business.

"Things moved along," he said. "All of a sudden, I was an adult. I was married, I owned a house, I was running a business. I had to be serious. I was twenty-six years old, and I can tell you, I didn't want to be serious. I wanted my old life back—the drinking, the smoking, the dancing until two in the morning, then sitting in the hot tub until the birdsong started. But Stephanie threw away my weed, and she decided that every Saturday night we'd have date night. I wanted date night every night, as well as two nights to go fishing and Sundays to golf. Stephanie worked in labor and delivery; all she wanted was a baby. I didn't want a baby. I *was* a baby! Stephanie went off the pill without telling me, and man, was I pissed when she told me she was pregnant. I left the island; I drove all the way down to Baltimore to see this friend of mine who had a job with the Orioles. We went to three ball games, ate a bushel of blue crabs, went to Hammerjacks to see a heavy metal band. It sucked; I was lonely. I went home.

"So then Cameron was born, and life changed even more, and all of a sudden I'm longing for the days when my only obligation was date night. Because having a child was tough on us. Steph was still working, and the baby was at day care and he was constantly catching something from the other kids, and I would have to stay home or Steph would, or we'd ask my mother to take him. And then, just as soon as he was older—walking, talking a little bit, solidly sleeping through the night—and things were a little bit easier, wham! Steph gets pregnant again. And whereas you're happy because you now know how great it is to have a kid, there is also this feeling of, *What the hell are we doing?* I felt buried. The business was doing fine, but it wasn't making us rich. I started having problems breathing, I couldn't suck air into my lungs or push it out. I went to the hospital for chest X-rays. I was convinced that one of the houses I worked on contained asbestos; Steph thought I had been out smoking dope. What did the doctors tell me? It was stress. So then it was like I got a doctor's note to go out and have fun. I joined the darts league at the Chicken Box; I was out every Tuesday and Thursday drinking beer with the guys I went to high school with. Steph didn't like it one bit; she had a little bit of the pregnant-woman paranoia going, where she thought maybe I was seeing someone else."

"Were you?" Tate asked.

"Nope," Barrett said. He paused, licked his lips. "There were months when we fought all the time, where we couldn't stand the sight of each other, and when she called my cell phone, I wouldn't answer. And then, when she was seven months pregnant, she dropped her coffee cup."

"Dropped her coffee cup?" Tate said.

"I don't want to talk anymore," Barrett said, burrowing his head into Tate's side.

He revisited the dropped coffee cup a few days later without provocation, and Tate was grateful. She didn't want to push, but she wanted to know. She felt like she was watching a movie and she knew something really bad was going to happen and then, at the critical moment when she was bracing herself, the reel broke and the screen went blank. Tate was caught up in a sense of sickening dread. *Just tell me!* If he could give her the nightmare stuff, then she could be his happy ending.

"She dropped the coffee cup and it smashed against the floor," he said. "And I thought she threw it out of anger, because that was where we were with each other. There was a lot of anger and resentment, and a smashed coffee cup wouldn't have been the worst thing that had happened. But Steph said she dropped it accidentally. She said her hand had stopped working."

This seemed odd, he said, but they ignored it. Steph's hands were numb, and then her feet. She had problems walking in a straight line; she weaved like a drunk. Her handwriting deteriorated because her fingers didn't work right. It was strange. She thought it was a symptom of the pregnancy; some women got acute carpal tunnel while carrying. It had something to do with the way the baby was positioned. When Steph mentioned the symptoms to her obstetrician—and added the fact that she kept biting her tongue—he suggested she fly to Boston for some tests. At first, Stephanie declined. They didn't have the money to go to Boston, she wasn't sure her medical insurance would cover the tests, she couldn't miss work. But the symptoms got worse, and she said she'd go. She went alone. Barrett had to work and pick up Cameron at day care.

"I should have gone," Barrett said. "But honestly? I wasn't that worried."

Stephanie was diagnosed with ALS, Lou Gehrig's disease, which was always fatal, though no one knew how quickly the disease would progress.

Always fatal.

Here, Barrett tried very hard not to cry, but his voice was thick and his lower lip trembled. Tate had seen the very same look on Tucker's face the day before when he fell down in the boat and skinned his knees.

"So we went from being one way to being completely another. She was *going to die.* I had one kid two years old and another kid not even born yet, and Stephanie knew she wasn't going to live to see them grow up. She wasn't sure she would live to see their next birthdays. I don't know if there is anything sadder than a mother who knows she has to leave her babies behind, but if there is, I don't want to see it."

He was crying, oh, God, of course, and Tate was crying, and she thought of Barrett Lee, five years old, sitting on the stern of his father's boat in his orange life preserver. You just didn't know what life was going to hand you. You didn't know what love you would find, what love would be snatched away.

They performed a C-section, Barrett said, got the baby out five weeks early. Tucker was on a respirator for six days, but he was fine. The doctors immediately went to work on Stephanie—drugs, therapies, experimental procedures meant to slow the sclerosis down. But the disease was brutal and aggressive. Tucker was born in February; by May, Steph was in a wheelchair. Cameron would ride his tricycle, and Barrett would push Tucker in his carriage with one hand and Steph's wheelchair with the other hand. They would go up the street, then down the street; it was the happiest they were during that time, but Barrett said he couldn't stand to think about it.

Steph lost the ability to speak, and she could no longer write. Still, she used a kind of sign language. A fist to the heart meant "I love you." Cameron still held his hand to his heart every time he and Barrett parted, and Barrett hoped he always would.

"The worst thing was that Steph had lucid thoughts. Intellectually, she was fully functional, the doctors said, but she had lost the ability to communicate. She was trapped in this failing body. And I just worry that she didn't get everything out. There were so many things she wanted to say—to me, to the kids." He looked at Tate. "I don't know how to raise them."

"Of course you do," Tate said.

"There were times after Steph died—like when Cameron got the chicken pox—when I would think, *You didn't tell me how to deal with this. Where* are *you?*"

Steph died in November, at home, thanks to a full-time nursing staff that Barrett borrowed a large sum of money to pay for. Stephanie had been bedridden since September and on a feeding tube since October. Barrett would bring the kids in to her and he would read stories aloud to all of them. Only funny stories. Happy stories.

"And then she died. Early in the morning, while I was

watching her. She looked at me and I could see her trying to move her arm, and the next second her eyes closed, and she was gone. And in a way I was relieved because I didn't have to be strong anymore. I cried every day for twelve months. I cried with the kids and I cried alone. I thought back on all the arguments we'd had and how angry we'd been, and I felt ashamed. But at the time those things were happening, they seemed unavoidable. We were young parents with young kids and no money and even less time. I always knew we were in a phase of our lives that would pass. I believed things would get easier and we would grow older and wiser and we would have our chance at perfect happiness."

Perfect happiness: Tate knew it was naive of her, but she believed in it. She had, for example, been perfectly happy on the beach when the kids came to Tuckernuck for the bonfire. Sitting on the cold sand, intertwined with Barrett, Tucker asleep across their laps, with the fire and her mother and India sitting bundled in blankets, and Chess throwing rocks into the water with Cameron, and the full moon and the stars above, Tate had thought: *Stop time. I want to stay right here.*

Once Barrett had finished the story, Tate lay beside him, humbled. She wasn't worthy of him. She hadn't survived what he had survived. She hadn't survived anything. Her life had been bloodless. Maybe that made her the ideal partner for him. She was whole and strong and unscarred; she could be a pillar for him, if he would let her.

Perfect happiness existed, but perhaps only in small increments. Because not two days later, Birdie—Tate's darling, beloved mother—spoke the words that drove a stake through Tate's heart. She called Tate and Barrett's relationship a "fantasy"; she called it "make-believe."

Tate was deeply hurt, and she was angry. She fled from her mother's words, and even though Birdie came up to the attic to apologize, she didn't take back what she had said. Tate wondered: *Was* her relationship with Barrett a fantasy? *Was* it make-believe? Why? Because it was summertime? Because she was supposed to return to her condo in Charlotte? Or was it something else? If Tate was in a relationship, it must not be serious. She was, in Birdie's words, "as naive as a child." Only Chess's relationships were to be taken seriously, such as her relationship with Michael Morgan. That relationship had been taken seriously—because they lived in New York City, because Michael Morgan owned his own business and wore a suit to work—and look what had happened there. Tate didn't know why Birdie would have said what she said, but Tate didn't dare probe deeper. She couldn't bear to hear Birdie say that Barrett wasn't good enough for Tate or that he was unsuitable because he hadn't been to college, or because he worked with his hands, or because he was a native islander and was therefore somehow a lesser person than Tate, who had been born and raised in New Canaan.

Everyone else was jealous, Tate decided. Her mother, her sister, India—and India was the only one who might admit it.

Tate decided that the three of them could go suck eggs (she was sad that she even had to think this about her mother). She would spend more time on Nantucket with Barrett and the kids.

When Barrett pulled up in his boat for his usual late-afternoon stop, Tate was waiting on the beach with her overnight bag packed.

"What's this?" he said.

"I'm coming with you."

His face registered a look she hadn't seen before (she had been cataloging all of his expressions): it was discomfort, unease, fear. Immediately, Tate felt like a fool. He had asked her four times in the past seven days to spend the night with him on Nantucket, and three of the four times she'd declined because she felt she should be with her family. Now here she was, ready to go, and he didn't want her.

"I'm not coming with you?" she said.

He shook his head. "I'm sorry," he said. "I had no idea you were planning—"

"I wasn't *planning,*" she said. "It was a spontaneous decision."

"I like spontaneous," he said. She knew this; he had told her this. "But there's something I have to do tonight."

"What?" she asked, though it was none of her business.

"Something for work," he said.

"That's awfully vague," she said. But he didn't elaborate. Instead, he did his job: he carried two bags of groceries and a bag of ice up to the house. There was an envelope in his hand. "What's the envelope?" Tate asked.

He said, "Boy, you are just full of questions today."

Tate didn't like the way he said this. They were lovers, right? They had made love and slept in each other's arms; they had told each other intimate things. She should be able to ask him anything and get a straight answer. But here he was, making her feel the way she'd felt most of her life: like a pesky ten-year-old boy. And to make matters worse, she had to follow him up the stairs with her overnight bag, which she would now have to unpack. Birdie, India, and Chess were all watching from their usual spots on the beach, and they would all guess what was happening.

Humiliating.

She trudged up the stairs behind Barrett, hating him, hating herself, hating her anger and her hurt. It could have been exactly the opposite: he could have been thrilled she was coming, and she could be waiting smugly in Barrett's boat while he made the delivery. Birdie and Chess and India would see this was *not* a fantasy, not a figment of Tate's goddamned imagination: it was real, they were in love, and Tate was going to Nantucket to spend the night.

Love was awful. It was unfair.

Tate stormed into the house behind Barrett and blew past him up the stairs. "Have fun tonight," she said. "Whatever you're doing."

He said, "The envelope is a letter for your aunt."

"I don't give a shit about the envelope," she said. She turned on the second floor and stomped up to the attic, where she threw her overnight bag willy-nilly into the air and it landed with a splat that she hoped Barrett heard. She threw herself facedown onto her bed. He would come up after her, right? This was their first fight. Certainly he would come up. She waited. She couldn't hear anything, and because there was only the one inaccessible window, she couldn't see anything.

What seemed like a long time later, she heard footsteps on the stairs and held her breath in anticipation.

Chess said, "Are you okay?"

Tate looked up. Her heart spluttered like a dying motor. Chess? No! "Where's Barrett?" she asked.

"He left."

"He left?"

Chess sat on the edge of Tate's bed. She looked concerned in a very annoying, older-sisterish kind of way. "Do you want to talk about it?"

The irony wasn't lost on Tate: Chess asking *her* if *she* wanted to talk about it. Ha! This was too good.

"No," Tate said. "God, no."

* * *

For the first time since they'd been on Tuckernuck, Barrett Lee didn't show up in the morning. At first, Tate didn't believe it. She ran as usual, she did her sit-ups from the tree branch as usual, she ate the breakfast that Birdie had prepared as usual—and the whole time her stomach was churning with nerves about the moment that Barrett arrived. Would he apologize? Should she?

Tate checked her running watch: 9:15, 9:29, 10:07, 10:35. At eleven o'clock, Tate took her running watch off and threw it into the living room, where it skittered under the lobster-trap coffee table like a mouse. It was pretty clear Barrett wasn't coming.

Birdie said, "I wonder what happened to Barrett. This isn't like him."

"Maybe one of the kids is sick," India suggested.

"That must be it," Birdie said. "Good thing we haven't run out of anything. Well, we only have one egg left. And I do like to read the newspaper in the morning."

Tate didn't comment. She doubted one of the kids was sick, and when they did get sick, Barrett's mother took care of them. So Barrett hadn't come...because of her? Because the unthinkable had happened and he didn't want to see her anymore?

He finally showed up at four o'clock. Tate heard the boat's motor; she had been listening for it so intently for so many hours that when it finally materialized, far away at first and then nearer and nearer, Tate feared it might be a figment of her imagination. She turned her head ever so slightly from its position on her towel and opened one eye. His boat. And—holy expletive expletive expletive—she couldn't believe it. He had a woman with him in the boat. Anita Fullin.

Tate closed her eyes. Her heart was slamming in her chest. He'd brought Anita Fullin.

Birdie said, "Who is that woman?"

India said, "She's very attractive."

Birdie said, "Oh, look, Barrett brought flowers again, Tate."

Please be quiet, Mother, she thought. She tried to put herself in a Zen state—for Tate, this was most easily achieved when she was in front of a computer screen—but she couldn't keep herself from listening to Barrett help Anita down off the boat, and Anita saying, *Honestly, those flowers are exquisite. Someone is very lucky!* And Barrett saying, *You wade on in. I've got to get these bags.*

Tate didn't move, didn't turn, didn't look. She heard Birdie get up from her chair.

"Hello, hello!" Birdie said in her meant-for-company voice.

"Hello!" Anita Fullin said. She had reached the beach; Tate could tell by the proximity of her voice. "My, what a wonderful property you have! I hope you don't mind my intruding, but I told Barrett I just *had* to see Tuckernuck. And he talks so much about your family, I feel like I know you."

Birdie clucked and cooed and Tate felt herself heating up. Her mother was *such* a pushover. "How about that! Well, I must say, it's nice to have a visitor. We're getting awfully used to one another around here. I'm Birdie Cousins."

"Anita Fullin."

"And this is my sister, India Bishop."

"Hello," India said. "Nice to meet you."

"And this is my daughter Tate. Tate!"

Tate wondered if she could continue with the charade of being asleep. Chess, lucky bitch, was actually asleep up at the house. Slowly, Tate rolled over. She lifted her head and had to go to the trouble of seeming surprised to find Anita Fullin on her beach.

"Hello." Tate now understood why Adeliza Coffin stood on her front step with a shotgun. "What are *you* doing here?"

The question was rude, Birdie would be positively *verklempt* about Tate's lack of manners, but Anita Fullin just laughed her deep, dusky storm cloud of a laugh and said, "I finally convinced Barrett to bring me over."

They all watched Barrett wading to shore holding a bag of groceries (Tate could see the newspaper and a carton of eggs peeking out from the top) and a massive bouquet of flowers. The flowers were grandiose, bordering on tacky; they were wrapped in plastic and tied up with a wide red and gold ribbon. The flowers weren't going to work this time, Tate decided. She wasn't a pushover like her mother. She wanted an apology and a good explanation for all of this. Although really, bringing Anita Fullin to Tuckernuck was unforgivable.

Birdie said, "Those are beautiful flowers."

Barrett said, "They're for you."

"For me?" Birdie said.

For Birdie? Tate thought. She was glad she was wearing her sunglasses, so that no one would see her eyeballs turning to little molten balls of hellfire. Tate watched as Birdie carefully opened the cellophane and plucked out the card. She needed glasses to read and so she borrowed India's glasses. Tate realized the flowers must be from the boyfriend, Hank, and she felt a second of pure, generous happiness for her mother before returning to self-pity. Nothing was fair.

Birdie said, "My law, they're from Grant."

"Dad?" Tate said.

"Grant?" India said.

"They're from Grant," Birdie said. She passed back India's reading glasses, and her cheeks took on a flush. "Well, he shouldn't have, but they're beautiful."

Barrett said, "I'll carry them up for you and put them in water. Is it okay if I take Anita on a tour of the house?"

"Certainly," Birdie said. "I'll come along. Tate, will you come?"

"Chess is asleep up there, you know," Tate said.

"I don't want to disturb anyone," Anita said.

"Don't be silly," Birdie said. "If Chess wakes up, she wakes up. She should wake up. She's been sleeping far too much."

"Well, that's kind of the point," Tate said. "I mean, she came here to rest." The world had now completely flipped upside down: her father had sent her mother flowers and Tate was defending Chess. Since there was nothing left to lose, Tate followed her mother and Barrett and Anita Fullin up the stairs and across the bluff to the house.

Chess was awake. She sat bleary eyed at the picnic table with a glass of iced tea. Tate tried to see her as Anita Fullin would see her. Chess seemed smaller than she ever had before. She wasn't wearing her blue crocheted cap and so her head, covered with blond stubble, was exposed. Despite all the time on the beach, she didn't have any color. Her face was pinched and her lips were chapped. She was wearing her dirty Diplomatic Immunity T-shirt and army-surplus shorts. Tate shook her head. She found herself longing to brag about her sister—food editor at *Glamorous Home,* the youngest editor for any Diamond Group publication—but the picture Chess was presenting now was not impressive, and in fact, Anita Fullin didn't even seem to notice Chess and might have walked right by her if Barrett hadn't stopped and said, "And this is the other lady of the house, Chess Cousins."

"Nice to meet you, Jess," Anita said.

Chess didn't bother correcting her, which either showed how little Anita Fullin mattered to Chess or how shocked she was to find this interloper here with Barrett.

She looked at Tate in alarm and confusion, and for the first time since they had climbed into their mother's Mercedes nineteen days earlier, Tate felt a connection with her sister. She raised her eyebrows at Chess and thought, *Oh, yeah, we're going to talk about this.*

Barrett said, "So this is the Tate house, built in 1935 by Birdie and India's grandparents, Arthur and Emilie Tate."

"Nineteen thirty-five?" Anita said. "My word! How did people get here in 1935?"

"By boat," Barrett said, and Tate, despite herself, smiled. "Back in the day, Tuckernuck had a schoolhouse. The people who lived here year-round were fishermen, or farmers."

"But not in our day," Birdie said. "In our day, it was just like this: privately owned by summer residents."

"You're quite the historian, Barrett," Tate said.

He looked at her for one quick second to see if she was being funny or mean, but she wasn't sure herself.

"This is the kitchen," he said. "There's a generator that provides running water, cold only, and the ladies have a half fridge that doesn't get very cold, I'm afraid. And a cooler of ice that I keep replenished. They cook on that camp stove there, or they grill."

"A camp stove!" Anita Fullin said. She was wearing a white T-shirt and bright orange Lilly Pulitzer pedal pushers and white thong sandals. Her toenails were painted tangerine. Orange was now a color that Tate officially detested.

"This is the living room," Barrett said.

"It's so charming," Anita said. "It's so *bare bones.*"

Barrett checked with Birdie. "Okay if I take Anita upstairs?"

"Oh, yes!" Birdie said, but she didn't look up. She was too busy arranging her flowers. There were too many flowers to fit in one vase, or even two, so she was divvying them up among old mason jars. The whole first floor smelled like a hothouse.

Barrett and Anita marched up the stairs, and Tate followed. "Two bedrooms," Barrett said. He swung the door open to Birdie's bedroom: twin beds, tightly made up with the prim yellow sheets, and chenille bedspreads, suitable for a convent. "And one bathroom."

"Does the toilet flush?" Anita asked. "Does the bathtub work?"

"Yes," Tate and Barrett answered at the same time.

"Cold water only in the tub," Barrett said.

Anita looked at Tate. "Honestly, I don't know how you do it. I have this fantasy about building a house over here, but the truth is, I probably couldn't handle it."

Tate thought, *You're probably right.*

Barrett swung open the door to India's bedroom. The squishy mattress was sliding off the box spring like icing off a cake. The bedclothes were disheveled and the room smelled like black lung. If Barrett and Anita didn't feel shameful at peering at India's private chamber, Tate did. Birdie's room was neat and tidy as a Holiday Inn, but viewing India's lair was voyeuristic. Unfortunately, Anita's gaze caught on Roger, who was manning his post by the bureau lamp.

"Look at that sculpture!" Anita said. "It is the most fabulous thing I have ever, ever seen. Who did it?"

Barrett was quiet. Tate hoped he was abashed at having brought Anita Fullin into their house and allowing her to observe them like they were a circus sideshow.

"My uncle," Tate said. And then, because pride got the best of her, she said, "Bill Bishop."

Anita Fullin gasped. "Bill Bishop is your *uncle?*"

"He was," Tate said. "He died."

"Of course," Anita said. "I know the story. I *thought* that looked like a Bishop, but then I thought, no way. It's too small... but there's something so *distinctive* about it." She smiled at Tate. "I have to say, I'm a bit of a fan. There was a Bishop outside our first apartment building in New York. Of the woman walking the dog. But so abstract. So *signature.* I felt like it was my sculpture, it spoke to me, and then we moved to the West Side, and I hardly ever saw it again, but when I did, I used to call out to her. Like she was a friend of mine."

Tate nodded. People felt that way about Uncle Bill's work. It was big and industrial and civic, but it was personal.

Before Tate knew what was happening, Anita Fullin pulled out her iPhone and took a picture of Roger.

Tate said, "Oh..."

Barrett said, "Anita..."

Anita said, "I hope that's okay. It's just for me, so I can remember this little guy. What's his name?"

"Roger," Tate said. Then she felt like she'd betrayed a confidence.

Anita slid the phone back into her pocket. "I'd like to buy Roger," she said.

"He's not for sale."

"I'll give you fifty thousand dollars."

"You can ask my aunt, but she'll tell you he's not for sale."

Barrett looked squeamish. He said, "Anita, would you like to see the attic?"

"The attic?" Anita wrinkled her nose. "Are there more Bishops hiding up there?"

"No," Tate said.

"Then no, I don't think so," Anita said.

Tate was offended. To her, the attic was the best part of the house, but only because it was her part. What would it seem to Anita Fullin but a hot, square room filled with beds and shadowy corners? Plus, Tate wanted Anita Fullin out of the house, off their property, off their island. Tuckernuck was unspoiled paradise primarily because there were no *people* to ruin it.

They descended to the first floor, where the flowers had been set around the house. Birdie, India, and Chess sat at the picnic table, waiting. They hadn't opened wine. Tate was relieved. If there was wine, they would have to offer Anita Fullin a glass. As it was, Anita could just go.

But she stopped at the table. Her eyes flicked between Birdie and India as if trying to figure out which one would be Bill Bishop's widow.

Anita said, "Your house is so authentic. It's redolent of summers well lived."

Birdie nodded. "Thank you. We're very happy here."

Chess rubbed at her tiny red eyes, the picture of happy.

Anita Fullin said, looking at India, "I noticed the sculpture upstairs. The little man?"

"Oh," India said, clearly taken off-guard. "Roger?"

"Yes," Anita said. "Roger." She said his name with such affection and reverence, he might have been a friend of hers. "I'd like to talk to you about Roger sometime."

India's eyes widened.

"But not right now," Anita said. "I can see you're busy."

Busy? thought Tate.

"And Barrett has to get me back to the big island," Anita said. "It was lovely meeting all of you."

"Good-bye," Birdie said.

"Good-bye," India said.

Good-bye, so long, thanks for coming! Tate was the most vocal of the four of them in bidding Anita Fullin adieu, and yet as she watched Barrett and Anita Fullin stroll toward the beach stairs, she couldn't believe she was letting Barrett slip away. She wanted to call him back, demand a private audience; she wanted to know exactly what was going on. Why had he rebuffed her the night before, and why had he not shown up this morning? What was the deal with Anita Fullin? Tate had thought she and Barrett were falling in love.

Had she been dreaming?

INDIA

She hadn't responded to Lula's letter. She couldn't afford to put anything in writing; Lula might hold it up as some kind of *evidence*. India was thinking as though a crime had been committed, and she was forced to reassure herself. There had been feelings, yes; there had been innuendo, yes; but India hadn't taken action, she hadn't crossed any boundaries. She hadn't transgressed. She couldn't be held accountable for wrongdoing, disciplined for wrongdoing, or, God forbid, fired for any wrongdoing. India had been careful. She had backed away from the fire at the final moment.

She didn't answer the letter.

What could she possibly say?

In response to India's silence came another letter. India saw the letter lying on the dining room table, left there by Barrett, and her breath quickened. Blood flooded her face. This reaction in and of itself told India there was *something* between her and Tallulah Simpson beyond the usual collegial relationship. But what was it between them? Jealousy? Sexual tension? Love?

India wanted to rip the envelope open, but instead she saved it for a quiet moment in her bedroom. India had a glass of wine and a cigarette; Birdie was downstairs fixing dinner. The window of India's bedroom was open; a breeze lifted the strands of Roger's seaweed hair.

Carefully, she slit the end of the envelope with her fingernail. She opened the letter, read the one line. Shut her eyes.

What do I have to do?

The nineties had not been kind to Bill Bishop. There was a sense in which he had fallen out of fashion and out of grace. It was a slow, almost imperceptible decline, which had begun back in 1985 with that piss-poor review of the sculpture in New Orleans. Bill's sculptures were copper and glass, blocky, abstract, funky but industrial. They were part of an era that included pin-striped suits, Wall Street moguls, Ronald Reagan, three-martini lunches. Bill knew nothing of the computer or the Internet; he didn't give a shit about the environment. And so he found his work becoming stodgy and outdated. Someone from the Art Institute of Chicago approached Bill about a retrospective pulled together for the year 1996 to mark the twenty-fifth anniversary of his first installation—which had been there, on Navy Pier.

A retrospective? Bill said. *That means you're dead, washed up. It's like a greatest-hits album. It means there isn't any new work, or the new work is irrelevant.*

Problems with his work tended to drive Bill's depression. Bill the sculptor and Bill the person were hard to separate from each other. And yet, India didn't wholly blame Bill's rapidly deteriorating mental state on his declining popularity. She was pretty sure he would have broken down even if work had been booming. His depression was chemical, she believed, and not situational. In the nineties, the boys were teenagers. The testosterone level in the house was high; they all lived in a fug of aggression and sexual drive. The four males were jockeying for position. Billy and Teddy battled nearly every day; there were fistfights, black eyes, bloody noses. India couldn't deal with it; she handed it over to Bill, which was a mistake, because Bill's anger was more formidable than ten Billys or twenty Teddys. He led by very poor example—screaming and yelling and throwing things against the wall, ripping up their homework, handing them coat hangers and saying, "You want to kill each other? Go ahead and kill each other."

India put Band-Aids on the cuts and ice packs on the bruises; she made pots of spaghetti and meatballs to feed the voracious appetites; she played classical music and took baths and read Jane Austen novels and refused to get involved. She could see the whole thing headed for disaster, but she followed a policy of nonintervention. *Why?* she wondered now. Anyone in the world could see that Bill was sick, that he needed a shrink and meds, and that the whole family needed counseling. What was keeping India from getting help? It was the Main Line, things were genteel and lovely—dogwoods flowering and croquet on close-cut lawns—but despite appearances, India knew other families who had hit rough patches. She could easily have found support. Was it inertia? Eternal optimism? Fear? Looking back, India believed that what she was suffering from in those days was apathy. She didn't care enough to step in. She wasn't motivated to save her husband. Was this possible? India had loved Bill with ridiculous ardor. He was her sun, her first thought in the morning, her last at night. But it was safe to say that by 1993 or 1994, she was worn down. The kids were giant, alien creatures who drank milk straight from the container and masturbated all over the sheets without bothering to hide it or clean it up; they watched horror movies and played lacrosse and fielded long, secret phone calls from girls they met while prowling the punk shops on South Street. And rather than get caught up in the who, where, when, how, and why, India took a step back.

In the fall of 1994, Bill had an affair with Teddy's math teacher, Adrienne Devine. From practically the beginning of the school year, Teddy had been failing trigonometry. The notices came home, and India addressed them with Teddy. Teddy said trig was stupid, it was nothing he would ever need to know, he had tried to drop the class but was told he needed it to graduate. India pointed out that not only did he need it to graduate but if he wanted to go to a good college, then he needed to get a decent grade, an A or a B.

He claimed he couldn't do it. India passed the buck to Bill.

You handle this, she said. Personally, she agreed with Teddy: trigonometry was stupid and useless.

Bill went in to meet the math teacher, Adrienne Devine, a hundred-pound, dark-haired twenty-four-year-old beauty, right out of the graduate teaching program at Columbia. When Bill came home and India asked how it went, Bill said, "I can't believe they have someone like her teaching those boys."

India didn't ask what Bill meant by this; she assumed the problem was dealt with, and indeed, Teddy's marks in math improved.

The affair, as it was later explained to India, started shortly after the parent-teacher conference, with Bill calling Adrienne Devine at home and telling her he would like to come to her apartment to make love to her.

Adrienne Devine, without hesitation, said yes. There had been a spark between them at the conference. She was intrigued by the fact that Bill was a sculptor.

(Intrigued by the fact that Bill was a sculptor? Surely she could do better than that? But no. She was so young, she didn't know any of his work.)

The affair continued, as many afternoons as they could manage, through the fall, through the holidays, into the new year.

Bill told India about the affair in January during a trip to Sweden. The City of Stockholm had offered Bill a commission for a series of pieces. It was the largest and most lucrative commission Bill had received in years. India knew he was bothered by the fact that from now on, most of his new work would be installed overseas, but that was how it was shaking out. His popularity was waning at home; he should have been grateful it was burgeoning in nations like Dubai and Thailand and Sweden, where having a Bill Bishop was considered a sign of American prestige (albeit one that Americans would find outdated—like a gold Rolex or a Cadillac).

On that trip to Sweden, Bill should have been energized and driven, but instead he seemed listless and sad. India asked him, innocently, what was wrong, and he told her about the affair.

India took the news quietly at first. She was curious about the details, and Bill was happy to provide them, though they weren't interesting because Adrienne Devine wasn't interesting—she was a twenty-four-year-old math teacher. The affair was about youth and sex; it was about anger against India and anger against Teddy. Bill was showing Teddy who was boss by screwing his math teacher. Were men really so stupid and shallow? India supposed they were. India realized that although she loved Bill, she had lost respect for him. It had been happening for years.

Indeed, the most upsetting thing about the affair was that Teddy hadn't learned any math; Adrienne Devine was giving him passing grades because of Bill.

Clearly, Bill expected a bigger reaction from his wife, and not getting a big reaction—or any reaction at all, really—embittered him. What could India say? She wasn't surprised. When she married Bill Bishop, she had expected that he would have affairs. He was a man with enormous appetites. That he had not had affairs before this was something that pleasantly surprised her. That he was having an affair now only made him predictable. She told him as much as they waited on the subway platform. He slapped her. She stared at him, and the Swedes stared at him, though no one intervened.

She whispered, "You're a coward, Bill." And she walked away.

She found her own hotel room for that night, and when she returned to their original hotel the next day, she found Bill in bed, naked, drunk, weeping. She realized, when she walked into the room, that this was exactly what she had expected.

In October, when Bill went to Bangkok to discuss a commission for the king of Thailand's summer palace, India stayed home. The affair with the math teacher had ended months before, but the aftereffects were toxic. The marriage was a shambles; India had basically moved into the guest room, her "sanctuary," and Bill often slept in his studio, and their bed became a surface where they stacked laundry and books and magazines and newspapers. They had gone to Tuckernuck that summer and they had been happy in the way that they were always happy on Tuckernuck—but when they returned to Pennsylvania, it was as if a storm cloud settled over their house. In September, Billy left for Princeton, and while

India missed him, having him out of the house was a relief. Teddy and Ethan were both playing football, and they got home so whupped and exhausted they didn't have the energy to beat up on each other. The house was eerily quiet. There was no conversation.

When Bill told India about the Thai commission, she was happy for him, but she said she would not go along. He begged her please; he wasn't doing well. Right, she knew he wasn't doing well. He had gained twenty pounds, he wasn't exercising, he was drinking too much. He had missed all of the football games without so much as an apology to the kids. India knew it was time for an ultimatum. Either he went to a shrink, or she was moving out. She needed to do something to galvanize the man, make him snap out of his funk, respond, act like a human being. But India didn't issue an ultimatum. She let him be. After all, she wasn't depressed. She had friends and lunches, and the boys to look after; she had her me-myself time, and plenty of personal space. She would not go to Bangkok because, quite simply, she didn't want to. She was sick and tired of being Bill Bishop's wife; she couldn't stomach a week in a hotel room alone with Bill; she couldn't stand to be that close to his mood swings. She was looking forward to Bill being gone. She was throwing a catered dinner for twelve women friends one night, and on a different night she was hosting a bonfire and pig roast for the entire Malvern Prep football team. India was looking forward to both events and the serene evenings that would surround them. She was looking forward to living in her house without fearing Bill, stalking the premises like a tiger.

He came into the guest room the night before he was to leave. It was late; India was asleep. She was frightened when she opened her eyes and saw his form looming over her like an intruder.

She said, "Bill?"

He didn't speak.

She said, "Bill, what's wrong?"

He climbed into bed with her and took her from behind. India and Bill had made love only a few times since returning from Tuckernuck, and a couple of those times, Bill had suffered from impotence. India remembered the sex that night as being thrilling in a twisted way; it had felt like sex with a stranger. She had lain in bed afterward, breathless and sweating, thinking, *My God.*

Bill, however, had started weeping. For such a big, powerful man, he cried like a child.

She said, "What's wrong?"

He said, "Come to Bangkok with me, please, India. I'm not going to make it on my own."

She shushed him, cradled his head, stroked his mane of hair. "You'll be fine," she said. "Just fine." She didn't voice any other thoughts—for example, that it would be good for them to have some time apart—because she didn't want to patronize him. She felt sorry for him, but she couldn't wait for him to go.

She took him to the airport. She waited with him at the gate. She kissed him good-bye as they used to kiss good-bye when they were younger—slowly, with tongue. He didn't seem to want to separate. She had to push him away; she remembered giving him a little shove. He handed the flight attendant his ticket; he disappeared into the mouth of the Jetway.

She remembered feeling free.

He waited until the final day. Quite possibly—India had to take this into account—it was the prospect of returning home that set him off. His trip, after all, had been a success: He had met the king of Thailand, he'd discussed his sketches with a team of the king's landscape architects and his cultural attaché, he had been paid in full and given the royal treatment—a dinner cruise down the Chao Phraya River on the king's yacht, a private tour of Wat Pho, Wat Arun, and the palace that contained the Emerald Buddha. He had been given a suite at the Oriental Hotel, where so many distinguished men had stayed before him: Kipling, Maugham, Joseph Conrad. Bill had also found time to venture into the underbelly of the Patpong neighborhood, where he found a prostitute and bought a handgun. The prostitute may have been his for the whole week, but the gun he saved for the last day. He paid the girl, dismissed her, and then shot himself in the head.

The butlers stationed outside of his suite heard the noise and knocked for entrance. They knocked and knocked and knocked, then entered with their own key.

A secretary of the king's called India at home. It was three o'clock in the morning. The catered dinner party for twelve women had ended only a couple of hours earlier. It had been a tremendous success, one of the most enjoyable evenings of India's life: the food had been delicious, the table had looked beautiful bathed in candlelight and swathed in linen, there had been good music—Carole King, Paul Simon, old Beatles—and too much wine—champagne, Meursault, syrah. The women had departed reluctantly, with hugs, vowing it was the best dinner party they had ever attended. India had cleaned up alone with loud Van Morrison playing. She had finished the wine and smoked cigarettes.

When the phone rang, she knew it was tragedy. She thought maybe one of the boys—both of whom were at sleepovers—had drunk himself into a coma. Or one of the women from the party had lost control of her car and killed herself or someone else. India didn't understand the heavily accented voice on the other line at first, but eventually she got it. She got it: Bill was dead. He'd shot himself.

It had been like falling into a well. Dark, cold, wet, scary, hopeless. Bill was dead. He'd killed himself. India remembered rising from bed, taking a handful of Advil, making a pot of coffee. Calling Birdie in Connecticut and sounding calm. *Bill is dead.* Birdie said she was on her way. She would stay and take care of the boys. India would go to Bangkok.

She didn't remember the flight; she didn't remember the cab from the airport to the hotel or what Bangkok had looked like out the window. She did, ridiculously, remember the outfits the bellmen at the Oriental Hotel wore—blue pantaloons with the crotches hanging down to their knees. Funny hats. Was it embarrassing for them to dress this way? she wondered. No sooner had India stepped from the taxi into the soupy heat than an official from the hotel—a Thai man in a pale beige linen suit—was upon her, bowing to her in the traditional *wai,* taking her hands. She looked at the man and could see that he expected her to cry or fall apart the way Americans did in the movies, and yet all India felt at that moment was contrition. Bill had, after all, killed himself in their fine hotel. It would have been a horrific mess and upsetting to the butlers who found him. (How had they gone home to their families and eaten their evening meal with the memory of Bill's brains splattered all over the plush carpeting?) India was as mortified as she would have been if the boys had thrown a raucous party and broken furniture or put holes in the walls. And beyond these surface concerns was a deeper shame.

The administration of the hotel and the representatives sent to the hotel by the king were somber and sympathetic. They didn't place blame; they didn't wonder what went so horribly wrong. They exuded acceptance, as if somehow they'd expected this might happen. The Thai people hailed Bill as a genius along the lines of Vincent van Gogh and Jackson Pollock, and geniuses were eccentric. Crazy. They cut off their ears; they overdosed; they blew their brains out.

India identified the body. She didn't remember doing this, but she did remember Bill in the casket. He was her charge; she had to get him home. She thought of the body in the casket as "Bill," though he was cargo now, he was luggage. And yet he was dearly familiar. She was a woman traveling home with her husband's corpse. It was surreal, she couldn't believe it was happening, and yet what choice did she have? She couldn't leave him in Thailand.

The boys and Birdie were all at the Philadelphia airport when India and "Bill" landed. The boys looked years younger; they looked like mere children, and they cried easily. Billy was the strongest, ever the leader, and he gathered India up in a hug, and Teddy and Ethan followed suit, and in the middle of Concourse C, the four of them became one rocking, sobbing mass.

Everyone had something in her life that put her strength to the test, and for India, it was Bill's suicide. For Chess, it was Michael Morgan's accident. Birdie had said that Chess "felt responsible," and India certainly knew what that was like. She held herself accountable for Bill's death as surely as if she'd pulled the trigger herself.

He'd left no note. But if he had left a note, what would it have said? *I asked you to come with me. I told you I couldn't do this alone. You should have gotten me help. Wasn't it clear I needed help? How could you forsake me? Why didn't you care? You knew something like this would happen.*

He could have written any one of those things and it would have been true.

India had eventually picked herself up and moved forward—and in rather spectacular fashion. She had, in some ways, made Bill's suicide work for her. She built a career, a persona; she created a self. And goddamn it, she was proud of this.

But she hadn't accounted for love. To love again was beyond her, right? She held Lula's note in her hand. *What do I have to do?*

India responded to this second letter immediately. She was no longer afraid of being caught by the officials at PAFA. She had already been caught by life's circumstances; she had nothing left to fear. *It's not what you have to do. It's what I have to do.*

Forgive herself.

Reconcile this and move on.

There was nothing harder.

CHESS

Day eighteen.

Nick stopped seeing Rhonda. I learned this, not from Nick, but from Rhonda, whom I saw on the elevator two weeks after the night I left Irving Plaza. She was coming home from Fairway, her arms laden with bags of groceries; I saw fennel fronds and artichokes. This was highly unusual for Rhonda: at home, she ate yogurt or Chinese take-out noodles.

I said, "Fennel?"

She said, "I'm cooking tonight for this new guy I'm seeing."

I took a metered breath. "A new guy? You mean Nick?"

She looked at me as if she didn't know who I was talking about. Nick? *Then she said, "Oh! Nick was a flash in the pan. We were together at his show, and then I never heard from him again. He vanished."*

"Vanished?"

"Do you ever hear from him?" she said.

"No," I said. "He and Michael aren't that close."

A few weeks passed. Michael got very sick with the flu, and I played nursemaid. I made him soup, I trekked to the pharmacy for his prescriptions, I did his laundry. I spent seven nights in a row in Michael's apartment, I bought all the groceries, I decorated with flowers.

Michael said, "I want you to move in."

I said, "The fever has made you delirious."

He grabbed me. "I'm serious."

I knew he was serious because that was the direction things were heading in: moving in together, marriage. If I was going to get out, I had to get out now. I studied Michael. He was a handsome man and he was a good man, and in so many ways, he was the right *man. I liked the way he dressed, I liked the way he smelled, we thought the same way, we liked the same things, we were wired the same way. We never fought, and when we disagreed, we did so respectfully. He was the man I had been groomed for. He was my friend. But I was not madly, hopelessly in love with Michael Morgan.*

I said, "Let's talk about it when you feel better."

The next day, I called Nick from work. I had never called Nick before for any reason; he sounded surprised, and wary.

I said, "Tell me to leave him."

"Excuse me?"

"Tell me to leave him."

"Who is this?"

I said, "If you tell me to leave him, I will leave him. Otherwise, I'm going to move in."

There was a long pause. I tried to imagine where he was: on the street, at a bar, in a soundproof recording studio, in his apartment, which I had never seen. I couldn't imagine. I didn't know him the way I knew Michael, and he didn't know me. There were so many parts of my life I feared he wouldn't understand: my love of food, my love of reading and writing, my adoration of creature comforts—taxis instead of the subway, good restaurants, spa treatments, the fifth floor of Bergdorf's. Michael fit in everywhere in my life. But Nick? They had been raised by the same parents, but Nick had been raised by wolves; he had a hunger, and a single-minded devotion to that which was pure and true. He loved music, he loved rock climbing, he loved the sweet high of gambling. There was no balance in his life, only flat-out passion. I wanted to live that way. Could I live that way? I considered myself to be in love with Nick, but was I in love with him or was he just the bad boy I lusted after? I didn't know if what I claimed to want was even real.

He said, "Meet me in the park in twenty minutes."

"That's not going to solve anything," I said. I would kiss him and become intoxicated and stumble away high with desire, but I wouldn't be any closer to an answer. "What are we going to do?" I asked him. "Meet in the park for the rest of our lives?"

"I am obsessed with you," he said.

Hearing him say it, anytime, in any way, knocked the wind out of me.

"But it doesn't matter," he said.

"What?" I said.

"Move in with him," he said.

I decided not *to move in with Michael for reasons that had little to do with Nick. I wanted to keep my own space. The thought of giving up my apartment terrified me. I didn't want to compromise my sense of self. Michael said he understood. He* did *understand; he was emotionally mature and incredibly secure. If keeping my apartment made me happy, he said, then I should keep my apartment.*

I kept my apartment. I tried not to think about Nick. It was pointless! Nick was obsessed with me and I with him, but what was that? It was stupid stuff, kid stuff; it was language borrowed from the movies. Nick was a coward and I was a coward, too. Otherwise I would have broken up with Michael for reasons that had nothing to do with Nick. But I didn't break up with him.

In October, Michael asked me to marry him. In retrospect, I should have seen it coming, and if I had seen it coming, I would have been prepared. It was our one-year anniversary and we were going for dinner to Town with Cy and Evelyn. Dinner was lovely; Cy and Evelyn were charming and fun. I loved them both with an ardor that should have unsettled me, but I didn't plan on losing them. After all, they were Nick's parents, too. After dinner, Michael said he had a surprise and he piled the four of us into a cab. We drove downtown to the Knitting Factory.

He said, "Diplomatic Immunity is playing."

Evelyn squealed with delight; she'd had some wine at dinner. She said, "Oh, goody!"

I was both thrilled and terrified, which was par for the course when we went to one of Nick's shows. Both of these emotions were heightened by the presence of Cy and Evelyn. What would they think if they knew?

We got drinks and muscled our way to the front row, where all of the groupies—most of them not of age—had coagulated. Michael seemed nervous, and I construed this as concern for his parents—not many sixty-year-olds frequented the Knitting Factory—but Cy and Evelyn were as hip and happening as movie stars. They were fine.

When Diplomatic Immunity came out onstage, the crowd went bonkers. Nick had the microphone in one hand, and with his other hand, he motioned for quiet. This was highly unusual; normally, he would have launched into "Been There" or "Kill Me Slow." He waited patiently while a hush came over the audience. Then he said, "This is kind of a special night, and before we get started, I'd like to call my brother, Michael, on stage."

I looked at Nick, not Michael. Nick, for all his rock-star bravado, looked green around the gills, like he was going to vomit, and I wondered if he was on something. Michael, like the natural athlete he was, leaped onto the stage using only one hand, and he took the microphone. There were the two brothers side by side—Michael in his blazer and Robert Graham shirt and Ferragamo loafers, and Nick in the Bar Harbor T-shirt we had brought him back that summer, and jeans, and a pair of black Sambas. Michael was clean shaven and professional looking; he might have been a motivational speaker. Nick slouched. He hadn't liked school the way Michael had, he hadn't been a team player like Michael, he didn't have a killer instinct for doing deals and making money, and his people skills were practically nonexistent. Who walked out on a family dinner? Who canceled on Christmas? Nick was brooding and sullen and gifted and the sexiest man I had ever, ever laid eyes on. The two of them side by side was a lesson for me, and if I had only had more time to study, I might have aced the exam, but everything was moving way too fast for me to catch up. I had no idea what was going on; I thought maybe Michael was going to sing, which would have been a bad idea. Michael couldn't carry a tune.

He said, "I'm going to be quick so that we can get to the real reason you're all here, which is not to see me propose to my girlfriend, but to see Diplomatic Immunity..."

The crowd cheered. I thought, What? *I'd heard him, but I didn't get it.*

Michael said, "I am in love with a woman named Chess Cousins." Here, he pulled a velvet box out of his blazer pocket, opened it up, and showed the audience a whopper of a diamond ring. He said, "Chess, will you marry me?"

The crowd roared. I wanted to look at Nick, but how could I? It would have given it all away. Cy and Evelyn were in my peripheral vision, and I could see Evelyn beaming with happy confidence. Of course she was. Had there ever been a woman who had been proposed to in public who had said no? Maybe there had been, somewhere, but that woman wasn't me. I nodded like an automaton and Michael smiled at me with incredible joy. Yes? *He said, "She said yes!" And he pumped his fist in the air. Nick gave Michael a hug; Nick's eyes were closed. The crowd was cheering. Michael dropped back down into the audience and Nick launched the band into "Okay, Baby, Okay," which he knew was my favorite song and which they usually saved for an encore.*

But it was not okay.

But it was as everyone expected it to be—Michael and I were getting married. That Michael had proposed in such a spectacularly out-of-character fashion baffled me. To put me on the spot in front of all those strangers? He said he wanted to surprise me. I always complained that he was predictable, that I could tell you the next words out of his mouth. He had thought of taking me to Per Se or Blue Hill alone and proposing with dessert, but that would have been what I expected, right?

Right.

Would my answer have been any different if we had been alone, if it had been just him and me and the truth floating somewhere around our heads? Would I have summoned the courage to tell the truth?

* * *

I didn't see Nick for six months. Something had been brewing the night of the Strokes concert: Diplomatic Immunity had found a legitimate agent with the same company that represented the Strokes, Death Cab for Cutie, Kings of Leon, and the Fray. They were going to sign a record deal—the agent loved "Okay, Baby, Okay," my song—but before they cut the album, they were going on tour for six months, opening in various B venues across the country for the Strokes and Kings of Leon.

Michael had been the one to accompany Nick to Port Authority. Nick had one duffel bag, Michael said, containing jeans, T-shirts, and his climbing gear. Michael had given Nick cash, five hundred dollars, and Nick said, "What are you, my father?" But he took it anyway.

Michael had said, "You'd better not fuck it up."

Nick responded, "You'd *better not fuck it up."*

I said, "What do you think Nick meant?"

Michael said, "Hell if I know."

Michael stayed at the station until the bus pulled away; this image haunted me.

I said, "Was it sad?"

Michael said, "Sad?"

It was over. Nick was gone; I was getting married. I couldn't seem to deal with the reality of getting married, however, so I asked Birdie to handle the details of the wedding. I was a little embarrassed about how honored she was to be asked to plan my wedding. I felt like all I had ever presented her with before were crumbs.

While Birdie planned the wedding, I worked hard and I played hard. I began to realize that my days of freedom were coming to an end. I spent more nights than ever in my own apartment; I couldn't bear the thought of letting it go. I asked Michael if it was okay if we kept my apartment after we were married. He laughed at me. I rekindled my friendship with Rhonda, who was, conveniently, between boyfriends. We went out once a week, sometimes twice, sometimes on the weekends. We drank a lot; we barhopped and skipped dinner; we went to clubs and hailed taxis in the breaking dawn. Rhonda was impressed by my endurance and my fire. She said, "You party like a woman who just got divorced, not like one who's about to get married."

I received postcards in the mail. Sometimes they came to my apartment, sometimes to my office. They were from Vancouver, Minneapolis, Boulder. Most of the time the postcards were left blank except for my name and address, but one had a smiley face sticker on it (Santa Fe) and another a drawing of a stick person with a gold foil star where the heart should be (Daytona Beach). The final postcard (Athens, Georgia) said, Yes, I do, *in what I knew to be Nick's handwriting.*

Yes, I do, too, *I thought.*

And then, in April, Nick came back to New York.

If Chess couldn't stand Tate when Tate was happy, she really couldn't stand Tate when Tate was upset. Tate upset was a running monologue that Chess couldn't endure. Barrett hadn't wanted Tate to come to Nantucket overnight. *Even though he begged me to come practically every other day and I turned him down because that's not why I'm here, and then the one time I'm waiting on the beach with my overnight bag, he says he has other plans. "What kind of plans?" I ask him. And he won't tell me. They're "secret" plans. He says, "Boy, you sure are full of questions today."*

Chess could only nod in response. This, to her, was not a real problem. Tate, to her knowledge, had never had a real problem.

Tate said, "I think he's having an affair with Anita Fullin."

Chess said, "What makes you say that?"

Tate said, "All kinds of things."

Chess thought about the word "affair." She thought about infidelity. Had the word applied to her? She had kissed Nick on three occasions, twice quite passionately, but they had not been having an affair. She hadn't slept with Nick except in her mind. She hadn't been "unfaithful" to Michael in the traditional sense. At least she had that.

Tate said, "Anita Fullin loves Barrett. She was all over him at the party. They danced together while I danced with Roman Fullin like some kind of hired escort. She kept calling Barrett 'gorgeous.' She's jealous of us because he comes to Tuckernuck twice a day. She said she hates us."

"Hates us?"

"She said it like she was kidding, but she wasn't kidding."

"Mmmm," Chess said. She had met Anita Fullin and had to agree the woman was beautiful in an older, sleeker, more "done up" kind of way; the hair and clothes and makeup formed a shiny enamel shell. "So you feel threatened?"

"Threatened?" Tate said. "No. Yes."

They were lying side by side on the shore of East Pond, just the two of them. East Pond wasn't as picturesque as North Pond—the sand was grainier, there were some flies, and the water had a marshy smell and moved with suspicious ripples that Chess thought were snapping turtles—but it was closer to the house than North Pond and they had yet to hang out here, which they always did at least once a summer in the name of tradition. The sun was warm and Chess felt herself melting into the sand. That morning, she had woken up with a tug at her heart. Only twelve days left before they would go home. When they had first arrived, the thirty days had seemed like a life sentence. Each of those first days had been so raw and painful, they had dragged—each minute an hour, each hour a day. But now every moment was sacred and fleeting; the sand was slipping through the hourglass way too fast. Tuckernuck had worked its balm into Chess's shoulders. She was able, if not to actually enjoy, then to relax. She hadn't confided a word to anyone, and it hadn't mattered. The house—with its bare sheltering walls, sloping floors, splintery beams, and familiar old furniture—was the haven Chess needed. The simplicity, which had frightened her at first, was now a way of life. Chess didn't have to worry about her cell phone or e-mails or neighbors or taxis or Shakespeare in the Park or where to go and what to do on the weekend. There were no taxes, no dentist, no shops, no dry cleaning, no errands, no obligations. There was nothing but the landscape, the ocean, and the sky. Her sister, her mother, her aunt.

What would happen when she went back? The only thing on the mainland that she wanted was Nick, and he wouldn't have her.

Tate said, "I'll ask him this afternoon if he's having an affair with Anita."

"I wouldn't," Chess said.

"You wouldn't?"

"I wouldn't."

"I can't believe he brought Anita here without asking," Tate said. "That was a professional breach."

"So what," Chess said. "Should we fire him?"

"She probably bugged him until he couldn't stand it anymore," Tate said. "You know she calls him to change the paper towel roll?"

"She does not," Chess said.

"Practically," Tate said.

A fly crept up Chess's thigh; she swatted, then tented

her knees. An airplane flew low overhead, the eight-seater Cessna, owned by a Tuckernuck resident, coming in for a landing. What would happen when she went back? Television, fast food, air-conditioning. She shuddered.

"Where do you think he *went* last night?" Tate asked. "Honestly. Do you think he went out with Anita?"

"Tate!" Chess said. Her voice was loud and aggressive. "Stop it! You have to stop!"

She thought Tate might be apologetic, or even angry, but Tate responded in a flat, calm voice. "I can't stop," Tate said. "This is what I do. I obsess."

Maybe she could stay another month. Maybe she could stay until Labor Day. Of course, she would be staying alone. Would that be okay? She would have to keep Barrett on; she had money in the bank, she could pay him.

"What are you going to do about Barrett when you leave?" Chess asked.

Tate groaned. "One thing at a time, Sister, please."

"Okay, sorry," Chess said.

Tate said, "What am I going to do about Barrett when I *leave?*"

BIRDIE

The flowers Grant had sent were extravagant. There were, in the mix, two dozen long-stemmed roses, a handful of Asiatic lilies, four Dutch blue hydrangeas, a dozen irises, ten fuchsia gerbera daisies, six calla lilies, and sixteen tall snapdragons in four colors. By Birdie's estimation, the bouquet had cost him two hundred dollars, a mere sniffle for Grant, and because of the breadth of variety, Birdie suspected that Grant had called the flower shop on Nantucket and asked for "a little bit of everything." This was business as usual. What was different this time was the message on the card. Grant had sent Birdie flowers dozens of times over the course of their marriage, and the card, written in the florist's assistant's hand, had always said something perfunctory and unimaginative: *Happy 48th birthday!* Or, *With love on our anniversary.* This time there was no occasion for the flowers. This time, the card had said, *I'm thinking about you. Love, Grant.*

I'm thinking about you. It was oddly intimate, more intimate, Birdie decided, than the abbreviated *Thinking of you.* It made Birdie believe that Grant was in fact thinking about her. But what was he thinking? Was he thinking romantic thoughts? (And what, for Grant, would be romantic? Birdie across the table from him at La Grenouille? Birdie coming off the eleventh green in her short golf skirt and visor, lightly perspiring, to join Grant for a Mount Gay and tonic?) Was Grant thinking sexual thoughts? (It was almost too mortifying to imagine, though at one time their sex life had been steady, if not particularly fulfilling.) Were the flowers a condolence, because of what had happened with Hank? Did Grant feel *sorry* for her? Or...was Grant lonely? Yes, Birdie deduced, that was it: Grant was lonely. It had been bound to happen. Work wasn't providing the same kind of visceral, macho thrill, and likewise, golf wasn't as good as it had been in the past. He was getting older and slower, his handicap was climbing. The waitresses at Gallagher's, who at one time had been like his concubines, were either older, lined, and cranky or else too young to realize that scotch was whiskey.

Birdie had come up from the beach early, leaving

India asleep in her chair. The girls had headed out to East Pond, and she missed them. She missed, too, the sense of purpose her afternoons had taken on when she'd been phoning Hank. It had been nice to have her own personal mission. She grabbed her cell phone from her bedroom. She decided she would call Grant to thank him for the flowers. He might be wondering if they'd even arrived.

The walk to Bigelow Point was invigorating, and she noted that she felt less morose and heart-sore than she had when she'd last spoken to Hank. *Hank was a jerk!* This was her battle cry, although she knew it wasn't true. Now that a few days had passed, she was able to look at things more generously. Hank had loved his wife, though he hadn't always been true to her; now that she was dead, guilt haunted him. Birdie could understand that. Losing a spouse under any circumstances was painful and all-consuming, and Hank, perhaps, didn't have the energy to deal with his grief and with his burgeoning feelings for Birdie. They had been a couple for only three months. Birdie would recover. She would meet someone else.

She didn't like to think of Grant lonely. She was protective of him. She marveled at how a spouse became so many things—a parent, a child, a lover, a friend. Grant hadn't been much of a friend to Birdie over the years; he had been too busy with work. Plus, he bonded more easily with men; even he would admit this. Birdie held out hope, however, that she and Grant could be friends in the future. He had been a friend to her since she'd been here on Tuckernuck, that was for sure, fielding her dejected phone calls after she'd called Hank.

When she reached Bigelow Point, she had to decide where to call Grant. At the office? On his cell phone? At the loft? She had no idea what day it was. Her phone said July 19, but was it a weekend? She couldn't remember. Tuckernuck gave no calendrical landmarks. She called Grant's cell phone.

"Hello?" he said. He'd picked up on the first ring. After all the nonsense with Hank, this was gratifying.

"Grant? It's Birdie."

"Hi, Bird," he said. "Did you get the flowers?"

"I did," Birdie said. "And I'm calling to thank you for them. They are beautiful. So lavish! Really, Grant, you shouldn't have."

"I wanted to," he said. "I'm glad you like them."

"The rickety old house smells like a *parfumerie,*" she said.

"How are things going?" Grant asked.

"Oh, you know," Birdie said. "Chess is the same. She's very quiet. She writes in her journal. She stares into space. And Tate has a boyfriend."

"A boyfriend?"

"Barrett Lee. She's dating Barrett Lee."

"Really?" Grant said. "How about that!" He sounded surprised but pleased. Birdie hadn't expected him to sound pleased. "I always liked Barrett."

"That's right," Birdie said. "You did. Of course, it's just a summer thing. I don't see that it has a future..."

"They're adults," Grant said. "They'll work it out."

"I suppose," Birdie said. "But you know how Tate is. She's so...*enthusiastic.* She's madly in love with Barrett and she's become attached to his children..."

"He has children?"

"Two boys, three and five. The wife died two years ago."

"Jesus," Grant said.

"Meanwhile, he and Tate have been dating less than two weeks, and we have less than two weeks left..."

"Birdie," Grant said, "don't get involved."

"Oh, I know, but—"

"Birdie."

"I know," she said.

"Tell me about you," Grant said.

"Me? What about me?"

"How are you doing? Have you talked to that bozo Hank?"

"No," Birdie said. "Hank is out of the picture."

"You're sure?"

"I'm sure."

"Well, good," Grant said.

"How about you?" Birdie asked. "Are you dating anyone?"

"Hell, no," Grant said. "Women are nothing but trouble."

"Right," Birdie said.

"Except for you," Grant said. "I don't mean you."

Birdie felt the sun on her face. What was happening here? She said, "So the card, with the flowers... you composed that yourself?"

"Composed?" he said.

"I mean, those were your words on the card. The girl at the shop didn't help you write it?"

"No, the girl at the shop did not help me write it," Grant said, sounding quasi-offended. "I wrote it myself. I've been thinking about you a lot."

Birdie pressed her lips together. She felt a flash of pleasure and she had to remind herself that it was *Grant* on the other end of the phone, Grant Cousins, the man she shared a bed with and served dinner to for thirty years. The man who had kept her emotionally at bay, who had thwarted her chance at a career and personal fulfillment, the man who made her become just like every other housewife in New Canaan, Connecticut: frustrated and lonely and overly devoted to her children.

Against the tide of these thoughts, she said, "I've been thinking about you, too."

He said, "Will you call me again tomorrow?"

"Yes," she said.

INDIA

She was alone on the beach when Barrett's boat pulled in. She had been asleep in her upright beach chair, her head lolling around on her left shoulder. She had heard herself snoring at the same moment that she heard the boat's motor, and she snapped awake and wiped the drool from her chin. There was nothing attractive about a woman of a certain age taking a nap. Her book, *The Red Tent*—she was only now reading the things that other women had read ten years ago—had fallen off her lap into the sand. She was wearing her sunglasses, and Bill's reading glasses were resting against her bosom.

She waved at Barrett, hoping he hadn't seen the grotesque spectacle of her asleep. He nodded at her; his hands were full. Groceries, ice. The poor kid. He was their slave. Then India remembered that she had something for Barrett: the letter for Lula and twenty dollars to ensure that it was FedExed to her. She was glad she was alone at the beach.

Barrett sloshed to shore. Normally, he headed right up to the house with the provisions, but today he trudged over to India. She dug madly through her bag for the envelope, addressed to Lula's apartment in Philadelphia.

She said, "I'm glad I caught you alone." She handed the envelope to Barrett; he set the ice down on Birdie's empty beach chair and accepted the letter and the twenty-dollar bill. "Will you mail this for me? Overnight it."

He nodded. He set the bag of groceries down in the sand and slid the letter into his front shorts pocket. He said, "I'm glad I caught you alone as well."

Something about his tone arrested India. He sounded like he was going to proposition her. God, was this possible? What about Tate? Having sex with Barrett Lee lived somewhere in India's deep-seated fantasy life, but only as a funny lark. It was a short, pornographic reel she played in her mind to amuse herself and to prove she wasn't *that* old.

"Really?" she said. She was tempted to look at Barrett over the top of her sunglasses in her best imitation of Anne Bancroft, but she declined.

He said, "Yeah. There's something I'd like to talk to you about."

He sounded nervous, which put her immediately at ease. She said, "Shoot."

He took a deep breath. He said, "My client Anita Fullin, who was here the other day?" He sounded like India might not remember Anita Fullin, but she had been the only visitor they'd had since they'd been here. How could India not remember? She nodded.

"She wants to buy the little statue in your bedroom."

"Statue?" India said. "You mean Roger?"

Barrett exhaled. "Yes," he said. "Roger."

"Ah," India said.

"She would like to offer you fifty thousand dollars for it."

"Fifty thousand," India said.

"She's a fan," Barrett said.

"Ah," India said. She didn't know how to respond. Fifty thousand dollars for Roger? She thought back to when she and Bill were first married. Bill had been an art teacher at Conestoga High School. They lived in a condo in Devon, right off 252. At night they'd listen to the rumble of traffic headed to the King of Prussia Mall, and occasionally they could hear a melody or two—Kenny Rogers or Bob Seger—playing at the Valley Forge Music Fair. They hadn't had two nickels to rub together. India's parents had been footing the bill for India to go to graduate school at Penn, but they were disapproving. How did Bill and India ever expect to make a decent living, enough to start a family? Well, India explained, they were counting on Bill's sculpture. He had the one installation on Navy Pier in Chicago, and another small one at Penn's Landing, which he had sold to the city for a fee of $750.

In 1992, when Bill created Roger, his sculptures—full-size civic installations—were going for more than a million dollars. But those took a year to fabricate. Bill had made Roger in one afternoon; Roger was only twelve inches tall. In India's mind, Roger was either worth five dollars or he was priceless.

"Hmmmm," she said. She wished Bill were here. She wished she could send *him* a letter, telling him that funny summer woman from Nantucket was offering India *fifty thousand dollars* for Roger. What would Bill say? She could practically hear him shouting, *Take it!*

But India couldn't take it. She would no sooner sell Roger than she would sell her unborn grandchild. Roger was the personification of her and Bill's happiness on Tuckernuck. She looked at Roger and thought of lying in Bill's arms on the beach-plum-jam-filled mattress. She thought of unbuttoning his pants in the Scout. She thought of Bill piling firewood, collecting shells, identifying shorebirds, checking the wind direction, admiring passing yachts, carrying the boys on his shoulders. She thought about how angry she'd been at Bill: he was perfectly fine on Tuckernuck, and a devastating head case at home. *Why can't we be this happy at home?* she'd screamed on the bluff that long-ago afternoon. *What the hell is wrong with you?* And Bill had said, *You! You're what's wrong with me!* They had been so vocal with their anger, Birdie had come up from the beach to shush them. There were the children to think of, as well as the rest of Tuckernuck. They were screaming so loudly that Birdie was afraid someone from the homeowners' association would hear them and drop off a written warning.

Bill had disappeared down the beach, and later that evening he presented India with Roger—a body made of driftwood, hair of seaweed, eyes of blue beach glass, nose and ears and teeth and toes fashioned from shells.

Roger was his apology.

"She may even be willing to go higher than that," Barrett said. "I know she really wants it."

India smiled. "Roger's not for sale."

"She'd probably go to seventy-five."

India shook her head.

"Really?" Barrett said. He sounded disheartened, like a little boy, and this surprised India. His wife had died. India thought that for this reason, he would understand. "Not for sale?"

"Not for sale," India said.

"And there's nothing I can do? Nothing I can offer you?"

"Nothing you can do," India said. "Nothing you can offer me. I'm sorry."

Barrett gazed out at the water. He looked so distraught that India wavered. She was something of a sucker, more like Birdie than she would care to admit. She would be more tempted to give Roger to Barrett for free just to cheer him up than she would be to sell Roger to a summer woman for seventy-five thousand dollars.

"She put a lot of pressure on me," Barrett said.

"That's perfectly awful," India said. "And again, I'm sorry. Roger has extreme sentimental value. My husband made him for me. I can't sell him."

"No, I get it," Barrett said. "I feel like a jerk for even asking."

"You're not a jerk for asking," India said. "If I had a way to do it, I would explain it to Anita myself."

"She's used to getting everything she wants," Barrett said morosely.

India wondered if Barrett was sleeping with this woman. Was that possible? Of course it *was* possible, but what about Tate?

"Well, this will teach her, won't it?" India said.

Barrett nodded and, without another word, headed up to the house. India hoped he wouldn't forget about her letter.

TATE

She wouldn't lose him. And so, Tate followed Chess's advice and let the whole thing go. She didn't ask Barrett what he had done the night he said he had plans, she didn't accuse him of having an affair with Anita Fullin, and she didn't upbraid him for bringing Anita to Tuckernuck uninvited. She pretended nothing had happened.

And everything was fine, or sort of. Barrett was still at the house when Tate and Chess got back from East Pond. Tate snuck up behind him, put her hands over his eyes, and said, "Guess who?" He turned around and scooped her up and they kissed. Chess pounded right up the stairs with a noise of disgust, but Tate didn't care.

She said, "I missed you."

He said, "Come with me now?"

Tate knew that Chess was cooking dinner for the first time since they'd been here—grilled swordfish with lime and chili, and an avocado sauce. It signified some sort of positive change. Would Chess understand if Tate missed it? She had just spent all afternoon listening to Tate bellyache. She would understand.

Tate said, "Yes. Let me get my bag."

She raced up to the attic. Chess was changing into her Diplomatic Immunity T-shirt and her army-surplus shorts. She hadn't once given the shorts or the T-shirt to Barrett for the laundry; any second now, they were going to get up and walk off on their own.

Tate said, "I'm going with Barrett."

Chess said, "You're missing dinner?"

Tate sat down on the bed and looked at her sister. "I am. I'm sorry. Are you mad?"

Chess shrugged.

Tate wavered. Should she stay? They had only so many days left; Tate was afraid to count exactly how many. Barrett was waiting downstairs. It was only swordfish. But Tate wasn't completely insensitive. It was more than dinner: it was a dinner that Chess was cooking.

Tate said, "I'll stay."

"You don't have to stay."

"I want to stay."

Chess looked at her sister, and then an amazing thing happened—something more amazing than her cooking. She smiled. She said, "You do not want to stay, you liar. So go—get going, go right now."

It was both permission and a blessing. Tate threw some clothes and her running shoes in a bag. She went.

She should have stayed home; that was apparent after just the first hour. The boat ride was fine, and Tate enjoyed it like a person who knew there would be a finite number of boat rides left. The sun was hot, but the spray from the ocean cooled her off. She soaked in the incredible beauty of the Nantucket shoreline on a summer day—the green of the eelgrass, the golden sand, the other boats, sleek and white. She thought of the women in her condo complex who sat by the pool all summer in the hundred-degree heat; she thought of the elderly man with double hearing aids who bagged groceries at Harris Teeter. She would soon be returning to that life. Was it possible? She had a job with a pretzel company in Reading, Pennsylvania, on August 1, and another job with Nike in Beaverton, Oregon, as soon as the pretzel job was finished. She could, maybe, do both jobs quickly and fly back and forth from Nantucket.

Barrett was wearing his visor and his sunglasses, but despite this, he was squinting. Tate sat beside him in the copilot's seat, but they didn't touch. This was normal: driving a boat was just as serious as driving a car. She couldn't distract him. And yet she couldn't help herself. She ran her finger down his spine and felt his body tense. She retracted her hand. They didn't speak.

He pulled into Madaket Harbor and tied up to his mooring. Tate clambered down into the dinghy. She was nimble and experienced at this. She waited in the dinghy with her overnight bag at her feet while Barrett got organized. He climbed into the dinghy and rowed for shore. He was still squinting; he looked like he was in pain.

Tate said, "Are you okay? You seem quiet."

He said, "I'm okay."

"So, how did Anita like Tuckernuck?"

Barrett said, "Let's not talk about Anita. Please."

Tate said, "Okay."

This was something of a conversation killer. Barrett was either annoyed or preoccupied, and all Tate wanted to do was bombard him with questions, but this would make the situation worse. When they reached the beach, Barrett tied up the dinghy and they walked to Barrett's truck in the marina parking lot. The inside of the truck was hot; Tate scorched the backs of her thighs on the seat. In the console was half a cup of coffee with a skin of milk across the top like pond scum. Tate lifted it up. "Want me to toss this? There's a trash can over there."

"Just leave it." Barrett turned the key in the ignition. The radio was on painfully loud. Tate turned it down.

Barrett said, "I told you, just leave it!"

Tate stared at him. "Why are you yelling?"

"I'm not yelling."

They drove in silence. Tate thought, *This is it. This is real life.* The floating, head-over-heels stuff was over; this was real, hot, boring, tired life with Barrett Lee. He'd had a bad day at work, or something else was wrong. She looked at him. He was so handsome, it hurt.

She said, "So what did you do the other night? You never told me."

He said, "Tate—"

"Is it a secret?"

"No, it's not a secret. I went to Anita's for a barbecue. Roman had a meeting or something in Washington, he couldn't be there, and she needed me to fill in."

Tate got a sour feeling in her stomach. "Fill in?"

"Right. Play husband. I grilled the steaks, opened the wine, sat at the head of the table, the whole goddamned thing."

"Did you sleep with her?"

"Jesus, Tate!"

"Did you?" she asked.

"I didn't. But thank you for asking. That really shows what you think of me."

"What am I supposed to think? I *knew* you were with her that night, and then the next morning you didn't show up at all, and when you did show up, you were with her. Now tell me, *what am I supposed to think?*"

Barrett said nothing.

The pieces of the puzzle fell into place too neatly for Tate to keep quiet, although that was what her brain was telling her to do. *Keep quiet! Don't push it!*

She said, "Why didn't you come yesterday morning?"

"I was busy."

"With Anita?"

He sighed. "Cameron had a dentist appointment."

"Really?" This sounded like a lie.

"Really."

She looked out the window as the old-gym-shoe smell infiltrated the truck; they were passing the dump. She wanted to ask him about the future or, at the very least, the rest of the summer. She wanted to move in with him, travel for the business she had to take care of, and return. Would he want this, too? She couldn't ask him now.

She said, "Do you want to go out tonight? Get wickedly drunk? Go to the Chicken Box and dance?"

"I'm too tired," he said. "I want to have a beer on the deck, grill some burgers, hang out with you and the kids."

This was real life.

"Okay," she said.

Tate was flexible; she could roll with any plans and be happy. They picked the boys up from Barrett's parents' house. Tate received a nice hug from Chuck Lee, who looked like an old man. Because of the stroke, he walked with a cane and his speech was slow and pained, so Tate waited patiently as he labored to ask after Grant, Birdie, India, Chess, Billy, Teddy, and Ethan. (He remembered everyone's name, which was amazing, and he remembered that Bill Bishop was dead, which was even more amazing.) Tate told Chuck that everyone was well, and that Birdie, India, and Chess were happy in the house on Tuckernuck.

Chuck said, "Your mother was a beautiful woman."

Tate said, "She still is."

"And so, for that matter, was your aunt."

"She still is, too."

"I'll bet," Chuck said.

She could have talked to Chuck Lee all afternoon, but she could tell Barrett was antsy for his beer on the deck, and the kids were whining. Tate backed toward the truck holding Tucker, promising she would see Chuck again soon.

Tucker cried when Tate buckled him into his car seat, and then Cameron started to cry.

Barrett said, "I have a goddamned headache."

When they reached Barrett's house, Tate helped unsnap the kids from their car seats and shepherded them toward the outdoor shower. The water made them cry harder.

Barrett said, "I'm going to run in and get them some pajamas."

Tate said, "Do you want me to wash their hair?"

"Would you?" he said.

She would, of course she would, she would do anything for Barrett and his two little foot soldiers. It felt happy and domestic—Barrett off to fetch the pajamas, Tate lathering the boys' hair with Suave shampoo for kids, which smelled like cherry pie filling, sweet and artificial. They cried, the shampoo got in their eyes, the water was too hot and then, when Tate turned it down, too cold. Tucker ran out of the shower and stood in the middle of the dry, dusty square of dirt that was the failed garden. His hair was white with soapsuds and now his feet were muddy.

"Tucker, come back here!" Tate called.

He was crying, and Cameron was whimpering, but at least he was clean and rinsed. Tate wrapped him in a towel. Where was Barrett with the pajamas?

"Tucker!" she said. "Come on, sweetie!"

He cried, rooted to his spot.

Tate ran out to the garden and snatched up Tucker, who wriggled and squirmed in her arms like a greased pig. She stuck him under a spray of water and he howled. Tate worried what Barrett would think, she worried about the neighbors, she worried that a woman not his mother forcing him into the shower would be a topic Tucker would revisit years from now, in therapy. She got him rinsed and in the process became soaked herself, but the warm water felt good to Tate, it felt magical, and she was tempted to strip down and shower herself right then and there, but that really *would* send Tucker into therapy.

She cut the water. There had been only one towel hanging in the shower, not two, so Tucker had no towel.

"Barrett!" Tate said. "Bring a towel, too!"

Barrett didn't appear. Cameron slunk in the sliding door while Tucker howled, buck naked and wet. Tate picked him up and carried him inside.

Tate called out again for Barrett. There was no answer. She followed Tucker to his room. On her way, she grabbed a towel from the bathroom and dried him off. He stopped crying and wandered over to his train table, naked.

Tate said, "Where do you keep pajamas?"

Tucker pointed to a row of hooks. Pajamas!

Tate got both kids dressed and collected the wet

towels. She felt like she had just run an obstacle course. Where was Barrett?

Cameron walked in and said, "I'm hungry."

Tate said, "We're getting dinner. Hold on."

She wandered up to the living room. If Barrett was on the deck with that beer, she was going to strangle him. But the living room was deserted, and the deck was empty. Tate went back outside to the shower, thinking maybe they'd missed each other somehow, but he wasn't there. She hung the towels from the clothesline like a good wife.

"Barrett?" she called. Nothing.

She wandered back into the house and checked on the boys, who were playing with Tucker's trains. "Have you seen your dad?"

Cameron said, "I'm hungry."

Tate moved down the hall to Barrett's bedroom. If he'd fallen asleep on top of his bed, she was going to strangle him.

The door to his bedroom was closed. She tried the knob; it was locked. She knocked. "Barrett?" She could hear him talking. He was on the phone. She knocked again. He cracked open the door, pointed to the phone at his ear, then closed the door again. She heard him say, "Anita, listen. Listen to me."

She walked back down the hallway and sat on the bottom step of the stairs. She thought about Chess, mixing up the lime and chili marinade, pouring it over the pearly white swordfish steaks, flipping the fish to make sure both sides were evenly coated. She thought about Chess in her blue crocheted cap, wearing Birdie's denim apron, moving about the small, campy kitchen with a sense of purpose for the first time in weeks. Was Chess smiling, whistling, ordering Birdie and India around like minions?

Tate tried not to cry.

* * *

Barrett stayed on the phone with Anita Fullin for nearly an hour. Tate, in the meantime, made the boys dinner: microwaved hot dogs cut into coins the way they liked them, served with ketchup. Each kid got a handful of pretzel Goldfish and a container of applesauce. They got Hershey's syrup in their milk because Tate was in charge. They ate dinner hungrily and happily, and Tate tried to conceal her growing anger and anxiety each minute Barrett was on the phone. What could he and Anita be talking about? Their relationship had moved out of bounds. Other caretakers didn't talk to their clients for an hour or more behind closed and locked doors, of this Tate was certain.

After dinner, Tate presented both kids with a pudding cup topped with a squiggle of whipped cream from the can.

Tucker said, "I like you."

Cameron said, "Where's Dad?"

When Barrett got off the phone, it was ten minutes to eight. He clapped his hands and used a cheerful, in-charge voice. *Where are my lieutenants?* Tate and the kids were on the sofa watching an episode of *Go, Diego, Go!* Tucker was nodding off in the crook of Tate's arm. Cameron didn't move his eyes from the screen.

Barrett touched Tate's shoulder. She didn't move her eyes from the screen either. Diego was trying to rescue a baby jaguar. If she looked at Barrett, she would growl. If she opened her mouth, she would bite him.

"I'm sorry that took so long," he said. He lifted Tucker up. "Let me put him to bed. I'll be right back."

Tate said, "When this is over, Cam, we have to go brush our teeth."

"Okay," Cameron said.

Tate oversaw the teeth brushing. She said to Cameron, "Did you go to the dentist yesterday?"

"Yes," he said. "I got a new toothbrush!" He held it up, grinning. So Barrett hadn't lied about the dentist. Tate felt strangely disappointed.

Cameron climbed into bed and Tate read him three stories. She was a wonderful mother. She kissed Cameron on the forehead, turned on the nightlight, and left the door open six inches, the way he liked it. There was an enormous sense of accomplishment in getting a child to sleep.

Tate poked her head into Tucker's room. Tucker was asleep, and Barrett was snoring beside him. It was impossible to be mad—the two of them were adorable—but she was mad. She didn't wake Barrett up.

She walked upstairs, opened a beer for herself, and foraged through the pantry until she found a can of Spanish peanuts. She settled on the sofa and turned on the TV. This was a luxury. She could watch any of her shows on HBO or Showtime; she could get sucked into the dramas of her old life—all fictional—and forget the dramas of her new life. But instead, she found the Red Sox—playing the Yankees!—and she was happy with that.

She picked up one of the photographs of Stephanie: a picture of her in a sundress. It had been taken from across a table, it looked like, at a restaurant maybe. Steph was sunburned, smiling, happy.

Had she ever had to deal with Anita Fullin–related nonsense? If so, had she left a handbook?

Tate fell asleep on the sofa with the TV on. She had worked her way through three Coronas and half the can of peanuts. When Barrett woke her up at 1:10, the evidence was on the coffee table: empty bottles, the open can of peanuts, Steph's picture.

"Hey," he said. He lifted her legs, sat down, put her legs in his lap.

"Hey," she said. She wasn't mad anymore. She was too tired to be mad.

"I'm sorry about the phone call," he said.

Tate was silent. She didn't want to say the wrong thing.

"I have some explaining to do," he said.

She stared at him in the dark. What was he going to say?

"Anita wanted to buy your aunt's sculpture. The little one in the bedroom that we saw the other day."

"Roger?"

"Roger," Barrett said. "She really wanted to buy it. And the thing is, when Anita decides she wants to buy something, it takes on incredible importance. She obsesses about it. Because she has nothing else to do. No job, I mean, and no kids. Acquiring things is her life's purpose."

Tate wanted to comment on how sad and pathetic this was, but there was no need.

"So anyway, I asked your aunt. I told her Anita wanted to buy Roger for fifty thousand dollars and would probably go to seventy-five. But your aunt said no. She's not going to sell it at all."

"She has plenty of money," Tate said. "And Roger belongs on Tuckernuck."

"Right. Any other person would understand that. But not Anita. She isn't used to being turned down. She isn't used to encountering things that aren't for sale because what's left in the world anymore that isn't for sale?"

"She's upset because she can't buy Roger?" Tate said.

"Devastated," Barrett said. "And you have to know Anita. She sees it as your aunt—and you, the four of you on Tuckernuck—having something that she can't have. And she's jealous of you for other reasons—because I come over twice a day, because I'm fond of your family, because you and I are dating. So she pulled a power play the other night and begged me to come for the barbecue. She said she'd pay me overtime, knowing that I could never turn that kind of money down. Then she made me promise to bring her to Tuckernuck the following day. I wish you could understand how manipulative she is. She doesn't leave room for me to say no."

"Have you slept with her?" Tate asked.

"No," he said. "I'm sure you find that hard to believe, but the answer is no. I am not attracted to Anita. She is pushy and inappropriate and a deeply sad and empty person."

"Okay," Tate said. "So that was the whole phone call? Anita being upset about not being able to buy Roger, and you explaining, and... what? Comforting her?"

"No," Barrett said. "Not exactly."

"So what else?" Tate said.

"She offered me a job," Barrett said.

"You have a job. You own a business."

Barrett sighed. "She offered me basically three times what I make in a year, plus health insurance, to work for her only."

"You're kidding me."

"I'm not kidding."

"Work for her, here on Nantucket? Or do you have to go to New York, too?"

"Here on Nantucket," he said. "I would do everything—oversee the house, the gardens, the boats, the cars. I would manage everything and everyone, get them a driver, make their dinner reservations, schedule their flights, make sure the newspapers are delivered, order the flowers, oversee the maids. I would be the house manager, the caretaker, their personal assistant."

"Would you still work for us?" Tate said. "Or any of your other clients? The AuClaires?"

Barrett shook his head. "Only the Fullins."

"Is this what you want?"

"It can't be about what I want," Barrett said. "They gave me *Girlfriend;* they could take her back. And another thing you don't know is that I borrowed a lot of money from Roman and Anita when Steph was sick. A *lot* of money. Two hundred thousand dollars."

"Holy shit," Tate said.

"I needed it to pay the private nurses," Barrett said. "So we could keep Steph at home at the end."

"Oh," Tate said.

"I was going to go to the bank and take out a second mortgage," he said, "but Anita offered. She said I could pay her back whenever I wanted. I didn't have to worry about defaulting and losing the house."

"Okay," Tate said.

"It was worth it," Barrett said. "Even if I have to take this job and give up my business, it was worth it to have Steph at home."

Tate looked at the photograph of Steph, smiling. *Of course,* she should say. *Of course you're indebted to Anita Fullin for the rest of your life because she gave you* Girlfriend *as a bonus, and she lent you the money that allowed you to keep your dying wife at home.* But this wasn't true.

"It's blackmail," Tate said. "Or something like that."

"I can't turn down the money," Barrett said. "Or the health insurance. I have two kids."

"I know you have two kids," Tate said. "I bathed them and dressed them and fed them while you were on the phone."

"Tate..."

"She's trying to buy you," Tate said. "Tell her you're not for sale. Tell her she's fired. You don't want her for a client anymore."

He laughed, but not nicely. "And what am I supposed

to do for money? And what about my debt? You can tell me she's trying to buy me, and you're right, she is, but I'm not a wealthy man, I wasn't born with money, I didn't grow up in New Canaan with a summer home on Tuckernuck. I am me, I need money. I'm taking this job, Tate, because I have no choice."

She wasn't buying it. "You do have a choice. You can choose to work for other clients. You can pay Anita back steadily or take out that second mortgage and pay her back all at once. I can see how you think working for Anita would be easier. It's the quick fix and there will be more money. But you will end up paying out more in the end. You'll be paying out your integrity. And your freedom."

Barrett stood up. "You don't know what you're talking about."

"Don't I?"

"Good night," he said.

At the first light of dawn, Tate sneaked down to Barrett's room and made love to him before he was fully awake. He accepted her, welcomed her, cherished her; she could feel the love in his touch. Desperation. Apology. Afterward, she cried on his chest. She was going to lose him.

CHESS

Day twenty.

Plans for the wedding were taking over my life. My mother was insisting on a floating island in her pond; she'd had a dream about it and she was determined to make it a reality. My father didn't want to pay for a floating island. I stepped in, I pleaded my mother's case, I pretended I really did want a floating island, though I couldn't have cared less. My father, perhaps, realized I couldn't have cared less, but he relented. I hung up the phone, then stared at it, thinking not only did I not care about the floating island, but I didn't care about any of the wedding plans.

I didn't want to get married.

I knew Nick was back in New York because Michael had told me. Evelyn wanted to have a family dinner honoring Nick's return, celebrating his record deal. She wanted to have it at the country club.

I said, "Nick will never agree to that."

Michael said, "He already has."

It was mid-April, and New Jersey had received springtime like a benevolent gift. The trees were that bright greenish yellow, and the country club had just cut the grass for the first time. They had beds planted with daffodils, crocuses, tulips the color of Easter eggs. Many of the members of the club were still down in Florida, but because of the balmy weather, there were people on the driving range. The country club was the Morgan family's second home; Cy and Evelyn had joined when the kids were small, and it had become for them a lush, quiet, safe haven where family life unspooled as it should. Nick, I knew, hated the country club, embodying as it did wealth and privilege and exclusivity. Michael loved it; I had to talk him out of holding the rehearsal dinner there.

We drove to the club in a rental car from the city. Cy and Evelyn, Nick, and Dora were to meet us there.

I was, despite the genteel surroundings, a complete basket case. But deep in my heart, I was convinced Nick wouldn't show. He had just toured the country for six months, playing in dive bars and underground clubs and seedy auditoriums; he wasn't going to sit down for a martini and prime rib with his parents. He would cancel, and my expectations would be roadkill once again.

I occupied my mind with work. I was throwing around an idea for an article on country club lunches: variations on club sandwiches and Cobb salads and chilled soups that you could serve in your own backyard. I watched my feet walk down the flagstone path to the entrance; my arm was linked through Michael's. We walked inside. The club smelled the same as country clubs across the country: french fries, pipe smoke, worn leather, polished brass.

"There they are," Michael said.

I looked over. In the foyer were Cy and Evelyn, Dora, and Nick.

Michael reached his brother first, tested a handshake, which became a bear hug. Michael said, "Man, you look great."

I kissed Cy automatically; then Evelyn, noting her perfume, which I loved; then Dora, who was home on spring break from Duke. I was moving toward Nick. I had to greet him, but I was afraid.

I said, "Hey, you."

He said, "Hey, yourself." And he kissed me like a proper brother-in-law. Side of the mouth. But he had my arm, too, which he squeezed so hard he might have left a bruise.

Evelyn said, "I can't believe we have the whole family together. I think I'm going to cry."

Cy said, "I think I'm going to order a cocktail."

Nick said, "I think I'm going to join you." His voice had a jovial expansiveness I had never heard before. "Lead the way."

He sounded like Michael, I thought. The anger was gone, the bad-boy vibe held in check. And he looked like Michael. He had cut his hair and he was wearing pressed khakis and a navy blazer. And loafers. He looked polished and proper. What was this? I wondered. I lagged behind naturally; the Morgan family were all gifted with long strides and an aggressive get-there-first gait, especially when there were cocktails involved. Nick turned around and winked at me.

I said, "Nice jacket."

"I wore it for you," he said.

He sat next to me at dinner, which meant I sat between him and Michael. I thought, I can do this. *And then I ordered a cosmopolitan instead of chardonnay. Cy gave a brief toast, welcoming Nick back; we all drank. There was a bread basket on the table with packets of crackers in plastic. Dora picked one packet out—two sesame breadsticks—and said, "This is so retro, but I love it."*

Nick talked about his tour—Charleston and Houston were his two favorite cities, and he was never going back to Ohio again if he could help it (sorry, Ohio). I listened with rapt attention. He was here next to me, this was him talking, *I could touch him, I did touch him, I handed him the shallow dish that held butter curls in an ice bath, and our fingers brushed. I thought,* What am I going to do? What am I going to do? *Nick had come to the country club, he had gotten a haircut and put on a blazer and loafers to show me something. To show me he could do it.*

Michael said, "Well, our wedding plans are coming along."

Evelyn said, "Oh, yes, they are! Tell Nick about the floating island, Chess!"

I said, "He doesn't want to hear about the floating island."

"Tell me about the floating island," Nick said.

I excused myself for the ladies' room.

The ladies' room had an antechamber, a sitting room with satin-cushioned seats in front of a long mirror. Under the mirror was a ledge that held glass ashtrays. I sat down and imagined the married women of suburban New Jersey sitting here to smoke and reapply their lipstick and gossip. No doubt they had had terrible problems themselves and excruciating decisions to make. They were unhappily married and having an affair, their husband was in danger of losing his job or had a drinking problem or gambled. They were carrying an unwanted pregnancy or couldn't seem to get pregnant.

I looked at myself in the mirror for a while, I don't know how long. Too long.

I thought, I don't want to get married.

There was a knock at the door. Michael, I thought, who had come looking for me. Evelyn would have just walked right in. I said, "Here I come!" And I opened the door.

Nick.

I looked around. A Hispanic woman in a maid's uniform was pushing a cordless sweeper over the dark red carpet.

I said, "I don't want to get married."

He said, "Then you'd better do something about it."

I wanted to grab him and kiss him, pull him into the empty ballroom and touch him, but I couldn't exactly do that in the middle of the Fairhills Country Club. We walked back to the table side by side, talking softly, like any regular soon-to-be in-laws.

I said, "You sent me those postcards."

He said, "I did."

I said, "You missed me?"

He said, "I did."

I said, "How much?"

He stopped in his tracks. A grandfather clock sounded the hour. He said, "I pined."

This made me smile.

He said, "You have a big job ahead of you."

I said, "You'll help me?"

"No. This is for you to do or undo. For your own reasons. This can't have anything to do with me."

I didn't respond.

"Do you understand?"

I did understand, but I felt abandoned anyway.

He laughed, not kindly. "You'll never do it."

* * *

I sat back down at the table, incensed. I had been dared. I was determined to win. The next time I ate dinner with these people, I decided, I would be with Nick.

But once I was ensconced in the car with Michael, I feared Nick was right. I was happy with Michael, happy enough. We belonged together, a wedding was in the works, tens of thousands of dollars had been spent on my behalf. I wasn't the kind of person to topple the apple cart. I wasn't the kind of person to change the course of history, however narrowly.

Michael went to California. Despite the demanding nature of his work, he almost never traveled for business. Having him gone was an unexpected luxury. The whole city seemed different. I was free! I called Rhonda and we made a plan: start with drinks at Bar Seine, move on to Aureole, the Spotted Pig, Bungalow 8.

I was happy that night. I called and talked to Michael on my way from Aureole to the Spotted Pig. I was very drunk; talking to him didn't seem real. He was in another time zone. He sounded serious and grumpy; he had not one but two candidates in the final three for a huge CEO position with a monster tech firm. I wished him luck. I hung up.

I was very drunk. I sent a text to Nick that said: Meet me at Bungalow 8. *There was no way he would ever do it. He had never met me anywhere. But then again, I had never asked him. I wondered if he knew Michael was out of town. I checked the Diplomatic Immunity website religiously; I knew Nick was free.*

No sooner had Rhonda unlocked our way into Bungalow 8 than I saw Nick. He had a drink; he was standing at the bar talking to a couple of young guys who seemed eager, like fans.

Nick saw me. I held up a hand. I needed a minute. I was with Rhonda, after all. It took her only thirty seconds to find someone she knew, some tall, dark Mediterranean guy who absorbed her like water into a sponge.

I said, "I'll be right back."

I grabbed Nick and we left.

He said, "Where do you want to go?"

"Central Park," I said.

He said, "It's not safe at night, Chess."

I said, "Walk with me."

We walked all the way uptown, nearly seventy blocks. I sobered up and we talked. What were we doing? Was it real? What would it be like? He was recording an album. He had already gotten a check and he was looking at new places to live. He would have to travel and he wanted me to go with him. Would I go with him? Would I quit my job? I said I would. He said, "You will not." But I would. I liked being the food editor of Glamorous Home *but there was something more for me out there, something bigger, deeper, wider. I wanted to leave Michael that very night. I would break the engagement—not for him, but for myself. I wanted Nick. Did he want me?*

He stopped me at the corner of Broadway and Thirty-third Street. Not a romantic corner in any respect. He took my face in his hands and said, "I want nothing but you. I will quit the band, quit music altogether, I will give up poker and rock climbing. I will give up red meat, beer, cigarettes, all of it, just to be with you. I will hold your hand and we will walk across this world, and I will sing to you and our babies, and that will be enough for me."

"Enough?"

"It's all I want."

We kissed. The world spun.

That night when I got home, I called Michael and broke the engagement. I broke it like a fistful of linguine over a pot of boiling water. Snap, in half. No putting it back together. I didn't waver; I didn't leave room for doubt.

Chess cooked dinner. This was a huge step; only a month earlier she had sworn she would never cook again. But look: chili-lime swordfish with avocado sauce, corn salad, heirloom tomatoes with blue cheese and bacon. It was a feast. Tate wasn't there, but Chess felt sorry for Tate rather than sorry for herself. Chess and Birdie and India lit the citronella candles and sat at the picnic table and drank and ate and talked over the sound of the waves. The sun set. Chess thought about the night at Bungalow 8 and walking all that way with Nick as though they were the only two people in Manhattan and the world was filled with brand-new possibility. Had it only been three months earlier? So much had changed. Chess cursed the way things had changed; she cursed the fact that Michael was dead, but cursing it, feeling angry about it, was a step in the right direction. *Throw those rocks. Get rid of the heavy stuff.*

Suddenly, Chess was crying. India and Birdie stopped talking about what a ghastly cook their mother had been (they had arrived at this topic after praising Chess's talents as a chef: the swordfish melted in your mouth), and Birdie reached out first, and then India moved so that the two of them were on either side of Chess, bracing her, and she was able to just cry. It had taken her nearly three weeks, but she was on her way toward something else—another state of mind, another way to be.

"Let it out, darling," Birdie said.

India said, "We've been waiting for this. We've been waiting for this exact thing."

Life was sad and difficult. We hurt the ones we love the most. Michael was dead. Nick was gone. Chess wanted to feel it all—the pain, the grief, the guilt. *Bring it on.*

* * *

She started walking. Tate was a morning person, but Chess liked to exercise in the late afternoon, right before cocktail hour. This was when she used to run in the city—after work, during the sacred hour that separated her daytime from her nighttime. She left the house at four thirty with a bottle of cold water, a hat, sunglasses, and her running shoes, which felt constrictive to her feet after three weeks in flip-flops. She would walk across Tuckernuck to the west coast and back. She would have liked to jog it, but she would have been out of breath in a few minutes, disheartened and discouraged. She used to run with Michael in Central Park; those were the times she had felt closest to him. He always matched her pace, despite the fact that he could have gone much faster. He didn't like to talk while running and neither did she. They communicated when necessary by pointing. It was both energizing and comforting to have Michael beside her, his stride in sync with hers, his heart beating at the same pace.

Tuckernuck was beautiful. It was, Chess decided, the most beautiful place on earth. The ocean, the blue sky, the simple dirt-and-gravel paths that cut across the acres of former farmland, which were now open space for rabbits and field mice and red-tailed hawks. There were houses here and there, family compounds; her mother and her aunt knew exactly who owned each one and when they had bought it. Those other people—some rich, some famous—had learned the secret of life, and for a flash, Chess felt like she knew it, too.

A blond girl with a ponytail rode toward Chess on her bicycle. Chess was walking up a short but steep dirt hill and the girl was coming down. The bike gained speed, the front tire wobbled. The girl said, "This bike doesn't have any brakes!" Her legs went akimbo, the expression on her face was comical, and in fact, Chess laughed, but she quickly realized that the girl was going to crash—and worse still, hit Chess. Chess jumped out of the way, but her foot caught on an exposed root and she fell into the brush. The girl and the bike went over with a clatter. The girl shrieked, then started to cry.

Chess stood up and brushed herself off. She went over to the girl, who must have been thirteen or fourteen.

"Are you okay?"

The girl had a scrape on her knee the size of a quarter that was dusty and bleeding, and her palms were skinned. She tried to get up, and Chess helped her lift her bicycle. The girl sniffed up her tears. "I'm okay," she said. She inspected her knee, wiped her hands on her jeans shorts, and gave Chess a weak smile. "Life is good," she said. She mounted her bicycle.

"Life is good," Chess said.

The next morning, Chess felt Tate rise from bed for her run, but Chess couldn't open her eyes. Tate had spent the night before last with Barrett on Nantucket and had come home in a fractious state of mind—something was going on. Last night, Chess had asked Tate if she was going to Nantucket overnight, and Tate had said no. She said, "Barrett has a big decision to make and I'm going to let him make it in peace." Chess was tempted to ask what the big decision was, but it was unfair of her to ask when she still hadn't disclosed anything about her own life, and so she didn't ask and Tate didn't tell. Chess murmured something like, *Have a good run,* but her mouth wouldn't move to form the words properly. She was covered in a blanket of sleep.

She woke at some point later. She *was* awake, she was fully conscious, but she couldn't open her eyes. She raised her hands to her face. Something was wrong with her face. It was rough and bumpy. She pried her eyes open and the dark room was visible through a milky film. Chess started to panic. What was going *on* here? She scratched the back of her hand, and at that instant, her whole body exploded in itch. Itch! Chess scratched at her arms, her neck, her face. She slid out of bed and stumbled for the door. She scrambled down the stairs and burst into the bathroom. What was wrong with her? She looked in the tarnished mirror and saw her monstrous face—covered with a landscape of rash. Her eyes were swollen to slits, but she could see well enough to know things were bad.

Poison ivy.

The inside of her ear itched. She imagined the canal to her ear coated with the sap she was so violently allergic to. She wanted to stick a toothbrush in her ear and scratch, scratch, scratch. She imagined her brain blooming with pink lumps. There was poison ivy on her brain. How could she scratch?

She clawed at her face. She wanted to rip it off. She was crying. Poison freaking ivy. The devil's scourge. She scratched her face until it bled, even though she knew this was the worst thing she could do. It was all over her—her face, her ears, her chest, her neck, her arms. It was between her fingers.

She crashed down the stairs to the kitchen. "Mom!" she said. "Mommy!"

Birdie turned and her eyes grew wide. "Oh, no, darling!"

"I fell yesterday. A bike was coming from the other direction and I jumped out of the way and I fell in the brush."

Birdie said, "What can I do? Get calamine?"

"Calamine?" Chess said. Calamine wasn't going to help, unless they were planning on pouring calamine in a vat and dipping Chess like a Salem witch. She needed to bathe in calamine. The half bottle of chalky pink they had upstairs wouldn't begin to address the problem. And what about her eyes? And what about her ears? And her brain? What about her brain?

"I need help, Mom," Chess said. "I need serious help."

"Barrett is still here," Birdie said. "He just left, I'm going to run, I'm going to catch him." She raced out the door shouting, "Barrett! Wait!"

Chess didn't particularly want Barrett to see her in this hideous state, but she had little choice. She grabbed her grandfather's floppy white fishing hat, which would cover her face better than the blue crocheted cap. She was wearing a nightgown. If she was going anywhere, she needed clothes, yet she couldn't make it back upstairs. She could barely see. She sat on the sofa shivering, even though she wasn't cold. She was hot and itchy. Just when things were starting to get better...what a mess! She scratched, then clenched her hands together to keep from scratching. She cursed. She cursed again, more profanely and at the top of her lungs. The homeowners' association would fine her if they heard.

She felt a hand on her back. Birdie.

"Barrett's here," she said. "He'll take you to the hospital."

"Okay," Chess said. She turned to face him.

Barrett said, "Holy shit."

She kept her head down for the boat ride. She had slipped on underwear and her army-surplus shorts under her nightgown. With her grandfather's fishing hat and the leprosy creeping across her face, she was a goblin. She would scare children. She tried not to scratch, but she couldn't stop; she would fixate on one area—the back of her neck, the undersides of her arms—and scratch until the pustules wept. This would only serve to spread the poison, but she couldn't help herself. She wanted to gouge out her eyes.

She didn't raise her face to Barrett. She couldn't see anything anyway. She felt the boat slow down and stop; she heard Barrett anchor. He said, "Okay, follow me." And he led her by the hand to the side of the boat. She would have to jump down into the dinghy. Barrett was holding her hand gingerly, and Chess worried about spreading her poison. Was Barrett allergic? When she gained the ability to speak again, she would tell him to wash his hands thoroughly with soap and water. She thought of the moment she fell, right into the evil, twisting, venomous plants.

Life is good, the girl had said through her tears.

Chess made it into the dinghy. Her scalp itched. She wanted to ask Barrett to douse her with gasoline and set her on fire.

She was wretched.

It took them twenty minutes to get to the hospital, twenty excruciating minutes where Chess did two things: scratched and tried not to scratch. Once she was inside the rarefied, air-conditioned, sterile air of Nantucket Cottage Hospital, once she was in a place where people could *help* her, things came into perspective: She had not fallen a hundred feet and broken her spine or crushed her skull. She had poison ivy.

Barrett directed her to admitting, where she dictated her information to a woman who wore a name tag that said *Patsy.* Chess's fingers were swollen and itchy, and Patsy didn't seem eager to hand over her pen, and Chess couldn't blame her. She and Barrett were then told to wait, and wait they did, as Chess resumed her manic scratching. Barrett's phone rang.

She said, "Do you have to take that?"

"No," he said, and he quieted his phone.

Chess said, "So how are things going with you?"

He said, "I can't begin to explain."

Amen, she thought.

She said, "Do you remember coming to see me in Vermont?"

He said, "Do I *remember?* Of course I remember."

"I was horribly rude."

"*I* was horribly rude," Barrett said. "I sprang myself on you without any warning. I should have called you to tell you I was coming."

"The least I could have done was have lunch with you," Chess said. "I've always felt bad about that."

"I think the reason I didn't call in advance was that I was afraid you'd tell me not to come," Barrett said. "I figured my chances were better if I just showed up."

"They weren't better," Chess said.

"No," Barrett said. "They weren't. You broke my heart."

"I didn't break your heart," Chess said. "We barely knew each other. We went on that one date where I *puked*..."

"I was glad when you puked," Barrett said. "Because in my mind you were this goddess, a year older than me, going to college, reading all those thick books. When you threw up, I was relieved. You were a normal person, just like me."

"It was gross," Chess said. "And I noticed you didn't try to kiss me."

"True," Barrett said.

They both laughed.

Barrett said, "But I did kiss you in Vermont. By my car, remember?"

"I remember."

"It fulfilled some kind of mission for me," Barrett said. "I drove away happy."

Chess filled with warmth. She and Barrett were resolving something here.

A nurse appeared and said, "Mary Cousins?"

"That's me," Chess said, standing up.

The nurse caught sight of Barrett, and a look of surprise rippled across her face. "Hey, Barrett."

Barrett said, "Hey, Alison." They looked at each other for a moment. Alison was dark haired, and very tall and thin and angular, like a runway model. She was in her early forties, too old to be an ex-girlfriend. But maybe not.

Alison said, "Okay, Mary, follow me, please."

Barrett said, "I'll be right here."

Alison the nurse gave Chess a shot of prednisone, which she promised would dramatically reduce Chess's discomfort. She didn't like to give the shot, because it tended to have nasty side effects—increase in blood sugar, increase in appetite, moodiness, psychosis—but Chess's case of poison ivy was so severe that Alison deemed prednisone necessary. Chess was grateful. What would a little more psychosis matter anyway? The needle didn't even hurt going in; it was delivering her salvation. She exhaled. She said, "How long will that last?"

"Twenty-four hours," Alison said.

"Can I come back tomorrow?" Chess said.

Alison laughed. Chess assumed that meant no. Alison said, "And I have ointment for you."

Chess said, "I need a barrel."

Alison said, "It's very potent." She whipped out a tube and squeezed some clear ointment on her finger and dabbed it gently across Chess's face. Chess closed her eyes and pretended it was a spa treatment. It seemed amazing to her that she had ever been relaxed, happy, and normal enough to receive spa treatments, but Michael had enjoyed giving her gift certificates for facials and massages. He would leave them on her pillow at night, or pretend to find them among the Chinese take-out menus. Michael had been a prince. Now he was dead, in a mahogany box.

Alison said, "If you don't mind my asking, what happened to your hair? Are you undergoing treatment?"

Chess flushed. "No," she said. "I cut it off. It was a decision made at a time of extreme mental instability."

Alison seemed unfazed by this blunt declaration of the truth. She was a professional. "Ah," she said, as though she had seen it many times before.

There was silence except for the sticky whispering of Alison applying the ointment. Chess thought, *New subject!*

She said, "How do you know Barrett?"

"I worked with his wife," Alison said. "Stephanie. She was a nurse in labor and delivery. She was one of the coolest people I have ever known. How do *you* know Barrett?"

"We're staying on Tuckernuck," Chess said. "He's our caretaker."

"Aha!" Alison said. "Well, he's a great guy. And a wonderful father."

"Yes," Chess said. She raised her chin so Alison could apply the ointment to her neck. The ointment was making her skin tingle and buzz, and she felt the prednisone coursing through her veins like rocket fuel. She was lulled and comforted. Alison applied the ointment to her forearms.

"I thought maybe you were his girlfriend," Alison said.

"Oh," Chess said. Her eyes twitched, but they were heavy and gummed with ointment. "No."

* * *

Alison walked Chess back out to the waiting room and presented her to Barrett. She had a tube of ointment in a white paper bag, as well as a prescription for more.

"She's going to live," Alison said.

"That's good," Barrett said. "How's everything going with you?"

"Oh, you know," Alison said. "It's summer. I've seen my share of moped accidents and acute sunburn. And poison ivy."

"I'm sorry," Chess murmured. She felt like a garden-variety tourist. She was grotesque in her nightgown, shorts, and ridiculous hat. Her skin was not only diseased but now slick and greasy. She wanted to get out of there.

"There's no reason to be sorry," Alison said. "It's my job." To Barrett, she said, "So how are you? How are the kids?"

"I'm fine," Barrett said unconvincingly. "The kids are fine. Swimming lessons, the dentist. Cameron will be old enough to go to the Boys and Girls Club in the fall."

"I think about Steph all the time," Alison said.

Barrett nodded. Chess had an incredible urge to drag her nails through the ointment.

Alison patted Barrett on the shoulder. To Chess she said, "You should be feeling better soon."

Barrett drove to Dan's Pharmacy and filled Chess's prescription. When he got back into the car, his phone rang. He checked the display and said, "I'm going to ignore that for a little while longer." He smiled at Chess. "Would you like to go to lunch?"

"*Lunch?*" she said.

"Yes, I think we determined that you owe me a lunch."

"Oh, God, Barrett. I can't be seen in public."

"Sure, you can."

"No, I can't. People will look at me and lose their appetite."

"Okay," Barrett said. "I'll tell you what. We'll get sandwiches from Something Natural and eat them at the beach."

"I probably shouldn't be in the sun," Chess said.

"I have an umbrella," Barrett said. "Any other excuse you want to try out?"

"No," Chess said. It was nearly one o'clock and she hadn't eaten anything. And all of a sudden, what Alison the nurse had said about prednisone causing an increase in appetite became crystal clear. Chess was suddenly *starving!*

"Okay, then," Barrett said.

She ordered a turkey BLT with avocado and swiss and extra mayo on pumpernickel bread. It was a sandwich the size of a dictionary, and still, Chess judged, it wouldn't be enough. Barrett had also bought her a bag of potato chips, an iced tea, and a chocolate chip cookie. Chess held her lunch in her lap, fighting the urge to dig in, as Barrett drove them out Eel Point Road. It was nice to be out in the wider world; it was voyeuristic—watching other cars and the summer homes pass. Once they pulled onto the beach, there were other people—mothers and their children, and a gang of college kids with a hibachi and a boom box. So many people! Barrett shifted his truck into four-wheel drive and drove to a deserted part of the beach. He put up the umbrella and set two chairs under it; then he came around and opened Chess's door.

"I feel like such an ass," she said.

"Please don't."

"I'm in my nightgown."

"Nobody knows that," he said. "And nobody cares."

He was right. Chess hopped out of the truck and landed in the hot sand. Her legs and feet were fine—smooth and clean, untouched by the scourge. She was eager for her lunch. She settled into the chair. Her upper lip was swollen and her face felt numb, like she'd been shot up with Novocain.

Barrett sat in the chair next to her. He pointed out across the water. "You see that land out there? You know what that is?"

There was, of course, only one answer, but it took Chess by surprise. "Tuckernuck?"

"Yep."

Chess stared at the distant green coastline. It was surreal. For the past three weeks, and for years and years before that, Chess had gazed out at Nantucket without any thought that people on Nantucket were, in turn, gazing at her. She could envision Tate lying on the beach, and Birdie and India in their upright chairs, eating their gourmet sandwiches on slender baguettes, reading, swimming, throwing the Frisbee, maybe walking the beach and finding a sand dollar or a whelk shell. Chess longed for them, much the way she longed for everyone else. She had the funny feeling she would never see them again.

"I feel like I'm on vacation from my vacation," she said.

Barrett unwrapped his sandwich, and Chess took this as the starting gun. She very carefully peeled away the layers of Saran Wrap around her BLT, trembling with anticipation. She took a bite—smoky, crunchy, juicy, tangy, crispy. God! She couldn't remember the last time eating had given her such pleasure. Before "all that had happened," eating had been Chess's passion. As Michael used to tease her, food had meant more to her than sex. There was truth in this; Chess took a very sensual pleasure in everything from salty chips and cold, creamy dip, to the velvety texture of foie gras, to the sparkling crispness of French champagne. She was partial to tomatoes, raspberries, corn on the cob, good cheese, fruity olive oil, rosemary, smoked paprika, and onions sautéing in butter. Her goal at *Glamorous Home* had been to create recipes that were both trustworthy and surprising: a really good pasta dish that could become a signature, a certain kind of birthday cake that became a tradition.

She took another bite of her sandwich, savoring it. After "all that had happened," Chess had lost interest in food. Food became gray, just like everything else. It was sad, but Chess couldn't bring herself to care. The return of her sense of taste, today, right now, was something not to herald with excitement but rather to coax gently along.

The prednisone, though, was kicking in. Chess ripped open her bag of chips and had to keep herself from inhaling them. She guzzled her iced tea.

She said, "Is everything okay with Tate?"

"Do we want to talk about Tate?" Barrett asked.

"Should we not?" Chess said. There was something about her face—under the shiny force field of the ointment—that made her feel safe. "Maybe we shouldn't."

They were quiet. Chess ate carefully. Because her upper lip was swollen, she couldn't chew normally. Bits of food fell out of her mouth onto her nightgown.

"Things were so good there for a while," Barrett said. "Now they've gotten weird."

"Weird?"

"Confusing."

"How so?" Chess asked.

"My client Anita Fullin—the one who came to look at your house?—wants to hire me full time. Which would mean I couldn't work for you anymore. Well, I could probably work tomorrow and maybe the next day, but then I'd have to subcontract someone to take care of you and the rest of my clients until you found a new caretaker while I worked for Anita."

"Is that what you want?" Chess asked. "To work for Anita?"

"God, no," Barrett said. "Not at all. But she has a stranglehold on me financially. I can't turn down what she's offering."

"Tate knows about this?"

"She doesn't think I should take the job. I'm not sure she understands the position I'm in."

"She's crazy about you," Chess said.

"I'm crazy about her," Barrett said.

"Are you in love?"

He winced. It was unfair of her, putting him on the spot. She said, "You don't have to answer."

"It's too soon to tell," he said. "But yes." He reddened, took a bite of his sandwich, then looked across the water at the coast of Tuckernuck. "I don't know what I'm going to do about it, though. She's leaving in another week. I can't offer to go with her. I can't uproot the kids."

"You could ask her to stay," Chess said. She drank some more iced tea. "You know what, this is none of my business."

"It's okay," Barrett said.

"Tate would hate it if she knew we were talking about her."

Barrett ignored this. "I'd ask her to stay, but what if she stays and she's not happy?"

"She'll leave."

"I have to think of the kids. I can't invite her into their lives and then have her walk out."

"Well, whatever you do, be careful with her," Chess

said. "This is the first time I've known Tate to be serious about anyone. I don't want to see her get hurt."

Barrett crumpled the plastic from his sandwich. "I'd never hurt her intentionally."

Right, Chess thought. *But people rarely hurt each other intentionally.*

Barrett's phone rang. "Goddamn it," he said.

TATE

When she arrived home from her run and discovered that Barrett had taken Chess to the hospital for her poison ivy, she felt psychotically jealous.

"Why did she need to go to the hospital?" Tate said. "Why didn't she just put calamine on it?"

"It was gruesome," Birdie said. "Her whole face, her neck, her arms, all covered. She had it in her ears. Her eyes were swollen shut into slits. She was scratching until it bled. Calamine wasn't going to be enough."

Well, then, why didn't they wait for me to get back? Tate wanted to ask. *I would have gone with them. Helped out.* But this was immature and unreasonable. The poison ivy was a quasi-emergency. Of course they weren't going to wait around for Tate. Barrett did the right thing. But Tate was consumed with jealousy, new and old. She lay on her towel at the beach, scanning the horizon for Barrett's boat, wondering where they were, what they were doing, when they would be back. It was nearly two o'clock. They had left five and a half hours ago. Were they still at the hospital? Had they gone somewhere else? Had they gone to Barrett's house? Tate's stomach churned. She remembered back thirteen years to that lunch with Barrett at the picnic table. How many times had he looked at Chess with naked longing? He had screwed up his courage to ask her on a date. If Chess hadn't puked off the back of the boat, they might have kissed. They might have become a couple that summer. Even this summer, Barrett had asked Chess out first. Why? Tate had never asked him; she had just been content to be the one he ended up with. But now Tate wanted to know. Had Barrett asked Chess out first because Birdie pushed him to, or were there vestiges of old feelings that remained? Was Chess the one he really wanted?

"How bad did she look?" Tate asked. "Did she look really bad?"

"Perfectly awful," Birdie said.

They didn't get back until four o'clock. Tate was standing on the beach with her hands on her hips, waiting for them. Barrett pulled the boat up, anchored it, and helped Chess down into the water. She said something; he laughed. Then he said something and she laughed. She *laughed.* Tate was in danger of displaying her anger in a really inappropriate way. She tried to rein herself in. Chess did look atrocious—she was still in her nightgown and those god-awful shorts and their grandfather's hat. As Chess waded in to shore, Tate could see that her face was a disaster area. It had been colonized by poison ivy.

Tate didn't get poison ivy. To Chess, *this* might seem unfair.

Tate said, "Jesus."

Chess said, "Well, you aren't going to win any sensitivity awards."

Barrett had a bag of groceries and a bag of ice. He waded in, staring at his feet.

Tate said, "So you're okay? They treated you at the hospital?"

"I got a shot," Chess said. "And some ointment." She held up a white pharmacist's bag for Tate to see. "I'm going up."

Barrett stopped in front of Tate. "Hey," he said. "How are you?"

"Me?" Tate said. "Oh, I'm fine."

"Listen," he said. "I'm going to take that job with Anita."

"Yeah," Tate said. "I figured as much."

"I know you don't understand..."

"I do."

"You don't, though..."

"You're in her grips, Barrett," Tate said. "She has you right where she wants you."

Barrett shook his head. *Touch me!* thought Tate. *Tell me you care about me!* Things had been so good, they had been so close, and it was like she had blinked and it was all ruined. It was the scene from *Mary Poppins* that used to make her cry—the beautiful chalk paintings on the sidewalk, washed away by the spring rains.

"How was your day?" Tate asked. "How was Chess?"

"It was okay. I took her to the hospital, then got her prescription. Then we went to lunch and she took a nap. Then I had to go to the grocery store for your mother, and Chess stayed in the truck. She didn't want anyone to see her face."

Tate was stuck back on *went to lunch* and *took a nap.* She thought of Chess, sitting in *her* seat in Barrett's truck.

"I don't think we should see each other anymore," Tate said.

Barrett looked stricken. Tate couldn't believe she had just spoken those words. She had said them impulsively, like throwing a glass across a room, and they resonated. Tate's thoughts were unreasonable and they wouldn't stop: Barrett loved her sister, he had always loved her sister, he had always longed for her, even when he was married to Stephanie, even when Stephanie was dying, his heart had been with Chess, who didn't deserve it.

"We only have a week left until I'm gone," Tate said. "It will be better to cut our losses now."

"Better to cut our *losses?*" Barrett said. "Is that what you *believe?*"

Tate shrugged. She didn't believe it, but she wouldn't backpedal. She wasn't going to fight for this relationship. She wanted *Barrett* to fight for it. She wanted Barrett to tell her he loved her. But if he had any feelings for Chess—and clearly he did—Tate couldn't stay with him.

He said, "Okay, well, then I guess I'll tell Anita I can start tomorrow. And I'll send Trey Wilson out to bring your supplies. He's a handsome kid. You'll like him."

"What is *that* supposed to mean?" Tate said.

Barrett dropped the groceries and the ice in the sand at her feet. He waded back out to his boat. Before he climbed in, he said, "I'll tell the kids you said good-bye."

The kids. Tate's heart felt like it was being pulverized in the boat's motor as Barrett started it up, swung the boat around like a cowboy, and sped away. *Boyfriend leaving in* Girlfriend, Tate thought. Then she thought: *The kids. Barrett.*

Barrett!

She wanted to cry out, but it was too late. She considered swimming—Nantucket was only half a mile away—but she was too weak.

She sat on the brand-new pressure-treated stairs made from sweet-smelling yellow lumber and cried.

She had been there ten or fifteen minutes when Chess came down.

"What happened?" she said.

"What *happened?*" Tate said. "What *happened?* You happened, that's what happened."

Chess said, "I don't get it."

"He has feelings for you," Tate said. "He always has."

Chess laughed once, sharply. "Jesus, Tate, look at me! He took me to the *hospital,* and then the *pharmacy.*"

"He took you to lunch," Tate said.

"He didn't take me to lunch," Chess said. "We got sandwiches and went to the beach. We talked for a while and then I fell asleep, which was a result of the shot. When I woke up, we went to the grocery store for Bird, and then we came back."

"What did you talk about?" Tate said. "Tell me exactly. What did you talk about?"

"I don't know," Chess said. "Things." She started scratching her throat; it was raw, red, and bumpy. Just looking at it made Tate's own throat itch. "I meant to tell you this before, the night of your first date with Barrett."

"Tell me what?"

"About how, back a million years ago, Barrett showed up at Colchester. To see me. And I was nasty. I basically kicked him out of town. And I always felt bad about it. So today was good. Today gave me a chance to apologize."

"What are you talking about?" Tate said.

"Barrett came to Colchester my sophomore year," Chess said. "He drove up from Hyannis." She then regaled Tate with the details: How she'd been working at the brat stand, how she ran with the cash box back to the sorority house, how Carla Bye was in the sitting room chatting with Barrett. How Barrett had driven six hours in the blue Jeep to see her. How she had turned him away.

The story left Tate breathless with shame for her sister; Chess was a snob, she was mean and stinky, treating

Barrett that way. The story also made her jealous—no, it confirmed her jealousy. She had a reason to be jealous: Barrett had loved Chess enough to track her down at Colchester. It made Tate livid: Why had Chess not told her this story before? And why had Barrett never told her?

"I tried to tell you the night you first went out with him," Chess said. "But you didn't want to hear it. And I'm sure Barrett didn't tell you because he'd forgotten all about it. It doesn't matter."

"Doesn't matter?" Tate said. "Except you felt the need to apologize to him today when you two were alone together. You ate lunch with my boyfriend. You took a nap with my boyfriend."

"Don't blow things out of proportion, Tate," Chess said. She was using her older sister voice now, her fucking food editor voice. "I took a nap in an upright beach chair while Barrett sat on the bumper of his truck and talked to Anita Fullin on the phone."

"So you know about Anita Fullin?" Tate said. "You know about the job offer?"

Chess didn't answer. She didn't *have* to answer. Of course she knew about the job offer; Barrett had confided in her. This morning, when Tate woke up, her biggest problem had been Anita Fullin. Now, her biggest problem was her sister.

"He had to tell me about the job," Chess said. "His phone kept ringing."

"I hate you," Tate said. She stood up on the stairs so that she towered over her sister. "I absolutely *hate* you! You ruin *everything,* you steal everything. You have been ruining my life since I was born. You have been taking everything good for yourself and leaving me with scraps."

"Tate—"

"Don't talk to me!" Tate was screaming now. "I *hate* you! I've loved Barrett since I was seventeen years old, but he's always wanted you. You are the prettier sister, I guess, the cooler sister, the *superior* sister. You get everything you want, you always have, and I'm sure you always will—"

"Tate, you know that's not true—"

"It *is* true!" Tate was hysterical; she could hardly catch her breath. She gazed out at Nantucket in the distance. She might never see Barrett again. She had stupidly, idiotically sent him away. "I can't breathe when you're around! You suck up all the oxygen. You are so self-centered, so self-*absorbed*—"

"Tate—" Chess said.

"You stole my boyfriend," Tate said. "You spent the day with him! You ate lunch with him, you took a nap with him, you ran errands together, he confided in you—"

"Yes," Chess said. "Yes, yes, yes. He confided in me. He told me he's in love with you."

Tate grabbed her sister's wrist. It was rough and lumpy with poison ivy. Tate wanted to wrench Chess's arm right off her body. "He told you that? He told *you* that? But he's never told *me* that. Do you see? Do you see how you're interfering and ruining everything?" She threw Chess's wrist back at her, and Chess took a stutter step backward and fell off the steps into the sand. Rather than apologize, Tate rushed her sister. She pushed both her hands into Chess and knocked her down.

"Tate!" Chess screamed. "Leave me alone!"

"You leave *me* alone!" Tate said. "You make me wish I had never been born!"

"I'm sorry!" Chess said. She was crying. "I'm sorry I got poison ivy, I'm sorry I had to go to the hospital. I'm sorry your boyfriend was the only one who could take me. I'm sorry that you feel I've ruined your life. I'm sorry you think my life is so perfect. I assure you, my life is *not* perfect. I assure you, I have *not* gotten everything I wanted. Not by a long shot."

Tate said, "Well, if there is something wrong with your life, why don't you *tell me what it is?* Tell me what happened with Michael! Tell me your horrible secret!"

"I can't!" Chess said. "I can't tell you. I can't tell anyone!"

"Did you tell Barrett?" Tate asked. "Did you tell him today?"

Chess pressed her fingers against her red and swollen eyes. Her face was a blotchy mess; the patches of poison ivy seemed to be growing redder and angrier. "You are so immature," Chess said. "You should listen to yourself. You sound like you're twelve years old."

"Shut up!" Tate screamed.

"You shut up!" Chess said. "And leave me alone!"

"I hate you!" Tate said. "I'm glad you're miserable!"

BIRDIE AND INDIA

India was in her bedroom when the screaming started. She could tell it was coming from the beach, but it took her another second to realize it was Chess and Tate. India sat on her bed and closed her eyes. God, the pain of having a sister, another girl, another woman, not you, but nearly you. A friend, a confidante, a rival, an enemy. She remembered the summer that... Billy was three, Teddy was fourteen months old, and India was pregnant with Ethan. They were here on Tuckernuck, down on the beach; India was in a low-slung beach chair with Teddy in her lap, and Billy was at the water's edge. India had been so tired, first trimester tired, she couldn't keep her eyes open, and then the next thing she knew, her eyes *were* open and she was watching Billy go under, whoosh, like he was being sucked into a vacuum. India tried to cry out—*Help! Billy!*—she tried to jump out of her chair, but Teddy was asleep and as heavy as lead in her arms. India's lethargic body was betraying her. She couldn't make herself move fast enough.

"Bill!" she shouted. Where was Bill? "Billy!"

Birdie had appeared out of nowhere. She had dashed into the water and scooped Billy up; he was sputtering water at first, then wailing. Birdie pounded Billy on the back, expelling the seawater, and then she was shushing him against her chest. India had hated Birdie in that moment, had hated that Birdie was the one to pull Billy out of the ocean, to save his life. And India had loved her, too. She had loved her with a depth and passion that she couldn't explain. When no one else was there, Birdie was there.

The screaming continued. India went downstairs.

Birdie was pouring herself a glass of Sancerre when the screaming started. At first, she didn't know what on earth...so she walked out to the edge of the bluff. It sounded like Chess and Tate. Could it be? She saw them at the bottom of the steps. She heard Tate say, *I hate you!*

Birdie turned and walked back to the house. With each step, her heart shrank. It was awful to hear her daughters speak to each other like that. It felt as bad as it must feel for a child to hear his parents fighting. At least she and Grant had never fought in front of the children. There wasn't a lot they could be proud of, but they could be proud of that.

India was standing at the picnic table as Birdie approached. She reached out for Birdie. Wordlessly, they embraced. Birdie smelled India's musky scent; she felt the bristles of India's short hair and the soft skin of her cheek.

They separated. India handed Birdie her glass of wine and then offered her a cigarette.

"Thank you," Birdie whispered.

"You're welcome," India whispered back.

CHESS

Nick and I had agreed: Clean break with Michael first. Clean, meaning I was not to mention Nick. This left me with no reason to break the engagement other than the stark and unapologetic I'm not in love with you anymore.

My conversation with Michael, which was a series of conversations, went something like this:

Me (crying): "I can't marry you."

"What?"

"I can't marry you." (I had to say everything six or seven times for it to sink in.)

"Why not? What happened?"

"What happened" was the big question—put to me by Michael, my mother, my father, my sister, by Evelyn, by my friends, by my assistant. When Michael called Nick to tell him the engagement was off, I wonder if Nick said, "What happened?" I was pretty sure he didn't say that, but I didn't know for sure. We had agreed not to speak again until the smoke had cleared.

"Nothing 'happened,'" I said. "I just don't feel the same way anymore."

"Why not?" Michael said. "I don't get it. Did I do something wrong? Did I say something wrong?"

"No, no, no," I said. I didn't want to make this his fault. The only thing he had done "wrong" was to propose in the public way that he did. It forced me to say yes. But I could have undone the proposal immediately after accepting; the knot had been loose at that point. No plans had been made, no bridesmaids asked, no deposits plunked down. I could have asked for time, then more time, and slipped out.

"I should never have said yes."

"Because you didn't love me even then?" Michael asked. "You never loved me?"

"I loved you. I love you now."

"Then marry me."

What I didn't say was this: I don't love you enough and I don't love you the right way. If I marry you, bad things will happen. Maybe not right away, but down the road. We will be at a family gathering and I will stare longingly at Nick. I will bump into him behind the shed in your parents' backyard, where one of our kids has thrown his Frisbee, and he will kiss me. And then, as we drive back into the city, I will be moody, and when we get home, I will pack my bags. Or I will have a full-blown affair with someone who reminds me of Nick but who doesn't have your best interest at heart the way that Nick does. This man will steal me away; he will steal your house and your children. You will be left with much less than you have now.

What I did say was: "I can't."

"You can."

"All right, then I won't."

He didn't understand. Nobody understood. Michael and I were so perfect together. We liked the same things; we seemed so happy. People fell into two categories: Those who understood the intangible quality of love and thought I was smart to get out while I could. And those who didn't understand the intangible quality of love. These people looked at

Michael and me and saw a match—perfect on paper!—and thought I was making a whopping, self-destructive mistake.

I explained myself until there was nothing left inside me except for the nugget of truth that I would not reveal: I loved Nick.

Michael suspected someone else. He asked me over and over again in every conversation: "Is there someone else?"

"No," I said.

And this was true. Nick wasn't mine in any real sense. He had no claims on me, nor I on him. But I knew he was waiting.

We talked after about ten days. I gave him the rundown, and he gave me the rundown. Because Michael wasn't only talking to me; he was talking to Nick.

Nick said, "Man, this is tough. This is weighing on my soul."

I said, "What should we do?"

He said, "I'm leaving for Toronto to make this album on June tenth. I want you to come with me."

"Come with you?"

"Come to Toronto with me. Live with me. Let's find out if this thing is real."

It meant leaving my job. It meant leaving New York. The job was easy enough. I had been food editor for three years; what had been the most exciting challenge of my life was now a spin on the lazy Susan. January/February: comfort foods. March/April: lighten up. May: foreign issue. June: garden fresh. July: BBQ. August: picnic. September: football tailgates. October: harvest flavors. November: Thanksgiving. December: Christmas/Hanukkah. I was ready to hop off.

We put the July issue to bed early, finishing at two o'clock. It was a lovely spring day and I gave my assistant, Erica, the rest of the day off. Then I walked into the office of my managing editor, David Nunzio, and told him I was leaving the magazine. From there, I walked to the office of the editor in chief, Clark Boyd, with David Nunzio trailing behind me saying he hoped I wasn't serious, I couldn't just leave, boom, like that, and what could they do to get me to stay? Did I want more money? I told Clark Boyd that I was leaving.

"Leaving?" he said.

"I'm done," I said. "I quit."

Both Clark Boyd and David Nunzio studied me for a moment, as if realizing at the same time that I might not be in my right mind. Indeed, some essential part of me was missing; I loved this job, I was good at it, and yet here I was, walking away.

Clark said, "I know you've been through a rough time..."

I laughed, but the laugh sounded like a hiccup. I wasn't even getting the laugh right. But I found it funny that Clark Boyd would have any inkling about my broken engagement, although of course the offices of Glamorous Home, *just like any other workplace, was a nest of gossip and rumors. I had tried to keep it under wraps; I hadn't taken a single personal call.*

"This has nothing to do with...," I said. Then I stopped. I didn't owe them an explanation.

"If you need time...," Clark said.

"I'm done," I said. "Finished. I'll get you a letter of resignation." Although this seemed such a stupid formality. I just wanted to walk free.

Once I was down on the street, I felt better. I watched the other New Yorkers in their spring suits and high heels carrying bags from Duane Reade and Barnes and Noble, and I thought, Okay, what now?

Nick and Michael were going rock climbing in Moab over Memorial Day weekend. Nick was going to tell him. He had to tell him because I was coming to Toronto. I wanted to travel to Canada secretly. Michael didn't need to know yet; *it would be wiser to give him time, to let him start dating again. But Nick was a straight shooter, and Michael was his brother. Nick would tell him when they were alone in the desert. Michael could yell as loudly as he wanted; he could throw punches. Nick would take them.*

It was the ultimate gamble. I was afraid that was what appealed about it to Nick. He never lost at cards, but what if he lost here?

"What are you going to say?" I asked him.

"The truth," Nick said. "That I love you. That I've loved you from the first second I saw you."

I had sublet my apartment to a friend of Rhonda's from the New School (that apartment was my baby, so I couldn't let it go) and packed my things and arrived on my mother's doorstep just about the same time that Michael and Nick were landing in Utah. I wasn't doing well. I was anxious, nervous, morose. I couldn't imagine being Nick, nor could I imagine being Michael. I tried to throw my phone away, but my mother picked it from the trash, thinking I would thank her later.

I slept most of the weekend. I hid behind Vogue; *I tried to read a novel, but the story of my own life kept inserting itself in the pages. I tried to remember who I had been before meeting the Morgan brothers. Where was the happy girl who had walked into the Bowery Ballroom that October night? I tried to come up with a plan; I had always been big on making a plan and sticking to it. I would go to Toronto, leave for Tuckernuck for two weeks with my mother and sister (I would tell them then), and then return to Toronto. And if the thing turned out to be real, if I was in love, if I was happy, I would go with Nick on tour. And do what for money? Freelance? Start a novel? It sounded so cliché. It sounded so* midlife crisis. *I was only thirty-two.*

* * *

When it happened, Nick called his parents first, me second. On the phone, his voice was calm; it was dispassionate. I didn't understand this. I still don't. Robin, my therapist, said he was most likely in shock.

In shock.

"Michael's dead," Nick said. "He fell. He woke up this morning at dawn and went climbing alone. He wasn't harnessed properly. He fell."

I didn't ask. I knew. I didn't ask.

Nick said, "I told him last night. He seemed fine with it. Angry, really fucking angry, yep, he punched a hole in the hotel wall, right through the plaster, and I thought, Okay, that's a start. *I told him the truth: We had kissed, but only kissed. I told him if I could change how I felt, I would, and I knew you would, too, but that we couldn't change it. It was there, it existed. I had big, scary feelings for you, and you had feelings for me. Yep, he said, he understood. We went out to a bar, drank beers, did shots of tequila, ate burgers. He got drunk and I let him. Why not? He was handling it okay, he was being a really good fucking sport, a gentleman as ever. We walked back to the hotel, he asked me if I hated him because things had always come easier for him, and I said, 'No, Mikey, I don't hate you. That's not what this is about, man.'*

"He asked me if I hated him because of the punch he'd thrown years ago, the punch that broke my nose. That fight had been over a girl, too, a girl at school named Candace Jackson. He'd won that fight and he'd won Candace. And I said, 'No, man, it's not about Candace or my nose.'

"He said, 'Okay, I believe you.'

"And then in the morning, he headed out to climb in Labyrinth by himself. It wasn't safe to climb Labyrinth alone and he wasn't harnessed properly."

Nick broke down crying. "Chess," he said. "Chess."

"I know," I said. "Jesus, I know."

"I told my parents he wasn't harnessed properly," Nick said. "But Chess?"

"What?" I said. "What?"

"He wasn't harnessed at all."

Michael hadn't died because his safety equipment failed. He had died because he went climbing without safety equipment.

The difference between these two realities, between the accidental and the intentional, was monstrous. It was the monstrous secret that now bonded me to Nick.

Chess closed the notebook. Her confession ended there. At the funeral, Nick stood on the altar and said to everyone in the church, *He really loved you, Chess.* He hadn't said, *I really love you, Chess.* He may have felt it, Chess knew he felt it, and wherever he was—in Toronto still, or on the road somewhere—he felt it right now the way she did, like an arrow shot through her from front to back, pain, longing, love, regret. But he didn't say it because Michael was his brother, now dead, and to say the truth out loud would be profane.

Tate took the Scout and disappeared in a cloud of dust and a spray of gravel. India and Chess sat at the picnic table while Birdie made dinner.

Chess said, "She'll never speak to me again."

India said, "Oh, you'll be surprised."

Tate missed dinner. She stayed out until sunset; she stayed out until dark. Birdie and India and Chess sat on the screened-in porch, Birdie doing her needlepoint, India doing her crossword puzzles, Chess pretending to read *War and Peace,* but really she was trying not to scratch her face and pretending not to listen for the car.

Chess said, "She can't stay out all night."

India said, "Don't worry, she'll be back. Getting some time away will be good for her. I'm sure she's doing some thinking. I'm sure she regrets the things she said to you."

But Chess knew she didn't regret the things she'd said. She had been waiting her whole life to say them. Chess, by virtue of being who she was, had always outshone and overshadowed Tate. She had stunted Tate's growth. But she had not done so on purpose, and she certainly hadn't meant to pose a threat with Barrett.

Birdie sighed. "I wish Grant were here."

Chess went to bed before Tate got home. She laid her confession on Tate's pillow.

When Chess woke up, Tate's bed was empty. It hadn't been slept in and the confession was right where Chess had left it.

Chess went to the bathroom and peered out the window. The Scout was in the driveway.

Chess slipped downstairs, her heart tiptoeing. Chess was afraid of her own sister. She felt guilty for years and years of infractions, involuntary as they may have been. She wanted absolution; she needed Tate's unconditional love, but it had been retracted. *I hate you! You make me wish I had never been born!* So Chess *was* toxic after all, as she feared when they started this trip. Chess had been slowly, silently poisoning Tate's drinking water, polluting her atmosphere. *You suck up all the air and I can't breathe!* This, Chess thought, was the awful end. She could lose Michael, she could lose Nick—they were boys—but she could not lose her sister.

When Chess got downstairs, she saw the scratchy crocheted afghan spread out over the ass-tearing green couch.

"Did she . . . ?"

"She slept on the couch," Birdie said. Chess couldn't tell what Birdie thought about this.

"Did she say anything?"

Birdie held out a plate with two eggs over easy and a piece of wheat toast, lavishly buttered. Chess accepted it.

"She's still pretty angry," Birdie said.

"I didn't *do* anything, Birdie," Chess said. She wanted her mother to understand this. "I'm not out to steal Barrett away from her."

"Oh, heavens, I know," Birdie said. "And she knows that, too. I think she's dealing with older issues."

Birdie wasn't helping set Chess's mind at ease. Birdie and Tate had always been closer than Birdie and Chess. Tate courted Birdie in a way that Chess found unnecessary. But right now, she realized, it would be nice to have her mother on her side.

"I guess," Chess said.

"Your sister has been jealous of you your whole life," Birdie said. "Just the way I've been jealous of India."

"Jealous of me?" India said, descending the stairs. "What the hell are you talking about?"

A few minutes later, a young man appeared in the doorway.

"Is this the Tate house?" he asked. He was about nineteen or twenty and he looked enough like a young Barrett Lee that Chess blinked in surprise. The blond hair flopping in his eyes, the lean build, the visor, the sunglasses, the flip-flops.

"Yes!" Birdie said.

"I'm Trey Wilson," the boy said. "I work for Barrett Lee."

India said, "You could be his stunt double."

Birdie said, "Where's Barrett?"

"He's at another job," Trey said. "So he sent me. I'll be doing deliveries from now on. He said I'm supposed to get your trash and your laundry and the... list?"

Birdie said, "I'm confused."

At that second, Tate walked in. She looked at Trey and did a double take; then she stormed up the stairs. Trey gathered a dripping bag of ice and a bag of groceries from the picnic table.

Chess took the ice. "Barrett has another job, so he sent Trey. Trey is going to be coming from now on."

"But what about Barrett?" Birdie said.

"He's *gone!*" a voice from upstairs shouted.

INDIA

India missed Barrett more than she expected she would. The new kid was cute—he looked enough like Barrett to be his long-lost little brother—but he didn't connect with people the way Barrett did. Trey Wilson was a kid who could drive a boat. He didn't care about Tuckernuck and he didn't care about them. There was no history and no intrigue. It was too bad, India thought, that they had to end the vacation this way.

There had been only one time that India could remember when Chuck Lee had failed to appear, and that had been India's fault. It was the summer after Bill had killed himself; India had come to Tuckernuck as usual, but from the beginning her heart wasn't in it. She had two of the three boys with her; Billy had taken a counselor job at a basketball camp at Duke for the summer. Birdie and Grant and the kids were there, and they went through the motions of doing the same things—the driving lessons, the clambake, the walks to North Pond and East Pond—but India always felt like she was watching from half a mile away. Chuck Lee had been the one coming twice a day then, though he frequently had Barrett with him, in training. When Chuck came alone, he always said something nice to India, complimented her hair or earrings, told her she was getting tan; on several occasions, they shared a cigarette down on the beach. In those days, there was no smoking up at the house because Grant hated the smell. Chuck never asked about what had happened to Bill, though India assumed he knew. Once, he picked a perfect sand dollar up off the beach and gave it to her. He said, "Here. Tuckernuck souvenir." India had kept the sand dollar—she still had it—because Chuck had given it to her and Chuck had been the first man she'd ever noticed, back when she still wore a training bra. She had thought that maybe—just maybe—something would happen that summer, but she was too buried to make a move, and Chuck had a wife on the other side of the water. Eleanor, her name was, Barrett's mother, Chuck's wife of a million years, a real battle-ax, he said, whatever that meant.

Near the end of their stay, Chuck showed up with bluefish fillets that he had caught; he presented them to India in a heavy-duty Ziploc bag, and India could tell by the set of his shoulders, and by the way he pretended it was no big deal, that it was a big deal. India acted very grateful. But the bluefish fillets were a lurid red, they were slick and oily, and India, as well as everyone else in the family, abhorred bluefish. India thanked Chuck profusely and promised they would grill the fish for dinner that night. Chuck seemed pleased by this, as pleased as he ever got, with the touch of a smile lifting the cigarette in his mouth.

"All right, then, good," he said. "I'm glad I brought them."

As soon as Chuck was gone, India threw the bluefish fillets out on the bluff, and the seagulls swooped in to devour them.

The next morning, India made a point of raving about how delicious the bluefish had been. Again, Chuck gave the half smile. And not five minutes later, India's youngest son, Ethan, came out, and when Chuck asked him how he liked the fish, he said, "Mom threw the fish out on the bluff and the seagulls ate it."

India was mortified. She remembered her face burning; she remembered being at a complete loss for words. Chuck wouldn't look at her. He collected the trash and left without the list. He didn't come that afternoon nor the following morning. Grant was bellowing about his *Wall Street Journal,* and India kept to her room, watching out the window, like the old Nantucket widows waiting for their husbands to return from the sea. She couldn't believe how bad she felt. She had already suffered through the worst of the worst; she hadn't believed that anything else could affect her. But she cared about Chuck. She explained to Birdie what had happened, and this helped because Birdie understood how India felt about Chuck Lee; Birdie felt pretty much the same way herself. Chuck Lee had been the romantic hero of their youth. Birdie and India fretted together; they worried he would never come back.

He did eventually return, but India sensed things had changed. He didn't like her anymore. Didn't he realize that she had only lied to spare his feelings? She couldn't confront him about it; he wasn't the kind of man you could apologize to. He was the kind of man you tried to keep happy because one slip and...

Well, it was never the same. There were no more compliments, no more shared cigarette breaks, no more offerings of sand dollars or fish. They left that summer, and when they returned the following summer, Barrett was doing the deliveries.

And now Barrett, too, was gone. India couldn't help feeling a bit bereft.

* * *

On the afternoon of the second day, Trey Wilson appeared with a package for India. He wasn't even sure which one of the women India was, so it was fortunate that India was sitting at the picnic table, smoking. Chess was down on the beach, Tate had driven the Scout to North Pond—the two girls still weren't speaking—and Birdie had gone for "a walk," which meant she was off to either secretly console Tate or make another one of her clandestine phone calls.

"India?" Trey said. He was so young that he rightfully should have called her "Mrs. Bishop," but they were on Tuckernuck, where things were insistently casual, and the kids' friends had always called her "India" anyway. Trey held out the small, flat package to her.

"For me?" India said. She put on Bill's reading glasses. The familiar handwriting, the absurdly sparse address. "Well, thank you."

"You're welcome," Trey Wilson said. He smiled at her. "What should I do with the groceries?"

"Just leave them on the counter, thanks," India said.

He did this, then loitered at her elbow as if he expected to be tipped. He didn't expect to be tipped, did he? India hadn't touched money in weeks; she wasn't even sure where her wallet was. She smiled at him, and he said, "Do you have anything for me?"

What was he asking?

"Trash?" he said. "Laundry? The list?"

"Oh!" India jumped up. Barrett had emptied the trash automatically, and he had taken the list from its usual spot—under the jar of shells and beach glass on the kitchen counter. India wasn't the woman of the house, but it was falling to her to teach this young man the ropes. Was there really any point, with only five days left?

She said, "The trash is here." She lifted out the liner and cinched its yellow plastic handle; then she set in a new liner, even though this was something Barrett had always done himself. "And the list is always kept right here."

Trey nodded glumly and accepted the list.

"Okay," he said. "Thanks."

"Thank *you,*" India said.

The boy loped away. India missed the real Barrett. And she missed Chuck Lee, the original man of her dreams.

At the picnic table, she turned the package in her hands.

She wanted a glass of wine or a cigarette—or preferably both—but there wasn't time. The others might appear at any second. *So open it, open it!*

It was a painting. Rather, it was part of a painting, part of one of the nudes of India, which Lula had cut into a five-by-five-inch square and reframed. India studied the small canvas; she turned it in the sun. Then she got it: it was the curve of India's hip, delicately shaded to accentuate the sensual sweep toward what lay south. India immediately knew which canvas Lula had cut up: it was the magnificent canvas that Spencer Frost had bought for the school. India gasped at the thought of that breathtaking painting now vandalized; Lula had snipped the hip from the painting like a woman clipping a coupon. But the act was anything but casual, India knew. Lula would have had to lift the painting off the wall and carry it to her studio. This would have been a fairly easy thing to do undetected; in the summertime, the halls of PAFA were deserted, and the school had zero budget for security measures for student work. Although Lula had withdrawn from the school, she wouldn't have to turn in her keys or vacate her studio space until mid-August.

India pictured Lula's studio: She had one of the coveted corner units, with a big window looking south over the city. She had a battered leather sofa, which was smudged with paint, and an old steamer trunk that she used as a coffee table. She had a half fridge, a full-size drafting table that she had salvaged from outside a big architecture firm, and stacks and stacks of art books and magazines—*Vogue, Playboy, Nylon*. She had a docking station for her iPod, and a makeshift closet, where she kept clothes so that she didn't have to go back to her apartment to change before she went out at night. The studio was her holy space. Lula had laid the canvas on the drafting table, perhaps, and studied it to decide where and how much to cut. Her procedure would have been as serious as a surgeon's. In cutting the painting, she was cutting herself. What she had sent, India realized, was her own version of van Gogh's ear. It was love and it was insanity.

In some ways, the small painting reminded India of the details of paintings shown in art history texts—portions of paintings were zoomed in on to show the reader the exquisite brushwork or technique. But in another way this small piece became something else. It could be the inside of a shell, or the swirl of a sand dune. Lula was, as ever, a genius. This small painting was its own whole.

There was a tiny white envelope with the painting, the kind used by florists when delivering flowers. India ripped it open. One word.

Try?

The question mark got her. Lula was asking, begging, pleading.

Try? Could she try?

Barrett kept a tool box in the bottom of the downstairs closet. India raided it and found a hammer and a nail.

Upstairs in her bedroom, she pounded the nail into the wall. Her first try punched the nail right through the plaster. She had to find a joist. She tried another spot, and the nail met with resistance. India hammered; the walls of the house shook, and India imagined them folding like a house of cards. She got the nail in, however, and she hung the painting. It was perfect here, she decided. It looked like the curve of Bigelow Point, or like the peachy inside of a whelk shell that the kids had picked off Whale Shoal.

She regarded Roger. "What do you think?" she asked.

His seaweed hair waved in the breeze.

BIRDIE

From the tip of Bigelow Point, she called Grant.

"He's in a meeting," his secretary, Alice, said. "Shall I have him call you back?"

"No," Birdie said. "That's okay."

She hung up the phone, immediately disenchanted. Now see? This was the Grant Cousins she had known for thirty years. In a meeting. On the eighth fairway. On a conference call with Washington, Tokyo, London. At dinner at Gallagher's. Unavailable. Can I have him call you back? Can I take a message? *Yes, tell him I need him. Tate pushed another child off the slide and that child has broken her arm. It will be a miracle if the parents don't sue. It's urgent. I'm miscarrying, again, on my way to the hospital. Please make sure he picks the girls up at preschool. It's an emergency. Tell him I'd like to speak to him about Ondine Morris. Someone overheard her praising Grant's fine physique in the ladies' locker room at the club. Have him call me immediately. I'm bored, I'm lonely, I should never have left my job at Christie's, I loved carpets, the stories they tell, the hands that knot them, he knew that. Why did he ask me to quit? Tell him earning ten million dollars a year doesn't mean he can effectively ignore his children. They're clamoring for him.*

I am clamoring for him. Please have him call me.

Birdie wanted to talk to Grant about the girls. He was their father. But when he learned the girls were fighting, what would he say? Would he be as concerned as Birdie was? Or would he wait, as always, for Birdie to tell him how to feel? She had thought, in the weeks since she'd been here, that she'd sensed a change in Grant. An emerging sensitivity. He had been sweet and attentive on the phone, supportive about her travails with Hank; he had been wistful and romantic. He had sent those flowers and worded the card perfectly. Birdie found it hard to admit, but she had been entertaining notions of being with Grant again. She would never, ever live with him, but they could be friends. They could do things together, alone, and with the children. She had thought she was immune to the old hurt. *He's in a meeting. Shall I have him call you back?*

But she wasn't.

She stumbled across Tate by accident, although Tuckernuck was small and Birdie knew where to look. At first she guessed Tate would be at North Pond, and when she wasn't there, Birdie guessed East Pond. East Pond was smaller than North Pond and not quite as beautiful, although it had its own charms; the part of the pond that was farthest inland was bordered by fragrant *Rosa rugosa* and beach plum. Birdie guessed that Tate was in the mood for East Pond, feeling smaller and not quite as beautiful herself.

Birdie was right. Tate was there, with her earbuds on. She was propped on her elbows, but when she saw

Birdie, she fell back flat. Birdie had half a mind to keep walking. Tate didn't want to see her, and Birdie didn't belong in the middle of whatever was happening between her daughters. When the girls were teenagers, Birdie had such a hard time with their squabbling that she went to see a family counselor, who advised Birdie to let the girls work it out themselves. Had she listened? No. They were her daughters; she wanted them to love each other. She had brokered the peace treaties then, and here she was, doing it now.

She marched over and sat next to Tate. She touched Tate's arm and Tate removed an earbud and sat up halfway.

"Hi," Birdie said.

Tate said, "Birdie, don't."

"Don't what?"

"Don't try to make me feel better. Because it's not going to work. This isn't something a mother can fix."

"Okay," Birdie said.

"I miss Barrett," Tate said. "I sent him away and now I want him back."

"I'm sure he misses you, too," Birdie said.

"You never thought we had a chance," Tate said. "But I did. Because I love him. I've loved him forever."

"It wasn't that I thought you didn't have a chance..."

"You thought it was a pipe dream. A stupid summer fantasy."

"Tate, don't be mean."

"You're the one who's mean. You and my sister."

"Tate."

"I told Chess I hated her, and I meant it. I hate her. Everything I wanted in life, she took away."

"That's not true," Birdie said.

Tate pressed her lips together, and Birdie saw her as a little girl, stubborn, defiant, angry. She had always been full of love, but she had also always been angry. Nothing Birdie had done in the past thirty years had been able to change that.

Birdie stood up and wiped her palms on her shorts. "I'm going to let you girls work this out yourselves," she said.

Tate muttered something as she flipped onto her stomach, but Birdie didn't hear what it was and she wouldn't ask Tate to repeat herself as she might have done when Tate was a teenager. But as Birdie walked the path back to the house, she wondered what Tate had said. Probably "Whatever," or "Yeah, right." Or maybe she had said, "Thank you," which was the best that Birdie could hope for.

TATE

That night, Tate left the house during the communal screened-in porch hour and descended the stairs to the beach. The moon, which had been fat and full the night of the bonfire, was now a waning crescent, which made Tate sad. Tomorrow there would be four days left, and the next day three—and then they would start to pack up. Across the water, the lights of Nantucket twinkled.

Barrett!

What was he doing tonight? Was he at home with the kids, or out with Anita at some fancy benefit because Roman was stuck in the city?

He had to be missing her. He had to be thinking about her. He was in love with her. He had told Chess he was in love with her (unless Chess was lying, but even she wouldn't cross that line).

Prayer worked, she reminded herself. And so she prayed. *Please please please please please please please.*

Tomorrow, Tate decided, he would come.

The next morning, Tate was standing on the beach when *Girlfriend* pulled into the cove.

Trey was driving the boat.

Tate thought, *So much for prayer.*

She said, "How's Barrett doing?"

Trey shrugged. "He's busy."

A few minutes later, she knocked on Aunt India's door.

"*Entrez!*" India said.

Tate stepped in and noticed something different right away. A painting. A small, square painting on the wall.

"What is this?" Tate asked.

"The inside of a whelk shell," India said. She was on her bed, smoking and reading.

"Oh," Tate said. "Yeah, I guess I can see that. Who did it?"

"A student at PAFA," India said. She exhaled smoke. "Are you visiting for a reason or is this a purely social call?"

"A reason," Tate said. She wasn't sure she could go through with this. She didn't like asking people for help. People asked *her* for help. That was her job; that was how she ran her life.

"Shoot," India said.

Tate sank onto the bed. The mattress was truly unusual. It was like it was filled with quicksand; you sat on it and it sucked you in. Tate was sure that if they ever cut it open, they would find it was filled with something bizarre and horrifying, like the blood plasma of all her dead ancestors.

"Barrett has this client, Anita," Tate said.

"I met her."

"She wants to buy Roger," Tate said.

"Yes, I know," India said. "Barrett told me. Fifty thousand dollars."

"So you told him it wasn't for sale, and he told Anita. And Anita got mad. And she pulled a power play where she offered Barrett a full-time job, working for her only, with a salary he couldn't turn down. He owes her a bunch of money anyway, from before, when his wife was sick and she needed private nurses."

"Oh," India said. "I didn't know any of this."

"Which is why I'm telling you," Tate said. "That's why Barrett doesn't come anymore. That's why he sends Trey."

"Ah," India said.

"And he doesn't come for me because I got angry that he was working for Anita." Tate stared at India's new painting. There was something compelling about it. "I guess you could say we broke up."

"Thank you for explaining," India said. "I wondered, but it's really not my place to ask. I'm just the aunt."

"No, you're way more than that," Tate said. "You're one of us."

"Well, thank you for saying that. And you know I love you and Chess like my own children."

Tate nodded. She swallowed. Her throat was coated with a film of despair. She said, "So anyway, I came up here to see if you would reconsider selling Roger."

India's eyes widened, but more in recognition, Tate hoped, than in shock or anger.

Tate said, "I thought if I went back to where the problem started, I could fix it. If you sold Roger to Anita, Anita would leave Barrett alone."

India said, "I want you to hold Roger."

Tate picked Roger up off the dresser—but carefully!

He was delicate and valuable. He was whisper-light, made of driftwood and dried seaweed, beach glass and shells. He had style, though. His hair looked like dreadlocks and his eyes were round, like funky Elton John glasses.

"How did Uncle Bill get the glass and shells to stick?" Tate asked.

"Chuck Lee lent him a glue gun. Secretly, I guess. And then he filched the electricity off the generator. Bill was resourceful."

Tate stroked the driftwood, which had grayed over the years, making Roger seem as if he were aging like a real person.

"Your Uncle Bill made him for me after we had a terrible fight," India said.

Tate nodded. A terrible fight.

"I can't sell him," India said. "He doesn't belong in Anita Fullin's house or in a museum. He doesn't even belong at home with me in Pennsylvania. He belongs here, in this house. He will stay here—forever, I hope. And that's the secret about certain pieces of art. They have their own integrity, and we, as humans, must respect that." She stubbed out her cigarette. "I would do anything for you, Tate. And I know you love Barrett and I know you're hurting, but I can tell you that selling Roger to Anita Fullin isn't going to bring about the kind of change you're looking for. Only you can do that."

Tate set Roger back on the dresser. Childishly, she felt hot tears of disappointment fill her eyes—like when she lost the hundred-yard dash at the Fairfield Regional Championships to Marissa Hart, whom she detested. Like when her father grounded her for a D in English and she missed seeing Bruce Springsteen at the Meadowlands. She hadn't progressed emotionally since she was a teenager—that was the problem. She needed, somehow, to figure out how an adult woman would act.

"I know," she said. "I just thought I'd ask."

"I'm glad you asked," India said. "I'm glad you feel you can come to me when you have a problem. And believe me, if I could help you, I would."

Tate nodded. The fact that Aunt India was being so nice made things worse. When Tate stood up, her eyes were drawn to the painting. The inside of a whelk shell? Tate could see that, sort of, but to her, the pale, flesh-colored curve represented something else: loneliness, desolation.

CHESS

Tate hadn't read the confession, and this was an infraction Chess couldn't forgive. Tate had said she wanted to understand about "all that had happened," and there it was, written down in minute detail, and yet Tate hadn't even opened the front cover. She'd moved the journal to the dresser, but Chess could tell it hadn't been opened.

There were only three days left. On the one hand, Chess was glad. She couldn't stand the tension between her and her sister. They weren't speaking except when absolutely necessary. Chess had accidentally opened the bathroom door while Tate was on the toilet, and Tate had barked, *I'm in here!*

And then at dinner, she said, *Pass the salt.*

The discord between Chess and Tate was a fog settling over the house. And yet Chess didn't want to leave Tuckernuck. One thing had become true: she was safe here. She wondered if she could stay here alone, and if she did stay here alone, what would happen? She would become some kind of strange hermit, unwashed and unshaven, who talked to herself. But she could read and write and cook certain things; she could take up astronomy or fly-fishing. She could be self-sufficient, and after a while, she guessed, her memories of other people would fade away.

After dinner, Chess retreated to the attic. Tate had taken the Scout and gone to watch the sunset off the west bluff; Chess wanted to go, too, but hadn't dared ask. She lay on her bed, knowing she should go downstairs to sit on the screened-in porch with her mother and her aunt, but she lacked the motivation. She shouldn't be allowed to stay on this island by herself; it wasn't healthy. She would have to go back to New York and start over. The mere thought exhausted her. She lay on her bed until the light faded and the evening purpled. Chess listened for the Scout pulling in. There was nothing but the thickening silence.

And then she heard a noise. A whooshing sound. A presence, there in the room. She knew what it was, somewhere around her head, the flap of black, scaly wings. She sat up in terror. *Oh. My. God.* Her whole life she had been afraid of this: evil black sacks unfolding into the vampire's spawn. A bat! It flew past her head; she could feel the air from its beating wings. And then another one. There were two of them, diving for her.

Chess put her arms over her head. She considered crawling under the covers, but she didn't want to trap herself. She needed to get out of the attic, but she was too terrified to move. Tate had always belittled Chess's fear of the bats—first saying there were no bats, then saying that even if there were bats, they echolocate and would never brush Chess's hair or face. But these bats must have been genetic mutants because they were going crazy; she could hear them keening, a sharp, high-pitched whine.

Chess didn't know what to do, so she started to shriek. She shrieked at the top of her register. *Aaaaaaahee-oweeee! Help me! Aaaaaaaaheeowee!* She waved her arms over her head. Then she was afraid she might accidentally touch one. She didn't want them near her with their beady eyes, their sharp little teeth, their creepy, black lace wings, which would cover her mouth and suffocate her. She screamed. The screaming felt good, letting it out, expressing not only her terror but her sadness and her anger. *Aaaaaaaaaheeeowee!* She shrieked until her throat was sore.

The door flew open and Tate burst in, wielding the broom from the kitchen. She was wearing work gloves, which she must have snatched from Barrett's tool box. She had always told Chess that bats ate mosquitoes, not people, yet if she believed this, why was she wearing work gloves? Chess wanted work gloves; she wanted a suit of armor. Really, she thought, she had never been so glad to see her sister.

Tate swung at the bats with the broom. They flew around her, dodging her attacks. There was a third one now—Chess was able to open her eyes and see three bats!

Tate said, "I'm trying to encourage them toward the window."

Chess nearly smiled. It was such a lovely word, "encourage," when what it looked like was that Tate was trying to beat them to death. Chess remained huddled on the bed while Tate ran around the attic with the broom, swatting in the bats' general direction. The one pathetically small window was open, but getting the bats to move toward it—toward open sky, night air, the all-you-can-eat mosquito buffet—didn't seem to be working.

Tate said, "I have another idea." And she left.

"Nooooooo!" Chess screamed. She tented her knees and hid her face, then covered her head with her hands, the preferred posture for most emergencies and natural disasters. "Tate! Taaaaaaaaaate!"

Tate returned with a long-handled net, the net their grandfather had used for fishing and crabbing. She ran around the room trying to scoop up the bats in the net, and as Chess watched her—Tate was still wearing the work gloves and now an ancient baseball cap from a tackle shop on Nantucket, probably long defunct—she realized that Tate was afraid of the bats, too. She was afraid! This made Chess feel better, and watching Tate chase the bats around the room with the net in what was clearly a fruitless endeavor suddenly seemed... funny. A chuckle erupted from Chess's throat; then she laughed. She laughed and laughed until she was holding her stomach and hiccuping.

Tate glanced at her and stopped dead still. She dropped the net to the floor with a clatter. Then she came over to the bed and hugged Chess.

She said, "I give up. Let them come and get us."

"Let them eat us," Chess said.

"Maybe we'll turn into vampires," Tate said. "Vampires are very hot these days."

They sat quietly, half-embracing, to see what would happen.

Chess whispered, "Where are Birdie and India?"

"On the porch," Tate said. "I told them whatever it was, I'd take care of it."

"Oh, you took care of it all right," Chess said.

They were quiet. The bats seemed to calm down.

They circled, they swooped, they did figure eights. They were graceful, Chess decided. The bats moved upward toward the ceiling, and then they would swoop down—one, two, three—in their own particular ballet. Their movements became hypnotic as Chess watched. What were they after? Chess wondered, though she knew the answer was prosaic: they were after bugs. The bats gathered in a cluster; for a split second, they seemed suspended in the hot attic air. And then, one by one, they discovered the open window, that square of opportunity, a gateway to their wildest dreams of freedom.

Chess and Tate stayed up most of the night. They were worried about the bats returning, so they closed the window and endured the stifling heat. Tate poked and prodded the far corners of the attic to make sure there were no more bats lurking. They were safe from bats.

Chess read Tate her confession by the beam of her flashlight, and Tate listened in rapt attention. It reminded Chess of long-ago years when she would read to Tate from their storybooks. Tate didn't comment on what she heard; she might have been appalled, or she might have been accepting, Chess couldn't tell. Tate just lay back with her eyes glued on Chess. The confession read like a story, a piece of fiction, and God, Chess wished, she *wished,* it were fiction.

After Chess shut the notebook and the truth was out, floating in the air around them, Chess said, "So what do you think?"

"What do *you* think?" Tate asked.

"I should have told Michael how I felt about Nick," Chess said. "But I wasn't sure my feelings were real, and since they were maybe not real, they were easy to hide." She looked at Tate, and even in the near darkness, she saw a new expression on her sister's face. Chess startled; it was almost like she was here in the attic with someone else. Tate looked serious; she looked thoughtful.

Tate said, "I know why you didn't tell Michael. You didn't want to. You liked Michael. You loved him. You didn't want to be the person who had an unshakable obsession with his younger rock-star brother. You never wanted to veer off-course, Chess. You got into this pattern, this mold, with Mom and Dad and everyone else, where everything you did was *right.* Michael was the kind of man you *expected* to marry. He fit right into your perfect life. If you had married Michael—do I even need to say it?—you would have had a six-thousand-square-foot house, a manicured lawn, gorgeous children—and you would have been miserable. You didn't betray Michael by not telling him about Nick. You betrayed yourself. You didn't want to be the person who had feelings for Nick, but guess what, Chess? You were that person. You are that person."

Chess stared at the woman lying across the bed, who may or may not have been her sister.

"You're right."

"I know I'm right."

Chess pinched the bridge of her nose. "I can tell you one thing, little sister." She said "little sister" with irony; in this instance, Tate was most definitely the big sister. "Love is not worth it."

"Ah," Tate said. "That's where you're wrong."

TATE

She wrote on the list for Barrett, which was now the list for Trey: *Don't leave without me!*

And when she got back from running, Trey, dutiful young man, was waiting for her on the beach. She hadn't said why she was going to Nantucket, and he didn't ask. He wasn't curious; he didn't care. This was for the best.

He had learned—from Barrett—that Tate was a Springsteen fan. And guess what? So was he! He wanted to talk about the Boss, the new albums, the old albums. This kind of conversation used to delight Tate, but now she could barely find a word to say about how much she loved "Jungleland" and found it a work of genius on the scale of *West Side Story.* The things that used to matter, the person she used to be, had been usurped. She had room in her mind only for Barrett.

Love is worth it.

After they arrived and anchored and after they paddled the dinghy to shore (it physically pained Tate to do these things with Trey instead of Barrett), Trey asked Tate if she needed a ride anywhere.

"I have *Born to Run* in my truck," he said.

She accepted a ride to town and they listened to "Thunder Road" and "Tenth Avenue Freeze-Out." Trey tapped the steering wheel and bobbed his head like the dedicated fan he was. Tate asked to be dropped on Main Street in front of the pharmacy.

He said, "How are you getting back?"

She said, "Taxi. I'll be at Madaket Harbor at quarter to four."

He gave her the thumbs-up and grinned. In his mind, they were buddies.

Main Street was bustling. There were people everywhere:

two lovely ladies outside Congdon and Coleman Insurance selling raffle tickets for a needlepoint rug benefiting the Episcopal church, a swarm of people surrounding the Bartlett Farm truck buying zucchini and snapdragons and corn on the cob, tourists with maps and strollers and shopping bags. Everyone looked happy. Had everyone on this street found love, then, except for her?

She wandered through town and stopped twice for directions to Brant Point. Gradually the streets became more residential, and then Tate found the familiar corner and she turned right. Inside, she was quiet, which surprised her. She was a calm, cool pond.

She found Anita's house with ease; it was impossible to forget. She peeked through the rose-draped trellis. The lawn and front gardens were peaceful and serene except for the whirring of the sprinklers.

Okay, so now what? Should she knock? Should she walk in?

She didn't see Barrett's truck. Was he running one of the countless errands that Anita Fullin and her house required? Tate studied the picturesque front of the house—the gray-shingled expanse, the many white-trimmed windows, the fat, happy hydrangea bushes with their periwinkle blossoms.

Tate opened the gate and marched to the front door. She was here to talk to Barrett; she wouldn't leave until she had. For Tate, men would forever fall into two categories: Barrett, and those who were not Barrett. She knocked with purpose. She waited. She thought about Chess and all that had happened. Chess believed that her chance to be happy was over; her system had crashed and couldn't be saved or restored. Michael was dead; Nick wouldn't be coming back. She would, Tate pointed out, meet someone else down the road.

Yes, Chess said. *But it won't be Nick.*

And Tate conceded: it wouldn't be Nick.

And Michael is dead.

Tate said, *Michael's death was an accident.*

Chess said, *It was a suicide.*

Tate said, *You don't believe that?*

Chess said, *Yes, I do believe that.*

Tate was ready for anything when Anita Fullin opened the door. Or so she thought.

Anita Fullin was wearing an orange bikini. Her hair was in a bun and her face was slick with sunscreen. She had been lying in the sun. Through the house, Tate could see an orange towel draped over a chaise on the back deck; she could see a Bose radio on the table and a glass of white wine. Was this how Anita Fullin spent her days? It wasn't fair of Tate to judge; she had spent the past twenty-five days doing pretty much the same thing.

Anita's expression was mildly pleasant, expectant, wary. Why was her sunbathing being interrupted?

She doesn't recognize me, Tate thought. *She has no idea who I am.*

Okay, this was infuriating. Her anger felt good; it felt like firepower.

She said, "Hey, Anita! Sorry to bother you. I'm looking for Barrett."

Anita smiled manically, and then she laughed once, like a gunshot. "Ha!"

Oh, dear, Tate thought.

Anita said, "Would you like to come in and sit down?"

Tate took a breath. "No, thank you. I'm just looking for Barrett."

Anita Fullin placed her index finger under her nose and inhaled. She said, "Well, you won't find him here."

"I won't?"

"He left this morning."

"Left...for where?"

"For where, indeed!" Anita Fullin said. "For his little business, for other clients, people who *need* him, he says. For his pathetic, lonely life, where he will never have the money to do anything interesting and never have the opportunity to grow into a real man. He left because he thinks I'm behaving inappropriately. I'm married, he says, and I'd better start acting like it or he's going to call Roman and *tattle* on me like a six-year-old." She let loose a trill of laughter, which fluttered like a flock of birds. "He thinks *he* can blackmail *me.* No, no, no, no, no, no, no."

Tate took a step back. Anita snatched her arm. "Please come in. We'll have a drink."

"I can't," Tate said.

"Please?" Anita said. "I'm not the monster he makes me out to be." She stepped back and opened the door a little wider, and Tate stepped over the threshold. Immediately she thought of Chess, doing what was expected of her instead of following her basic instincts. Tate knew better than to step into Anita's home territory—but what did she do? She walked right in.

Anita seemed energized by Tate's presence. She shut the door firmly behind her and said, "Come, come, sit right here and I'll get you a glass of wine. Is chardonnay okay?"

"Um," Tate said. It was not yet ten o'clock. "Do you have any iced tea?"

"Iced tea?" Anita said. She disappeared into the kitchen and came back a few seconds later with two glasses of wine. "Here you go," she said brightly. "Please sit."

Tate was perched tentatively on the arm of a chair, which she realized was quite rude, but that was all the commitment she was willing to give. She didn't want to sit. Anita set the glasses of wine on the glass coffee table and plopped down ever so casually on the sofa, and what could Tate do? She had been raised by Birdie. She sat in the chair and smiled at Anita and said, "Your house is lovely."

Anita picked up her wineglass. "Cheers!" she said. She reached out to clink Tate's glass, forcing *cheers* upon her. That was fine, but Anita couldn't make her drink. Tate brought the glass to her mouth. Anita was watching her. She took the tiniest sip, just enough to dampen her lips.

"You like it?" Anita said.

"Delicious," Tate said.

Anita said, "You look nervous. Are you nervous?"

"Kind of," Tate said. "I didn't mean to interrupt you."

"Oh!" Anita said. "You aren't interrupting a thing. I was just relaxing in the sun. I'm really very lazy." She smiled as she said this and Tate thought she was joking, so Tate laughed what she thought was the appropriate amount. But Anita set her wineglass down harshly on the glass table, and there was a noise like a dissonant bell. And Tate thought her laughing must have been inappropriate; she should have said something soothing instead, like, *Well, you are on vacation.* Tate wasn't great with social cues despite Birdie's tutelage. Anita said, "Roman thinks I'm completely useless, sitting here on Nantucket, going out for lunch, going out for dinner, spending his money, not working, not contributing to my local community or what he refers to as 'the wider world.' So we've separated, he's in New York and I'm here, we're no longer a couple, and that is *fine* with me."

"Oh," Tate said. "I'm sorry to hear that."

"Sorry?" Anita Fullin said. "*Sorry?*" She threw back

some more wine and her hair fell into her face, and Tate wondered exactly how much Anita Fullin had had to drink that morning already. Had she poured a glass with her Grape-Nuts? "So of course what Roman doesn't know, what I could never have told him, is that I had hopes for Barrett. I became *very* close with Barrett when his wife was dying and then even *closer* after she died. I lent him a lot of money, but that didn't matter because I *adore* Barrett and would do anything for him. And then, just recently, last week, when I hired him to work for me exclusively, I thought it would be a good opportunity to make him into something."

"Make him into something?" Tate said.

"Make him into a successful man," Anita said. "Introduce him to the right people, find him a job..."

"He has a job," Tate said. "He owns a business."

Anita stared at Tate. Her face was tan and absolutely unlined. Her lipstick was perfect. "He can do more. He can be like Roman: An investment banker, a man of the world. A man with money and power. He deserves that. He deserves so much more than what's befallen him."

"You think so?" Tate said.

"Yes," Anita said. She finished her wine. She stared at Tate's untouched wine, and Tate nearly offered it to her. "I do."

Something about the way Anita said these last two words made Tate realize that, for Anita, men fell into the same two categories: Barrett, and men who weren't Barrett.

Anita said, "But he blew it today. He walked out on me. I've decided to give him until noon to come back. Otherwise I'm going to sit down and make the calls."

"Make the calls?" Tate said.

"I'm going to call all of his clients and tell them what a selfish bastard he is. I am going to call all of my friends and have them call their friends. I'm going to repossess his boat. I'm going to speak to my attorney about the money he owes me. I'm going to cut off all his other options so he has no choice but to come back here." She picked up her empty wineglass and stood. "I would have called you, too, but you don't have a phone." She smiled. "So it's lucky you stopped by!"

Tate excused herself to use the ladies' room. Anita repaired to the kitchen for more wine. Tate walked to the end of a long hallway, past the powder room, onto a sunporch. It didn't have what she was looking for. She tried another door and found a sitting room with two yellow cats reclining on a love seat. Tate turned around and saw a set of back stairs. She climbed the stairs and crept around—master bedroom, guest room, guest room—until she found the study. The home office. She sat down at the desk in front of the computer and lightly tapped the keyboard. The screen jumped to life. Tate grinned; it was a good, expensive model, a Dell, one of Tate's favorites. Tate felt like she was seeing an old friend. She checked out the configuration of the desktop and got to work. Her fingers flew. She could do this in her sleep. It was scary, really, but being a computer genius cut both ways. She heard Anita downstairs calling out, "Hello? Hello?" Tate scrambled to work faster and faster until she had the system on its knees; if she pushed one more button, she would wipe out the entire hard drive—all the documents, all the e-mails, all the pictures, all the music, everything. Wipe it out! Tate was giddy.

"Hello?" Anita called up the stairs. "Tate?"

Tate waggled her fingers in the air above the keyboard, a piece of personal theater she liked to use to remind herself of the witchcraft she was capable of. Just having the ability to visit a technical hurricane on Anita Fullin was good enough. Tate stood up from the desk. She experienced a bloom of unexpected satisfaction. Anita Fullin knew her name.

Tate descended the stairs. Anita was waiting at the bottom.

"I think you'd better go," Anita said.

Tate held up her hands to show she hadn't stolen anything. Upstairs, the computer waited, hanging by a thread. Maybe Anita Fullin would push the magic button herself.

"I think you're right," Tate said.

Tate walked down the hot street toward town. This was where Barrett was supposed to appear and scoop her up so they could drive off into the midday sun. He had quit Anita Fullin; he had set himself free. But where *was* he?

She bought two bottles of cold water in town and walked all the way back to Madaket Harbor. It was sunny and hot, and unlike on Tuckernuck, the bike path here was paved and populated; people zipped around Tate on bikes, chiming their bells. *On your left!* Cars zoomed past, and she thought each one might be Barrett. But no.

She reached Madaket Harbor at two o'clock. She bought a sandwich and another bottle of water at the Westender store, and she ate on the dock with her feet dangling in the water. She wanted to swim but hadn't brought her suit. She considered jumping in in her shorts and T-shirt—but she was determined, from this point forward, to act like a grown woman. Not a woman like Anita Fullin or like Chess or like her mother or like Aunt India—but like the woman that was inside herself.

Then she thought, *The grown woman inside me is hot and sticky.* And she jumped in.

She was asleep on the deck in her drying clothes when Trey nudged her with his Top-Sider.

"Hey," he said.

She opened her eyes, then closed them. When she opened them again, it would be Barrett standing over her, and not Trey. She understood then why Chess slept all the time: when life wasn't going your way, it was much easier to snooze.

"Come on," Trey said. "We're going."

Tate sat up, bleary eyed. Madaket Harbor was spread in front of her like a painting. Blue water, green eelgrass, white boats. Trey had a bag of ice and a bag of groceries; he was untying the dinghy. She stumbled down onto the beach. Her clothes were stiff with salt, and she didn't even want to think about her hair.

They got situated in the boat, and Tate said, "*Where* is Barrett?"

Trey said, "He went to the airport to get the husband."

"The husband?"

"That's what he said."

"Meaning Roman? I thought he was all done working for Anita."

"He'll never be done working for Anita," Trey said.

Tate's heart tumbled. This was probably right. Anita must have called him to lay down the ultimatum: *Come back by noon or I will ruin you.* And Barrett would have done the only thing he could and gone back. He had the kids to think of. He was like a bluefish that Anita had hooked painfully through the lip. No matter how hard he struggled, she wouldn't release him.

* * *

When Tate got back to the house, she found Birdie, Aunt India, and Chess sitting at the picnic table, drinking Sancerre and eating Marcona almonds. Tate's eyes welled up with grateful tears.

Birdie said, "How was your day?"

Tate said, "Awful." And she sat down in the fourth spot, where she belonged.

Chess and Tate set the table. Normally, with only a couple of nights left, Birdie would throw together bizarre combinations of leftovers such as scrambled eggs with corn and tomatoes, but tonight they were having steaks, campfire potatoes, salad with buttermilk dressing, and rolls.

Chess set down the place mats and Tate followed behind her with the silverware. Chess said, "Did you find Barrett?"

"No," Tate said.

"Are you okay?" Chess said.

"No," Tate said.

Pssst. There was a noise like air leaking from a tire.

Tate looked around, fearing it was the Scout.

Pssst.

Coming up the beach stairs was Barrett.

It *was* Barrett, right? And not Trey looking like Barrett?

He was windmilling his arm, beckoning her over. "Monkey girl!" Yes, she was coming, she was running, just like in the movies, running into his arms, God, he smelled good, she kissed his neck, he tasted good, he was real, he was here, she loved him, she *loved* him. His arms were around her and he was laughing. She kissed his mouth. He...let her kiss him, but he didn't kiss her back, at least not in the fully passionate way she wanted him to. Something was off, something was wrong. He was going to tell her he was still working for Anita. Was that it? And what would Tate say? Could she live with that? *Could* she? He looked happy, that was for sure. He was grinning.

She said, "Oh, my God, I've never been so glad to see anyone in all my life."

He squeezed her. He whispered. "I have a surprise."

A surprise? She heard footsteps. He had brought someone. Again? Tate's neck stiffened. She tried to pull away; Barrett held her. She peered around him at the person huffing up the stairs.

It was her father.

BIRDIE

She supposed it would become part of the Tuckernuck family legend, the day she nearly set the house on fire.

It took Birdie a second to figure out what, exactly, was happening. She was startled to see that Barrett had returned; she was delighted for Tate. Of secondary concern was who Barrett had with him. An older man, tanned, trim, good looking. A man who reminded Birdie of...who looked just like...who was...Grant! It was *Grant!* Here on Tuckernuck! Here! Then Birdie realized she was smoking and she couldn't let Grant see her smoking, so she flicked her cigarette to the ground, which was very unlike her. She hadn't meant to litter; she just wanted to get rid of the cigarette before Grant saw her holding it. By chance, it landed, not in the dirt at her feet, but in the paper bag where they kept the newspapers for recycling. The bag and the newspapers went up in flames in a matter of seconds.

India pointed and shouted. Birdie was too addled to notice; she was assaulted by an avalanche of thoughts, rolling, tumbling. Grant looked good, he looked *fantastic,* he had lost weight, he was tan, he looked different. He was wearing a white polo shirt, blue and white seersucker shorts, and *flip-flops?* The most casual Grant ever got was golf shoes and driving moccasins. But here was Grant in flip-flops, looking relaxed, at ease, and present in the moment, three things Birdie had asked for for thirty years.

Then Birdie smelled smoke—not grill smoke but *smoke* smoke—and she saw the flames licking the shingles of the house. Birdie had a momentary vision of her grandparents' beloved house burning to the ground. She looked at Barrett in panic. There was a fire truck on the island, with a 250-gallon tank, everyone who lived on Tuckernuck knew this, but what Birdie didn't know was who drove that truck or who to call to get it to their property.

Grant, meanwhile, was striding right for Birdie.

"Back up," Grant said. "For God's sake, Birdie, back up!"

He picked the water pitcher up off the table and dumped it over the flames. There was a hiss and a billow of bitter smoke. Grant checked to see that the fire was out. He grabbed the Sancerre off the table and doused the smoldering remains. Birdie thought, *Not the Sancerre!* But of course this was the right thing to do.

Barrett and India and the girls were looking on, mystified. Birdie was embarrassed. She said, "I threw my cigarette in the bag by accident."

Grant said, "You were smoking?"

"Kind of," Birdie said.

India laughed. "Kind of," she mimicked.

Birdie said, "What on earth are you doing here, Grant Cousins?"

Grant took her hands. His eyes were a clearer blue, it seemed, and his hair was longer than he liked to keep it; it curled at the ends. He looked "cute" in the way that teenage girls thought rock stars were "cute"—he was shaggy and sexy.

He said, "I came to see you."

Birdie found she couldn't speak. Her mouth gaped open. He kissed her—Grant Cousins *kissed* her in front of everyone. And further surprise: desire stirred. God, she had forgotten all about it.

INDIA

She regarded her bed—that squishy sinkhole with the five firm new pillows to compensate—and knew she wouldn't sleep. She had felt her insomnia coming on; it was a ghost ship on the horizon drawing nearer and nearer. Her head held an electronic buzz; it felt like someone was grabbing her by the back of the neck and wouldn't let her go.

Grant's arrival had thrown everything off. India hated him for showing up unannounced and stealing the spotlight. Birdie was ecstatic, the girls were elated, Barrett was impressed. The *man* of the house had arrived! As if what they had been waiting for all these weeks was a man. *Hardly,* India thought. They had been just fine here, the four of them, on their own. As far as India was concerned, Grant was an egregious interloper.

Grant had approached India nervously, and she

thought, *You'd better be nervous! You'd better be shaking in your boots!* This was the Tate house, their house, not Grant's house; he had done nothing, in the years of India's memory, but defile the Tuckernuck lifestyle by spending hours on his cell phone on the bluff and poring over the sheaf of documents FedExed to him each day. He used to turn the picnic table into his personal office, weighing down papers with rocks from the beach, asking Birdie to bring him more coffee. Birdie had obeyed like a dutiful wife, but deep down, India knew, she found it as despicable as India did.

Grant said, "India, I'm sorry for horning in here..."

He was about to make an excuse or give a good reason, but India shook her head at him. At PAFA she did this to great effect.

Grant lowered his voice. "I came for Birdie."

India wasn't sure how to take this comment. He came for Birdie. Meaning he came to get Birdie, claim her, take her home? Or he came because Birdie asked him to. Birdie had gone on a lot of mysterious errands with her phone, so this last interpretation was not unfeasible.

India was old enough to be self-critical. She wondered if what was really bothering her about Grant's arrival was that he had come for Birdie—and no one had come for her. Her anger was based in the sibling rivalry of nearly six decades. Birdie was happy—she was luminous!—and to begrudge her this happiness was also despicable.

They might have been stretched at dinner, but Tate left with Barrett. In addition to feeling jealous about Grant and Birdie, India also felt jealous as Tate and Barrett sped away in the boat called *Girlfriend*. Barrett had returned, the romantic hero, and had whisked away the young, beautiful niece. He had given India a kiss on the cheek and she, in turn, had pinched his behind. Then she thought, *Woman, get a grip on yourself!*

* * *

After dinner, they all retreated to the screened-in porch. Grant had brought a bottle of scotch for himself and a bottle of vodka and some tonic for India. (He knew who his toughest critic would be, calculating motherfucker.) Since there was no reason to hold back, India got wickedly drunk. She and Grant got into a storytelling contest in which all the stories were about Bill. For a while there, Bill and Grant had been involved in some serious prank one-upmanship: short-sheeting the beds, hanging a bluefish from the doorway of the bedroom, stealing each other's alcohol, cigarettes, and cigars, putting fiddler crabs in the beds, water in the beer bottles, itching powder in the talcum, condoms in the salad. Grant, being a man's man, had an enormous appetite for this kind of practical joking, but Bill was the creative one. They had been well matched, worthy adversaries, proving their love for each other by how much time, thought, and effort the prank took.

The reminiscing left India close to tears. Grant had orchestrated a Lazarus-like return from the dead, but Bill couldn't. And Michael Morgan couldn't either. Chess might have been thinking this exact thing, because she stretched, stood, and excused herself. She kissed her father first, and said, *I'm glad you're here, Daddy.* Then she kissed her mother. Then she came over and hugged India fiercely, as if in some kind of solidarity, and India felt the tears fall despite her most fervent wishes, and she wiped at them quickly, and said, "I'm going to retire, too."

And when India set eyes on her bed, she thought, *There is no way I am ever going to sleep.*

She had been granted twenty-seven nights plump with sleep, eight, nine, sometimes ten hours at a stretch, a smooth white kingdom of sleep. Now, she was faced with the cold hand, the red room, the buzzing alarm in her brain. The insomnia was a taskmaster, a torturer. She took off her clothes and lay upon the strange mattress that had given her so many gifted hours of slumber. Slumber lumber, she had slept like a fallen tree. She was drunk—maybe that was the difference. For the first time in weeks, she had moved beyond wine; it was the vodka keeping her up, or the tonic, or the quinine in the tonic. It was Grant. Not Grant, but Grant's stories about Bill. It was Bill keeping her awake. It had always been Bill that kept her awake. He was piloting the ghost ship on the horizon; he wanted her for some reason. He wanted her to do something. He wanted her to listen. He needed to tell her something.

Fine, she thought, angry now. *Just say it: It was my fault! You did it because of me! You did it to keep me captive! You saw me retreating, you needed to reel me in, hold me prisoner. I am your prisoner! I have been your prisoner for fifteen years!*

Her thoughts were interrupted by a sound. Sounds, noises: At first India didn't know what it was. A bang, something dropping to the floor or hitting the wall, followed by a voice. Grant. Then there was a rhythm, permeating the wall in waves. Then Birdie's voice, a cry or a whimper. They were making love. India closed her eyes. She couldn't believe this was happening. Of course it was happening. She had to leave her room, go downstairs, smoke on the porch, or leave the house altogether—walk to the beach or take the Scout for a drive. But she found she couldn't move; she was pinned to the bed. She thought of all the nights when she and Bill had made love on this Gumby mattress, never caring who heard them. She had known back then that Birdie and Grant were lying cold and stiff in their narrow, coffinlike twin beds, listening (or in Grant's case, oblivious, snoring), and that had turned India on. She was getting some and Birdie wasn't!

This, then, was her just deserts, and she accepted it as such.

She fell asleep for two minutes, three, four—this always happened on her sleepless nights, and it was agonizing. A taste of something unspeakably sweet—sleep, real sleep!—and then she lost it. It was a kite string ripped from her hand. She rose from bed; the other room was quiet, and India imagined Grant and Birdie entwined in one of those spinsterish beds, spent and happy.

Something in the room was calling to her. Okay, she was nuts, she was as mentally ill as Bill had been at the end. Inanimate objects had spoken to him all the time. That was what it was like to be a sculptor: he heard forms speak. It was then his job to give the voices a body.

Fifteen years he had held her captive.

She looked out the window. She didn't have the good view; Birdie did. Because this was, truly, Birdie's house; their parents had left it to Birdie, and India had gotten the equivalent in cash, which she used to buy their house and acreage in Pennsylvania. It was all fair, and Birdie never mentioned that the house was hers, and she took on all expenses and never asked India for a dime and India was free to use the house anytime. Birdie was a good egg, a tiny woman with a solid-gold heart. She deserved to have the man she had divorced out of frustration return to her on his knees.

Something in the room was calling to her. There was nothing outside, no suitor beneath her window, no meandering drunk neighbors or rowdy teenagers on ATVs, nothing but Tuckernuck, its dirt trails, its mysteries.

Was it Roger? He stood on the dresser, small and

light and perfect. She picked him up as she might a baby chick and cradled him in two hands. *Are you talking to me, Roger?*

Silence. She was losing her mind. She set Roger down. Roger wasn't a real person; he wasn't a talisman or a mystical object. He wasn't a totem or an idol. He was a sculpture.

Something in the room was calling to her. She listened. Was it Chess from the attic? Was there another bat? Was there a bat in this room? Or a mouse? Or a garter snake? Or a black widow? India removed Lula's painting from the wall. It was the only foreign presence in the house; aside from the pillows and linens Birdie had ordered this summer, every other object and piece of furniture had been there for decades.

It was so dark India couldn't see the painting, but that didn't matter: she knew what it looked like. It was, after all, her body. Her hip, the shallow bowl beneath her hip. A sand dune. The inside of a shell. She remembered lying on Lula's white suede sofa; the memory itself was as strong as sex. Lula sketching, her pencil ravishing the page. It had been sensual, Lula's eyes devouring India, Lula's hair falling in her face, her skin lightly perspiring, the kohl around her eyes smudged. There had been a scent in the room, the smell of women, of sex—it had been her musk, or Lula's, or hers and Lula's intermingled. She had been fantasizing about sex with Lula—whatever that might look like—but Lula had been thinking of work. India's body was Lula's work, her greatest work to date, the subject of her genius. India had never been Bill's muse in that way. His work was too blocky, too masculine, too civic. But she had been Lula's muse.

Was I wrong about you?

What do I have to do?

Try?

What would a life with Lula look like? It would be unconventional, shocking even. In a few short weeks, India was to become a grandmother: Could a woman with a new baby grandchild take a female lover half her age? What would her sons say? What would the faculty, the administration, the board of directors—Spencer Frost!—say? (Spencer Frost would approve, India decided. He was a worldly man, with European sensibilities.) What would Birdie, Chess, and Tate say? Did India care what other people thought? Did she, at the age of fifty-five, care?

Something else was standing in her way, keeping her from embracing happiness, from saying, *Yes, I'll try.* It was the pilot of the looming ghost ship. It was the ghost himself.

Something in the room was calling to her. India hung the painting back on the wall. She cast around the room. The voice was getting stronger, louder; she was getting closer, like a child in a game of Marco Polo. She lay on the bed. Her eyes were burning. Her eyes. She turned to the nightstand—her book lay there, and... Bill's reading glasses. *His glasses.* They were practically glowing. The lenses caught light from the moon out the window, except there was no moon. So where was the light coming from?

India picked up the glasses. They were cool to the touch, as they should have been. The frames were green plastic, a mottled jade green that people commented on. *I love your reading glasses. Oh, thanks. They belonged to my late husband.*

India had taken the glasses from the hotel room in Bangkok. They had been on the night table next to a small pad and pen, standard issue from the hotel. India imagined Bill wearing the glasses as he held the pen over the blank page, trying to decide what to write. If there had been a suicide note, she would have taken that, but because there had been no note, because Bill had not found a single word to say in his defense, India had taken the glasses. They were nothing remarkable. India knew Bill had gotten them at the CVS in Wayne. But she took them as her memento of her husband, and for fifteen years they had hung around her neck. They had rested against her heart.

India opened her door, stepped out into the hallway, and tiptoed down the stairs. She passed through the living room and kitchen and out the door. The night was brilliantly dark. There was a sprinkling of stars—diamonds against the obsidian—but no moon. They had outlasted the moon. India should have gone back for a flashlight; she couldn't see a goddamned thing. But this was Tuckernuck: she could make it to the beach blind or sleepwalking. She floated across the yard and felt for the railing at the top of the stairs; it was right where she knew it would be. She descended to the beach. The new stairs were sturdy. She remembered the summer that Teddy put his foot through one of the old boards and got a wicked splinter. Bill had pulled it out with his sculptor's tweezers. There was a memory for everything, India realized; it was pointless to try to escape the memories.

But that didn't mean she had to spend the rest of her life haunted by the ghost of her dead husband. She was still young. She didn't have to spend the rest of her life looking at the world through Bill Bishop's eyes.

By the time India made it to the water's edge, the glasses had warmed in her hand. *Try?* she thought. *Try?* She cranked her arm back in a classic windup (she had pitched so many balls to the boys through endless seasons of Little League. She had been a good mother and she had been a good wife. She had been a good wife, damn it!) and wheeeeeeeeeeeeeee . . . she let the glasses fly.

She heard them plunk in the water and hoped they had landed far enough out for the tide to carry them away. If they washed up on shore, she decided, she would bury them.

She headed back up the stairs lethargically. Her eyelids were drooping. The alarm had been shut off; the room in her head was dark and hushed. She was ready for bed.

TATE

She awoke in the morning in Barrett's bed, with Barrett holding her.

Perfect happiness, she thought.

The kids were asleep in their rooms. When Tate walked in last night, they jumped into her arms, they cheered and made happy noises, and Tate felt like Bruce Springsteen. She felt loved. It was intoxicating.

Barrett wanted to tell her exactly what had happened. He was talking quickly, and Tate had to tell him to slow down.

Slooooooooow down.

He had promised himself, no matter what happened, that he would work for Anita for three days. It started out oddly, he said, with Anita leading him up to her bedroom, flinging open the doors to Roman's closet, and telling Barrett he could wear whatever he wanted. There was, he said, a Jay Gatsby collection of beautiful shirts handmade in London. There were cashmere sweaters, golf pants, Italian loafers.

Barrett said to Anita, "I don't need clothes. I have clothes."

She implored him to wear a pink shirt of Roman's, a simple polo shirt, but still, it was Roman's. Barrett felt uneasy. What was Roman going to do when he saw Barrett wearing his shirt?

Anita said, "Oh, don't worry. Roman isn't coming back."

She then explained that she and Roman had separated. They were going to test it out; he hated Nantucket anyway. That was one of the reasons Anita had hired Barrett full-time. She was on her own now.

Barrett wore the shirt. He hung a new painting for Anita, then cleaned her Hinckley picnic boat bow-to-stern and took Anita and her girlfriends on a cruise around the harbor. There was a catered lunch on the cruise, but the women ate nothing except for the stray lettuce leaf and a few grapes, so Jeannie, the cook, offered the entire gorgeous lunch to Barrett. He stuffed his face and would take the rest home.

"It wasn't bad," he said to Tate. "That part."

At five o'clock, when he had to go pick the kids up from his parents' house, Anita didn't want him to leave. She wanted him to stay and have a glass of wine. She wanted him to give her a massage.

"A *massage?*" Tate said.

Anita had a masseuse come to the house every day, but the masseuse had been canceling a lot lately, he had canceled that day, and Anita's neck and shoulders were sore. Wouldn't Barrett just rub them a little? All she needed was a pair of strong hands.

No, Barrett said. He wouldn't. He couldn't stay for wine either. He had to pick up his kids.

She pouted but seemed to accept this answer.

The next day, he said, there was another shirt. Blue, with white stripes.

He said, "Is there something wrong with what I have on?"

She said, "Please wear it."

He considered it a uniform of sorts. A uniform to make him look like her husband. It didn't feel right, but he couldn't find anything blatantly *wrong* with it. She sent him to the post office to mail a box to her sister in California; he drove her to the Galley, where she had lunch with the same friends from the day before. He offered to wash the windows of the house, and she said, "I'll hire someone to do that."

He said, "You did hire someone to do that. Me."

She said, "Don't you dare wash the windows. I'll call someone."

He said, "Let me do it, Anita. There's no reason to pay someone else."

She said, "Are you the boss here or am I?"

While she was at lunch, he started washing the windows. The windows that faced the harbor were coated with a salty grime. When Anita got home, she found him on a ladder with a squeegee. He had changed into his own shirt.

She stood at the bottom of the ladder with her hands on her hips. From the look on her face, he could tell that she had had wine with lunch.

She said, "What are you doing?"

He said, "What does it look like I'm doing?"

She stormed into the house.

On the third day, she stayed out of his way. There was a list of mundane things on the counter—take the recycling to the dump, order the flowers, run to Bartlett

Farm for lobster salad and broccoli slaw. (She liked to have these things in the fridge, though she never ate.) At the bottom of the list, it said, *Dinner 7 p.m.*

She stayed on the deck off her bedroom for most of the day, and to interrupt her would be like waking a sleeping lion. As he wrapped things up at five o'clock, she came down the stairs in a white waffled robe. She was holding a navy blazer. He got a bad feeling.

She said, "Where are you going?"

He made a show of checking his watch. "Home to get my kids."

"But you'll be back at quarter to seven?" she said. "We're expected at seven."

"Expected where?"

"Dinner at the Straight Wharf. The Jamiesons and Grahams invited me and I can't go alone."

"Well, I can't go with you."

He thought she might pull a power play. He thought she would remind him how much she was paying him. (He reminded himself of that constantly. It was a lot of money.) Instead, she said, "You can't?"

He said, "The kids."

She said, "Can't you get a sitter? This is important to me."

He relented.

"Why?" Tate asked him. "Couldn't you tell she was using you?"

He felt bad for her. She was deeply unhappy. He called a sitter for the boys. He wore his own navy blazer. He met Anita at the restaurant. She kissed him on the lips in greeting. She touched his leg under the table. He moved away. He talked to the other men at the table about fishing. He was the resident expert; the other two men listened intently. Barrett had thought he would be outclassed at this dinner, but he ended up feeling good about himself. These people wanted the real Nantucket; he was the real Nantucket.

Anita had been hitting the red wine pretty hard throughout dinner, and then with dessert, she had a glass of champagne. She was drunk, blurry-slurry, sloppily affectionate. Barrett drove her home. She tried to persuade him to come inside; he declined. She asked him to walk her to the door. Okay, he would walk her to the door. She lunged for him.

He said, "Good night, Anita."

"So those were the three days," Barrett said to Tate.

"And then what happened?" Tate said. "You just decided to quit?"

"No," he said. "Then your father called."

Grant Cousins called Barrett at eleven o'clock at night, as Barrett was driving back home to Tom Nevers. Mr. Cousins was going to surprise the ladies on Tuckernuck. He would land at five o'clock the following afternoon and needed to be picked up at the airport and transported to the island.

Barrett said, "I'll send Trey. He's the kid who works for me now."

Grant said, "If it's not too much trouble, I'd like *you* to come, Barrett."

Barrett was about to say that he no longer ran the caretaking business day-to-day. He was about to say it would have to be Trey or nobody. But Barrett found he *wanted* to be the one to deliver Mr. Cousins to Tuckernuck. He said, "Okay, yes, I'll see you at five."

In the morning, Barrett told Anita he had to leave fifteen minutes early. He explained why.

Anita said, "But you don't work for that family anymore."

Barrett said, "Right, I know. This is a personal favor."

Anita said, "Well, you're not leaving here one minute early to do a personal favor *for that family*."

Her tone bothered him. He said, "What did they ever do to you?"

Anita sniffed. She said, "Will you change the paper towel roll in the kitchen, please? We're out."

Change the paper towel roll? He had become the butt of his own joke.

"That was it?" Tate said.

"That was it," Barrett said. "I left. Anita made her phone calls starting at 12:05, just like she promised she would, and by two o'clock in the afternoon, five people had called and hired me as caretaker."

"You're kidding," Tate said.

"Including Whit Vargas, who has a huge estate in Shawkemo, and who said he will pay me double what Anita was paying me just *because* I left Anita. He said he's very good friends with Roman Fullin and he's a client of your father's as well. He asked if we were still dating."

"And what did you say?" Tate asked.

"I said yes."

Tate felt both elated and panicked. She had Barrett back! But she was going to lose him.

She said, "I leave tomorrow."

He said, "I know."

She thought, *Ask me to stay! Ask me to move in! I can help you pay Anita back! I can help you with the kids! I can fit right into your life here! I can, I can, I can!*

Slowly! she thought.

She said, "I start a job in Reading, Pennsylvania, for Bachman pretzels on Monday."

He squeezed her. "How long will that take?"

She said, "It depends on how bad it is. Five or six days?"

"And then you'll come back?"

"Back...?"

"Back here?" he said. "Will you come back here when you're done with that job? I know it's expensive, but..."

"Oh, my God!" Tate said. "Expensive? I don't care if it's expensive. I don't care if I have to fly back and forth a dozen times. Being with you is worth it. You, Barrett Lee, are *worth it!*"

He shushed her and pulled her close. He didn't want her to wake the children just yet.

BIRDIE

She had heard of couples who divorced and then remarried each other. Everyone had heard of such couples. The story had a romantic ring to it, especially for the couples' children, who had the singular experience of watching their parents get married. But in the case of her and Grant, Birdie wasn't going to be such a sucker. She wasn't going to be a pushover or a Pollyanna. She had divorced Grant for a reason: after thirty years of emotional wasteland, she was moving on. She would either live alone and have a full and stimulating life, or she would find someone new who enjoyed the same things that she did.

Birdie allowed herself one last, long, wistful thought about Hank.

Hank!

Grant Cousins was a known quantity to her. Lawyer,

strategist, financial wizard, expert in accounting loopholes, golfer, aficionado of scotch, aged beef, cigars, and high-end automobiles. He had been an adequate father, she supposed, though only with Birdie's direction. He was a generous provider, she would give him that.

How likely was it that, at the age of sixty-five, Grant Cousins was going to change? Not likely. It was more likely that a mountain would change, or a glacier. And yet the Grant Cousins who had shown up on Tuckernuck was a different man from the man Birdie had been married to.

The mere fact that he had shown up at all! Spontaneously!

"What are you doing here?" she asked him. "Really."

"I told you," he said.

"What about work?" she said.

"What *about* work?" he said. "I'm due about five years of vacation and I'm going to take it."

"Yeah, right," she said. She sounded like a sullen teenager, but could anyone blame her?

Later, after dinner, after an hour of reminiscing on the screened-in porch with India (Birdie noticed how kind Grant was with India, telling all those funny stories about Bill), they faced the awkward decision about where Grant would sleep. His suitcase remained in the living room.

Birdie said, "You can take the other bed in my room."

"Are you sure?" he said.

"I'm sure."

He had changed, Birdie thought. Either that or she was being duped. He had mellowed; he had loosened and lightened. And his hair! It was so long.

They climbed the stairs together. Birdie had consumed her usual glasses of wine, but because of Grant's presence, she drank more—or because of his presence, it affected her differently. She felt tipsy, giddy, girlishly nervous like she hadn't since those long-ago weekends in the Poconos when Grant used to visit her room in the middle of the night.

In the bedroom, she changed into her white cotton nightgown. She gave thought to changing behind the closed door of the bathroom, but that seemed ridiculous. Grant had been her husband for thirty years. He had seen her naked thousands upon thousands of times. And still, she felt self-conscious and shy, especially since she heard the rustlings of him changing on the other side of the room. When she was in her nightgown (it wasn't exactly lingerie, but it was new that summer—bought for nights with Hank—and pretty and feminine) and he was in his pajamas (ones she had bought him at Brooks Brothers years earlier), they looked at each other and smiled. She was nervous!

"Here," he said, beckoning. "Come sit with me on the bed."

She obeyed, grateful for the directive. She sat on the bed and Grant sat next to her and the bed groaned and Birdie thought they might snap it in half. They had made love in these very same beds. Birdie remembered those occasions as ones of fulfilling a spousal duty; she remembered being worried that the children would hear or Bill and India would hear (because Birdie and Grant could certainly hear them) or her parents would hear. She remembered the acrobatics and flexibility required to copulate in these narrow beds. She wanted Grant to speak before she embarrassed herself.

He said, "I meant what I said about taking a five-year vacation. I'm retiring, Bird."

She gasped. Men like Grant didn't retire. They worked and worked until they had a massive coronary sitting at their desks. "When?"

"At the end of the year."

She was tempted to express some skepticism; he wasn't *really* retiring. He would say he was retiring, but he would still go in to the office each day to keep tabs on his clients and his cases.

"Honestly?" Birdie said. "I can't believe it. I never thought you'd retire. I thought you'd die first."

He said, "My heart's not in it anymore. The fire has gone out."

"Really?" Birdie said. She was tempted to ask where his heart was and what would restart the fire, aside from her flicking away her cigarette.

"Really," he said. He turned her face and kissed her. He kissed her like some other man. God, it was weird—this *was* Grant, right?—and it was thrilling, too. They fell back on the bed and Birdie realized she was going to make love to her ex-husband and she nearly laughed at the amazing wonder of it. Grant!

Later, when it was over and she lay spent and lightheaded on the bed, and Grant was heavy and snoring on the other bed (sleeping together in the same bed had seemed unnecessary), Birdie wondered about other couples who had divorced and then remarried. Had they been drawn back to their marriages out of loneliness, because they could find nothing better? Had they been drawn back out of habit? Or had they been drawn together as if they were two new people with new things to discover and appreciate about each other?

As she fell asleep, Birdie prayed for the latter.

They had one full day left, and one half day. Normally, Birdie spent the last day packing up, cleaning, gathering laundry, and cooking strange meals with the odds and ends left in the fridge. But as Grant reminded her, a cleaning crew came in after they left, and if they ended up throwing away half a stick of butter, the world wouldn't end. Grant wanted to make a few sandwiches, walk to North Pond, sit on the beach, swim, and do a little fishing. He wanted Birdie to come with him.

"And look," he said, setting his BlackBerry on the counter, "I'm leaving my phone here."

Birdie said, "What about Chess? And India? It's our last day..." It was all well and fine for Grant to want a romantic day with Birdie alone, but she had come to the island for a reason, and that was to spend time with her daughters and her sister.

"We'll all go," Grant said.

Birdie made coffee and bacon and blueberry pancakes. Grant ate seconds, then thirds. He smacked his lips and said, "I've missed your cooking, Bird. I haven't had a home-cooked meal since we split."

Birdie tried to think of a response to that (she didn't believe him), but before she could, Tate and Barrett walked into the kitchen. Birdie beamed. She had feared Tate wouldn't come back, but of course, here she was. She wouldn't miss their last day.

"Breakfast?" Birdie said.

"Starving," Tate said.

Barrett dropped off the final bag of ice as well as the cleaning supplies Birdie had requested. "This is it," he said. "The last drop-off."

India descended the stairs. "I think I'm going to cry."

"It must have been quite a month," Grant said.

"Oh, it was," Tate said.

"Can you come for dinner?" Birdie asked Barrett. "And bring the boys? Please?"

"And spend the night?" Tate said. "Please? The boys can sleep in the bunks."

"The boys are with their other grandparents this weekend," Barrett said. "But I'll come for dinner. And that means I can spend the night. But I'll sleep on the sofa."

"Damn right you'll sleep on the sofa," Grant said.

"I want to sleep with Chess anyway," Tate said. She misted up, and Birdie handed her a paper towel; they were all out of Kleenex. "I can't believe this is over."

They still had today. One last, brilliantly blue Tuckernuck day, which seemed incredibly precious. Birdie had let other days slip by carelessly, it seemed now. She hadn't appreciated them enough; she hadn't wrung the life out of each minute; she hadn't lived as fully as she might have. So much time wasted longing for stupid old Hank!

She would not squander today! She made lunches for everyone and packed chips, drinks, plums, and cookies. They walked together along the trail to North Pond. It was a bright, hot day, though the air was pure and clean and decidedly less sticky than it had been, and Birdie thought that what she would miss the most when she was back on the mainland tomorrow was the sterling quality of this air, the absolute purity of it. She wondered if Grant could appreciate the unadulterated beauty of this island now that he wasn't consumed with the SEC's pending case against Mr. So-and-so. There were wild irises blooming and red-winged blackbirds and the pervasive scent of *Rosa rugosa*. Tomorrow, Birdie would be back on I-95 with the Cracker Barrels and the Olive Gardens and the Targets; even the rarefied acreage of the New Canaan Country Club and her favorite bistro and independent bookstore would seem like offensive, man-made artifice. Would she be able to bear leaving? She had no idea. It felt like this every time she left: like her heart was being ripped out.

They reached the pond and they set up camp: chairs set firmly in sand, towels spread, lunch cooler placed in the shade of the chairs. Grant had brought his fishing pole and he took Tate with him to the other side of the pond. India wanted to walk out to Bigelow Point; she couldn't finish her book, she said, because she'd lost her reading glasses.

Birdie was aghast. "You lost *Bill's* reading glasses?"

"Lost them," India said. She seemed strangely unconcerned. The glasses she had treated like a pet—washing them with Windex and a paper towel each morning, keeping them around her neck at all times except when swimming and sleeping—were *lost?* "They might turn up, but I kind of doubt it."

India then wandered off toward the point in search of whelk shells. That was what she wanted to bring home to everyone as a gift: perfectly spiraled bone white whelk shells with satiny peach insides. She wanted one for the president of the board, Spencer Frost, as well as one for her assistant, Ainslie, and one for a student.

"Are you playing favorites?" Birdie asked.

"Sort of," India said.

That left Birdie alone with Chess, who was lying facedown on her towel. Birdie suddenly felt the pressure of twenty-nine days. She hadn't had the talk with her daughter that she'd meant to have. She hadn't heard the whole story, or any of the story. To force a talk now would be awkward and unfair. Wasn't that typical of the time on Tuckernuck, or of any summer vacation, for that matter? The hours had stretched out like an endless highway, and then all of a sudden, they were gone. Evaporated. And here was Birdie on the very last day, trying to cram it all in.

She sat down in the sand next to Chess's towel.

"Chess?" she said.

There was no response. Chess's breathing was deep and steady. Her sleep seemed peaceful. Birdie didn't have the heart to wake her.

CHESS

Everybody was going to get a happy ending but her.

Her parents were reuniting. That was what was happening, right? Her father had come here to Tuckernuck, a place Chess would have said he'd never liked in the past—but now he was liking it. And he was looking at her mother in a way that Chess had never seen him look at her before. He was attentive—doting, even; he carried the chairs and the cooler to the pond; he ran after Birdie's straw hat when it blew off down the dirt trail. He set up Birdie's chair and rubbed lotion onto her shoulders. He kissed her on the lips in a way that was very tender, which left Chess embarrassed. She knew her parents had slept in the same bedroom the night before, and when she saw the kiss, she thought, *Sex.* Her parents had had sex. She felt confused—possibly more confused than she'd felt when they told her they were separating. The divorce had hurt her somewhere deep inside, but it had made sense. This reunion made her happy somewhere deep inside, but she worried. If her father disappointed her mother again, it would be far worse than if some other man disappointed her mother. If her father was coming back, he was going to have to do everything right.

He would; Chess felt this in her bones. Theirs would be an unlikely love story, one to be envied. Chess wished it was Nick who had shown up out of the blue. If it could be her father, why couldn't it also be Nick?

Tate had Barrett. She told Chess the story of Barrett and Anita Fullin as they walked to the pond.

Chess said, "So what are you going to do? Stay here?"

"I have a job in Pennsylvania on Monday. I'm going to work there, then come back for a few days, then go out to Beaverton to do a job for Nike, then come back. I'm trying not to think too far ahead. Do you know how hard that is?"

Chess did know. She was facing a vacuum. But she'd had one idea, like a spark in a dark room. She wanted to cook. She had a culinary degree, after all. She knew the restaurant life was punishing—the hours, the heat, the chauvinism—but a little punishment would suit her. Cooking was the first thing she had felt a stir of passion about since Michael died. Cooking—somewhere good, somewhere market driven, clean, consistent, uptown, downtown, East Side, West Side. She would have choices.

Choices: it wasn't true love, but it was something.

Chess stood at the edge of North Pond and threw rocks into the water. *Get rid of the heavy stuff. Get rid of it.* Then she lay in the warm sand by the pond. She had only one more day to nap in the sun.

She awoke to Birdie staring at her.

Chess thought, *She wants to see me smile. She wants to know I'm going to be all right.*

Chess smiled.

Birdie smiled. She said, "I love you."

Chess said, "I love you, too, Bird."

And what about India? India had been the wild card when they started out on this vacation, an unknown quantity. Chess knew her better now. India was really and truly strong; she had gone through what Chess had gone through, only worse, and she had come out on the other side whole. She would pursue a relationship with the female painter or she wouldn't, and either way, India would be okay. India was the person Chess was the most envious of. India was the person Chess aspired to be: she was her own happy ending.

BARRETT

Thank God for his sunglasses. No one could see how close he was to tears.

There were logistics to deal with: Emptying the cooler and defrosting the refrigerator, checking and double-checking that the windows were shut and locked, gathering the sheets and towels for the Laundromat, shutting down the generator, storing the propane gas from the camp stove, buttoning up the Scout and hanging the key back on the hook by the front door. Storing the picnic table and, finally, taking down the *TATE* sign and stowing it away in its place in the kitchen drawer. A cleaning crew would come in after they were gone; later, Barrett would bring the sheets and towels back wrapped in plastic, and he would weatherproof the windows and doors.

Grant had taken a load of luggage down to Barrett's boat. This left Barrett and the four women staring forlornly at the front of the house.

"Is it going to be another thirteen years before this island sees you again?" Barrett asked.

A sob escaped—from Birdie. Suddenly she was in Barrett's arms, hugging him.

"I don't know what we would have done without you," she said. "I just don't know what we would have done."

India was on him now, too, hugging him from the left. "Those days you sent Trey were a complete hell," she said. "He just wasn't as *cute* as you were. I couldn't even bring myself to whistle at him."

Chess grabbed his right side. "Thank you for taking me to the hospital," she said. "You saved my life."

And from behind, Tate grabbed him. His girl. "I love you," she said.

The four of them were on him at his cardinal points: north, south, east, and west. They hugged him and squeezed him and someone pinched his butt; he suspected it was India.

Grant came huffing up the stairs. India said, "Grant, take our picture! Quick—the four of us with Barrett!"

India handed Grant her disposable camera, and Barrett and the women arranged themselves into a pose and smiled.

"Life is good!" Tate said.

"Life is good," Birdie said.

"Life is good," India said.

There was a pause. Grant was waiting before he took the picture. Barrett himself was too choked up to speak.

"Life is good," Chess said.

Grant snapped the picture, then another one for backup. He looked at Barrett over the top of the camera.

"You are one lucky guy," he said.

EPILOGUE

September 25 marked the day that Mary Francesca Cousins was to have married Michael Kevin Morgan.

TATE

Tate was at Fenway Park. She had left her seat to go to the bathroom and pick up popcorn for Tucker and an ice cream for Cameron. The popcorn stand was near the bathroom, but the ice cream—the kind that Cameron wanted, served in a mini batting helmet—was half a stadium away. Tate found the ice cream vendor eventually, but she waited so long in line that she couldn't remember if she should go left or right to get back. She didn't have her ticket stub and she had left her cell phone in her purse, which was back at her seat. There were hundreds and hundreds of people streaming past her, all of them different and yet somehow the same in that they were all strangers.

God, there were so many people in the world. How could you ever be sure you'd found the right one?

She had talked to Chess once the afternoon before, acknowledging that that was to have been the night of the rehearsal dinner, tapas and caipirinhas for a hundred close friends at Zo, Chess radiant in her orange polka-dot dress—but it was not to be. Acknowledging this, they both decided, was better than ignoring it. Chess had sounded weepy, but she ended strong; she was on her way to work. She had gotten a job as the sous chef at a popular French Vietnamese bistro in the Village; the kitchen staff was all-female and the head chef was a woman named Electa Hong, who had become a friend to Chess. Chess had moved back into her old apartment, but she was thinking of moving someplace closer to work. Too many memories in the old place, she said.

Tate had called Chess that morning and they had acknowledged that, had life gone differently, they would be in their mother's house, half-dressed, their hair in curlers, drinking mimosas and, most likely, bickering.

Tate asked Chess if she had plans for the day. Chess said that she was working a double shift. The restaurant was a safe place. Fair enough, Tate thought.

She said, "I miss you."

And Chess said, "I miss you, too."

Kevin Youkilis from the Red Sox got a hit and the crowd roared. Tate looked out at the thousands and thousands of people in the stadium and her heart sank. She had only two and a half innings to find her seat; the ice cream was melting in her hand. She chastised herself for not paying closer attention to the section or row number, but it had felt good to let Barrett lead the way. When they arrived at the park, Tate had taken Tucker to the bathroom, and a woman had said, "Your son is adorable."

Tate said, "Thank you."

Tate walked around to the left; she passed a hot dog and sausage stand that she thought looked familiar. Someone was selling Italian ices. Then Tate passed the Legal Sea Foods concession, where there was a long line for chowder. A woman with sunglasses on top of her head said, "I can't believe the summer is over."

Tate couldn't believe it either. In the car, on their way here, Cameron and Tucker had been talking about their Halloween costumes.

My sister's wedding, she thought.

Section nineteen. That was it! Tate turned left and descended the stairs. Even from the top of the section, she could see the back of Barrett's head. He was sitting between Cameron and Tucker; Tucker was sitting in a plastic booster because he wasn't heavy enough to keep the folding seat down.

Barrett twisted in his seat and craned his neck, scanning the stands behind him. He was looking for her, Tate knew. She had been gone forever.

She waved to him, madly, the way people waved to each other in stadiums. *Here I am! I'm right here!*

He saw her. He grinned. He made a fist and put it over his heart. *I love you.*

INDIA

On September 21, the autumnal equinox, William Burroughs Bishop III was born at the Hospital of the University of Pennsylvania, weighing in at nine pounds eleven ounces and measuring twenty-two inches. Heidi had battled in labor for nearly twenty hours before they took the baby in a C-section. Both mother and baby were doing fine.

India had been to the hospital each day to visit her grandson. He was a beast as far as newborns went; he looked like he was already a month old. But still he was a tiny, tiny person, a nub, a nugget. India held him and she wept and she laughed, and she looked at Billy and Heidi and said, "Bill would have loved this. Holding this child would have made him *high.*" There was something about a grandchild. What was it? Well, first of all, India was relieved of the heavy burden of parenthood, the impossible responsibility of raising a child—navigating the pitfalls and wonders that life presented each and every human being. And, too, there was something about a grandchild that made India feel immortal—like she would live on, one-quarter of her in this child, one-eighth of her in this child's children. It humbled and amazed her.

On September 25, the day Chess was to have been married, a fact that didn't escape India, she visited the baby on his first day at home, and she brought Lula with her.

Lula was nervous. She had her hair up in a bun, then she released it so that her hair flowed over her shoulders, and then she whipped it back up again. She checked her eye makeup in the mirror on the passenger side of India's Mercedes. India didn't have the heart to say so, but how Lula's eye makeup looked or whether her hair was up or down would matter very little. The fact that she was a *woman* in her *twenties* and was having a relationship—the parameters of which would be nebulous to Billy and Heidi—with India would matter a great deal. India had had half a mind to keep her burgeoning relationship with Lula a secret, at least from her sons. (Everyone at PAFA, and she meant *everyone,* knew that India and Lula were a couple and that this was why Lula had reenrolled. Spencer Frost had pitched a purple fit when Lula destroyed the canvas he had purchased for the school, so Lula spent the final part of her summer painting a different canvas to hang in its place. Ultimately, Spencer Frost was relieved Lula hadn't defected to Parsons. The girl was going to be famous and PAFA was going to claim her.)

India had changed her mind about introducing Lula to Billy and Heidi only that morning when she awoke, realized the day, and thought about Chess. Life was too short, she thought. She would take Lula with her, come what may.

India and Lula walked up the brick path that led to Billy and Heidi's impressive stone house in Radnor. Lula was holding the gift she'd brought—a pair of small denim overalls, a striped shirt, a tiny pair of sneakers. And because she couldn't help herself, she had bought the baby some brightly colored clay. He wouldn't use it for two or three years, but who cared?

India had called Billy and Heidi that morning to say she was coming and bringing a new friend.

"Oh," Heidi said, sounding intrigued under her exhaustion. "Someone special?"

"Someone special," India confirmed.

India knocked, and together she and Lula stood at the door, waiting.

Billy opened the door, saw India, saw Lula, smiled, and said, "You can just walk right in, Mom. I thought you were Avon."

She said, "Billy, this is my friend, Lula Simpson. Lula, the firstborn, Billy Bishop."

Billy extended a hand. "It's nice to meet you, Lula."

Lula said, "I've heard so much about you. Congratulations on your new addition."

Billy grinned. "Thanks. We're thrilled. Tired, but thrilled."

Heidi was sitting in the library with Tripp in her arms, asleep.

"Don't get up," India said.

"Okay, I won't," Heidi said, and they all laughed. Heidi looked at Lula, but there was no change in her expression, no widening of the eyes or pursing of the lips, no hesitation in her smile. Perhaps they had expected that when India brought "a special friend" to meet them, it would naturally be a young, beautiful Indian Iranian woman. Ha! India nearly laughed. She said, "Heidi, I'd like you to meet a very special friend of mine, Lula Simpson."

"Hello, Lula," Heidi said.

Lula touched Heidi's shoulder in a way that was just right, but her attention was captured by the baby.

"My God," she said. "He's *beautiful.*"

"Would you like to hold him?" Heidi said.

"Could I?" Lula said.

As Heidi placed William Burroughs Bishop III in Lula's arms, India was sure she could hear Bill laughing.

She's going to want children, India, she heard Bill's benevolent ghost say.

Oh, shut up! India said back to him. But she smiled in spite of herself.

BIRDIE

She and Grant woke up in the morning to mellow sunshine. Birdie loved nothing more than Indian summer. But today, for Chess's sake, she had been hoping for rain.

Grant repaired to the kitchen and came back, moments later, with two cups of café au lait. It had become his custom to bring Birdie her coffee in bed, even on mornings when he went in to the office. She loved the gesture, the attention, and the coffee Grant made—he warmed the milk on the stove—tasted better than any coffee she had had in her life.

He sat on the bed next to her.

She said, "Beautiful day for a wedding."

He said, "That it is."

They had planned things to keep themselves busy. Brunch at Blue Hill, which was positively exquisite, and then a long drive to look at the emerging foliage. They happened across a few antique stores, where they stopped to putter. Grant used to loathe puttering, but now he meandered through the shops with ease, holding up one thing and then another, wondering what Birdie thought.

She thought, *I can't believe this is the same man I married.* He hadn't mentioned golf once all day. And the Yankees were in the playoffs and were playing later that afternoon, and he hadn't mentioned that either.

She thought, *He has pretty good taste.*

They pulled back into their driveway at quarter to five. The sun was behind the trees already; the long days of summer were over. Birdie couldn't help thinking...the ceremony was to have been at four, and at quarter to five they might have been standing in the receiving line or posing for the photographer. If she was feeling so bereft, how must Evelyn Morgan be feeling?

Birdie said, "I'm going to call Chess."

"In a minute," Grant said. "Right now I have a surprise."

A surprise? Grant?

He led her to the backyard. It was so beautiful, it hurt. The elms were half-green, half-yellow, and the Bradford pears were starting to turn. Grant stopped at the wrought iron table, and there was a portable CD player, which Birdie recognized as something Grant had purchased for his "loft" apartment in South Norwalk. He pressed a button and Gordon Lightfoot started singing "If You Could Read My Mind." This had been their wedding song.

Grant led Birdie to the pond, and they crossed, single file, over the bridge the landscape architects had built to reach the floating island. The floating island was a perfect circle in the middle of the pond, covered with lush grass that had grown in while Birdie was away on Tuckernuck. Grant took his shoes off and Birdie followed suit.

"You promised me a dance," he said.

CHESS

She had considered taking the day off from work and visiting Michael's grave at the cemetery in New Jersey, but after giving it some thought, Chess decided that would be too painful and, if she got right down to it, disingenuous. She didn't need to go to Michael's grave to honor her memory of him. She would honor Michael's memory by continuing to forge ahead in her new life, such as it was. She would honor herself by being direct and honest: this might have been her wedding day, but it hadn't worked out. So... she could sit on Michael's grave and cry, or she could make herself useful.

She had agreed to work a double shift, lunch and dinner, which entailed arriving at the restaurant at eight in the morning, checking that the correct orders had been delivered, and getting the rest of the kitchen staff started on their *mise en place.* She took the worst job: artichokes.

When Electa came in at ten, she placed a hand on Chess's lower back. "Thanks for getting things rolling," she said. "How are you doing?"

Electa knew what day it was. Chess had confided in her one night after service, over an impossible-to-come-by bottle of Screaming Eagle cabernet.

"I'm okay," Chess said, and she was surprised to find this was true. Her job didn't allow time for thinking. The orders came in one on top of another like balls she was expected to juggle. Because it was Saturday, the restaurant was packed—full house with a wait—and the kitchen was moving at an amphetamine pace. Chess prepped and plated crab and mango summer rolls and the roasted beet salad with ginger vinaigrette. Then Nina, a very tall and lean Lithuanian cook who worked the sauté station, reached for a pan on the stove without a side towel, and she burned her palm. Chess slid over to cover Nina's station and man her own station. Under normal circumstances, this would have sent Chess into a tailspin, but today, she was grateful.

There were a couple of lulls in the midafternoon, where thoughts drifted in like fog under a door. It was her fault, all of it. She had hurt Michael. But was she responsible for his reaction? Climbing without a harness. Without a harness! *Why were you so reckless? You wanted to break some rules? Act out? You didn't care what happened to you?* Chess no longer believed that Michael wanted to die. Michael loved his life too much, he was good at life, he was a leader, he met challenges, he succeeded. If Nick was going to steal his fiancée, Michael would find another fiancée, a better fiancée, a supermodel who was also a Rhodes Scholar, a beach volleyball champion who was a member of Mensa. There were all kinds of beautiful, wonderful women out in the world, waiting. Michael would never, ever have fallen intentionally. If he had gone climbing without a harness, it was because he believed he was invincible.

Chess was crying now, over her smoking pan of fluke in lemongrass broth.

What happened wasn't Michael's fault. It was an accident; he fell. What happened wasn't Chess's fault. She had liked Michael enormously and she had grown to love him as a person. She had wanted to be a woman who was in love with him, who could marry him and have children and be happy. She hadn't been that woman, but she had tried.

She had tried.

She finished her shift at ten thirty that night. The other cooks had knocked off nearly an hour earlier, but Chess had stayed on to clean the stations, mop the floor, get everything ready for brunch service the next day. Electa appeared and asked Chess if she wanted to sit at the bar and have a drink.

"No Screaming Eagle tonight," Electa said apologetically. "But we can have lychee martinis?"

Chess shook her head. "I'm going home."

"You sure?" Electa said. "Well, you've had a long day."

Long day, yes. Chess removed her apron and threw it in the laundry bin. She ran her hands through her hair. It had grown back in, spiky at first, then softer. She'd decided to keep it short, which was convenient for kitchen work. In the very front now was a tuft of pure white. White hair at age thirty-two: it was either a punishment or a badge of honor.

Chess arrived in the lobby of her building at quarter past eleven. She was bone tired—too tired to paint her toenails, iron her clothes, or think. This was a good thing. She grabbed a week's worth of mail from her box and headed up to her apartment.

Chess turned on a light, collapsed on the sofa, dropped the mail on the coffee table. *Now what?* she wondered.

She was as limp as a dishrag and yet she feared she wouldn't be able to sleep. She thought of Aunt India, and then her mother and Tate, the four of them on Tuckernuck together. Her eyes burned with tears. She might as well admit it to herself: she was lonely.

Then she saw it. A postcard, resting on the top of the pile of mail. A postcard of Central Park in autumn, the trees ablaze with color. In white script across the top, it said, *New York City*.

New York City? Chess thought. Who would send her a postcard of New York City when she lived in New York City? She felt a buzzing along her hairline, and her head snapped up. Central Park. She flipped the card over.

It said: *Okay, baby, okay.*

Chess's heart fell to her feet, like a stone she could pick up and throw.

Nick.

She stood up and walked into her kitchen. Her fridge was nearly empty—she ate breakfast from a street vendor and her other meals at the restaurant—but she had been saving the bottle of Veuve Clicquot that Tate had given her on Tuckernuck for an extraordinary occasion.

She pulled it out. It was shockingly cold.

Okay, baby, okay.

She popped the cork.

ACKNOWLEDGMENTS

There are two challenges in writing about Tuckernuck Island. One is that it is difficult to set a novel in a place where not much happens. (When I asked longtime Tuckernuck residents what they *do* on Tuckernuck, a popular response was, "Do? Why, we visit!") The other challenge was gaining access to Tuckernuck, because the island is privately owned. So the first people I would like to thank are Mark Williams and Jeffrey Johnsen, who took me to Tuckernuck on one of the most beautiful days of the summer last July. I fell madly in love with the place, and that was largely due to my wonderful guides. Everyone who has ever stayed or lived on Tuckernuck has a story to tell about it, and I heard a lot of those stories, the most colorful of which came from my agent, Michael Carlisle, whose family owned land on Tuckernuck for something like centuries. The summer residents of Tuckernuck are private people, and my hope is that this book celebrates the place where they live rather than exploits it.

Moving from country to city, I would like to thank all of the amazing people I have met at the Pennsylvania Academy of Fine Arts, or PAFA, most especially Gerry and Rosemary Barth (aka Mary Rose Garth), who introduced me to the world of PAFA, as well as board member Anne McCollum and president of the board of directors Don Caldwell and his wife, Linda Aversa (aka Spencer and Aversa Frost). Huge thanks to Stan Greidus, for giving me the lowdown on student life, and to the president of PAFA, David Brigham, who gave me a comprehensive tour and made me feel like part of the family.

In New York, I would like to thank my dynamic-duo agenting team of Michael Carlisle and David Forrer at Inkwell Management, as well as all of the brilliant and generous minds at Little, Brown/Hachette, including my editor, Reagan Arthur, Heather Fain, Michael Pietsch, David Young, and the wizard-guru of all things trade paperback, Terry Adams.

On Nantucket, I send a big hug and a kiss out to my Inner Circle—you know who you are—who have stood by me through a couple of roller-coaster years. Of special note this year are Wendy Hudson, rock-star independent bookseller and owner of Nantucket Bookworks (who gave me the Tuckernuck story of riding around the island on a bike with no brakes!), and Wendy Rouillard, author of the Barnaby children's books, who has tirelessly talked publishing with me for more than a decade now. A loud and enthusiastic shout-out to Chuck and Margie Marino, simply because they are two of the finest people walking the earth and I love them to bits.

Thank you to my summer nanny, Stephanie McGrath, for smiling even after a hundred-and-one trips to the Delta Fields and forty-two trips to the Hub for bubble gum. A huge thank you to Anne and Whitney Gifford for use of their house on Barnabas Lane—no book would ever get written if it weren't for Barnabas! And thank you, always, forever, in extremis, to Heather Feather, for her love, support, friendship, and positive life force.

On the home front, thank you to my husband, Chip Cunningham, the best Mr. Mom in all the world; to my spirited, creative, and very funny sons, Maxx and Dawson, who really know how to rock out (!); and to my singing, skipping daughter, Shelby, who fills our house with sunshine each and every day.

This book is for my mother. Not only does she allow me to move back home for a month each fall so I can revise in peace, but she taught me absolutely everything I know about unconditional love. Thanks, Mom.

ABOUT THE AUTHOR

Elin Hilderbrand is the proud mother of three, a dedicated Peloton rider, an aspiring book influencer, and an enthusiastic cook (follow her on Instagram to watch the Cringe Cooking Show). She's also a grateful eight-year breast cancer survivor. *The Island* is her ninth novel.

Keep reading for an excerpt from Elin Hilderbrand's latest novel, *Golden Girl*.

Martha

She receives a message from the front office: A new soul is about to join them, and this soul has been assigned to Martha.

Martha puts on her reading glasses and finds her clipboard. The soul is arriving from...Nantucket Island.

Martha is both surprised and delighted. Surprised because Nantucket Harbor is where Martha met her own fateful end two summers ago. She thought the front office was intentionally keeping her away from coastal areas so she didn't become (as Gen Z said) "triggered."

And Martha is delighted because...well, who doesn't love Nantucket?

Martha swoops down from the northeast, so her first glimpse of the island is the lighthouse that stands sentry at the end of the slender golden arm of Great Point. Martha spies seals frolicking just off the coast (and sharks stalking a little farther out). She continues over Polpis Harbor, where the twelve-year-old class of Nantucket Community Sailing is taking lessons in Optis. One boat keels *way* over and comes dangerously close to capsizing. Martha blows a little puff of air—and the boat rights itself.

Martha dips over the moors, dotted with ponds and crisscrossed by sandy roads. She sees deer hiding deep in the woods. A Jeep is stuck in the soft sand by Jewel Pond. Next to the Jeep, a young man lets fly a stream of swears (*My, oh, my,* Martha thinks) while his girlfriend tries to get a cell signal. She's sorry, she says, she just really wanted the early morning light for her Instagram photos.

Martha chooses the scenic coastal route along the uninterrupted stretch of the south shore. Despite the early hour, there are plenty of people out and about. A woman of a certain age throws a tennis ball into the rolling waves for a chocolate Lab of a certain age. (Martha misses dogs! She's far too busy to ever make it over to the Pet Division.) A white-haired gentleman charges into the water for his morning swim. There are a handful of fishermen out on Smith's Point, a cadre of young (and *very* attractive) surfers at Cisco, and a foursome—*thwack!*—teeing off from the first hole at the Miacomet Golf Club.

As Martha floats over Nobadeer Beach, she sees the town lifeguards gathering in the parking lot. Their conditioning session starts at quarter past seven, and it's nearly that time now. Martha has to hurry.

She has one more minute to appreciate the island on this clear blue morning of Saturday, June 19. The sun glints off the gold cupola atop the Unitarian church, and a line chef at Black-Eyed Susan's runs full speed down India Street, late for his shift. Across the island, irrigation systems switch on, sprinkling lawns and flower boxes, except for out in Sconset, where residents like to do things the old-fashioned way: They don gardening clogs and grab a watering can. People are pouring their first cup of coffee, reading the front page of the *Nantucket Standard*. The thirty-five women who will be getting married today open their eyes and experience varying degrees of anticipation and anxiety. Contractors pull into Marine Home Center because they have punch lists that need to be completed *yesterday;* the summer people are arriving, they want their homes up and running. Charter fishing boats motor out of the harbor; the first batch of sugar doughnuts is pulled from the oven at the Downyflake—and oh, the aroma!

Martha sighs. Nantucket isn't heaven, but it is heaven on earth.

However, she isn't here to sightsee. She's here to collect her soul. The pinned location on Martha's map is Kingsley Road, almost at the intersection of Madaket, but not quite.

Martha arrives with a full thirty seconds to spare, which gives her a chance to inhale the heady fragrance of the lilacs that are in full bloom below. There's a dark-haired woman with fantastic legs jogging down the road, singing along to her music, but the rest of Kingsley is quite sleepy.

Fifteen seconds, ten seconds, five seconds. Martha double-checks her coordinates; it says she's in the right place...

In the time that Martha takes her gaze off the road, tragedy strikes. It happens quickly, the literal blink of an eye. Martha winces. *What a pity!*

All right, Martha thinks. *It's time to get to work.*

Vivi

It's a beautiful June day, the kind that Vivi writes about. In fact, all thirteen of Vivian Howe's novels—beach reads set on Nantucket—start in June. Vivi has never considered changing this habit, because June on Nantucket is when things *begin.* The summer is a newborn; it's still innocent, pristine, a blank page.

At a few minutes past seven, Vivi is ready for her run. Since her divorce ten years earlier, when she moved into Money Pit, she has taken the same route: down her dirt road, Kingsley, to the Madaket Road bike path. The path goes all the way to the beach, though Vivi hasn't made it that far in years. Her hips. And also, she doesn't have time.

Vivi is agitated (!!!) despite the sunshine, the bluebird sky, and the luscious bloom of the peonies in her cutting garden. The night before, Vivi's daughter Willa had called to say that she's pregnant again. This marked Willa's fourth pregnancy since last June, which was when she and Rip got married.

"Oh, Willie!" Vivi said. "Yay, hurray, good, good news! How far along are you?"

"Six weeks," Willa said.

Still very, very early, Vivi thinks. Willa basically *just* missed her period.

"You took a test?"

"Yes, Mother."

"More than one?"

"Two," Willa said. "The first was indecisive. The second had two lines."

What Vivi did *not* say was *Don't get your hopes up*. Willa had miscarried three times. The first pregnancy had progressed to fifteen weeks. Willa started bleeding while she was giving a tour of the Hadwen House to a group of VIPs from the governor's office. She ran out on the tour and drove herself to the hospital. It was a horrible day, the most physically painful and difficult of the three miscarriages. After the third, Willa became convinced there was a problem.

A thorough examination at the Brigham and Women's fertility clinic in Boston, however, showed nothing wrong. Willa was a healthy twenty-four-year-old. She had no problem getting pregnant. When Rip looked at her, they conceived.

Privately, Vivi suspected the miscarriages had something to do with Willa's type A personality, which Vivi and her ex-husband, JP, used to call her "type A-plus personality" because regular As were never good enough for Willa.

"If this doesn't work out, why don't you and Rip take a break? You're so young. You have years and years, decades, even, to conceive. What's the *rush*?"

Predictably, Willa had become defensive. "What makes you think this won't work out? Do you think I'm a failure?"

"You succeed at everything you do," Vivi said. "I just think your body might benefit from a reset..."

"I'm *pregnant,* Mama," Willa said. "I will give birth

to a perfectly healthy baby." (She sounded like she was trying to convince herself.)

"You *will* give birth to a perfectly healthy baby, Willie. I can't wait to hold her." Though Vivi didn't feel quite old enough to be a grandmother. She was only fifty-one, and in terrific shape, if she did say so. Her dark hair, which she wore in a pixie cut, didn't have one strand of gray. (Vivi checked every morning.) She might be occasionally mistaken for the child's mother. (Well, she could hope.)

The conversation had ended there, but for Vivi, an unsettled feeling lingered through the night. *Are children ever punished for the mistakes of their parents?* she wondered, *or was that just her novelist's mind at work?*

Vivi had woken up at five thirty, not only because it was June and sunlight streamed in through the windows like it was high noon, but also because she heard a noise. When she crept out into the hallway, she saw her daughter Carson stumbling up the stairs, smelling distinctly of marijuana.

Vivi had last seen Carson the afternoon before, dressed for work in cutoff jeans and her marigold-yellow Oystercatcher T-shirt, her dark hair still a little damp, neat in two French braids. Carson was the most attractive of Vivi's three children, though of course Vivi wasn't supposed to think that. Carson alone favored JP—the dark hair, the clear glass-green eyes, the fine pointed nose, and teeth that came in white, straight, and even. She was a Quinboro through and through, whereas both Willa and Leo favored the Howes. They'd inherited Vivi's overbite and crowded lowers and had spent years in braces.

Carson was still in her cutoffs, but she had downgraded her T-shirt to something that looked like a silver-mesh handkerchief that just barely covered her breasts and left her midriff and back bare except for one slender chain. She was barefoot; her hair was out of its braids but held kinky waves. When she saw her mother standing at the top of the stairs, her eyebrows shot up.

"Madre," she said. "What's good."

"Are you just getting home?" Vivi asked, though the answer was obvious. Carson was walking in at five thirty in the morning, when her work shift had ended at eleven. She was twenty-one, fine, so she'd had a drink at work, and she probably went to the Chicken Box to catch the band's last set, then either to the beach with friends or she hooked up with a random stranger.

"Yes, ma'am." Carson sounded sober, but that only served to make Vivi angrier.

"The summer isn't going to be like this, Carson," Vivi said.

"I hope you're right," Carson said. "Work was slow, my tips were trash, the guys at the Box all looked like they were on the junior high school fencing team."

"You can't stay out all night, then come home reeking of marijuana..."

"Reeking of marijuana...," Carson mimicked.

Vivi searched for extra patience, which was like trying to find a lost shoe in the depths of her maternal closet. *This is Carson.* Ten years earlier, when Vivi learned that her husband had fallen in love with his employee Amy, Vivi moved out. The three kids took it hard—but especially Carson. Carson had been eleven years old and was unusually attached to Vivi. Vivian's novel that year, *Along the South Shore,* had been something of a breakout book, and Vivi, wanting to escape the inevitable divorce fallout—people asking "what happened," people asking "was she okay," people telling her she was "brave"—had gone on a twenty-nine-stop book tour that kept her away for seven weeks (and she'd missed the first day of school and Carson's birthday). By the time Vivi got back, Carson had changed from the funny little spitfire of the family to a "troubled child" who threw tantrums, swore, picked fistfights with her siblings, and generally did everything in her power to get attention. Vivi blamed the transformation on JP's affair (which their couples therapist insisted they not disclose to the children), and JP blamed it on what he called Vivi's "abandonment."

Ten years had passed. Carson was no longer a little girl, but she still had her challenging moments.

"This is my house," Vivi said. "I pay the mortgage, the taxes, the insurance, the electric bill, the heating bill, the cable bill. I do the shopping and make the meals. While you're sleeping under this roof, I don't want you out all night, drinking, smoking, and having sex with complete strangers. Do you know how that *looks?*" Vivi stopped just short of reminding Carson that they'd already battled chlamydia once, the previous summer. "You're setting a rotten example for your brother."

"He doesn't need me to set an example," Carson said. "He has Willa. I'm the screwup. It's my job to be a hideous disappointment."

"No one said you were a hideous disappointment, sweetheart."

"I'm twenty-one," Carson said. "I can drink legally, I can smoke pot legally."

"Since you're so grown up," Vivi said, "you can move out on your own."

"That's the plan," Carson said. "I'm saving."

You're not *saving,* Vivi wanted to say. Carson made good tips at the Oystercatcher, but she spent them—on drinks, on weed, on clothes from Erica Wilson, Milly & Grace, and the Lovely. Carson had finally dropped out of UVM after struggling through five semesters—her cumulative GPA was a 1.6—and whereas Vivi was initially aghast (an education makes you good company for yourself!), she knew college wasn't for everyone.

"I'm not giving you a curfew," Vivi said. "But this behavior won't be tolerated."

"This behavior won't be tolerated," Carson mimicked. It was the response of a seven-year-old, and yet it brought the reaction Carson wanted. Vivi took a step toward her, arm tensed.

"Are you going to spank me?"

"Of course not," Vivi said, though she kind of wanted to. "But you have to clean up your act, babe, or I'll ask you to leave."

"Fine," Carson said. "I'll go to Dad's."

"I'm sure Amy would take *very kindly* to you coming home like this."

"She's not as bad as you think," Carson said. "When you demonize her, you show how insecure you are."

Vivi stared at her child, but before she could come up with a response, she smelled something.

"Did you...cook?" Vivi asked.

Carson stepped into the bedroom, slamming the door behind her.

Vivi flew down the stairs to the kitchen, which was filling with black smoke. Vivi's brand new All-Clad three-quart sauté pan was on a lit burner. The sausage-and-basil pasta from last night's dinner. Vivi turned the burner off, grabbed a towel, and carried the smoldering pan outside, where she set it on the flagstone path. The bottom of the pan was charred black. It was so hot, it would have scorched the deck or the lawn.

Brand-new pan, ruined.

The sausage-and-basil pasta in a luscious mustard-cream sauce, which Vivi had been thinking of taking over to Willa's as a peace offering, ruined.

And what if Vivi hadn't gotten out of bed? What if the kitchen had caught on fire, what if flames had engulfed Money Pit while Vivi—and Leo—were sleeping? They could all be dead!

Back in the kitchen, Vivi caught sight of her bottle of Casa Dragones tequila on the side counter, along with a shot glass. She felt a formidable strain of fury brewing inside her. That tequila was *hers;* she wouldn't even let her (almost ex-) boyfriend, Dennis, make margaritas with it. Carson had come home, put the pasta on over a burner, done two—or three?—shots of *Vivi's* tequila, which Carson knew was *not for public consumption,* and then she left the pasta to burn on the stove.

Vivi marched back up the stairs and pounded on Carson's locked door.

"You left the pan on an open flame!" Vivi said. Leo would definitely be awake now, which Vivi felt bad about on a Saturday morning, but oh, well. "What is *wrong* with you, Carson? Do you honestly not think about *anyone* but yourself? Do you not think, period?" There was no response. Vivi kicked the door.

"Please go away" came the response from inside. "I'm trying to sleep."

"And you drank my tequila!" Vivi said. "Which you know is off-limits. You did that just to infuriate me."

"I didn't drink the tequila," Carson said. "I haven't

had a drink since I left the Chicken Box, and that was hours ago."

Vivi blinked. Carson sounded like she was telling the truth, and she had seemed sober. "Who drank it, then?"

There was a pause before Carson said, "Well, who else lives here?"

Leo? Vivi thought. She looked at Leo's bedroom door, which was shut tight. Leo had been going to high school parties since he was a sophomore, but a run-in with Jägermeister had propelled him away from the hard stuff. He drank Bud Light, and the occasional White Claw.

Vivi turned back to Carson's door. "You are scrubbing that pot, young lady," she said. "Or buying me a new one."

After Vivi poured herself some coffee, opened all the windows, turned both sailcloth ceiling fans to high, washed the shot glass, and hid what remained of the Casa Dragones in the laundry room (her kids would never find it there), she calmed down a bit. She was the mother of three *very young adults,* and parenting very young adults required just as much patience as parenting very young children. No one ever talked about this; it felt like a dirty little secret. Vivi had always imagined that by the time her kids were twenty-four, twenty-one, and eighteen, they'd all be drinking wine together around the outdoor table by the pool, and the kids would be cooking, clearing, and giving Vivi sage investment advice. *Ha.*

Vivi ties up her running shoes and stretches her hamstrings, using the bumper of her Jeep—then she clicks on her iTunes and takes off.

ALSO BY ELIN HILDERBRAND

Barefoot

"Settle back and prepare to be charmed.... Hilderbrand's women move in and out of passion, rivalry, and solidarity in one unforgettable summer, finally reaching that state of wonder and gratitude that comes with sheer survival."

—Susan Larson, *New Orleans Times-Picayune*

"It's *Beaches* meets *The Graduate*." —*Self*

"Engrossing." —Melinda Bargreen, *Seattle Times*

"Summer reading fun.... Twenty pages in, you'll be ready to drop everything and head for the beach yourself."

—*Boston*

"*Barefoot* deftly portrays the bittersweet journey of three women." —*Redbook*

"You will almost be tempted to check your own shoes for sand by the end of this engaging story about a season of change on Nantucket."

—Beverly Meyer, *Free Lance–Star*

ALSO BY ELIN HILDERBRAND

A Summer Affair

"Claire has it all—and then she gets *more!* Will new love destroy her great life? *A Summer Affair* is voyeuristic fun."

—*People*

"A perfect summer cocktail of sex, sun, and scandal."

—*Kirkus Reviews*

"A gem of a summer read with a glamorous location, elite lifestyle, and Hilderbrand's appealing take on the constant stress that fills the lives of women everywhere." —*Booklist*

"This story of one woman's midlife crisis is an emotional and heartfelt journey. It's a captivating tale of heartache, happiness, confusion, and love. By the end, it seems as though we're hurtling through time at breakneck speed, and readers will find themselves rooting for the heroine."

—*Romantic Times Book Club*

"Characters are as complex and fragile as glassblowing artist Claire's creations in Hilderbrand's latest Nantucket tale." —*Library Journal*

BACK BAY BOOKS

Available wherever paperbacks are sold

ALSO BY ELIN HILDERBRAND

The Castaways

"Hilderbrand provides the perfect summer read as she explores love, loss, and, ultimately, absolution."

—Patty Engelmann, *Booklist*

"A juicy novel.... Hilderbrand captivates with a racy narrative and characters who are both familiar and memorable."

—Joanna Powell, *People*

"*The Castaways* is a sensitive portrayal of the complexities of friendship. Hilderbrand's characters illustrate the alliances, insecurities, and joys that color adult relationships.... When it's done well, as it is here, reading about other people's problems is ever so satisfying."

—Kristi Lanier, *Washington Post*